"What do we do with the dog while we're gone?"

"It's about time you started using her name instead of calling her *the dog*. Angel will go with us and I'll have Freya ride next to her. You'd be surprised how much a smart dog can learn by observation."

Sean chuckled. "What makes you think Freya won't learn to act up from watching Angel?"

"I'll take my chances," Zoe said, returning his smile. She was beginning to realize she might be willing to take a chance on caring for Sean again, too. He might have broken her heart once, but he wasn't the same macho guy he had been. He was a wounded warrior whose invisible scars needed the balm of love and faith, both in himself and in the God he had recently denied.

It was her fondest hope that she could lead him back to a realization of both.

She cared for the man deeply. They had both been through a lot since their youth. Above all, she was going to make sure he stayed safe, no matter what it took.

USA TODAY Bestselling Author

Valerie Hansen

and

New York Times Bestselling Author

Lenora Worth

and

Terri Reed

Christmas Rescue

Previously published as *Rookie K-9 Unit Christmas*
and *Classified K-9 Unit Christmas*

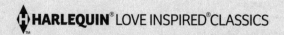

HARLEQUIN® LOVE INSPIRED®CLASSICS

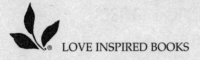 LOVE INSPIRED BOOKS

Recycling programs for this product may not exist in your area.

ISBN-13: 978-1-335-14308-2

Christmas Rescue

Copyright © 2019 by Harlequin Books S.A.

Rookie K-9 Unit Christmas
(Surviving Christmas and Holiday High Alert)
First published in 2016. This edition published in 2019.
Copyright © 2016 by Harlequin Books S.A.

Classified K-9 Unit Christmas
(A Killer Christmas and Yuletide Stalking)
First published in 2017. This edition published in 2019.
Copyright © 2017 by Harlequin Books S.A.

Special thanks and acknowledgment are given to Valerie Hansen and Lenora Worth for their contribution to the Rookie K-9 Unit miniseries and to Lenora Worth and Terri Reed for their contribution to the Classified K-9 Unit miniseries.

www.Harlequin.com

Printed in U.S.A.

CONTENTS

Valerie Hansen was thirty when she awoke to the presence of the Lord in her life and turned to Jesus. She now lives in a renovated farmhouse on the breathtakingly beautiful Ozark Plateau of Arkansas and is privileged to share her personal faith by telling the stories of her heart for Love Inspired. Life doesn't get much better than that!

Books by Valerie Hansen

Love Inspired Suspense

Emergency Responders

Fatal Threat
Marked for Revenge

Military K-9 Unit

Bound by Duty
Military K-9 Unit Christmas
"Christmas Escape"

Classified K-9 Unit

Special Agent

Rookie K-9 Unit

Search and Rescue
Rookie K-9 Unit Christmas
"Surviving Christmas"

Visit the Author Profile page
at Harlequin.com for more titles.

SURVIVING CHRISTMAS

Valerie Hansen

For He shall give His angels charge over thee,
to keep thee in all thy ways.
—*Psalms* 91:11

Many thanks to Lenora Worth for her friendship and expert advice as we put these two novellas together.

And continuing love to my Joe, who is with me in spirit, looking over my shoulder and offering moral support as I write. He always will be.

ONE

Sean Murphy hated to close his eyes. A terrifying past waited for him in sleep, a past that sometimes invaded even his waking hours. Love for his six-year-old son, Patrick, was what kept him sane, kept him battling to return to normal. Patrick needed him, now more than ever. All they had left was each other.

The St. Louis apartment Sean had rented on his return to the States was small but adequate for the present. The future would take care of itself. At least Sean hoped so. There had been a time when he'd believed God was guiding him through life. Now, he felt adrift.

Fog of sleep dulled his senses, but not so much that he failed to hear a strange sound in the dark. He froze. Listened intently. Heard nothing more. Sighing, he wished he knew how to stop being so jumpy. Every creak of the old building brought irrational fear.

A cadence of soft steps followed. Sean sat bolt upright. "Patrick?"

The sound ceased. Sean slipped out of bed, wishing he still had his rifle and full battle gear. St. Louis might not be Kandahar, but that didn't mean there was no danger. Yes, his emotions were raw. And, yes, chances were that he was merely imagining a threat. There was only one way to find out. He must see for himself.

Since Patrick's near-drowning accident in the swimming pool at his maternal grandparents' estate, the boy had been having trouble with speech as well as motor skills. Therefore, he sometimes sought out his daddy without explanation. That was probably what Sean had heard. Still, he refused to disregard an instinctive warning.

Barefoot, he tiptoed to the open bedroom door and waited in the shadow from the night-light in the hallway. A low mumble reached him. How could Patrick be talking in his sleep when he had so much trouble doing so awake?

Sean pressed his back to the jamb and slowly eased forward. The voices were clear. For an instant he wished they weren't.

"I ain't killin' no kid. You got that?" one person grumbled.

"We aren't supposed to. Just the father."

"Fine. What if the kid sees us? What then?"

"Nobody'll know we're here if you shut your yap," the other prowler whispered. "Come on."

Sean tensed. He was strong, ready to defend himself, but anything might happen if Patrick awoke. The boy's most frequent utterance was a high-pitched squeal of fright and frustration. If he began to carry on like that, the attackers might change their minds and harm him, too.

Going on the offense was the answer. Sean grabbed the junior baseball bat he'd bought to help Patrick regain coordination and braced himself.

The first man led with his pistol, giving Sean a one-time chance of disarming him. Wood in the child's bat cracked as Sean brought it down on the assailant's wrist. The man dropped the gun, doubled up and howled. His partner didn't wait for him to recover. Instead, he fired blindly in the dark, then turned tail and ran.

Sean dove for the gun and connected. Its owner leaped onto his back and tried to wrest it away. He might have succeeded if he'd had both hands in working order—or if his cohort had stuck around to help.

Sean continued to struggle with the man in the confines of the narrow hallway. His temple hit a doorjamb. Flashes of light, like exploding mortar shells, blinded him. Noises of war filled his ears. The acrid smell of gunpowder and the portent of death seemed to be everywhere.

A trickle of blood wet his close-cropped hair as survival instinct locked his fingers around the cold metal in his hands. At that moment, nothing could have pried open his grip.

There was a muted crash, then a tinkling, rustling sound. Clarity returned enough to suggest that the first man had stumbled over the Christmas tree he and Patrick had just decorated.

A child screamed.

Patrick!

Lunging, Sean knocked the intruder aside and struggled to his feet, gun in hand. That was enough. The injured man scrambled away, rounded the corner into the living room and disappeared out the door.

Sean wanted to follow. To capture at least one of the thugs who had declared their intent to kill him. But he didn't. Patrick needed him more. The child came first. Always had. Always would.

So, now what?

* * *

Police officer Zoe Trent had recently graduated from Canyon County K-9 Training Center in Desert Valley, Arizona, with her Belgian Tervuren, Freya. Being partnered with a specialized K-9 had been a goal of hers ever since completing the police academy. Now that it was time to return to her regular assignment in Mesa, Arizona, however, she knew she was going to miss the new friends she'd made during the twelve-week K-9 training program.

Wishing there were an easy way to keep in touch, and knowing they would surely drift apart as normal life resumed, she'd struggled to fall asleep tonight. A Christmas carol ringtone on her cell phone startled her awake.

Freya barked to accompany her muttered, "Hello?"

"Zoe?"

"Yes." Coming alert, she raised on one elbow.

"It's me again. Sean Murphy. Sorry to bother you, but you did tell me to call if I needed anything."

Instant worry for her college chum infused her. "Of course. What's wrong? You sound awful. Have you had another PTSD flashback?"

"It's worse than that."

Her dark eyes narrowed, and she raked stray tendrils of long brown hair away from her face with her free hand. "How can it be worse? It's not Patrick again, is it?"

"He's okay, so far. There's nobody here I can trust, and I really need help. Somebody's trying to kill me."

"What?" How could she express doubt without jeopardizing their seasoned friendship? "Are you sure? I mean, you told me you'd been a little confused since your medical discharge."

"I know what you're thinking," he countered. "I had the same misgivings. I've been awake for hours since this happened, trying to figure it out. Two guys broke into my apartment, and I fought with one of them."

"Did you call the police?"

"Of course. You know how it is in a big city. If the prowlers had succeeded in shooting me, I'd have gotten more attention."

"The men were armed?"

"Yes. One is now sporting a broken wrist, I hope. I disarmed him and he ran. So did his partner."

Zoe paused to choose her words carefully. "Okay. You had a break-in. What makes you think these guys had murder on their minds?"

"I heard them say they were there to kill me." He hesitated, then added, "I know I wasn't hallucinating because of what happened next. When I hit one on his gun hand, the other fired and left a bullet in the ceiling. The cops took all the evidence. Since nothing was stolen and nobody got shot, they acted like they didn't hold out much hope to catch the guys."

"Unless the ballistics match another case," she said. "Do you think these assailants might have been old friends of Sandra's?" Zoe hated to bring up his late wife but felt compelled to ask. After all, the woman had overdosed while her innocent son was floundering in the deep end of a swimming pool.

"I can't see why drug dealers would have it in for me," Sean said. "Their business was with Sandra."

"Agreed. So, how can I help you?"

"You can get me into that service dog program you

mentioned when I was first discharged. I need to get my emotions under better control if I intend to survive more real life attacks."

"Okay. I'll see the director, Ellen Foxcroft, and put your name on her waiting list."

"That's not enough. Not after last night."

Zoe could tell from his tone that he was approaching an emotional crossroad and wished they were face-to-face so she could judge his condition more accurately. "Are you and Patrick out of danger now?"

"Temporarily. I threw some clothes and stuff into the pickup, and I've been driving around, thinking, ever since the police left. I can't take him back to the apartment. Whoever came after me last night may try again."

"What about going to your in-laws? They have plenty of room for both of you, don't they?"

"I'd rather hole up in a cardboard box on the street than rely on them," Sean said. "The Shepherds were so concerned with excusing Sandra's addiction and transferring blame, they laid it all on me."

"Okay. Tell you what," Zoe said, hoping her growing concern was masked, "why don't you come on down to Desert Valley to visit me? I was going to head back to Mesa soon, but there's no hurry. I don't start my new assignment until after the first of the year, and the Desert Valley PD can use a few substitute cops here while their regulars take holiday time off."

"What good will a few weeks do me?"

"It'll give you a chance to chill out, for one thing. Besides, once Ellen meets you and Patrick and realizes how special your needs are, maybe she'll make an exception and work you in."

The quiet on the other end of the line troubled her.

The Sean Murphy she'd met in college was nothing like this traumatized widower. Coming home from combat with PTSD was bad enough without having to face the death of his spouse and near loss of his only child.

"All right," Sean finally said.

She almost cheered. Instead, she said, "I'm looking forward to it. And to meeting Patrick."

Silence again. Then, "He's not himself yet. He may never be. Doctors keep reminding me there are no guarantees."

"That doesn't matter."

Anger tinged his reply. "Of course it does."

"No," Zoe told him tenderly. "It doesn't. He's your son and you love him. That's enough for me."

Although Sean's goodbye was terse, she could tell he was touched by her total acceptance. She didn't have to see the boy to know he merited a good life with the parent who was willing to sacrifice anything to help him. Everyone deserved a fighting chance at happiness.

Even babies who are born with fatal birth defects, she added, blinking rapidly. She had not wept for her nameless baby brother since she was five years old and a stranger had come to take him away. Mama had cried then, but Daddy had stood dry-eyed, staring at the tiny, imperfect bundle wrapped in the blue blanket.

That was the last time Zoe had been permitted to talk about the absent baby. It was as if he had never been born, which was apparently exactly what her parents had wanted.

The sense of injustice and concern for the helpless had begun then and had built throughout her formative years, perhaps even directing her path into law enforcement. She didn't trust easily, but she did have a soft heart for the downtrodden.

Like Patrick. And like his daddy.

Sean's next stop was the bank, where he withdrew all but a few dollars of his savings via the drive-through window. If there was any chance he was being tracked or followed, cash would be a necessity.

And speaking of being followed...

A black SUV seemed to be dogging them. It was back several car lengths, yet changed lanes whenever he did. His hands tightened on the wheel. His little boy was strapped in, of course, but that didn't mean it would be safe to take evasive action, particularly if excessive speed was involved. Where were the cops when you needed them?

Sean whipped around a corner, determined to find a patrol car or police station. He checked his mirrors. The SUV was gone. Had he merely imagined it trailing them? *Imagined* was the key, wasn't it? His mind was good at seeing enemies around every corner and behind every door, the way they'd been in Afghanistan. His body had come home, but part of his mind was still over there, still caught up in the fighting.

He couldn't afford to show signs of instability. If the authorities concluded he was an unfit parent, they might take Patrick away. Worse, with no other close relatives available, they might place him with his negligent maternal grandparents.

The only thing that mattered to Sean was his own assurance that Patrick was absolutely safe with him. If he'd thought otherwise, he'd have stepped back and voluntarily relinquished custody.

Glancing in the rearview mirror at his curly haired look-alike strapped into the narrower backseat he smiled. "You getting hungry, buddy?"

Patrick nodded.

"How about a quick burger? You like those, don't you?"

Another nod.

"Sorry," Sean said, urging speech the way the therapist had. "I don't quite understand you. Can you say yes or no?"

The little boy looked back at his daddy with eyes as blue as the sky, smiled and said, "No."

"Did you just make a *joke*?" Sean's eyes misted.

Patrick's grin spread as he said, "Yes," and Sean was so excited by the possibility he almost let his pickup truck drift to the curb.

In moments, however, his pulse returned to normal. Patrick began to chant, "Yes, no, yes, no," as if neither word meant anything to him.

Monitoring the traffic behind him, Sean picked up some fast food, then headed for the highway that would take him southwest to Desert Valley. He might not have an abundance of friends willing to stand with him, but at least he had one.

He'd checked his side-and rearview mirrors repeatedly and had seen no sign of the SUV that had worried him before. Nevertheless, the sooner he reached Zoe Trent, the better.

"Sean's an old college friend who just got out of the army on a medical discharge," Zoe told lead K-9 unit trainer Sophie Williams. "I was hoping you could have a word with Ellen Foxcroft and see if she can work him in to the therapy dog program."

"And leave who else out?" Sophie was scowling.

Zoe knew her position as a rookie K-9 officer from Sophie's most recent graduating class gave her very little influence. Nevertheless, she had to keep trying. "Maybe, since I've offered to hang around DVPD until after the holidays and sub, I could volunteer my services to you in my downtime and we could squeeze in an extra student and dog. There's no place else I need to be, and I don't have to report to work with Freya until after the first of the year."

Looking for moral support, Zoe laid her hand on the Belgian Tervuren's head and scratched behind her silky, erect ears. Fellow students had teased her about being assigned to a dog whose fur almost matched her own dark brown hair. That was fine with her.

"All right. I'll speak to Ellen for you," Sophie said.

Zoe thought she'd better give Sophie a little more information about Sean, including that he and his son would be staying with her. She explained about the PTSD. "And he's a widower. His wife overdosed while she was supposed to be watching their son, Patrick. The boy survived almost drowning but was left with brain damage. It's a really sad story."

"Well, sounds like he has a good friend in you," Sophie said. "All right. As soon as your friend gets settled, bring him in for an interview. What do you intend to do with Sean's son while he's being assessed and maybe trained?"

"I thought I'd see if Marilyn and Josie would accept him in their day care. Patrick does have special needs, though."

Sophie nodded. "Lily likes it there, and Ryder and I are pleased with the facility. She's not my stepdaughter yet but it won't be long."

"Hey, if the police chief approves the place and so do you, I'm sure that'll put Sean at ease." Encouraged and uplifted by her trainer's support, Zoe laid a hand lightly on Sophie's arm. "Thanks. This means a lot to me."

"Don't thank me," Sophie said. "Nothing has happened yet."

"But it will, God willing," Zoe countered with a grin. "This is the perfect time of the year. Patrick can go to Sunday school and maybe even participate with other kids in the Christmas pageant."

"We can always use another shepherd or angel," Sophie said. "Lily and I are playing Magi. I'm working on camel costumes for Ryder's old dog Titus and another yellow Lab. Probably Tristan McKeller's Jesse." She paused. "Come to think of it, Tristan's a former soldier. Maybe he can offer your friend some advice."

Zoe stopped smiling and shook her head slowly, thoughtfully. Tristan, a Desert Valley police officer, was a good guy, but… "I don't know. Sean may not want to air his problems. It will all come out if and when he qualifies for the Canine Assistance program, of course, but since I didn't ask if I could tell anyone else, would you mind keeping the story to yourself?"

"Of course," Sophie said. "You did mention he had some kind of trouble in St. Louis, though. If it follows him here, I will need to share his story with Ryder."

"I understand. And thanks." Sighing, Zoe remembered her old friend Sean and his boyish good looks. She'd had a crush on him from the first moment she'd laid eyes on him, and when he'd proudly announced

his plans to marry coed Sandra Shepherd, it had nearly
broken her heart.

*Hopefully whoever broke into his apartment doesn't
figure out where he's gone*, she thought, realizing she
did believe his story of the attack. If thugs came after
him here, their actions would certainly be taken seriously. The advantage she—and Sean—had while in
Desert Valley was her close ties with the police department and the Canyon County K-9 Training Center.

Nobody was going to pull the wool over the eyes
of the officials here, let alone fool trained dogs whose
senses were so well honed.

The previous batch of rookies and their K-9 partners
had helped nab a serial killer. If anyone should be scared
of coming to Desert Valley, it should be criminals.

Zoe smiled. Strangers here stood out like bright blos-
soms on a Cholla cactus in December. Nobody was
going to bother Sean and his son. Not while she and
her friends were on duty.

TWO

Despite the terrain in Desert Valley being anything but Christmas-like, Sean noticed red and green decorations hung from every light post, and twinkling lights festooned the fronts of businesses along the main street of the small Arizona town.

As he looked for a place to park, he glanced in the rearview mirror at Patrick, who was still fast asleep in his car seat, then pulled to the curb in front of the only official-looking building he saw. He let his truck idle while he called Zoe's cell. "I'm here. Where are you?"

"Already? What did you do, drive night and day?"

"As a matter of fact, yes. I'm in front of the police station. I'd planned to go in and ask for you, but Patrick's asleep and I'd hate to wake him."

"I'm at the training center. It's about a quarter mile east, on the same road. Can you see the sign from there?"

He peered into the brightness of the rising sun. "I think so. Stay put. I'm on my way."

The hair on the back of his neck prickled as he looked in the side-view mirror to check for oncoming traffic. There was nobody in sight, yet his senses remained on high alert, as they had been since the break-in. Every dark SUV seemed to be on his trail, not to mention a few other models and colors. The sensation was akin to driving on drifting sand that might be hiding an improvised explosive device. Yeah, been there, done that.

His focus shifted. *There she was!* Sight of the slim, dark-haired woman with a large dog at her side raised Sean's spirits immeasurably. How could he have forgotten how lovely his old friend was? How pleasing it was to be around her?

Zoe waved. Sean's heart beat faster. This reunion felt more like coming home than he'd imagined it would. He was older and wiser, of course. Well, at least older. If he'd been at all wise, he'd have realized how much Zoe had meant to him in the first place.

Cruising to a stop at the low curb, Sean sat behind the wheel and tried to regain control of his emotions. This wasn't another flashback of the kind that left him frightened and fearful. This was the kind that made him want to weep and wrap Zoe in an embrace that should be reserved for close family—or the woman he loved. She was neither, and yet…

Her grin was wide, her dark eyes sparkling. He didn't notice she was decked out in a police uniform and fully armed until he'd climbed out of the truck. Some men might have found that off-putting, but it pleased Sean greatly.

The decision of whether or not to hug her was taken from him the instant she threw herself into his arms. All he could do was hang on and blink back tears.

To his surprise and relief, her eyes were moist when she released him. She swiped at her cheeks, grinned and sniffled. "Bright sun will do this to me every time."

"Yeah. Me, too." He was so glad to see her he was nearly speechless. The urge to kiss her was too strong to resist, so he brushed his lips against her cheek before straightening to say, "You're looking good."

"Not so bad yourself," she countered with a blush. "You've packed on more muscle since we were in college."

"Compliments of Uncle Sam." His gaze drifted to his truck. "I wish I'd known before, what I know now."

"Yeah, well, time has a way of wising us up whether we like it or not."

"You never married?" he found himself asking.

Zoe laughed softly. "If you asked my chief back in Mesa, he'd say I'm married to my job. I like to think it's worth it." She sobered. "Did you have any trouble getting here?"

"Not that I know of. I kept thinking we were being followed, but it was probably my imagination. I tend to do that. If I hadn't actually fought with those two guys in my apartment, I'd be wondering if the attack was real."

"I asked the chief here, Ryder Hayes, to send for a copy of your incident report," Zoe said. "There wasn't much to it."

"Did it say whether there was news on the ballistics?"

"Not yet. Don't get discouraged. We'll keep an eye on your case."

He scanned her khaki uniform. "Are you working here?"

"Not today, but I do sub. Just getting the dog used to seeing me ready for duty and doing a bit of extra training. Why don't I get my car and you can follow me home. I'm sure you'd like to get Patrick settled and get some rest yourself."

"Home with you? I figured I'd rent a motel room."

"Don't be silly. I have plenty of space."

He eyed the panting dog at their feet. "What about your K-9? Will she be okay with a kid?"

"Yes, she'll be fine. That was part of her training. These dogs can differentiate between felons and friends."

Still concerned, Sean leaned closer to speak more privately even though they were alone. "Patrick is not typical in any sense of the word, Zoe. We're going to have to be very careful when we introduce them. The poor kid has had it rough."

"I understand. I really do," she said. "But didn't his doctors warn against babying him too much?"

"Ensuring his safety is not the same thing. If those guys who broke into our apartment had seen him acting up, they might have shot him just to make him be quiet." Sean squelched a shiver. "When he gets scared and can't communicate, he tends to panic."

"Maybe Freya can help with that, too," Zoe said. "This evening, after supper, I'll invite my trainer and the K-9 cop who founded the assistance dog center to join us for coffee and dessert. That way Patrick won't have to sit through a whole meal with strangers if he isn't able, and they'll still get a good idea of your needs. Okay?"

"Sounds like you've worked it all out."

"I'm doing my best."

"I know you are." Starting to turn toward his truck he said, "Let's go. I'm ready."

Traffic was predictably light all the way to the rented house. The place was actually too big for one person but was all that had been available, so she'd leased it. Looking back, she wondered if God had arranged the extra room for this purpose. True or not, the notion was comforting.

She motioned Sean to pull into the driveway ahead of her. Instead, he drove onto the sorry excuse for a lawn and left room by the garage for her.

"I meant for you to use the driveway," she said, approaching his truck.

"It all looks the same to me."

"So I gathered. You parked on what's supposed to be the lawn when it gets proper watering."

"Sorry." An eyebrow arched. "Is it always this cold here? When I think of the desert, I picture heat."

"It depends on the elevation and time of year," Zoe said. "A light jacket is usually enough for us, even in the winter. When there's snow in Flagstaff and around the Grand Canyon, it can feel colder, though. It generally warms up during the day and cools off when the sun goes down."

She leaned to peer into his truck and smiled broadly at the little boy who'd just awakened. "You must be Patrick." When the child hid his face, she added, "My name is Zoe."

"That's right," Sean said. "This is the friend I told you about while we were driving. She's a very nice lady."

Still, the child cowered. "I'll go get my partner," she told Sean, adding a smile at Patrick. "Then we'll all go inside together."

Forcing the little boy to act sociable would have been wrong no matter what. Since he was clearly afraid, Zoe wanted to make certain this first meeting with her K-9 went smoothly. Therefore, she ordered Freya to heel and kept her on a short leash.

Sean was carrying Patrick and waiting at the front door of the simple, one-story, stucco home. The boy had his face pressed to his daddy's shoulder, hiding his eyes as if doing that made him invisible.

Sensing his uneasiness, the dog whined and wagged her tail. Zoe was about to silence her when she saw a big blue eye peeking out to see what was making the noise.

"This is Freya," Zoe said. "She lives and works with me. She's really friendly."

The key turned in the lock. Zoe pushed open the door and stood back. "After you."

A small hand reached back, and both of the child's eyes peered over Sean's shoulder. "Da."

"Dog? Yes, she's a dog. A very nice dog," Zoe said. "Would you like to meet her?"

"Da!"

Zoe laughed. "I think it's time you put Patrick down, Sean. He may not be ready to accept me," she whispered, "but it looks like he's more than ready to have a fur buddy."

"I don't know."

"Let's try it," she suggested. "Put Patrick down so he and Freya can meet on the same level." A flat hand in front of the eager K-9's muzzle kept her from lunging and overwhelming the child the way most dogs would.

As soon as the boy's shoes touched the floor he ducked behind his daddy's leg, holding on at the knee. Zoe wasn't worried. She caught Sean's eye and shook her head to keep him from interfering, then sat on her heels.

"Patrick, this is Freya." She looked to her panting partner. "Freya, this is Patrick. *Friend*."

There was no doubt the dog agreed. Although she kept her distance as ordered, she began to wiggle as if seated on a hill of swarming ants.

"Put your hand out like this and let her sniff you," Zoe said, demonstrating. "She can tell you like her by the way your fingers smell."

Sean interrupted. "Is that true?"

"In a manner of speaking. She can sense fear and pick out gunpowder residue, plus all sorts of icky things I won't mention. The key is this introduction. It will be your turn as soon as Patrick is done."

"Maybe I should…"

"Trust me?" she said.

A soft chuckle preceded Sean's reply. "Since when did you get so bossy?"

"Since I was trained and know what I'm doing."

"Humph. Okay. You're the police officer."

"Yup," she said with an echoing laugh. "Watch and learn, civilian."

Another hand signal caused Freya to lie down. Patrick reached forward. She sniffed his fingertips, then licked them. He giggled. "Like me."

"Yes, she does. And so do I," Zoe said. As if on cue, the dog rolled over, tail still wagging, legs flopping wide. "She trusts you and wants you to scratch her tummy," Zoe told the boy. "Go ahead. Her fur is really soft."

He had to come out from behind Sean and squat to reach the dog's stomach. Zoe couldn't have been happier at his rapid response. She grinned up at Sean. "Okay. Your turn. She wouldn't have rolled over if she was worried about you, so join the party."

Sean began by crouching, then dropped all the way next to his son, keeping one arm around him. Patrick eased into his father's lap, followed closely by Freya. The idyllic scene was the kind that made Zoe wish she could snap a photo without disturbing them. Father and son were hugging each other while the dog leaned against Sean's chest and reached up to lick under his chin as if they had known each other for years.

He laughed. "As Patrick said, I think she likes me."

"I'd say so. It's a good thing her main training is in search and rescue. You might be ruining her if she was an attack dog."

"Really?"

Because he looked worried she admitted to teasing. "No. Not really. But it is unusual to see her take to anybody so fast."

"She knows we're the good guys, right, Patrick?" Sean said. The boy nodded his agreement.

Zoe slowly rose. "Tell you what. After you put your things in your room and we go shopping for your favorite foods, maybe I'll have time to teach Patrick how to brush her. Would you like that, honey?"

Again a nod, this time with a shy smile. Zoe had no quarrel with his medical diagnosis. She simply saw more to Patrick's reticence than brain damage. In her opinion, he needed to be showered with love in order to be more confident, to blossom the way she felt he could.

Whether there would be time for her to help enough to matter was not up to her, it was up to her heavenly Father. She was beginning to suspect that Sean's need to come to Desert Valley was not limited to one objective. There was healing here for him. And for Patrick. And, God willing, for her, as well.

It had been a long time since she'd actually looked forward to having free time and not concentrating on her job 24/7. Truth to tell, she sort of felt like a puppy that had just been let out into a big play yard for the first time. If she hadn't been afraid of frightening Patrick she might have pumped a fist in the air and danced around the room.

THREE

After a quick tour of the house, Sean agreed to ride with Zoe and Freya rather than drive separately to the grocery store. If she had been anybody other than an armed police officer, he wasn't sure what he'd have done. He'd been so used to taking care of himself and being the only responsible adult in his son's life, it felt odd to not stay in full control.

She glanced over at him and smiled. "What's wrong?"

"Nothing."

"Right. And I'm Santa Claus. Talk to me, Murphy. I know something's bugging you."

Shrugging, he smiled at her. "Actually, I just realized I can relax a little when I'm with you. It's hard to accept."

"What is? Relaxing or trusting me?"

"Not being in command. Since I got back to the States, I've had to do it all. Believe me, the Shepherds didn't like most of my decisions."

"Such as?"

Sean lowered his voice and glanced over his shoulder at the backseat where his son and the dog were having a whispered conversation that included a lot of face licking on Freya's part. "Whether or not to bring Patrick home, for one. They wanted him to either stay in rehab or go to their house for private treatment. When I saw how unhappy he was in the hospital environment and how much better he acted with me, I decided to spring him."

"What did his therapists say?"

It hurt to repeat the negative opinions. "They felt he had made all the progress he probably would, and it didn't matter whether I left him there or took him with me."

"Then you have no reason to feel guilty." Zoe smiled. "Right?"

"Right. All I have to do is get my own act together so I can be a good father to him. If I keep having flashbacks, I may have to relinquish custody—for his sake."

"And give it to whom? I remember when your mom and dad were killed in that auto accident during my second semester of college." She arched her brows. "Surely you wouldn't consider your wife's parents after what you've told me!"

"No, no. Never them. They've already indicated that their idea of handling his problems is to overlook how much he needs love." Although he wanted to turn his face away and retreat, Sean remained stoic. "I had no idea how bad things had gotten while I was in the service. Sandra told me she'd gone home to her family's estate because she was lonely, not because she intended to stay stoned all the time and wanted Mommy and Daddy to watch Patrick."

"That's what happened?"

"Yeah."

"So, you asked for a discharge?"

"It wasn't that simple. I was on my way to the airport, ready to fly home because of Patrick's accident, when one of my buddies drove over an IED. The explosion took out half the Humvee and killed two men. I was thrown clear. By the time I got out of the hospital, I'd been diagnosed with PTSD, Sandra had died from an overdose and Patrick was still struggling to recover."

"Wow."

Sean nodded soberly. "Yeah. My sentiments exactly."

"You should be thankful you were able to get him away from your in-laws for this trip. I'm sure they didn't like it."

"I didn't tell them. They act as though I'm the reason for everything that went wrong." His jaw set. "Actually, they aren't the only ones. I had a long layover in Minneapolis during the trip home and used the time to pay a condolence visit to the family of one of the men who'd been with me in the Humvee. They slammed the door in my face. I guess they blamed me since they had no one else around to be mad at."

"I'm so sorry."

"As they say, 'No good deed goes unpunished,' right?"

Zoe pulled into the supermarket parking lot, found a space and turned to stare at him. "Could *they* have been responsible for sending the thugs to harm you?"

"I can't see why. Or how."

"What about Sandra's folks?"

"No. Violence is definitely not their way of handling problems. They have enough money to hire the best lawyers and sue for custody if they want me out of the picture."

He saw her hands fist on the steering wheel as she asked, "Do you think they might resort to that?"

"Unless I can get a grip on my flashbacks and prove I'm stable, it's a possibility. That's another reason why I need the help of a service dog. I've seen for myself what a difference one of those can make. Guys who were hardly able to leave their houses are working again and leading fairly normal lives."

"You managed to drive all the way down here. Are you sure you qualify?"

"I don't know whether I could have made myself act if it hadn't been for Patrick," Sean said flatly. "Whatever I did, I did for him. And that's what I'll keep doing for as long as I'm able."

She patted the back of his hand. "I believe you."

The grocery store was crowded. Zoe grabbed a cart, wiped it down to eliminate germs and stood back. "There you go, Patrick. All ready."

The child buried his face against his father's shoulder and clung to him.

"Wait right here," she said. "I'll be back in a sec."

There was no rule against taking her K-9 partner with her anywhere she went. She had left Freya in the car to simplify their shopping trip but could now see that had been a mistake. Freya was Patrick's temporary service dog, had been since the moment he'd laid a small hand on her back and let her lead him from room to room in the unfamiliar house.

A working vest identified Freya the way a badge gave Zoe authority. She buckled it on and the dog assumed a more cautious demeanor.

"Good girl. Heel."

Patrick's face lit with a smile. His eyes twinkled. "Da."

"That's right, Patrick," Zoe said. "The dog is coming with us. Can you show her how nicely you sit in the cart?"

She was afraid Sean might balk when it came time to let go. Thankfully, he didn't. Patrick's feet slipped through the leg openings, and he grasped the cart handle as if preparing to ride a bucking bronco.

"Freya will stay right here next to us while we shop," Zoe said. "Will you help me watch her to make sure she behaves?"

The child nodded. "Good da."

"That's right. She's a very good dog."

Sean took up a position on the side opposite the dog so they flanked the boy well. Zoe supposed she couldn't blame him for caution, but some of his choices seemed excessive. Maternal instinct kept insisting that there was no way any child could reach full potential when he or she was kept so close, so guarded, yet she could also identify with the urge to protect Patrick.

As they worked their way through the store, however, her opinion softened. Sean was gently but firmly requiring the boy to at least try to name whatever food he wanted them to buy. Truth to tell, she would have lost patience if she hadn't known how important the exercise was.

"I didn't think we were ever going to get those tangerines," she commented on their way to checkout. "You did a wonderful job working through the name."

"I watched the doctors," Sean said. "It seemed to me they were making things too simple until I realized that breaking the words into syllables was the way to go." He stepped ahead of her and took out his wallet. "Let me get this. Most of it's for us, anyway."

"I don't mind."

"I know. Humor me."

His smile warmed her cheeks enough that she backed off and let him pay. Freya stayed at the rear of the cart as they both bent to unload it. Zoe was concentrating so completely on Sean, it took her a few seconds to notice the dog's low growl. She grabbed his arm to still him and froze, herself.

His response was immediate, his voice raspy. "What?"

"The dog. Look."

Instead of facing them, tongue lolling and tail wagging, Freya had turned so that her back was to Patrick and the adults. She was staring past the next person in line and focusing on one of the aisles.

Zoe rested the heel of her hand on her holster and straightened. "You finish checking out while I go see what's wrong."

"No."

The command was so forceful, so packed with emotion, she stopped. He was right. If the dog was sensing danger and had put her back to them, then she was reacting to an unseen threat inside the store. As an off-duty police officer, it was still Zoe's duty to protect and serve. Should she protect her friends and serve the community by calling the station and reporting a possible problem? Maybe. The trouble was, without any visible threat she'd be out of line to do so. Nevertheless, she made the call.

Staying on full alert, Zoe kept her eye on her dog and the other shoppers while Sean loaded the bags in their cart and paid the cashier.

"Ready to go," he said behind her.

"Okay. You lead the way. Look for anybody from

your past or things that seem unusual. I'll bring up the rear."

"It was dark when I was attacked in my apartment. I didn't get a good look at either of those guys."

"Doesn't matter," she said. "You know how to judge body language from being in combat. This isn't a lot different."

She heard him sigh before he said, "Yeah, providing I don't see an innocent person and read more into their posture than is really there."

"Better safe than sorry." As soon as the automatic door slid closed behind them she moved to shield the boy despite the fact that Freya had settled down.

Sean noticed. "Looks like the dog is okay now."

"Yes. The threat was apparently inside. Go ahead and load Patrick and the food into the car while I stand guard. We'll leave as soon as a local unit arrives."

"How soon will that be?"

"Hopefully, not long." She used her cell phone again, then told him, "ETA less than five."

"Why didn't you radio?"

"Because I'm not actually on duty now." Waving to an approaching patrol car she stepped away. "Here they are. Be right back."

Sean watched her jog across the parking lot to speak with the other officers. He'd managed to quell unreasonable fear inside the store and was feeling even less jittery now that they were out. Patrick was already in the backseat, as was the working dog. Some of the plastic grocery bags were piled on the floor while others shared the bench seat with the child and the K-9. Sean was surprised to see Freya sitting quietly instead of wiggling as before and stepping on perishables.

"Ah, you're still in uniform, aren't you," he muttered. "Of course. You think you're on duty."

At first, he assumed the dog's ensuing reaction was to his voice. She slowly rose, growling and bristling. The effect of her hair standing up made her look twice as big. And dangerous. But she wasn't looking at him. Or at his son. Again, she was focused beyond them.

"Zoe!" Sean shouted.

She whirled, her hand hovering over her holster. "What?"

Sean turned to follow the dog's line of sight. A beefy man wearing a dark vest was walking past in the distance. He could have been anybody. There was no reason for concern. Or was there?

By the time Zoe rejoined him at her car, the stranger had climbed into a dusty red pickup.

She touched Sean's arm. "Did you recognize somebody?"

"No." Frowning, he kept watching as the truck pulled away. "It was your dog again. She really doesn't like that guy in the dirty truck."

"She may have picked up the scent of gunpowder or drugs coming from him. Whatever is wrong, I'd trust her opinion over that of almost any human."

"Okay." Still peering at the truck, Sean caught his breath and reached for Zoe's arm. "Look!"

"What? What do you see that I don't?"

"The passenger," Sean gasped. "His arm. On the open window. It looks like it's in a cast!"

"Why would...?"

"Because I hit one of my attackers with Patrick's baseball bat. Remember?"

"You told me you fought them off. You never mentioned a bat." She was already running back to direct the patrol car. Those officers jumped into their unit and started in pursuit.

"Do you think they'll catch them?" Sean called as she returned.

A solemn shake of her head was all the answer he got. All he needed. Given the delay starting the pursuit, chances were not good.

"Sorry," Sean said. "I shouldn't have put Patrick in the car. I just thought it would be safer."

"It was. It is. I wouldn't have chased after them in a private vehicle, anyway. It's dangerous enough with red lights and sirens."

He nodded.

"Believe it or not, we don't usually go around acting wild like the cops on TV and in the movies. I have yet to take a class on how to jump onto the top of a speeding car and disarm the suspects inside."

"No?" Despite the recent fright, he couldn't help smiling slightly at the mental picture. "That's too bad. I'd have liked to watch."

"Then rent a DVD. I'm not doing any leaping."

"Not even to entertain Patrick?"

"No, but I do have some ideas for him. If we get you into a class soon, I can recommend a local day care. The police chief's daughter goes there, so you know it's very safe."

Sean had to take a deep breath before trying to answer. "I never thought about having to leave him. I figured he could stay with me. He'll behave. I know he will. Particularly if he gets to watch dogs."

"And not be allowed to play with them? I doubt it," Zoe said. "But let's not get ahead of ourselves. We still have to convince Ellen Foxcroft to put you in her program."

"You're right. One thing at a time," Sean said. "Let's go home."

"And keep an eye out for that red truck on the way."

"Oh, yeah." He had already buckled up and was braced to keep watch, front and rear.

Had the would-be assassins really tracked him here? Were they that clever? Was he that careless? He hadn't thought so, but it was beginning to look as if the danger he'd wanted to escape was still with him.

If only he knew why somebody wanted him dead. Knowing *why* might point him to *who* and he'd know what to do next. There had to be something. There had to be. He needed to survive for Patrick's sake. Surely God wouldn't punish an innocent child for the mistakes of his parents.

If he still believed in the power of prayer, he might reach out. Beg for protection for his son. However, he had prayed repeatedly for Sandra's redemption and look what the result had been. How could he trust a God who let a child nearly drown? Who deprived the boy of a mother?

That thought brought him up short. In the case of Sandra's untimely death, perhaps that was the only thing that had protected Patrick from her drug-induced mania. But then the pool. Why the pool?

Sean's mind was whirling, stunned by myriad possibilities, none of which made sense to him. He was a civilian now, ready to take care of his son, but he wasn't whole, either. How could a loving heavenly Father expect to use an earthly father who was so damaged?

And then it hit him. Without Patrick, without purpose, there would be no reason to fight anymore. No reason to try to heal. No reason to have come to Desert Valley, to have reunited with the extraordinary woman seated beside him.

He gazed at Zoe. Right now, he needed her help. Maybe, when all this was over, he'd be able to repay her kindness. He certainly hoped so because now that he had seen her again, he didn't intend to let more long years pass without keeping in closer touch. If he had not had her to reach out to when his life fell apart recently he didn't know how he'd have managed.

Something flashed in the rays of the setting sun, as if glinting off a gun barrel. Sean yelled. Ducked. Unsnapped his seat belt and threw himself over the back of his seat toward Patrick just as a shot rang out.

Freya closed her mouth on Sean's shoulder to stop him but didn't bite hard enough to break the skin.

Zoe swerved toward the curb. "Anybody hit?"

"No," he shouted. "I saw a reflection just in time. Get us out of here!"

"Hang on!"

Temporarily steering with one hand, she punched a button on her cell phone. "Trent here. Possible shots fired. We're almost to my house. It's the old Peterson place on Second, not far from Sophie Williams's. We took fire about a half-mile south. Can't pinpoint the exact location."

Sean barely had hold of the buckle on his seat belt

when she dropped the phone and fisted both hands tightly on the wheel. Her jaw was set.

"What did they say?"

"They're on the scene. Found the red truck, abandoned, close to where we were shot at. It was stolen. If the guys took off on foot, they were probably our shooters."

"That makes sense."

"Maybe. Maybe not. Either way, I'm getting you and Patrick back inside where you'll be safer. They can't hit you if they can't see you."

"I'm sorry I dragged you into this," Sean said.

"You didn't drag me into anything. I walked in with both eyes open. This is what I do. Why I got into this business. What good is all my special training if I don't use it?"

He recalled one silly way they used to tease each other in college and revived it, hoping his breathlessness wasn't too evident. "So, where's your superhero cape?"

"At the cleaner's," she shot back as she slid the car around a tight corner in perfect control. "I use a badge and a gun, now."

Sean sighed. "That's my Zoe. Saving the world, one friend at a time."

He wasn't happy with the role reversal. Men were supposed to rescue damsels in distress. He snorted quietly. That was not likely to happen when the woman in question was his old friend, Zoe Trent.

FOUR

Zoe didn't slow much as she entered the open garage. If she hadn't been concerned about the whole situation, she might have laughed when Sean braced himself on the dash with both hands.

"I've been taught defensive driving," she said. "Don't panic."

"Defensive is one thing. Driving through the back wall of a garage is another."

"Ya think?" A soft chuckle erupted. "Don't worry. I have complete control."

"So you say. If you don't mind, I'll get out now."

"I don't mind a bit." She was lowering the mechanized garage door behind them with the push of a button. "This side door to the house isn't locked. Go on in with Patrick. I'll bring Freya and the groceries."

"You get the dog. I'll get the food."

"Now who's being bossy?"

"I am." He'd already bent and picked up his son when she joined him and asked, "Is there a problem with his motor skills, too?"

"Some. Why?"

"Because I thought it would be good for him to walk more. He can lean on Freya again if he needs support."

"He falls easily."

"And how did he learn to walk in the first place?"

She noted Sean's sigh. Perhaps she was being too out-spoken. Then again, maybe bluntness was just what he needed. It was possible to love someone or something so much you didn't give it the opportunity to learn and grow. The same was true of the canines in the various programs. If they weren't pushed, they'd not only fail to make progress, they might regress. Training was a daily necessity, as was affection. Each had its place and time.

Leading the way, Zoe entered with the dog at her heels, leaving the door open behind them. When she turned, Sean was gently lowering Patrick to the floor and bending to speak to him.

"I'll be right back, buddy. I have to go get your tangerines and the other stuff we bought. You watch the dog for us like you did at the store, okay?"

The tousled, blond head nodded without hesitation. "Good da."

"Dog." Sean put emphasis on the final letter. "Daw—guh."

To Zoe's surprise and joy, Patrick repeated it perfectly. She would have cheered if she hadn't seen moisture gleaming in his father's eyes. Every small step was a triumph, every properly annunciated word a victory.

"Thank You, Lord, for letting me be a part of this amazing healing process," she whispered, blinking back her own tears. She'd thought her offer of assistance was meant for one person, and it was actually going to benefit at least two.

Make that three, she added. Not only had her heavenly Father reunited dear friends, He had placed her in a position to render aid and share blessings. No amount of threat, no lowlife with an evil agenda, was going to steal that from her. Not now. Not ever again.

The scheduled visit with lead K-9 trainer, Sophie Williams, and Ellen Foxcroft, the founder of the assistance dog program, took place as scheduled at Zoe's house. Sean liked both women, and Zoe's introduction of him and his disabled son wasn't maudlin. As a matter of fact, it was so uplifting he wondered if she'd talked her associates right out of helping him.

"I never claimed to be totally helpless," he told the women with a nod toward Patrick. "But as you can see, there are special circumstances. I not only need to be able to function for my own sake, I need to be there for my son. As much as it pains me to admit it, I'm not myself." His elbows were propped on his knees, his hands joined between them while he toyed with his wedding band.

Ellen mirrored his pose. Her reddish hair hung in a single braid down her back. Her gaze was tender. "I know how hard this is for you, Mr. Murphy. The human body sometimes deals with intense trauma in ways that go against everything we expect. That doesn't make us less of a person. It's how we cope with the aftereffects of disaster that will define who and what we become. By asking for help you've taken a big step, and I want to tell you how impressed I am."

"Just get me well for Patrick," Sean said with passion. "I don't care what it takes. Whatever I have to do, I'll do it. I promise."

"I know you will." She glanced at Sophie. "What do you think of giving Angel another chance?"

The lead trainer smiled and shook her head. "It's

easy to see why the folks who donated her named her Ding-a-ling. She really is a sweetheart, but do you really think she's salvageable?"

Zoe had been fidgeting. Now she spoke up. "Why Angel? I mean, she's lovable and partially trained in several disciplines, but she's also terribly headstrong and easily distracted."

"Exactly why she needs a strong, forceful, determined man as her partner," Ellen replied. "Mr. Murphy is right about not being as badly affected as many of our clients, so why not let him give Angel a try? It's that or wash her out of all our programs."

Watching his old friend's expression, Sean could tell she was mulling over the suggestion. A misfit dog for a misfit soldier. What could be better?

Zoe finally nodded. "Okay. How can I help?"

"We'll do introductions first thing in the morning. Bring everybody involved to the training center with you but don't wear your uniform. We want that meeting to be as casual as possible so we can judge Angel's reactions. If she passes that test, we'll make up a training schedule."

The women stood, as did Sean. "Thank you, both," he said.

Sophie nodded and shook Sean's hand, then paused and looked to Zoe. "By the way, what was the disturbance at the market all about? I understand from Ryder that a threat may have followed Mr. Murphy to Desert Valley, after all."

Sean knew she was referring to the chief of police, Ryder Hayes, the same person who had sent for the report about his break-in back in St. Louis.

"It started when I thought I saw somebody who had

caused me trouble in St. Louis," Sean explained. "It turned out they were driving a stolen truck and ditched it right before somebody took a potshot at Zoe's car."

Ellen nodded. "I heard we tried using James Harrison's bloodhound, but he lost their trail. Do you think the incidents were connected?"

"I'm sure beginning to," Zoe said. "Freya reacted to one of the guys when we were all in the store."

Sophie nodded. "We'll all need to be on alert. See you tomorrow morning at eight."

Sean hung back as Zoe walked her friends to the door. Patrick had curled up on the sofa with Freya. The dog opened one eye, studied him for a second, then closed it, sighed and relaxed. If the new dog he was about to meet was half the canine companion Freya was, he'd be more than satisfied.

It suddenly struck him that canine senses were going to be the answer. If he felt threatened and the dog did not, then he'd know his imagination was in charge. If, however, the dog reacted as well, he could begin to trust his own senses. To trust himself.

What might it be like to actually lighten up and enjoy life again? Considering the way he'd been feeling, the concept sounded both enticing and out of reach.

Sean shivered, remembering the words of his attackers. They had been sent to kill him. That was all there was to it. If they were here, in Desert Valley, there was no way he'd ever be able to let down his guard. Not if he expected to live long enough to raise his child.

Zoe took a brief phone call later in the evening. She'd watched the tension building on her friend's face as she'd listened, so the first thing she did was set Sean's mind at ease. "That was Chief Hayes."

"What now?"

"Good news, actually," she said, smiling. "They were able to get usable prints off that stolen red truck. They belonged to local kids who have been in trouble here before, not hit men from St. Louis."

"They're sure?"

"Positive."

"But, the guy we saw in the parking lot was no kid."

"Maybe. Maybe not. In any case, they're also running a partial palm print through the AFIS database to see if there are any matches."

It pained her to see some of the starch go out of Sean's spine. "You can't convince me it's all in my head, so don't even try."

"That's not what I meant. We didn't find any shell casings today, but the bullet in your apartment ceiling was plenty real."

"True. I wish I had a better idea of who has it in for me. I haven't been home long enough to have made new enemies, so it has to be somebody from my past."

"Or Sandra's," Zoe said. "Did you pick up any of her stuff from her parents?"

"Nothing except clothes for Patrick and a few toys."

"Could she have hidden drugs in those?"

"If she did, the proof is back in my old apartment. I left too fast to take much with me."

"I could have Chief Hayes contact the St. Louis department and suggest they do a thorough search. The problem is, if they do turn up illicit drugs, it will look as if you were hiding them."

"I hadn't thought of that."

Zoe shrugged. "At this time it's a moot point. Any-body who thought you were hiding drugs has probably already ransacked the place. You can check when you're done training here and then involve the police if you need to after Christmas. In the meantime I'll be keep-ing careful watch, just in case. So will my colleagues."

"Mentioning Christmas reminds me," Sean said. "I can understand why you haven't put up holiday deco-rations, but would you mind if I did a few things for Patrick?"

She clapped her hands. "I'd love it! I wasn't even considering Christmas when I left Mesa in September."

"Do you know where we can get a tree?"

"I do. The church youth are having a sale. And re-hearsals are starting for the outdoor Christmas pageant, too. We can get Patrick involved in that when we go to church on Sunday."

The off-putting look on his face was disappointing. "We don't go to church."

She made a face. "Why not? You used to."

"Things change. People change." He lowered his voice to add, "I've changed."

"Fine. God hasn't. And whether you admit it or not, your little boy needs to learn about faith. If you won't go with us, Freya and I will take him."

"I could stop you."

"You could try." Although she no longer wore her holster or uniform, she struck a dominant pose, feet apart, hands fisted on the hips of her jeans, shoulders back. Yes, she was being pushy. And, yes, Patrick was Sean's responsibility. But she cared so much for both of them it was hard to stand back when she thought there was something she could do or say that would help.

"You're actually serious." Sean was frowning.

"You're right. I am."

"Okay, I'll think about it."

"You do that. And while you do, I'll be praying that you come to your senses."

"Why do you think faith makes sense?"

Zoe began to smile. "The very definition of faith is belief without seeing. You had it once." She jabbed a finger at his chest. "It's still in there. All you have to do is look."

"I have," Sean argued.

She wasn't about to back down. Not when she was convinced he needed his former faith in order to complete his healing. "If I could loan you some of mine I would, but it's an inside job. You can't borrow it or catch it like a cold. You have to seek the Lord yourself."

"God gave up on me long ago," Sean said flatly.

Zoe couldn't help smiling. Instead of continuing to argue, she merely said, "Then you might want to ask how you got here and why you escaped death when the bomb went off on your way to the airport and when those guys tried to kill you in St. Louis and since then, because it seems to me He's rescued you over and over lately."

The expression on her old friend's face was painful to look at when he focused on his only child and said, "I'd gladly have traded those supposed rescues for Patrick's well-being."

Why *did* bad things happen? She had no idea. But she was certain of one thing. The only way she'd have survived the tragic loss of her baby brother was through a belief that they would someday be reunited in heaven.

And in the meantime, she intended to stand up for

earthly justice as best she could. It was foolish to try to discern divine wisdom or assume she could figure out everything that was occurring. All she knew for sure was that she was glad Sean had come to her and brought his son. Anything beyond that would work out for the best.

Zoe didn't know why she was so positive, but she wasn't about to argue with her conclusions. If it became necessary for her to act as the law enforcement officer she was, then so be it. Rookie or not, she was ready.

Mulling over the recent call about the fingerprints in the stolen truck, she realized Sean was right. The figure they had seen get into it was no teenager. He'd not only looked like an adult, he'd moved like one. Heavy. Purposeful.

Dangerous? Maybe. Probably. She felt a shiver climb her spine like a squirrel skittering up the trunk of a ponderosa pine. At the same time she was encouraging Sean to relax, she was going to have to double her guard. And keep him from realizing it.

FIVE

Their first stop the following morning was to be the training center. Sean had made pancakes for all of them while Zoe tended to the coffee and helped Patrick dress. He had only allowed her to assist the boy because the doctors had recommended changing off caregivers to encourage independence. It had apparently worked because when she entered the kitchen, Patrick was holding her hand and walking. His gait was stiff and somewhat awkward, but he seemed far more capable than previously.

"We came for pancakes." Zoe helped the boy into a chair and tucked a napkin under his chin.

When she paused and looked to Patrick, Sean heard him say, "Please."

"My pleasure." Deeply moved, Sean was turning away to tend the stove when his son added, "Please, Dad-dy." The frying pan faded for a moment while he regained control of his emotions.

When he looked back at the table, Zoe was beaming. "Good, huh?"

"Very good. Thanks for helping."

"Freya helped, too. She pulled on the toes of his socks while he tried to put them on. Patrick had to really fight to get them up."

"By himself?" Sean was astonished.

"Yup. All by himself."

"That's wonderful."

Zoe joined him at the stove. "Why don't you let me finish cooking while you two eat? I'm used to grabbing a quick cup of coffee and whatever I can chew on the run."

"Are we in a hurry?" Sean asked, suspicious.

"You do want to get started with your new dog, don't you?"

His brows knit. "Yes. But I'm getting the idea that there's more to your suggestion than you're letting on. What is it?"

"Nothing. Just..."

"Just what, Zoe?" Instead of going to the table, he lingered close to her. "You may as well tell me. I'm not going to eat a bite until you do."

"All right." As she raised her face, he saw concern mirrored in the dark depths of her eyes. "They got a hit on the ballistics from the bullet fired in your apartment."

"And?"

"And that gun had been used before. In multiple murders. Whoever came after you was no novice, even if he did behave like one that night."

"Hit men? Somebody sent professional hit men after me? Why?"

"It's anybody's guess," she said. "The only good thing about the information is that they're unlikely to have left the metropolitan area and followed you here."

If she had not been trembling slightly, Sean might have felt more comforted by her conclusion. Taking her elbow, he guided her to the table and urged her into one of the chairs. "Sit. I'll bring you breakfast. And then we'll go get my dog so I can be on my way."

"It doesn't work like that," she insisted. "If you're paired with one of Ellen's assistance dogs, you have to stay in Desert Valley for training."

Sean hesitated. Of course he had to stay. There was no way he'd get the help he needed unless he played by the rules. He filled three plates and delivered them to the table, then busied himself cutting Patrick's food into bite-size pieces while he processed his dilemma.

"I see your point," he finally said. "And I suppose it won't help if I keep running. I was just trying to remove the danger from around you."

"I'm not the one you should be worrying about," she said. "After we see how Angel reacts to Patrick, we'll take Patrick to the day care that I think is best."

"I don't want…"

"I know. You don't want him away from you for a second. I get it. I do. But he'll be safer mixed in with other kids than he is if he stays with you all the time. You're the target, he isn't."

"Apparently. I just wish I knew why. The only important thing in my life is my son."

Zoe frowned. "As far as you know. There has to be something else going on. Someone hired the hit men for a reason. And the guys who are after you seem to be high-end. Who do you know with money to burn?"

"Sandra's parents, Alice and John Shepherd. But like I said, they'd hire a lawyer, not a thug."

"If you say so." She stuffed a bite of pancake into her mouth and licked her lips, momentarily distracting Sean and making him wonder what it would feel like to kiss that sweet mouth for real instead of only in his imagination. Shaking off the unwarranted thought, he said, "Okay. You're right. We'll go visit the day care. But I won't promise I'll leave him."

"Fair enough." Zoe licked her lips again, then reached for his mug. "More coffee?"

Sean was still staring at her tender, sweet mouth. "Huh?"

"Pay attention, Murphy. Do you want a refill?"

Sean merely nodded. He'd been paying attention, all right. To the wrong thing. The more time he spent with Zoe, the more he realized what a fool he had been to marry Sandra. He'd apparently been deluded by his youthful desires and had made the biggest mistake of his life; one it was too late to correct.

Or was it? Studying Zoe and admitting his own shortcomings, he concluded they would never be a good match. Not now. Not when she was so capable and he was damaged goods. Sadly, their chance for happiness had passed. He was simply pleased she'd stepped into his life long enough to render the kind of specialized aid for which she'd been trained.

Those thoughts led him further into the doldrums and left him wondering if she would consider looking after Patrick if something bad happened to him. It wasn't fair to even suggest it, of course, yet he desperately wanted to be able to count on someone he trusted. To know his son would be loved and cared for if the assassins finally succeeded.

Maybe later he'd bring up the subject, Sean decided. If he lived long enough.

A gentle touch on his arm drew him back to the present. Zoe had put down his steaming mug and was leaning closer, staring as if he'd just had an episode of regression. If he turned his head just a little, maybe…

"Earth to Murphy. Are you all right?"

"Fine." He swallowed hard. "Thanks for the coffee."

"Where were you just now? You didn't seem to be fighting a war again."

"Not the shooting kind." He laid his hand over hers and lowered his voice to speak more privately while Patrick happily stuffed himself, ignoring the adults. "I was just imagining the future if something happened to me."

"Well, something won't, so cut it out."

"If something did—" he cleared his throat and continued in a hoarse whisper "—would you consider becoming Patrick's guardian?"

"Me?"

"I know it's a lot to ask, but…"

"I'm not refusing. I'm touched, that's all." She eyed the content child and smiled. "He's the most important person in your whole life and you're offering to trust me to take care of him. Of course I'd do it." She placed her free hand over where theirs were joined, and sniffled.

The moisture glistening in her eyes brought a similar reaction in his as he said, "Thank you."

Next to them, grinning and sticky with syrup, Patrick giggled and echoed, "Tank you," interrupting their moving exchange and destroying the romantic mood.

Zoe recovered first, pulled away and pointed to the boy. "Your daddy will clean you up while I clear the table."

"I will?" Sean lifted an eyebrow.

"Oh, yeah. I may have offered to look after him in an emergency, but I'm not starting now. You fed him pancakes, so you get to wash off the sticky."

"You drive a hard bargain, Officer Trent."

She laughed. "You'd better believe it."

Sobering, Sean lifted his son into his arms. "You meant what you said? You'll step in if..."

"Absolutely. And if you're as serious about it as I am, we need to see an attorney and make it official."

It occurred to him to tease about marrying her, instead, then decided it would be cruel to even suggest such a thing. He was not going to place her in an untenable position, nor was he going to take the chance she might actually agree, for Patrick's sake.

"Fine," Sean said, as he left the kitchen. "You make the arrangements, and I'll keep my head down until it's legal."

"You'd better plan on keeping it down a lot longer than that," Zoe shouted after him. "I understand puppies a lot better than I understand little kids."

It was a delight to tour the training facility with Patrick. Every dog excited him, especially the pups he saw when Zoe kenneled Freya.

Crouching, she pointed to a pile of K-9 vests. "Remember how Freya acted different when she was wearing a police jacket and badge like those? Some of the dogs we have here are not very friendly even when they aren't all dressed up, so you shouldn't try to pet them without asking first. Understand?"

Patrick's head bobbed, his expression solemn. "Uh-huh."

"Good. Now let's go find my friends." She stood and offered her hand. "We need to introduce you and your daddy to Angel."

Judging by the way his eyes widened and he tugged

on her hand, Zoe assumed the reference had confused him. She explained. "That's her name, honey. She's not a real angel, like in the Bible."

He seemed to be searching for a word. "Wings?"

"No, Patrick. No wings. She's just a really sweet dog. Come on. The trainers are waiting for us."

A wry smile on Sean's face reminded her that Sophie and Ellen had warned him about possible problems. If he wasn't open to accepting Angel, Zoe wasn't sure he'd have a second chance. Of course, he wasn't the only one who needed to display camaraderie. The dog's reactions were as important as the human's.

"I'll take care of Patrick for a few minutes while you go with Ellen," Zoe said as soon as pleasantries had been exchanged. "We'll be right out here, watching."

He eyed her casual attire. "You're not armed today."

"Not visibly. This place is always full of officers, so there's no need to worry. Most of the previous rookie class is still here, working for the DVPD, and some of those in my group stayed over to sub so officers like Shane Weston could go home to Flagstaff for Christmas. I think you'll like Tristan McKeller when you meet him, too. I mentioned him—he's a former soldier, same as you."

"The same? I doubt that." He hesitated. "You do understand why I won't carry a gun, right?"

"Because you don't want to have a flashback episode and make a terrible mistake. I get it. But if you think about all that's happened here and the way you've been protected, you'll see there's no need to be armed."

"I suppose gut feelings don't count."

"Not if they're yours. Sorry," she said, smiling to soften the comment even more. "Give it time. Heal.

Work through your nervousness with a service dog by your side. Then you won't even want to be armed."

Sean sighed noisily. "I hope you're right."

"Haven't you heard? I am *always* right." Nudging him through the doorway after Ellen, she lifted Patrick and balanced him on her hip. "Wow. You're heavy today. Must be from all the pancakes you ate."

"Uh-huh."

As his small arms circled her neck and squeezed, Zoe felt a surge of emotion she had not anticipated. He was all shampoo and soap and syrup and...and love. How had that happened? She'd liked him from their first meeting but had attributed those feelings to her friendship with his father. This was different. This was personal. And very dear.

Toting Patrick to the one-way viewing window, she told him to watch while his daddy met the dog that might provide their deliverance. Having a bond develop during an initial meeting was iffy, at best. The quirk on Angel's side was her overabundance of love. She could track fairly well, but was more likely to lick a criminal she apprehended than to growl or bite him as she was supposed to. That was what had ultimately washed her out of the K-9 cop program.

Sean was seated in a chair in the center of the room. A side door opened. Sophie started to lead Angel in and was almost jerked off her feet when the dog realized there were other people present.

"You may as well release her," Zoe heard Ellen say.

"Da!" Patrick didn't take his eyes off the leaping, dancing, pulling canine. "Da-gh."

Zoe gave him a squeeze. "That's right. Dog. Very good."

"Daddy."

Tears pooled in Zoe's eyes as she watched the scene unfold. Unleashed, Angel left the trainer at a run, made a dash to Sean and almost knocked him over backward, chair and all, when she tried to jump into his lap.

Of course he did everything wrong after that, including hugging the affectionate dog and letting her lick his face. She made several circles around the room, her nails scrambling on the slick floor, then returned to him to greet him with more exuberance.

All Zoe could do was whisper, "Thank You, Jesus," and swipe at her damp cheeks. They still had a lot of work ahead of them, but Sean and Patrick Murphy had their service dog. They would be staying in Desert Valley for training.

The two trainers had managed to corral Angel, fit her with a working harness and put her back on a long leash so Sean could walk her in the fenced training yard.

"How did you know she'd take to my son so fast?" Sean asked Zoe.

"She loves everybody. That's her problem. She'd rather give and receive affection than settle down and work."

"And that makes her good for me how?"

"We'll have to wait and see. If she forms a strong enough bond with your family, she may naturally provide protection."

"Suppose she doesn't. What then?"

Zoe surprised him with a sock on his shoulder. The dog was so busy wiggling and trying to lick Patrick's face she didn't even seem to notice the playful blow.

"Hey. What did you hit me for?"

"Because of your rotten attitude. How can you expect good results when you think so negatively?" She waved her hands in front of him as if erasing the comment. "Never mind. Forget it."

Watching the interaction between Angel and the boy, Sean realized she had a valid point. "You're right. I was being a downer. Sorry. It's just…"

"I know. Let's take it one day at a time." She eyed the happy dog. "This morning is off to a great start."

"Can I let her go soon?"

"Why? Don't you like being pulled along like a musher on a sled in Alaska?"

"Not particularly. I know Ellen said she needed a strong man to control her, but doesn't she ever quiet down?"

"Actually, letting her run off some of that excess energy might be good." Zoe grabbed the leash near the harness and firmly commanded, "Sit."

Angel plunked down, trembling with excitement but sitting all the same. As soon as the clasp clicked, she tried to bolt, but Zoe still had hold of the harness. In a few seconds she gave the command of release.

Patrick clapped his hands as his new furry friend took off in a dead run, circling him as if corralling a herd of sheep.

"That's natural instinct," Zoe said. "Angel was a rescue. Her former owners insisted she was incorrigible. Because border collies are known for their intelligence, Sophie decided to put her in training and give her a chance."

"It's going to be hard to find her some sheep to chase around in St. Louis." As soon as he'd mentioned his former home, he saw Zoe's smile vanish. He didn't blame her. Thinking about their parting didn't make him happy, either. She was right about his mind-set, though. He needed to keep up his spirits for everyone's sake, especially Patrick's.

Forcing a wide smile, he tried to encourage his old friend. "Maybe I should buy a ranch."

Her brows arched. "Can you afford one?"

"No. Sandra kept insisting she had some kind of a trust fund to fall back on, but she never proved it to me. I imagine it was the drugs talking. If she'd had money, she could have gone anywhere instead of complaining about the housing I had provided on base and moving in with her parents."

"Did you ask them about it?"

"No way. They already thought I married her because they were wealthy. The last thing I want to do is mention piles of money, particularly before I get back on my feet and get a job to supplement my temporary disability." He shaded his eyes to watch the dog, saw her circle again and head straight for Patrick.

The boy opened his arms. Angel plowed into him and sent him sprawling. With an angry shout, Sean raced to the boy and tried to shove her away.

Instead of giving ground, however, she stood fast, feet braced and curled a lip at him while Patrick laughed so hard he was gasping for breath.

"Stop," Zoe ordered. "Freeze. Look at the dog."

Sean rocked back on his heels once he realized the child was unhurt. "What's she doing?"

"Protecting him. From you. You came at him shouting, and she sensed you were upset so she stood guard."

"She's supposed to look out for me, too."

"I think she will, once you two have bonded more.

Right now, I want to tell Ellen what just happened." She pulled out her cell phone. "This is amazing!"

As Sean relaxed and dropped into a sitting position beside the dog and child, he saw the canine back off, too. Given that he wanted to help Patrick as much as himself, he couldn't argue with what he'd just seen. If Zoe was pleased, so was he.

Deep breaths calmed him further. Scanning the yard, he noticed obstacles and jumps and all sorts of strange contraptions that he assumed were part of the training regimen. As soon as Zoe finished reporting to the service dog trainer, he planned to ask her how the equipment was used.

Definite joy filled her conversation. "That's right. She stopped to defend Patrick. I know. It's wonderful. Okay, we'll…"

When she broke off in midsentence Sean turned to look at her. Saw her pointing. Whipped around to follow her line of sight.

"The west fence," Zoe continued, this time cupping a hand over the phone to mute her words. "There's a guy standing out there now. He looks just like the man in the stolen red truck, the one they chased near the grocery store!"

SIX

Zoe wished she'd worn her Glock and had Freya by her side. The best she could do was corral everybody and move them inside. According to what she'd been told about the trouble in town back in August, assailants had arrived in a car and shot at Sophie with a rifle. At least this guy was on foot and had no visible weapon. If he'd been closer, she'd have drawn her concealed Ruger .380, but at this distance she might as well throw rocks.

Running up to Sean she shouted, "Inside. Now!"

"What's wrong?"

"I'm not sure. Just move."

Sean was already on his feet and scooping up his son. She could tell by his expression that he was going to follow her orders. "Hurry!"

"What about the dog?"

He needn't have asked. Angel was right on his heels.

Zoe slammed the door. Breathless, she took a moment to regain the proper demeanor. A police officer was supposed to remain calm in a crisis, rookie or not. "There was somebody loitering out by the farthest fence," she explained. "We had a shooting incident in the training yard about four months ago, and I didn't want to take a chance this time."

"Thanks, I think." He, too, acted out of breath. "You could have told me with a little less drama. You scared me good."

"Badly. I scared you badly."

Sean huffed and shook his head. "Those aren't the first words that popped into my head, believe me." He eyed his son. "I cleaned it up for both of you."

"Good." She went to one of the windows and peeked through the blinds. "I don't see him now."

"I never did. What did he look like?"

"One of the guys at the market that made you so nervous," Zoe said. "I thought for sure you'd seen him standing there."

"Nope. I was watching the dog until I heard you holler. After that, it's a blur."

"Well, at least you didn't have a flashback." She studied him. "You didn't, did you?"

"No. I didn't." He seemed both pleased and concerned. "I can't get well before we qualify for Angel."

"I'm sure it won't happen quickly. You just didn't have the right triggers this time. Besides, there's an outside chance Patrick can also qualify. You won't need two service dogs."

"True." He joined her to peer out the window as redand-blue flashing lights reflected off the glass. "Is that every patrol car in Desert Valley?"

"Looks like it. We have so little crime around here the officers tend to respond whenever they can."

"You said there was a serial killer?"

"Not anymore. It's a long story. The former police department secretary turned out to be a psycho who was targeting cops. She was mentally unbalanced and thought she could make Chief Hayes fall in love with her if she got rid of all her rivals. In the process, she also killed officers who happened to resemble him because they didn't ask her for a date. It was a nightmare."

"Sounds like it." Sean stepped back. "I've been thinking. Since nobody has bothered Patrick, how about we take him to that day care you mentioned? I suspect you're right about him being safer if he's not around me."

"Granted. And I'll stop by the house for my other gun." She displayed the Ruger .380 in her palm. "This is only for close quarters."

Sean visibly tensed. "You'll keep it locked up when Patrick is around, right?"

"Absolutely. And I'll make sure it's unloaded."

"What do we do with the dog while we're gone?"

"It's about time you started using her name instead of calling her *the dog*. Angel will go with us, in a portable kennel, and I'll have Freya ride next to her to set a good example. You'd be surprised how much a smart dog can learn by observation."

Sean chuckled as he eyed the still-excited canine. "What makes you think Freya won't learn to act up from watching Angel?"

"I'll take my chances," Zoe said, returning his smile. She knew he was referring to the dogs, yet her reply had a double meaning. She was beginning to realize she might be willing to take a chance on caring for Sean again, too. He may have broken her heart once, but he wasn't the same macho guy he had been. What he needed to realize was that his inner strength was still there, still evident in his actions to protect his son. He wasn't less of a man than he had been. He was merely a wounded warrior whose invisible scars needed the balm of love and faith, both in himself and in the God he had recently denied.

It was her fondest hope that she could lead him back to a realization of both. She wasn't fooling herself. Her goals were not nearly as noble as they sounded because she had a vested interest in this matter, too.

She cared for the man deeply. They had both been through a lot since their youth. Above all, she was going to make sure he stayed safe, no matter what it took.

Sean's first opinion of Desert Valley Day care was not particularly good. It looked more like the usual private home, decorated for Christmas, than a professional place. There was a wreath on the front door, and twinkling lights hung from the porch, just like every other house on the block.

Meeting the two main caretakers, however, helped set his mind at ease. Marilyn Carter and her niece, Josie Callahan, had achieved a welcoming, family atmosphere and were offering sensible parental guidance to the children without a lot of unnecessary shouting.

The roomful of kids was noisy, of course. Most were younger, like Patrick. A brunette, dusky, blue-eyed girl of about ten stood in the background, acting as if she considered herself everyone's big sister. She was helping younger kids build a castle with blocks and gently admonishing them to share.

He inclined his head toward the group of children and spoke to Zoe. "Who's that? She looks old for day care."

"Maisy is Officer Dalton West's daughter. She's here after school because he's been in K-9 training classes, too," Zoe said. "Dalton is staying in Desert Valley over Christmas vacation, so she'll probably be here a lot."

"Maisy will make a good teacher someday," Josie added, sounding wistful.

Zoe sobered. "I suppose she tends to mother the little ones more because she lost her own mother."

Sean laid his hand on Patrick's head while the boy leaned against him. "I understand. It's hard."

Josie nodded and began to smile. "That's why Aunt Marilyn and I stay open so late and accept parents' flexible schedules. We know what a struggle it can be."

"Do you have children?" Sean asked.

"No, but Marilyn does." She turned away. "If you'll excuse me, I need to check the bathrooms."

"And I suppose I'll need to fill out enrollment paper-work." Sean looked to Zoe. "Can I use your address?"

"Sure." She paused. "It would be a good idea if you agreed to put Patrick in Sunday school, too. That way everybody can get to know you and feel more comfort-able with you guys being a part of the day care."

"Sunday school? I gather you'll want me to go to church with you, too."

"Well…"

"I get it." Sean sighed noisily. "All right. You win. Church it is, but don't expect me to suddenly go running down the aisle and repent. God gave up on me long ago."

"Whatever you say."

He could tell she didn't mean it. Nevertheless, he would try to make things easier for her while he was there. She had opened her home and arranged for his training. The least he could do was go to church with her.

But it would be hard, he knew. Facing the faith he

had rejected and being bombarded with pleas to reconsider was liable to creep into his mind and cause untold
problems and spiritual confusion.

How did he know? Because it already was.

Zoe was glad to see Patrick being assimilated into
the group. As soon as Maisy West had noticed his difficulty walking steadily, she had taken his hand and
begun to lead him from child to child, making introductions. What an adult would have taken days to accomplish, Maisy had done in the space of an hour.

"I think we can leave now," Zoe said. "Go tell Patrick what we're doing so he won't worry."

Seeing his reticence, she laid a hand of comfort on
his arm. "He will be fine here. Very safe. You know
he needs the company of other children. They're not
judging him the way adults might and he hasn't even
looked at us for ages."

"Yeah. I see that."

Zoe stood back and watched her old friend approach
the group of children, crouch and speak to his son as the
others listened nearby. One of the boys spoke up, then
Maisy followed with further assurances. By the time
Sean stood, Patrick was already headed for a play area
filled with large wooden blocks and obstacles.

"That gives me a great idea," Zoe told Sean as he
returned to her. "We can run Angel through her paces
in the training yard and encourage Patrick to do some
of the exercises with her. The physical agility will undoubtedly help him."

To her chagrin, Sean scowled. "My son is not a dog."

She had to laugh. "No, but some of his best buddies are. Think of how encouraged he'll be if he can do what they do?"

"Such as?"

"Oh, I don't know. We won't ask him to climb, of course, but I imagine he'd love crawling through tunnels and under barricades." Enthusiasm for her brainchild grew until she wanted to clap her hands and jump for joy. "It's a wonderful idea. As a matter of fact, once Angel is certified as a therapy dog for you, you may want to continue training her and take her on visits to hospitals and rehab centers."

"Whoa. Hold on, lady. We haven't even taught her to stop jumping on me. Let's not get ahead of ourselves."

What she wanted to do was remind him that the Lord could accomplish anything, and that believers should always try their best, but she kept silent. He'd get there eventually. At least she hoped and prayed he would. If she looked back with honesty and candor, she could see how far Sean had already come. It would be wise to concentrate on that rather than focusing on how far he still had to go.

Whatever happened, she vowed to be there for him. How and when was unknown, yet nothing was impossible for God. Even if she had to quit her beloved Arizona job, she would. Hopefully it wouldn't come to that. Right now, her fondest wishes were a jumble of unknowns and confused thoughts, so she couldn't begin to decide what to ask or expect.

In her heart, she knew indecision was okay. No matter how much her mind argued, she would trust in her faith, in her Lord. All she really had to do was exercise patience.

That thought almost made her burst out laughing.

There was a joke among believers about *never* praying for patience unless you wanted to be presented with long, long trials. Well, here she was, in the midst of just such a dilemma, with no end in sight. *Welcome to God's boot camp.*

She and Sean left the day care together and checked to be sure the dogs were comfortable in the car. Zoe slid behind the wheel while Sean got into the passenger seat. "Back to the training center?"

"Fine with me. I forgot to ask. Do they feed the kids lunch and snacks?"

"Yes. Are you hungry?" She pulled into traffic.

"I'm not sure. I feel kind of funny, as if I should go back and get my son no matter how safe and happy he is. Does that make sense to you?"

"Of course. You're getting used to your new life, and he's a big part of it. You'll settle down more after you bond with Angel and the three of you become a team."

"I hope you're right."

Zoe chuckled softly. "Don't you know I'm always right, Murphy?"

"Yeah, well—"

Instant shattering of the side windows on her car interrupted him. Dual instincts made him duck and Zoe tromp the gas pedal to the floor.

She hadn't seen or sensed danger until it had been obvious. In order to have broken both windows simultaneously, a bullet must have passed from one side of the car to the other. Missing them both. *Praise God!* And thank Him that Patrick had not been present.

Eyes wide, head swiveling back and forth, Sean was bracing himself on the dashboard and shaking as if he'd been hit. "Where's the shooter?"

"I don't know," she shouted back. "Grab my phone and report it while I drive."

The desert air felt icy as it rushed through the broken windows. In the rear, the dogs barked, futilely warning intruders to stay away.

Zoe dodged through traffic and headed straight for the police station, hoping whoever had fired at them would be stupid enough to follow.

She slid into the open lot behind the station and jumped out to take up a defensive position behind the car door.

Sean circled the front of the vehicle to join her as cops raced out the back exit and surrounded them.

To her disappointment, whoever had shot at them had been smart enough to disappear. Chief Hayes tapped her on the shoulder and drew her away with Sean while others looked over the vehicle damage.

"We went back and rechecked that stolen red truck after we received the ballistics report I told you about. Most of the prints we lifted belonged to the teenagers we arrested, like I said, but there was one palm print that was unidentified. We ran that through AFIS. I have bad news for you."

"You got a match." Zoe wasn't asking. She knew.

"Yes," the chief said. "Whoever left that print has a record as long as your arm, including charges of homicide."

"So, the bullet in St. Louis is from an assassin's gun, and the print proves he or someone like him is here," she concluded.

"Afraid that's how it looks."

"Then how about putting a guard on Marilyn Carter's day care for us?" She was speaking to the chief but looking at Sean. "Sean's son Patrick isn't the only child who deserves protection. Your own daughter is there."

Hayes agreed. "Very sensible. What about you two?"

"I'll keep my guard up and so will Sean," Zoe said. "When we're not at my house, we'll be at the training center. It probably wouldn't hurt to keep a close eye on that, too."

"Will do." Chief Hayes offered his hand to Sean and they shook. "Don't hesitate to call if you even *think* you've seen something odd."

Before Zoe could explain for him, Sean spoke up. "I'm here because of a diagnosis of PTSD." He held out his trembling hands as a demonstration. "Are you *sure* you want me to call?"

The other man clapped him on the shoulder. "Absolutely. I'll tell you if it's too often. I don't want any more losses on my watch. Got that?"

"Yes, sir."

Sean's forceful agreement echoed his time in the military. So did his stiff posture. This was the first time Zoe had been privy to such a clear picture of his background. A lot had been imprinted. A lot would need to be mitigated because it could never be erased. He was the product of his past, as was she. They all were.

The secret to healing, as far as she could tell, was learning to face tragedy and figuring out how to find happiness despite whatever had happened. Service dogs helped in some cases. Counseling and meds in others.

But she wanted more for Sean. She wanted him to have true peace and joy with his son by his side. To accomplish that, she and her fellow officers were going to have to do more than pat him on the back or give him a place to live or even find him the perfect canine companion.

They were going to have to end the reign of terror begun by the thugs who wanted to kill him. And then they were going to have to track down whoever had hired those men to keep it from recurring.

Given the enormity of that task, she didn't see any way to make it happen without calling upon divine intervention. Whether Sean believed or not, she was going to pray and keep praying. Fervently.

She was also going to stay armed. If God chose to work through her, she'd be ready.

SEVEN

The next few days kept Sean busy training with Angel. At night, when he took her home with him, she managed to settle down with Freya and avoid tearing up Zoe's house, much to his relief.

The progress Patrick had made was the most astounding of all. Sean wasn't sure whether to give the credit to Angel or Freya or the day care, particularly ten-year-old Maisy West. The few times he'd spotted her father in the distance and thought about praising the girl, however, the man hadn't looked approachable.

"Tell me about that guy, West," Sean said when he and Zoe were straightening up the kitchen after supper. "Why does he look mad at the world all the time?"

"Probably because he is." She sighed. "His wife was killed as the result of a home invasion. It's possible the perpetrators were after him, instead. I don't doubt he blames himself. I feel sorry for Maisy. She's kind of lost both parents at once."

"Well, she's sure been good for my son. I can't believe how well he's walking."

"Speaking of Patrick, where is he?"

Sean slipped the last slices of pizza onto a plate and

refrigerated it. "Watching TV with the dogs while we do the dishes."

"Um, I don't think so."

"What do you mean? Of course he is. That's what they've done every evening."

She gestured with her chin since her hands were in soapy water. "Then where did she come from?"

Freya was peeking around the corner as if hoping he'd drop leftovers. There was no sign of Patrick.

Scowling, Sean ran past the dog so rapidly she edged her way to Zoe and sat at her feet, apparently waiting for orders.

"Did you find him?" Zoe was drying her hands when Sean returned.

"No. He's not in the living room or the hall or the bathroom."

"Well, he can't have gone far. Has he run off before?"

"Run?" Sean was incredulous. "He can hardly walk. How can he possibly be gone?"

"Calm down. We'll find him. He can't be far away."

Sean's trembling had returned, this time without flashbacks, and he raked his fingers through his short hair. "Not on his own, he can't. What if somebody kidnapped him?"

"With the dogs in the same room? Highly unlikely."

"Then what? Where is he?"

"I suspect he's using his newfound ability to walk better to explore the house. Let me get Freya's working harness on her and we'll do a professional search."

Sean knew he was being unreasonable but couldn't help shouting at her. "Why are you smiling?"

"Sorry," she said, although she continued to look

pleased. "I'm just in my element right now. I'm not worried. I know the dog will track him down."

"Fine. You do this your way. I'm going to keep looking."

"If there is a scent trail, the less you muddle it, the better," Zoe said. "But suit yourself. You've both been all over the house, anyway." She held Freya's leash and straightened. "Wait a second. Where's Angel?"

"How should I know? She's always on the move." His scowl deepened, his fists clenching.

"There's a good chance she followed Patrick," Zoe said. "You stay here while I conduct my search."

"In a pig's eye. I'm coming with you."

"Why am I not surprised?" Pausing long enough to lay a hand lightly on his forearm, she waited until his gaze met hers before she spoke. "Intense emotional reactions can affect everyone, including service dogs. I know it's hard for you to control your feelings. Everybody has trouble sometimes, particularly when a loved one is involved, but I'm going to ask you to really try this time. Take a deep breath and let it out slowly."

"You're wasting time."

"If I thought Patrick was in real danger, I'd already be on my way. Calm down and think rationally. The doors are locked. He can't have gotten out. And neither dog barked, so we know nobody broke in."

It took every ounce of Sean's strength to stand there and listen, to comprehend and consider that she might be right. Deep, slower breathing did help some. "All right. I'm as calm as I'm going to get. Can we go now?"

"Yes. Freya, find Patrick."

Tail wagging, tongue hanging out, the Belgian Tervuren looked up at her human partner as if asking for further instructions.

"Patrick." Zoe grabbed the boy's sweater off the back of the sofa and held it down for the dog to sniff. "Find."

Sean stepped aside as the pair passed. Zoe was not the only one who looked happy. The dog seemed just as pleased to be working. She entered the hallway, made several course adjustments, then headed for the room Zoe had given to her guests.

"I already looked in there," Sean insisted.

Zoe wasn't deterred. Neither was the K-9. She snuffled around the bed, then raised her head and made a beeline for the closet.

"They're in there," Zoe told Sean. "Open the door."

Ready to do battle because he didn't believe Patrick could have walked that far unassisted, he grasped the knob. Turned it. Heard muted giggling just as he jerked on the door, then froze. There they were. His son and Angel. Sitting on the closet floor and wrapped in the blanket they'd shared in the living room. Patrick's eyes were sparkling. The dog was alternately panting and licking the boy's cheeks as if agreeing that they had pulled off a great trick.

"How did you get in there?" Sean shouted.

Patrick's grin faded, and his eyes began to glisten. He not only lowered his head, he buried his face in the border collie's black-and-white ruff.

Sean immediately dropped to his knees. "I'm sorry, son. I didn't mean to scare you. I'm not mad. I was just so worried I yelled without thinking first." He opened his arms. "Come here."

Although the child moved slowly, he did go to Sean. So did Angel, which made the otherwise poignant mo-

ment more comedy than drama. Patrick had his arms
around his daddy's neck, holding tightly. Angel was
determined to kiss every face within reach.

Keeping one arm around his son, Sean looped the
other over the dog's shoulders to help hold her still and
avoid her wet tongue. Sort of. There was no way to keep
her under full control, and, truth to tell, he didn't care
if she showered him with doggy affection. She had not
only followed his handicapped son, she had stayed with
him despite the other dog's absence.

She might be too easily distracted as the trainers had
reported, but she was loyal. And instinctively protective.
No matter how hard he had to work to transform her
into a good service dog, he was determined to succeed.

A shiver shot up his spine as his thoughts expanded
on the premise. Would she be effective enough against
enemies when her natural gift was for friendship?
Should he ask for a more formidable-looking dog like
a German shepherd or a Doberman, instead?

It didn't take long to reason that the likelihood of
being assigned to a dog like that were slim and none.
If Angel had not been available when he'd arrived at
the training center, chances were he'd have been turned
away. Therefore, she had been meant for him. For Patrick.

What he disliked most about that conclusion was the
inference that a higher power may have arranged their
pairing. Undoubtedly Zoe thought so. And perhaps the
other trainers did, too. But that didn't mean he had to
agree with them.

Trouble was, he was wondering if he might be wrong
and they might be right. The fact that his enemies had
driven him to Desert Valley, to the help he so desper-

ately needed, was enough to upset his preconceived notions. Add to that the amazing assets that had awaited him here and you had a real conundrum.

Sean scooped up his son and carried him into the living room, where he settled with him on the sofa, pretending to watch TV while his mind sought answers that probably didn't exist.

Angel plopped down at his feet and rested her chin atop the toes of his shoes. All Sean said was, "Good girl."

Zoe gave man and boy a few moments alone before joining them. "Mind if I sit here, too?"

"Of course not."

She'd locked up her regular sidearm and was able to comfortably collapse next to them on the couch. "Long day."

"Yeah. Especially this last part."

Nothing could have kept her from smiling at the pair. "You should be thankful, you know."

"I know. It's just so unbelievable. A month ago he was barely able to stand. He was unresponsive for weeks before that."

"Kids are resilient. I understand the water in the pool hadn't been heated. That was in his favor, too."

"So they tell me. The younger the child and the colder the water, the less lasting brain damage is done."

"Right." She produced a small electronic tablet and laid it in her lap. "I thought, if you're up to it, we could go over a few things. We need to figure out who is upset enough with you to want you dead."

"Beats me."

"Let's start with the families of the comrades in arms

you visited after you returned to the States. Where did they live?"

"One was in Chicago. One was in Minneapolis. The other survivor had moved with no forwarding address. The folks in Chicago did talk to me, although they certainly didn't welcome me the way I'd hoped. It wasn't my fault the Humvee hit an IED. All I was trying to do was get to the airport so I could fly home to Patrick."

She saw his arms tighten around the drowsy child. "I could try to track down the soldier who moved as well as check on the backgrounds of the others if you like."

"Okay. Gentry was the family I couldn't find. Smiths were in Chicago. Yarnells were from Minneapolis. They were the ones who acted the most upset."

"I'll have Chief Hayes put out a few feelers and see what he can come up with. How about your late wife's connections?"

"Those are a lot hazier. And far more likely to be with criminals. She was deeply involved in drugs."

"Do you know if there was an investigation after she overdosed? I'd think they'd at least look into identifying her supplier."

"So would I. Her parents, however, apparently pulled some strings to keep the whole thing hush-hush. No doubt they were embarrassed by Sandra's poor choices." He blew out a noisy sigh. "Including me as a husband."

Mulling over the information, or lack of it, Zoe finally asked, "Is it possible they just want control of Patrick?"

"Only an outside chance," Sean said flatly. "As I've said before, they could always sue for custody. I'm actually kind of surprised they haven't. Which reminds me, you and I haven't seen an attorney yet."

Her body moved imperceptibly as her mind retreated. "I think you should hold off on that. It's not that I don't want to help out, it's just that I suspect you'll find somebody special before long and build a new family. I don't want to stand in the way."

Waiting, barely breathing, she willed him to encourage her, at least by including her in the pool of eligible mates. He did not. Staring at the television, he acted as if he hadn't heard a word she'd said. Not speaking was more telling than denial. Silence told her that Sean was willing to view her as a buddy and accept her assistance in a pinch, yet not expand that image to include a lifelong commitment.

Okay. She got the picture. It hurt all the way from the roots of her dark brown hair to the tips of her toes, but she understood perfectly. They were friends, period.

That would do. It would have to.

Companionable stillness enveloped Sean. Patrick had fallen asleep in his lap, so he had no qualms about bringing up Christmas plans. Anything but face the touchy subject Zoe had tried to discuss.

"Do you want me to get a tree and ornaments, or will it create too much excitement for the dogs?" he asked.

"I've given that some thought. I'll pick up a small one and put it on the table in the kitchen. That way they'll know it's off-limits." She sighed. "What about presents for you-know-who? I have no idea what to buy him."

"You don't have to give him anything."

"I want to. He's a real sweetheart. Why wouldn't I give him something for Christmas?"

"I just don't want you to feel obligated."

"In that case, I'll cross you off my list. Patrick is getting presents."

"Okay, okay. Don't get huffy."

"*Huffy?* You want to see huffy, you just try to stop me from making this the best Christmas he's ever had."

Sean partially let go of the boy in order to raise one hand in surrender. What in the world was wrong with Zoe? She was usually so even-tempered and level-headed. "No argument here," he said. "I was just trying to make things easier for you."

"I love Christmas, okay? If I were home in Mesa, I'd have my whole apartment decorated, even the cactus in front of my picture window. I do it every year."

"And instead, you're stuck here with us."

"I'm not stuck anywhere, Murphy. I'm here because I choose to be, and you're staying in my house by my invitation, so don't go imagining me as some suffering martyr. I'll buy some decorations that I can easily take home afterward. You can pick up anything else you want. It makes no difference to me."

Eyeing her and sensing continued animosity, he decided it was best to merely nod. He'd never been big on a lot of tinsel and colored lights. Hadn't even had a tree since childhood. Sandra's parents, Alice and John Shepherd, had always gone overboard on fancy decorations, and she had dragged him to their house whenever he was home on leave around holiday time. They hadn't done all the work themselves, of course, and the result had always been so perfect he'd found it off-putting.

Finally he ventured a comment. "Do you think we could talk a couple of your police friends into shopping with us? I'd feel safer if others were along."

Zoe nodded and arched an eyebrow. "That's a good idea. I'll ask Dalton or Tristan if they're available."

"I know about West. Who did you say the other guy was?"

"A former soldier who recently married one of the local school teachers. He's been raising his teenage niece, too. You and he have more in common than some of the others."

"Have you told him about me?"

It surprised him to hear her say, "No." The reasons were even more impressive. "I hadn't asked you if I could share your story with anybody except the dog trainers, so I didn't. If you want to make it public, that's up to you."

He knew he was staring when she said, "What?"

"Nothing. I just figured the whole town knew by now."

"Gossip can spread fast in a close-knit community, but they didn't learn any secrets from me."

"Thank you."

"You're welcome." Zoe got to her feet and stretched, arms over her head. "Turn off the lights when you decide to go to bed."

"Good night." Sean wanted to say so much more. To tell her what she'd meant to him, now and in the past. To compliment her on her expertise and choosing a career of service. To thank her again and again for opening her home to him and her heart to his son.

His cheeks warmed when he pictured himself thanking Zoe with a hug as she left him. Instead, he gently eased the boy off his lap and laid him on the couch, then made the rounds of windows and doors, rechecking the locks before doing it all a second time. Yes, he was paranoid. That was only crazy if nobody was after him. He knew the danger remained, just as he knew his nerves were balanced on a knife-edge between self-control and sheer panic.

Every time he peered out into the darkness, he thought undefined objects moved. Shifted. Inched closer. Then he'd blink and the supposed danger would vanish.

He flicked off the kitchen lights and paused at the window over the sink. Moonlight cast parts of the yard in darkness while gleaming off bare rocks and crags in the distance.

A shiver shot up his spine. Instinct pushed him back into the interior shadows. Held him there. Made him wonder if his mind was playing tricks as it often did.

Then he saw a pattern of light and dark pass across the bare floor. It lingered only for a second. Was this for real? Was someone watching? Waiting for him to make a mistake?

Edging closer to the window frame, Sean held his breath and continued to scan the yard for intruders. Nothing presented itself, not even a passing noctur-nal animal.

He left all the interior lights off to keep from high-lighting himself, then once again made the rounds of all the windows. His musings progressed from a height-ened sense of danger to an assurance that his damaged mind had been responsible for the fright.

"All right," he mumbled, sighing. "So there was nothing there this time." That didn't matter. He was not about to let down his guard. Not if folks called him crazy for the rest of his life. Which, hopefully, would be a good long time.

EIGHT

Sunday morning came early for Zoe. Even Freya seemed inclined to sleep in—until Angel nosed open the door and came barreling into the room, caromed off the edge of the bed and sped back out. If her barking had not been so high-pitched and playful, Zoe would have worried.

Instead of reaching for her sidearm, she stretched and yawned. Freya did the same. This was a special day. A morning filled with promise and possibilities.

A silly notion made her smile and mutter, "Yes, as long as nobody tries to shoot us." That attitude made her shake her head at herself. How could she hope to convince Sean to trust God if she went around making jokes about divine intervention? Then again, humor was good medicine. The Bible said so.

By the time she'd dressed, the aroma of freshly brewed coffee and sizzling bacon had drifted down the hall. There was a lot to be said for a guy who pitched in and cooked.

She breezed into the kitchen, smiling. "Wow. Something smells great!"

Judging by the way Sean stopped moving and stared, she'd either made a good impression or a very bad one. She whirled, arms out. "What do you think? I love this red sweater."

"It's—it's pretty."

A slight blush accentuated his approval and appreciation of her efforts. She seldom wore more than lipstick, but this morning had splurged using eyebrow pencil and a touch of eye shadow. Gold hoop earrings replaced the plain gold studs she wore while training and working.

"Thanks. I didn't bring a skirt from home, but at least I'm not wearing jeans."

"I don't have fancy clothes," Sean said, looking down at his jeans and boots. "Maybe I should just stay here."

"Not on your life." Zoe grinned. "I figure, if a church doesn't accept people for who they are instead of what they wear or how much money is in their wallets, then they shouldn't bother opening their doors."

"I have to warn you, I'm not comfortable in crowds."

"We can sit all the way to the rear, with our backs against the wall. Will that help?"

"Hopefully. Just don't be surprised if I have to take a break during the service."

That's fine. We'll include Freya for moral support."

"Not Angel?"

She wanted to jump for joy. "If you want her with us, that's fine. The Community Church is used to handlers bringing their dogs. Nobody will think it's odd."

"That's a relief. I was afraid I'd stand out."

Zoe wanted to comment that he'd stand out simply because he was so attractive, despite his often somber mood, but she refrained. The less attention they called to themselves, the better. Plus, there would be plenty of police officers at the morning service, both in the sanctuary and posted in the hallways, just in case of trouble from outsiders. Therefore, she saw no need to strap on her duty weapon or tuck a spare gun at her waist and spoil the way her red pullover fit.

"Okay." Zoe took a place at the table next to Patrick. "Let's eat so we can get this show on the road. Right, kiddo?"

The child paused and inclined his head for a moment before he said, "At-rick."

Sean whipped around. His jaw gaped. "Patrick?"

Pressing her lips together and leaning closer, Zoe made the sound for *P*, then followed it with the rest of his name. She thought she and Sean were both going to cry when the little boy echoed, "P-atrick."

Because of the broken windows in Zoe's car, they took Sean's pickup to church. The parking lot was far more crowded than Sean had expected. He chose a spot on the fringes.

Sean recognized Dalton West because he was with Maisy. Patrick spotted her and led the way to the pair by tugging on his daddy's hand and leaning.

"Your daughter has made quite an impression on my son in day care," Sean said, trying to keep Angel from jumping all over the children and licking their faces.

"New dog?" Dalton eyed the border collie.

"Very new. So am I. She's supposed to help me with PTSD."

"I can tell that from her vest." Dalton shot a concerned look toward Zoe, then said, "May I?" and reached for Angel's leash.

"Sure," Sean said. "She's settled down a lot at home but still gets really excited in new situations."

Instead of answering, Dalton faced the dog, pointed

a finger at her, then quickly brought it to his own face. "Look at me. Look. Sit."

She not only obeyed the calm, firm instructions, she sat still at West's feet and kept staring into his eyes. He didn't babble or keep repeating her name, nor did he make unnecessary motions. He merely exuded authority.

Sean was flabbergasted. "Wow. What did you do to my crazy dog?"

"Took command," the other man said as he passed the end of the leash back to Sean. "You can learn to do it, too. It just takes time."

"Thanks for the lesson." Eyeing the children, Sean asked about Sunday school.

"Maisy usually sits in church with me," Dalton said.

The dark-haired ten-year-old tugged at her father's hand. "I can take Patrick to the kindergarten class and stay with him today, can't I? Please?"

"If it's okay with Mr. Murphy."

"I'll— We'll walk with you," Sean said. "Lead the way." A backward glance at Zoe made Sean wish she were by his side. No. Zoe was too wonderful. She needed a man who was perfect, not an emotionally wounded one like himself. She deserved better. He just wished…

What? What did he wish? That he had been wiser as a younger man? That he had realized how ideal Zoe was when they were college students? That he had waited to marry? His imagination paused before adding, *That Patrick was her son.* Hers and his. And that she'd be the one to help raise him.

Entering the church with the others, Sean hardly noticed where he was. Someone tried to hand him a bulletin. Angel promptly accepted it for him, gave it a shake, then carried it as she trotted obediently at his side.

Short hair at Sean's nape began to prickle. He fought off the sensation. It kept building. If he had been sitting down, he knew he would have had to get up and move. To flee his invisible enemies.

Zoe touched his arm. "Are you all right?"

"No. It's claustrophobic in here."

"Okay. I'll finish escorting Patrick to class. You can wait for me outside."

"He'll be scared without me."

"It'll be worse if you suddenly have a flashback and he has to watch," she said tenderly. "Go. If anybody asks, tell them the dog needed to go out. That way you won't be embarrassed. I'll join you in a few minutes."

"If you have any trouble, bring Patrick back to me. Promise?"

"I promise."

Turning on his heel, Sean headed for the exit. Angel gave him no argument, sticking to his side as if she'd suddenly realized he needed her. Perhaps she had. Whatever the reason, he was relieved to not have to drag her or fight to keep her from jumping on others.

The glass door swung open. Sean was barely able to hesitate long enough to permit a couple with small children to enter before he sidled past them with his dog and burst out into the open. His heart was pounding, his breath shallow and quick. One stride. Two. Then more, until he reached a place where he could be alone enough to regain his composure.

Exhausted, he leaned against the side of his pickup bed and forced himself to inhale deeply, slowly. He'd almost waited too long. Almost embarrassed Zoe in front of her friends. Instincts for self-preservation were supposed to keep a person out of trouble, not cause it, and his were clearly wide of the mark.

Watching for Zoe and Freya, Sean reached down and laid his hand on Angel's soft fur. Stroking her head seemed to calm him, and when she tried to give him the soggy church bulletin he almost smiled. "Yes, you're a good girl. It would be nice if both of us weren't wonky but you're coming along well. I guess we will work out."

The glass side door reflected sunshine and vehicles as it swung open again. Sean started to straighten before he realized it wasn't Zoe passing through. He relaxed and looked away. Then his head snapped around. He'd almost failed to recognize the beefy hit man wearing Sunday clothing. And there was a telltale bulge under the arm of his sports jacket to confirm that he was armed.

Sean eased around the pickup and kept his head down as he watched the would-be assailant. A uniformed officer of the DVPD had followed him outside and was resting his palm on the butt of his sidearm while calling, "Wait!"

If the hit man replied, Sean didn't hear it. He didn't have to. He saw enough. The man hailed a dark SUV and climbed inside, leaving the cop standing alone in the lot.

It was impossible to ID the driver due to darkly tinted windows. When the vehicle accelerated out of the parking lot, Sean expelled his breath in a whoosh. They were gone. For now.

As he started to stand, his innate wariness kicked in again and he muttered, "Assuming there are only those two."

Zoe had trouble spotting Sean so she commanded Freya to find Angel. That was all it took.

She hurried up and greeted him with a smile in spite of his frown. "The kids are all set. Are you ready to go back inside?"

"I'm not sure. Not after what I just saw."

Waiting, she raised an eyebrow. When he failed to volunteer information, she asked. "What did you see?"

"One of the guys who came to Arizona after me."

A frisson of fear shot up her spine as she wheeled to face the church. "Where? When?"

"He came out and got into a black SUV with a second man. They drove away in spite of one of the cops calling to him."

"When?"

"Just now."

"You're sure it was the same guy?" She hated to question Sean's judgment, but his record of being correct was less than perfect. He was, however, apparently ultrasensitive to danger. The key was learning to differentiate between the real thing and figments of his imagination.

"As sure as I can be under these circumstances," Sean said dryly. "Being paranoid doesn't mean there's nobody after me. Your car did get shot up."

"True." Continuing to scan their surroundings, Zoe kept Freya at heel. "You're sure you saw them leave?"

"Yes. I don't know why they were here in the first place. I mean, if they wanted to harm me, why not shoot when I came out here?"

"Maybe they didn't see you leave."

"It's more likely that," Sean agreed. "I wouldn't want to cause trouble in a church full of cops."

"So, you're ready to come back in with me?"

"I have to. Patrick is in there."

"Right," she said. "I'll alert church security to watch

for the SUV, just in case. We can find seats in the rear of the sanctuary and sneak out just before the altar call so we're waiting when his class dismisses."

Although Sean agreed by not arguing, she could tell he was far from settled. As before, she would take one moment at a time, ready for intervention if necessary yet hopeful that his troubled mind would allow him to actually benefit from the pastor's sermon. Beyond that, she had no plans.

"Freya, heel," she said, stepping out to lead the way. Was Sean following? She wanted to look back to be certain. Instead, she kept walking until they reached side windows on the building where she could see their reflections. Her pulse jumped. Sean's posture looked good. Straight, tall and in command. Was wishful thinking influencing her, or he had actually made some progress? That didn't matter as much as the fact that he was functioning well despite his recent scare.

When she'd first spoken with him about coming to Desert Valley, he had not seemed nearly as sure of himself or able to cope. Research had told her that his traumatic past might always color his future, but she also knew that some degree of healing was possible. *With God, all things are possible.*

If she had ever doubted that biblical truth, she didn't anymore. Truth to tell, nobody but God was in charge of their future.

All Zoe prayed for at this point was her friend's happiness and well-being. If Sean's life was to include her, she would be overjoyed. If not, she would somehow accept that, too. She either trusted her heavenly Father in all things, including the long-ago loss of her ill, helpless baby brother, or she didn't.

For years she'd assumed that childhood disappointment had cost her the most dearly of any. Now, realizing how much she cared for Sean and his son, she knew better. Losing him, for any reason, was going to hurt so much she might never recover. The mere thought was enough to tie her stomach in knots and make her wish she had skipped breakfast.

He touched her elbow. "Are you all right?"

A shiver zinged up her spine and tickled the back of her neck.

"Of course. Why?" Their eyes met in the mirrorlike window glass. His body language spoke of protection. His height and strength giving her an instant sense of awareness that made her insides quake.

"You seemed different," he snorted. "Don't tell me *that* was all in my head, too."

"No." She turned to look directly at him and tried to smile. Their lips were so close, the idea of initiating a kiss so tempting, she swayed, fighting to keep from leaning toward him. Suppose he was resistant? Suppose he wasn't as enamored of her as she hoped? Suppose she ruined their close friendship by taking it to a new level before he was ready?

Zoe sighed. "I was thinking too much, that's all."

"About me?"

What could she say that would be the truth, yet not reveal her burgeoning love for man and boy? Imagining his tender kiss was already bad enough, so she turned his question into a gibe. "If I say yes, will you get all sappy on me?"

Sean gave a wry chuckle. "I think you're safe. I'm too busy trying to keep this dog in line and make sure nobody is trying to sneak up and shoot me while I'm distracted. I don't have room in my brain for excess sentimentality."

Although she said, "That's a relief," she was disappointed. Her brain certainly had enough room to entertain romantic notions while still doing her job.

"Well, this threat can't last forever," Sean said, adding, "I hope."

In Zoe's mind a worst-case scenario began to form. If they didn't manage to nab the thugs or figure out who had sent them in the first place, the only other way this story was all going to end was if Sean was killed. There had to be a different answer. Anything was better than that.

Witness protection was out because Sean didn't qualify. And he certainly couldn't go back into the military. Not with PTSD. Neither could he join her profession. Besides, if he wasn't around anymore, who would look after his little boy?

That brought her back to their verbal agreement about custody.

Zoe sighed as she started into the main sanctuary and led the way to seats in the rear for Sean's sake. The more she was with him, the greater her affection grew. Did he suspect how she felt? Was it possible he was falling for her, too?

The shake of her head was barely perceptible. If Sean cared for her, he would be sending out clues, and she wasn't getting any hints at all. Perhaps it was time to quit hoping their pact about Patrick's care would be fulfilled by a mutual love and take the legal steps they had discussed in the beginning. The drawback was that that might satisfy Sean and keep him from considering alternatives.

Such as marriage.

NINE

Maisy not only led a giggling Patrick into the hall outside his classroom after church, she also made a convincing speech about the benefits of letting the boy participate in the children's Christmas pageant.

"He can be a shepherd," she insisted when Sean began to slowly shake his head. "He'd get a cane to lean on and everything. And I'll be right there." She began to beam. "I'm playing Mary."

"How much time would he have to practice with all the others?" Sean asked. "It might take him a while to catch on."

"We'll all help him." The tenderhearted child took Patrick's hand. "He can do it. Please, please, please?"

Sean was about to make more excuses when Patrick smiled up at him and said, "Peas?"

What could he do or say at that point? "All right. What about practicing? When do you do that?"

"Tonight during church for grown-ups," Maisy said. "My dad helps. So does Chief Hayes."

Zoe was agreeing. "That's right. And I can be there, too, if you're worried. Sophie's acting the part of one of the Magi with the chief's daughter, Lily, and a couple of dogs. It should be worth watching just to see a Labrador retriever pretending to be a camel."

As far as Sean was concerned, the added exposure was foolish. However, he could also see how much progress toward normalcy Patrick had made since being allowed his freedom among a group of helpful children. Maisy, alone, was a godsend.

That conclusion brought him up short, particularly the definition his subconscious had chosen. To imagine that God had sent anything his way seemed odd. Still, anyone who was privy to the events that had brought him and his son to Desert Valley had to be thinking the same thing. A happy coincidence was one, maybe two, actions that were of benefit. He was seeing dozens, from the original accident to Patrick all the way to this very moment. Along the way, a myriad of connections had been made and people were in places where they would not normally have been. Take Zoe. She should have been at work in Mesa, yet here she was, just where and when he needed her.

Stunned, he had to admit that there may have been a divine hand guiding him to Desert Valley. Many questions remained, though. Such as, why did the boy have to suffer and why was his own mind affected adversely—and why was somebody so determined to harm him?

Sean blinked rapidly to clear his head and realized he was standing in a crowded hallway with all sorts of people milling around and pushing past, laughing and talking. It was too much. An assassin could be right next to him, and he wouldn't know until it was too late.

He looked at Zoe. "We need to go."

"I see that. Give me Angel's leash and bring Patrick."
She started to steer both dogs toward the closest exit.

"The truck's on the other side of the church," Sean
reminded her.

"I know. I thought it would be best to get outside
ASAP and then circle around. Besides, the dogs need
room to move, to stretch their legs."

And so do I. Sean inhaled deeply, trying to force a
calm he wasn't feeling. They broke into the sunlight,
and the warmth on his face bathed him in peace. When
the time came for him to look for employment, finding
work outside was probably going to be best.

"Assuming I can keep it together long enough to
look for a job," he muttered, half disgusted with himself even though he knew his brain had been affected
by a trauma he could not have anticipated or avoided.

Zoe overheard him. "You're thinking about a job?
Good for you. That's a step in the right direction."

"Yeah. All I have to do is add a dog to my résumé."

"Stranger things have happened." She paused and
shaded her eyes. "I think you're doing very well."

"What about the incident in the parking lot before
church started?"

"That's only a bad thing if it was all in your head.
You're still sure you recognized the guy?"

"Oh, yeah. It was him all right."

"Then stop beating yourself up about it. The only
thing you can really influence is your own actions.
We'll face the rest when and if it happens."

"If?" His eyebrows arched. "You act like you think
my problems are just going to vanish. Well, they're not.
I'm a basket case, my son is half the kid he once was
and I'm in more personal danger than I was overseas."

"I don't know that I'd go that far," she countered. "Here, you have the whole police force—and me—on your side."

"And by being here I'm putting you in jeopardy," Sean said. He'd have reached for her hands if she hadn't been holding both leashes and he hadn't had hold of Patrick.

Instead of acting the way he'd expected, Zoe smiled. "There is no place you could possibly be that would be better for self-defense than this town. And there is no better lookout than a dog. Your senses may not be up to par, but Angel's are. Stop borrowing trouble. This will all work out for the best."

"How can you believe that?"

"Because I've seen it happening all around me, ever since I became a Christian," she said. "You'd see it too if you'd just open your eyes and your mind."

"What about the bullet that took out your car windows?"

Laughter bubbled, leaving Sean astounded, particularly when she said, "It missed *us*, didn't it?"

Evening church was a more casual gathering, and although there was a short sermon, Zoe didn't mind skipping it in order to accompany Patrick and his father to the rehearsal for the Christmas pageant.

They gathered with the children and an assortment of dogs in the fellowship hall. Although the simple drama was to be staged outside under special lighting and with background music, rehearsals were handled inside.

She stood back as one of the volunteers fitted Patrick and several other boys with brownish robes and head coverings. Sean had accompanied them into the large hall that was half meeting room and half gymnasium, depending upon the current need. Children's chattering and laughter filled the space.

Zoe leaned toward Sean. "So far, so good?"

"I'll live. I think."

"That makes one of us." Grinning, she looped Freya's leash over her wrist and covered her ears with both hands. "I don't know why schoolteachers don't have headaches all the time."

"Maybe they do. I wish Patrick had had more time to learn what to do."

Zoe wasn't worried. "Don't sweat the small stuff. It looks as though Maisy has arranged for the newest shepherd to be shepherded by at least two others. Look, they're even sharing their crooks. He'll be fine."

"He does seem happy."

"And that's what matters," Zoe reminded him. "This is for Patrick more than us." Realizing that she had inadvertently joined herself with Sean as a couple, she blushed and hoped he hadn't noticed.

There was no denying how she felt. If she had been around the boy from the time he was a baby, she didn't think she would love him more than she already did. *And his daddy? Oh, yes.* No matter where Sean went or how much he did or did not recover, she loved him dearly.

In her deepest heart, she knew she always had.

Supervisors moved the children outside as soon as the Sunday-school director announced, "We have time for one run-through with the manger."

Sean kept his eye on his son and followed closely. So did Zoe. Angel wasn't behaving as well as Freya, but she'd quit straining at the leash and trying to kiss every kid she saw. As far as he was concerned, that was a big breakthrough.

He touched Zoe's arm. "I don't like moving them outside."

"You know we have security on duty whenever church is in session. Besides, nobody knew we were going to be staging on-site tonight. The actual dress rehearsal was set for Tuesday night with performances on Wednesday and Friday evenings."

Sean didn't hide his concern. "I hadn't considered that much exposure. Maybe I should pull Patrick out."

"Don't you dare. He's going to have this wonderful experience if I have to hog-tie you to keep you out of it."

"Hey, tell me what you really think." He managed a smile for her benefit. "Okay. But one sign of trouble, and we're out of here."

"What could possibly happen in a group of great people like these? Look how the boys his age are helping him find his place and sharing the shepherds' crooks."

"I see." Sean sighed. Zoe was probably right. She had been so far. It was just that his skin kept crawling, and the hair at his nape prickled with warnings. Yes, he was not normal. And, yes, the church people had been great to accept him and his son. Yet there remained a sense of uneasiness that refused to go away no matter how much assurance he got.

The children assembled, ready to march up to the manger beneath the makeshift shelter. Mary and Joseph sat beside each other, gazing fondly at the baby doll, while older girls dressed as angels with impressive white wings sang along with recorded Christmas carols playing loudly in the background.

It was time for the shepherds' entrance. Sean could see the crooks sticking up above the costumed heads of the children. From where he stood it was hard to pick out Patrick, so he looked for a halting gait, instead. None stood out.

Sean scowled. Shaded his eyes against the floodlights illuminating the tableau. One, two, three, four... He grabbed Zoe's wrist. "How many shepherds are there supposed to be?"

"Five?"

"That's what I thought." He shoved Angel's leash at her and shouldered closer to the costumed boys. There were exactly four dressed as shepherds.

His son was not one of them!

"Patrick!"

Zoe would have beaten Sean to the front if she hadn't had to manage both dogs. Even Freya was acting out. Little wonder, with Angel leaping against the constraints of her harness and making a terrible racket, half barking, half whining and howling.

"Maisy," Zoe called over the swell of the music, "do you see Patrick?"

The girl stood. Looked into the background. Shook her head—and immediately abandoned her part as Mary to press in among the younger children.

After that, pandemonium reigned. Joseph was yelling at her to come back. Shepherds milled around, unsure whether or not to follow Mary, and the Magi broke ranks, with Sophie and Ryder's old dog, Titus, in the lead.

Sophie shouted to Zoe. "Circle to the left. I'll take the right with my dog. Everybody else freeze."

Without question, teachers rounded up the children and kept them in a tight group around the staging.

Passing through, Sean was yanking the head coverings off any child who even slightly resembled his son. Zoe could tell he hadn't found Patrick because he kept going until he had removed them all.

She joined him, facing the parking lot. Beyond lay a stand of ponderosa pines surrounded by rocks and dust and uninhabited desert. Was it possible the little boy had gotten that far? If so, he was liable to be stunned by the cold the winter night brought, not to mention the possibility of a slight snowfall. Thankfully, all the children had been costumed over their jackets and sweaters, but that didn't mean Patrick would stay warm all night.

Sean's blue eyes sparked with anger. And fear. "Where is he?"

"He's probably just playing hide-and-seek the way he did when he hid in the closet. We'll find him." She believed they would. They must. The only real worry was how long it might take.

Sophie came up with Titus and began stripping the old yellow Lab of his costume. "I've called the station and requested more dogs and handlers. Until they get here, I'm going to start Titus. He's not the tracker he used to be, but there was none as good when he was younger."

She looked at Zoe and Sean. "Do either of you have anything of the boy's? A scarf, hat, glove? Anything?"

Sean reached into his jacket pocket. "He took his gloves off when they put his costume on him."

"Perfect." Snatching the small, padded mittens, Sophie presented them to the old dog, let him sniff for a few seconds, then said, "Find."

Knowing what to expect gave Zoe comfort. Unfortunately, that did not transfer to Sean. He started to follow Titus.

Zoe grabbed a handful of his jacket. "No. Let them work. If you interfere, you'll confuse the dog."

Anger flashed from his eyes. His body was so obviously tense, so primed for action, she was surprised her efforts even slowed him down.

She'd looped the ends of both leashes over her wrist to free her hands and used both on his arm to hold him back. "Stop. Think. That dog is trained and you're not. Let him work." As his focus shifted to her she added, "Please?"

"I'll give you to the count of ten, then I'm going. Understand? Patrick could barely walk a week ago. There's no way he got far on his own."

"I know. I agree, up to a point. But he's been doing so well since Maisy started encouraging him, I think you may underestimate his abilities."

A shout came from the dimness. Dogs barked. Zoe's heart jumped along with her body. Releasing her hold on Sean, she started to run toward the sound, and in the process lost hold of Angel.

Freya paced Zoe while Sean and the border collie raced ahead. It was easy to keep Angel in sight due to the bright white parts of her coat. Zoe could have cheered and wept at the same time when she saw the dog stop and circle.

They'd found Patrick. It had to be him. It just had to be. *Please, God, let him be all right.*

Sean was on his knees by the time she got to him. His arms were wrapped around his son, his face buried on the child's shoulder. Angel kept circling, and Titus was barking, proudly announcing news of his success.

A sobbing Maisy tugged on Zoe's jacket. "It's—it's all my fault. I told him I'd help him go get another crook for the boy who gave him his. Only I meant later. Will my daddy be mad at me?"

"I'll explain for you," Zoe assured her. She looked at Sean and noticed how tense he appeared. "Relax. We found him. No harm done."

"That's what you think." Gesturing at several uniformed officers and their K-9 partners who were disappearing into the shadows of the trees, he said, "Patrick didn't walk all the way out here by himself. He says a strange man promised to help him find a long stick and carried him this far."

"What man?"

"Exactly. I strongly doubt it was a member of the church. That leaves only one other option."

"Impossible," Zoe insisted. "If kidnappers had taken him, they'd still have him. They wouldn't have let him go."

"That was my first thought—until he told me somebody else told the man to put him down and wait for me."

"Wait for you? Did he say why?" There was no real reason to ask that question, but Zoe had to hear for herself.

Sean's eyebrows arched. "Why do you think? They'd probably still be waiting here to ambush me if the police response hadn't been so overwhelming and fast. And if there hadn't been dogs in the lead."

He stared into the woods where the officers and other working K-9s had disappeared in pursuit. Patrick was hugging his daddy and acting as insecure as he had when Zoe had first met him. Poor kid. He gets a little independence back, starts to enjoy it and his whole world falls apart.

Finally, Zoe held out her hand to the boy. "Come with me, Patrick. We need to go back to rehearsal."

"No way." Sean cupped the boy's tousled head. "He's through standing around outside where I can't hold on to him."

"Whoever bothered him is long gone with half the DVPD on their heels. There's no place safer than the church right now."

"I said, no."

There was enough ire in Sean's voice to have made a grown man quail, so Zoe wasn't surprised that the little boy began to sniffle and cry.

She stood as tall as her slim frame would allow and tried to appear formidable. "I understand your concern, but stop and think about it. If everything you say is true, then it's you who needs to stay out of sight, not your little boy." Signaling with a nod toward the church she added, "Move, before I have you handcuffed and put in protective custody for your own good."

"You wouldn't dare."

Facing him with every ounce of courage she possessed, Zoe managed to sound convincing when she said, "I will do anything I need to in order to keep you safe, Murphy. Even make you mad at me, if that's what it takes."

A shout from the woods and intense barking brought Sean up short in the church parking lot. He looked to Zoe. "Hear that?"

"Yes. It sounds as though they caught him."

"I almost hate to get my hopes up."

Ellen Foxcroft joined them, waving a radio and grinning. "Did you hear?"

"Hear what?"

"They got the guy. And he's the one who left the palm print on the stolen truck!"

They're sure?" Sean asked.

"Positive ID."

Mirroring the other K-9 officer's grin, Zoe glanced at Sean. "See? I told you this police force was good."

"What about the second man?" Sean asked. "Did they spot him, too?"

Ellen sobered. "Not yet. We're close. As soon as the suspect in custody talks, we'll pick him up, too."

"Was this guy driving a black SUV?"

"Yes. They're dusting it for fingerprints now. Should have AFIS results on any partners he may have had before the end of the night."

Zoe whispered, "Thank You, Jesus."

Sean swallowed hard. He was almost ready to agree.

TEN

Sean went back to training Angel with Ellen and Sophie the following week, trusting his son to the day care. Now that they were aware of Patrick's improved mobility, everybody would be taking more precautions. He actually felt sorry for ten-year-old Maisy West. She'd taken a personal interest in helping Patrick and therefore blamed herself for his mistakes.

After careful consideration, Sean had come to the conclusion that Maisy's tender mothering had helped the boy a lot more than anything and anybody else had, including himself. He and Dalton, her father, were in similar circumstances. Both children lacked a parent. Perhaps Maisy needed Patrick as much as he needed her.

And what do I need? Sean asked himself. A lovely image appeared in his mind. It was Zoe, of course. Who else would it be? He could picture her fitting into many areas of his life, including becoming Patrick's mother. She'd be good at it. If he weren't so imperfect, he might even seriously consider asking her to marry him.

For Patrick's sake? Sure. Partly. But there was another reason, one that kept needling him, awake or asleep. He didn't want to be separated from his dear friend ever again. *Because?* Because, like it or not, he was in love with her.

Patrick made it through the second dress rehearsal without a glitch. To the boy's credit, he didn't seem at all nervous when Wednesday night arrived. Happily, someone had come up with a fifth shepherd's crook, so each little actor was similarly equipped.

Angel went everywhere with Sean, as per instructions, and had settled into her job with amazing ease. No matter how relaxed and calm she seemed to be, her ears were always perked, her eyes keeping watch. For Sean, it was like being surrounded by a cadre of alert bodyguards. Nobody was going to sneak up on him— or his son—with Angel on duty.

The change in his outlook had occurred quickly, and although he knew anything could still upset his peace, he felt 100 percent better. So good, in fact, that he didn't stop himself when he got the urge to hold Zoe's hand while they watched the pageant performance.

As her fingers slipped between his, a sense of rightness flowed over and through him. Not only had she failed to object, she was returning the affectionate gesture.

Her shoulder bumped his. "Look. Here they come."

"I see. All five of them, thankfully."

"Exactly. Thanks to the good Lord, all is well and getting better. Right?"

Sean shrugged a little. "Okay. I'll give you that. And thanks to the Desert Valley police, one of my assailants is off the streets. Any word on the other guy?"

"Not yet. He may have hit the road when his buddy was picked up. He's not exactly able-bodied with one arm in a cast."

"Unless he's ambidextrous, it's his gun hand, too."

"True. Is that why you seem so much better?"

"That, and the dog," Sean said. "Having Angel with me makes a lot more difference than I'd thought it would. All she really has to do is be there and keep watch. Now that she's used to me and Patrick, she's taking her job very seriously."

"As she should." Zoe leaned on him, shoulder to shoulder, and squeezed his hand. "Aren't the kids cute? Look at that angel in the back. She keeps yawning and knocking her tinsel halo crooked."

"Here comes the hero dog, or should I say camel. I can't imagine why they'd retire a great dog like Titus."

"Arthritis and stamina, mostly," Zoe said. "Chief Hayes took him home to be a pet for Lily. His new dog, Phoenix, knocked over their Christmas tree but Titus is a good boy."

"That reminds me. We never shopped for the decorations I promised you."

"One project at a time," Zoe whispered. "The most important thing is getting you and your dog squared away and making sure that last suspect is captured. Then we'll shop or hike or whatever you want. I still have a couple of weeks left on my lease. We may as well enjoy the desert while we can." She shivered. "Even if it does get cold after dark."

The Magi with their canine camels filed in, led by Titus and Sophie and followed by another yellow Lab who didn't act nearly as complacent about having extra gear strapped to his back. Zoe giggled. "That's Tristan McKeller's dog, Jesse. He's a lot younger than Titus."

"Aren't there supposed to be three wise men?"

"There are. Maybe the third camel had to go on duty and miss this performance."

"I'll sure be glad when all this stuff is over." Sean gave her fingers a gentle press. "I know it's good for Patrick but…"

"I do understand. The thing is, you can't expect him to make progress if you continue to baby him. We've seen great results in the few weeks you've been here."

He made a face. "Yeah. I don't like admitting it, but you're right."

"Of course I am. Humble, too."

Muted chuckles apparently made Angel look up at Sean. He didn't react to her movements until she stood and bristled. Could she be jealous of his feelings for Zoe?

"The dog," Zoe said. "Look at your dog."

"I see her. What do you think is wrong?"

"I don't know." She gathered Freya on a tight leash and scanned the crowd. "You stay here and keep an eye on Patrick. I'm going to circle around to the back of the set and investigate."

"He's fine," Sean said.

Only when he looked again, he didn't see his son. Four crooks stood tall in the rear of the tableau. The fifth was gone.

Zoe was already on her way when she heard Sean shout, "Patrick!" Nobody had to explain. Panic was so evident in the man's voice she knew the child was out of sight. The question was, where had he gone this time? Had the second thug taken him despite all their precautions? That seemed impossible. Patrick had been warned about strangers, so he wouldn't have willingly submitted. Something else must be going on. But what?

Circling wide, Zoe thought she glimpsed several dark figures fading into the trees at the edge of the parking lot. Freya zeroed in on the distant forms and did her best to drag her handler closer.

Out of the corner of her eye, Zoe saw a flash of white. Angel was on her way, too. One dog might be mistaken, but both were probably right. The struggling at the edge of the lot involved their missing little friend. He hadn't wandered away. He'd been kidnapped again!

Every nerve in her body fired, driving her forward at a run. She hadn't heard any shots. But if she didn't get to Patrick before his father did, Sean could fall into the same deadly trap he'd avoided the last time. Surely he must realize that, yet he was still running toward danger.

He was gaining, on her right, trying to keep pace with the barking, straining border collie.

Zoe pulled her gun and shouted, "Stay back."

Sean ignored her. All he seemed to care about was Patrick. Reaching him was his only goal.

At that point, Zoe broke a rule, praying she wasn't making a terrible mistake, and let go of Freya's leash. The Belgian Tervuren took off as if she were rocket propelled, paws barely touching the ground, fur flying, teeth bared.

Zoe was close enough to see a gun barrel rising. The muzzle-flash came fractions of a second later. Her heart had already been hammering. When she saw someone fire at her beloved K-9 partner, she thought it might pound right out of her chest.

Freya never faltered. She hit the shooter hard, carrying him back and down, then standing on his chest and growling into his face, mere inches away. He tried to bring his pistol to bear on her again.

Gasping, Zoe pushed the last few feet. The gun was rising. Aiming at Freya. She wasn't going escape injury this time!

In a flurry of fur and shouting, a booted foot kicked the man's arm hard enough that she heard the cast crack. He screamed. Angel joined Freya by crunching down on the already broken arm and shaking it the way she would a rat.

That fit. The rat was human, and he was down and disarmed. That left only whoever was restraining Patrick.

Zoe trained her gun on the prostrate shooter and ordered, "Freeze," while Sean picked up the man's gun and pointed it at the other adult.

A crowd from the pageant had followed and was beginning to gather close by. Someone shone a beam of light on Patrick and his captor. It was a woman. She wasn't elderly, nor was she as young as Zoe. Her clothing was pristine. Her hair perfectly coiffed. Her nails manicured. She would have presented a comforting picture if not for the look in her eyes. It radiated pure evil.

"Alice! What are you doing here?" Sean shouted.

"I came for my grandson."

"You can't have him."

"Oh, really?" she snorted derisively. "It looks like I already do."

"You know what I mean." Sean lowered the gun rather than take the chance he'd accidentally harm Patrick.

"I know more than that," Alice screeched. "Now all

your friends will know it, too. You don't care for this boy. You just want control of his fortune."

"What fortune?"

"Ha! You can't fool me. You know all about the trust. Sandra left everything to her son. She told you. I know she did. She said so before she died."

"I have no idea what you're talking about. Sandra was so confused after she got hooked on drugs she told wild stories all the time. I quit paying attention long ago."

"Liar!" Alice's grip on the boy tightened. She brandished a knife and pressed it against the side of his small neck.

Sean put down the assailant's gun and held up both hands, palms out, to demonstrate submission. "I'm not armed. You don't need that knife."

She gestured at the man on the ground. "Give him back his gun and back off."

When Sean's glance met Zoe's he knew that wasn't going to happen. It was a standoff. He looked around. "Get these kids out of here so they don't have to watch. You, too, Maisy. Patrick will be all right. Go back to the pageant."

The girl was sobbing to Alice. "Please let him go."

"He'll have a wonderful life with me and my husband. And he won't have to worry about his crazy daddy," the older woman shouted back.

Sean's fists clenched. If not for the knife at his son's throat, he'd jump her and end this. Since Patrick could easily be cut, he had to hold himself in check. He had to.

Flashes of invisible light nearly blinded him. Mortar shells exploded. Sean shut his eyes and covered his ears against the mental bombardment of war. All he could think, all he could do, was call out to the God he had denied and pray from the heart. So he did.

There was no instant relief, but he did begin to breathe more slowly, to feel a sense of encroaching peace. It was as if he were an outside observer, watching a life-and-death struggle over which he had no control.

Blinking, he forced his eyes to open. To focus. Alice was still holding Patrick, still grimacing as if she were readying herself to plunge the knife despite her need to keep her grandson alive.

"If—if you hurt him, you'll never get custody," Sean managed to choke out.

"I will if you're dead. That was the original plan, but those idiots I hired failed."

"Suppose I sign over the trust. Will that do?"

"You can't. That's not legal. We'd been administering it for Sandra, and we'll keep doing it for the boy."

Sean was desperate. He shouted, "I don't want any money! Got that? You can have it all. Just let go of my son."

"You can end this right here and now," Alice said. "If your cop buddies won't let my associate shoot you, you can shoot yourself."

During the time in the past when he had initially struggled to regain his mental equilibrium, Sean had toyed with the idea of suicide. Now, he had somehow crossed a line and desperately wanted to live. To make a new life and begin to enjoy it. That's what his counselors had tried to tell him during his darkest hours. There was life and happiness and a future waiting on the other side of his illness. To have purposely ended his life early would have been a selfish, foolish act that would have hurt his loved ones beyond measure.

Nevertheless, he could pretend to agree to stall for time. Surely the officers who had been at the church tonight must be getting ready to act.

Zoe shouted, "No!" as he lifted the gun slightly.

While Alice was holding tight to Patrick, her attention was on Sean, so the deranged grandmother failed to see what was happening behind her. A few armed officers, in and out of uniform, had cut off her escape. That was a start. All Sean had to figure out was how to get her to release the boy without harming him.

The sight of his border collie, Angel, creeping along on her belly like a commando startled him. He knew that breed instinctively herded animals, but he'd never seen her crawl before. Not only was she sneaking up on Alice, she was getting away with it! Above all, he must not let himself give away the dog's position by staring at her.

A glance at Zoe told him she had seen Angel, too. Was it possible? Could the intelligent dog be acting on her own to end the stalemate? It sure looked that way.

"Well?" Alice screeched, obviously near her breaking point. "What are you waiting for?"

His arm raised a little more. The older woman began to smile. Angel was almost in position. Was she going to succeed in distracting Alice? The idea seemed preposterous to Sean until he remembered his tortuous, rambling, silent prayer.

A deep breath preceded a whispered, "Please, God," just as the dog's jaws clamped hard on Alice's ankle the way they would have on the hock of a misbehaving sheep.

She screamed, let go of the boy and slashed wildly at the attacking canine.

Angel was quicker. She ducked, parried and ran back to deliver a second nip before dashing off again and barking.

Officers reached Alice and restrained her. Sean shoved the unfired gun at Zoe. Patrick dived for his father and ended up grasped tightly, lovingly.

As father and son embraced, Sean felt the arms of a third party wrapping around them. Zoe's tears of relief mingled freely with theirs, and the rightness of the moment was inescapable.

She was kissing his cheek. He turned his head slightly and did what he'd been yearning to do ever since their reunion. He finally kissed her properly. Seriously. And oh, so lovingly.

It was not only the best kiss he'd ever experienced, but her eager response proved that he hadn't made a mistake. The only difficulty was stepping away when the police were ready to clear the scene.

ELEVEN

Zoe kept remembering Sean's kiss and wondering if he had merely been reacting to the emotions of the rescue. The more she thought about it, the more confused she became.

By the time they were finished with their debriefing at the police station, Alice had been booked, as had her remaining hired thug. Her husband, John, had been notified and had disavowed any knowledge of her scheme to usurp the trust, one way or another. It was not up to the Desert Valley Police Department to ascertain whether or not he was telling the truth, since that part of the crime had occurred in another state.

Zoe covered a yawn on the way to the truck. "Sorry."

"You're entitled. It's been a long night."

The child sleeping against his shoulder stirred. "For all of us."

"Right. The hero dogs, too. I'm so glad they weren't hurt." Smiling at the memories, she bent to pet them both. "No kidding. I was sure Freya had been shot. And when Angel bit your mother-in-law, I almost fell over. That's the way her breed handles sheep, but I never dreamed she was smart enough to put her instincts to use the way she did."

"Speaking of being smart," Sean said, "I have something I want to discuss with you. Everything that happened tonight made me realize how important it is. I'm just not sure how to put it."

"Simply would be best."

"Okay. I think you and I should get married."

"Whoa! After one kiss? I admit it was amazing, but that's a little too simple."

"What I mean is, Patrick needs a mother and you're fond of him, right?"

Zoe didn't like the way this was developing. "Yes."

"Well? I've talked to Dalton about applying for a job with his family's construction company, so I won't be freeloading. He says I can work outside and even pick my job sites, so you can go back to your position in Mesa without any conflicts if that's what you want."

"You've worked it all out, haven't you?"

There was hope in his expression. "I think so. How about it?"

Zoe almost choked up when she shook her head and said, "No."

"No? I'm getting better. You said so yourself. And I thought…"

"What? What did you think, Sean? That I'd sign up for a lifetime with you because I felt sorry for your son?"

"No, I…"

If she'd had any way to escape being with him, she'd have taken it. Unfortunately, they had ridden to the church and later to the station together.

Head lowered to hide her silent tears, Zoe turned away.

Sean opened the truck door, belted Patrick in safely, then straightened and placed both hands on her shoulders. "Something tells me I need to start over."

She didn't move. Could barely breathe.

He turned her to face him, continuing to hold her in place while he said, "I love you, Officer Trent. Probably always have, but I was too dense to realize it. I know we can make a marriage work. I just can't bear the thought of losing you again, especially since God went to so much trouble to bring us together."

"Go back," she said haltingly. "You love me?"

"With all my heart. I thought that kiss proved it."

"And you want to marry me?"

"More than anything."

Beginning to grin, Zoe slipped her arms around his neck and tilted her face. "Why didn't you say so in the first place?"

Sean's initial answer was the second best kiss she'd ever had. When she finally leaned back to gaze into his eyes, she saw her old friend looking back at her. His spirit was still in there, still alive, and he loved her.

There was nothing more she could want. No other prayers that remained unanswered. He'd made his peace with God, and that would help him make peace with his traumatized mind. In the meantime, she'd be by his side, supporting his efforts. She and Angel.

"Then, yes," Zoe whispered. "I love you, too, Sean. I'll marry you." Her tender gaze swept past farther to his sleeping son and lingered as she began to smile. "Both of you."

"That's the best Christmas present I've ever received," Sean said.

Zoe smiled. "Me, too."

* * * * *

With over seventy books published and millions in print, **Lenora Worth** writes award-winning romance and romantic suspense. Three of her books finaled in the ACFW Carol Awards, and her Love Inspired Suspense novel *Body of Evidence* became a *New York Times* bestseller. Her novella in *Mistletoe Kisses* made her a *USA TODAY* bestselling author. Lenora goes on adventures with her retired husband, Don, and enjoys reading, baking and shopping...especially shoe shopping.

Books by Lenora Worth

Love Inspired Suspense

Military K-9 Unit

Rescue Operation

Classified K-9 Unit

Tracker
Classified K-9 Unit Christmas
"A Killer Christmas"

Rookie K-9 Unit

Truth and Consequences
Rookie K-9 Unit Christmas
"Holiday High Alert"

Capitol K-9 Unit

Proof of Innocence
Capitol K-9 Unit Christmas
"Guarding Abigail"

Visit the Author Profile page
at Harlequin.com for more titles.

HOLIDAY HIGH ALERT

Lenora Worth

And the work of righteousness shall be peace;
and the effect of righteousness quietness
and assurance forever.
—*Isaiah* 32:17

To my dear friend and fellow writer Valerie Hansen.
Thank you for your guidance and your friendship!

ONE

Desert Valley Day care was quiet now.

Then why did she keep hearing things?

Josie Callahan did one more check, but all of the children and the rest of the staff had gone home. All but one. Once rookie K-9 Officer Dalton West came to pick up his ten-year-old daughter, Maisy, all of the children, ranging from six months to twelve years old, would be home with their parents. Dalton had completed the winter K-9 training session but had decided to stay in town until after the holidays to gain more experience and fill in for some of the senior officers.

Tired, Josie shook off the creepy feeling and went about shutting down the building. She typically didn't allow any of the staff to stay here alone, including herself, but she'd sent them all ahead tonight. Christmas was only a week and a half away, and everyone needed extra time to shop. But Dalton was running late. Nothing unusual there. The man lived for his work.

A piercing pain stabbed at her heart. She had no one to go home to, anyway.

A noise in the back parking lot sounded like a motor humming near the covered drop-off area. A car door slammed, the sharp sound echoing around the building. Footsteps pounded against the asphalt.

That might be Dalton now.

Wondering why he parked in the back, Josie glanced up the hallway to where Maisy sat reading a book in the big reception room. "Your dad's on his way, Maisy. I think I heard his car."

Maisy nodded and tugged at her long dark brown ponytail, her expression stoic. "He works too much."

"I know, honey. But he's one of the good guys. He has an important job. He's been training so hard, and now he's gaining even more experience helping out the local police."

"And he has Luna," Maisy replied, rubbing at her nose. "She makes him smile."

"You make him smile, too," Josie said, her heart turning to mush each time she thought of the handsome, no-nonsense widower who'd enrolled his daughter in the after-school program about three months ago. Luna, a brindle black-mouth cur with some chocolate Lab thrown in, was his K-9 partner. Luna was an expert tracker. Dalton and Luna were still considered rookies since they'd been partnered at the Canyon County K-9 Training Center for intensive training, but Josie could tell that Dalton West already knew his stuff. He'd been a detective in another town before he decided to become a K-9 officer. And he'd be going back to Flagstaff soon.

Listening, Josie heard a tap on the kitchen window. Dalton must be in a hurry. Not that she blamed him. He'd want to pick up his daughter and head home for the evening.

Josie hadn't locked the front door yet, but she'd locked the back one after she'd gone out and secured the playground gate. She headed to the back to let him in, Josie's thoughts returning to the dedicated police officer.

Dalton West didn't smile much, but he loved his little girl. And when he did smile at Maisy, Josie couldn't help but get caught up in seeing that love.

He had a beautiful smile.

Get back into the here and now. She'd have a rare night at home. Since her aunt, Marilyn Carter, who was also her partner in this new venture, had four rambunctious children, Josie always stayed for the late-shift workers if they had kids here after regular hours.

No one tonight, however. Just one girl awaiting her a-little-late father.

When she heard someone moving around outside again, she called out, "Coming, Dalton. Just let me check a few things."

She peeked into the various rooms, turning off lights and checking cabinets to make sure the supplies were put away properly. Halfway to the back door, she heard heavy footsteps hitting the tiled walkway leading to the playground.

"I'm coming, Dalton," she called again, her hand on the door.

The door shook with a jarring flurry.

Impatient man! "Just a minute."

Her hand on the doorknob, Josie inserted the key into the dead bolt. But the front door swung open, causing her pulse to rush into high-speed.

She whirled. "Dalton?"

Maisy ran and hugged her daddy. Josie backed away from the door with a funny feeling. Needles of fear moved down her backbone. She thought she'd heard footsteps running away. Who'd been out there?

"Sorry I'm late," he said. Taking Maisy by the hand, he strolled toward the kitchen, his alert gaze raking over Josie. "Hey, you okay?"

She forced a nod, glancing toward the playground. "Yes, I'm fine. I thought you were at the back door."

"No. I parked out front."

"Someone was there," she said. "They shook the door handle several times. I'm worried they were trying to break in."

"Do you have any other kids here?" Dalton asked, his gray eyes darkening as he went on alert.

"No, just Maisy," Josie replied. "Maybe someone thought their child was still here."

"But they know to call you on your cell," he said, well aware of the rules.

"I'm sure it was nothing," Josie said for Maisy's benefit, trying to hide the shudder moving down her spine. "Maybe someone got the wrong address."

Dalton gently shoved Maisy toward Josie. "You two stay here. Luna and I will take a look."

Josie didn't argue. They were all still jittery after one of the new kids at the day care, six-year-old Patrick Murphy, had almost been kidnapped by his maternal grandmother.

Josie was still shaken by that episode, which had happened the night of the Christmas pageant at the church, so she was probably overreacting. The grandmother hadn't come here to snatch Patrick, but Josie couldn't afford for the parents to think the day care might not be completely safe. Patrick stayed here almost every day, and his dad, Sean, trusted her to take care of Patrick since the boy had special needs.

"Is there a criminal out there?" Maisy asked, her gray-blue eyes full of fear.

"I don't think so," Josie replied, her tone steady in spite of her heart's constant bumping. Maisy knew as much police lingo as anyone, and the girl had a keen awareness that broke Josie's heart. "Your daddy wants to be sure everything is okay before we go home."

Maisy held her book tightly to her midsection. "A criminal killed my mom."

Josie bent, her hands on Maisy's slender arms. "I know and I'm so sorry. But your daddy is trained to help us with things like that."

"Then why didn't he save my mom?" Maisy asked, her solemn expression full of despair.

Josie had a degree in education and a minor in child care administration, but she didn't know how to answer that question. So she went with her instincts. "Your daddy tried his best to help your mom, Maisy. But sometimes, no matter how hard we try, we can't save the people we love."

"He's making up for it," Maisy said. "He wants to keep us safe. I try to be good all the time so he won't worry."

Josie inhaled a breath. Maisy had probably never told her daddy these things. "Yes, he does want to keep you safe." Touching a finger to Maisy's nose, she added, "But you, Miss Maisy, don't need to try to be good. Your daddy knows you are one of a kind. He loves you so much."

And, yes, he was making up for not getting to his wife in time. She'd heard the horrible story about how a drug dealer had broken into their home looking for Dalton, who'd been an undercover detective in Flagstaff at the time. Instead, they'd found his wife and taken her, leading to a high-speed chase that ended with the car flipping and his wife being killed. Thankfully, Maisy had hidden in a bathroom.

When she heard Dalton coming back inside, Luna with him and in her official K-9 vest, Josie hugged Maisy close. "We'll be okay, honey."

Maisy clung tightly to Josie. Then she looked up at Josie and whispered, "I'm the one who has to make sure he's okay."

Dalton gave Luna the space to do her job, the leash loose in his hand until they moved toward the back of the house. When they reached Josie and his daughter, Luna immediately let out a low yelp in greeting to her best buddy.

"Hey, Luna," Maisy said, reaching to pet the dog's brown-and-gold brindle coat.

"She has to work now," Dalton explained. Glancing at Josie, he nodded. "Unlock the door and then take Maisy to the front of the house. I'll need the playground keys, too."

She nodded, her green eyes full of trust in spite of the frown marring her heart-shaped face. "I'm sure it's nothing." Her gaze moved to Maisy in a warning, the curve of her auburn bangs shadowing her expression.

"No, a precaution," he said to reassure both of them. "Standard procedure, right, Maisy?"

Maisy stared up at her dad with solemn eyes. "If you say so."

"I say so." He waited for Josie to turn the lock. "This

won't take long, and then we can order a pizza and call it a day."

"Can Miss Josie come with us?" Maisy asked in a tone full of hope underlined by demand.

Dalton's gaze clashed with Josie's. "Uh...we'll have to see. Let me take care of this, and then we'll talk."

His daughter, the little matchmaker.

Dalton leaned down to Luna. "Search, girl," he ordered.

Luna took off, her head lifting up, her nostrils flaring. Then she lowered her head to the ground around the door before running toward the chain-link fence that enclosed the playground area across from the drop-off driveway.

Luna turned away from the fence, her nose going back down on the ground now. She followed the driveway all the way to the street and then whined an alert.

"They were in a vehicle," Dalton noted, his gaze scanning the street that ran along the left back side of the Tudor-style building.

They must have driven up to the drop-off area and gotten out to check the back door. Anyone could have pulled up to the door and touched the handle. Maybe a child had lost something and a parent had come looking, thinking the whole place was locked up. Thankfully, the door had been locked.

"I need something solid," he said to Luna.

They went back over the entire yard, even the playground area they'd skirted before. Dalton unlocked the gate to the playground, careful to hold Luna's leash around one wrist. It didn't look as if the lock had been tampered with. He could dust for prints, but there had to be hundreds on the door handle. He'd need something more isolated and specific.

He followed Luna around the playground, past the swings and climbing gyms. The muscular dog halted at the corner of the fence where an outcrop jutted high enough for someone to make it over the heavy, wooden security fence.

"Parked on the street, came to the door and then managed to sneak around the corner to hop this fence to get into the playground?" Luna moved through the rubber mulch under the various gym sets, castles and curving slides. She stopped short near one of the smaller forts, her nose sniffing at something lying on the mulch inside the miniature enclosure.

A white folded piece of paper, taped together.

Dalton dug in his equipment belt for a pair of plastic gloves. Telling Luna to stay, he let go of the leash and pulled the gloves over his hands before picking up the heavy-grade paper.

It was addressed to Josie Callahan.

Josie sat with Maisy, talking about anything to keep the little girl's mind off what was going on out in the backyard.

"Yes, this used to be someone's home," she explained. "But this whole area was rezoned for commercial use."

"What does that mean?" Maisy asked, her backpack right by her feet. The child was very precise about her belongings.

"It means that the town allowed this building to be used for a business instead of a home. I moved to Desert Valley to be close to my aunt, and when we found this huge old house for sale, we changed it into an official day care for children."

"Mrs. Carter," Maisy supplied. "Your aunt is nice."

"Yes, she is. And she loves children." Josie was thankful for her aunt Marilyn and thankful that Desert Valley was a long way from the small Texas town where she'd lived all of her life. A town she'd been forced to leave. "She watched children in her home, and since I'd always wanted to do that, too, we decided to open our own place. This building always reminded me of a gingerbread house, so we thought it would be perfect for children."

Maisy gave her a rare smile. "I love coming here."

"Me, too," Josie admitted with pride. "We worked hard to make it perfect."

They'd hired a contractor, gutted walls, installed the necessary equipment to bring it up to code and had gone through lots of forms and permits to make their day care a reality.

"I hope my dad's okay," Maisy said, craning her neck to see down the hallway.

Before Josie could come up with a reassuring answer, she heard the back door swing open and then the *tap, tap* of Luna's nails hitting the tile.

"There they are now," she said, releasing the breath she'd been holding.

"Daddy, is it okay to go out?" Maisy asked, jumping up.

Josie could hear the tremor of fear in the girl's question.

"It's safe," Dalton said. "But I do need to talk to Miss Josie."

"Can I hear?"

"Why don't you read your book for a bit more," Dalton said in a firm tone. "Then we'll figure out dinner."

Josie didn't like that tone. It meant he needed to speak to her in private.

"A word in the office," he suggested. Then he turned to Luna. "Stay with Maisy."

Luna dropped to the floor and stared up at Maisy with adoring brown eyes.

Dalton escorted Josie across to the office through what used to be the living-dining area. They could see Maisy and Luna through the glass window.

"I found this on the playground near one of the slides," he said.

When she saw her name spelled out in cutout letters on the folded sheet, she inhaled a deep breath. "Someone left this for me?"

"It looks that way," he said. He handed her a pair of latex gloves. "Put these on and open it."

Josie did as he asked, her heart pounding so hard the lace on her blouse kept fluttering. When she saw the cutout words pasted against the stark white, her heart took off again.

Who so sheddeth man's blood, by man shall his blood be shed. Genesis 9:6 (The wicked shall pay.)

Dalton's gray-eyed gaze met hers. Josie saw the concern in his expression.

Then he leaned in and lowered his voice. "This is obviously about more than a parent dropping by after hours. This was deliberate. And if I hadn't arrived when I did, you and Maisy could have been in serious danger."

TWO

"Daddy, I'm ready for pizza."

Josie carefully folded the paper and pivoted when she saw Maisy standing at the office door. "Your dad will be done soon, honey."

Maisy's big eyes widened. "Are you coming with us, Miss Josie? Please?"

Josie didn't know how to answer that. She didn't want to disappoint Maisy but…she had no business going to eat pizza with these two. She knew to keep her professional life and her personal life separated. "I…uh…"

"I have an idea," Dalton said, his eyes bright for Maisy's sake. "How about we follow Miss Josie home and we can order pizza from her house."

Josie sent him a shocked, questioning glare, her thoughts rolling over each other. "Really?"

"Really," he said. "It never hurts to see where my daughter's favorite after-school teacher lives. You know, to make sure things are okay?"

He wanted to check her home?

The dread Josie felt over the last few minutes increased twofold. Her stomach knotted, and her breath stopped cold. She rambled on, trying to recover. "It's been a while since I've had any company besides my aunt and uncle. I moved in next to them after Whitney married David and moved to a bigger house."

Whitney was also a K-9 officer and her husband, David, was a physician's assistant planning to go back to med school to become a full-fledged doctor. They lived around the corner in a new subdivision and were raising Whitney's little daughter, Shelby, a regular here at the day care.

"I'd heard that," he responded, his tone neutral and calm. "I'd like to see where you live."

He wasn't leaving her room to say no. Maybe it was a good idea to have him do a sweep, in case. In case of what? She didn't want to think about that.

"Of course," she said. "Let me finish locking up."

"And Luna's coming, too," Maisy said, her tone truly happy for a change. The young girl probably needed some motherly companionship.

"I wouldn't have it any other way," Josie said, thinking this was an interesting turn of events. And a disturbing one. She worried about what had happened, and for some reason she didn't want to examine too closely, she also fretted about being near Dalton West. The man cut an intimidating swath.

Just get home and think this through, she told herself. There had to be an explanation for that cryptic message.

And there had to be an explanation for the pitter-patter of her heart every time Dalton came to pick up Maisy.

Together she and Dalton double-checked the doors and windows. "All clear," he said after she'd locked the main entry. "I need to bag this letter, and then we'll be right behind you. I'll dust it for prints later. Might find some on the tape if not the paper."

After he'd settled Luna in her backseat kennel and Maisy in the front, seat belt secured, he turned to Josie. "I'm going to watch the streets between here and your house. And when the pizza comes, I'll answer the door. Better to be cautious than careless," he added. "I'm following you home and that's that. And we can talk about what might have provoked this."

"I'll see you there, then."

"Be careful," he said. She felt him watching her until she was in her car.

What a bossy man! No, more than bossy. Serious and commanding. Trustworthy. Good at his job. Josie sent up a prayer of thanks. Dalton had probably saved her from a break-in or a possible robbery. She should be relieved. Someone had pinpointed the day care and left that note for her to find.

Knowing that a police officer with a highly trained K-9 partner was following her home and coming inside to check her house made her feel a lot better about things. Because if she thought too long and hard about that note, she'd fall to pieces and… Josie wasn't going to give in to that notion.

She wasn't that woman anymore.

Dalton eased the old patrol car against the curb in front of the little house where Josie lived next to her aunt and uncle. The Carters were good people. Marilyn loved children, and her husband, Jack, ran his own auto repair company and worked on keeping all the old patrol cars running smoothly.

Josie Callahan obviously had the same work ethic

as her relatives. He'd heard the stories about the old rambling house that was now the day care. Whitney and David had recommended it to Dalton when he'd needed after-school care for Maisy. And not a moment too soon. They moved here not long after the day care had opened.

A good idea since everyone around here needed a safe place to leave their children. He especially considered the place an answer to his prayers since he didn't like leaving Maisy alone in the house, even with a nanny or teenage sitter. Maisy still had nightmares about her mother's death, so she needed to be in a safe and fun environment.

Up until now, he'd believed the Desert Valley Day care had been that place. But after Patrick Murphy's close call a couple of weeks ago with a vindictive, unhinged grandmother who thought he should be with her instead of his dad, Sean, and now this situation, he needed to find out what was going on.

Why would someone target the day care? Or rather, why would someone target Josie Callahan?

"This is a cute house," Maisy said, all smiles since they'd pulled into the neighborhood. "Look at the lights, Daddy."

"I see," Dalton responded. The lone fake Christmas tree he and Maisy had decorated a few weeks ago looked sad compared to this display.

The little beige stucco cottage was neat and clean. A small rock garden in front held a scrawny palm tree with top-heavy fronds and several varieties of cactus bushes, all of which were decorated with colorful Christmas lights. A pretty tree stood at the front window, and a palm-tree-embellished wreath hung on the front door. The woman must have a thing for desert palms.

But Dalton wasn't focused on the decorations. He glanced around the neighborhood, checking the cul-de-sac and scanning the street. A few vehicles were parked here and there, but he couldn't see anything that looked suspicious. Leashing Luna, he ordered her out, and they all headed up the drive to meet Josie at the door.

"Come in," she said, her tone unsure. "I have some pizza coupons."

Dalton scooted Maisy ahead of him, noting she had her favorite purple backpack. That thing seemed to be her security blanket these days. Luna followed, sniffing the new location with interest, her dark eyes full of curiosity.

Dalton scanned the tiny den and kitchen, making sure nothing was out of order. Neat and sparse with old but tidy wicker furniture and one big, comfortable-looking, puffy beige side chair. He watched as Josie moved around and fluffed pillows, her actions guarded.

"Make yourself comfortable," she said, clearly *uncomfortable*.

Maybe he shouldn't have forced the issue, but he couldn't shake the wariness gnawing at the pit of his stomach.

Regardless, they were here now so he'd do his job.

"Thanks." He motioned to Maisy. "Sit down, honey. You can put your pack on the coffee table."

Maisy did as he told her, her big gray-blue eyes gazing around the room with delighted interest. At least his daughter was enjoying this diversion.

Now Dalton had to wonder what had really prompted him to insist on coming to dinner at Josie's house. That threatening note, of course. Someone had gone to a lot of trouble to plant that. What if a kid had found it? Depending on what the kid would do with the note, Josie might have never known about it or the whole day care could have gone into a panic.

Both dangerous concepts.

He needed to follow through and get that note to the lab, but Dalton doubted anything substantial would be found on the paper. He might be able to question Josie after dinner if they could find a distraction for Maisy and Luna.

"Your place looks nice," he said when Josie came over with her cell phone and a handful of coupons. "Whitney loved it here, but she and David are happy in their new house from what I hear."

"That's good," Josie said. "Whitney told me they went through the wringer when they first met." Glancing at Maisy, she smiled. "But they made it through."

Dalton nodded, glad she didn't go into detail in front of his daughter about drug dealers and the town doctor who'd turned bad. "Yeah, they seem very happy."

"Shelby is so cute," Maisy said, clearly interested in the adult conversation. "She's funny when she walks. She falls and then gets right back up."

"She loves to run, but sometimes her feet get ahead of her," Josie said. "Even at eighteen months, she's a go-getter like her mama."

The silence that followed seemed like an eternity. Dalton wished he'd thought this through a little better. He'd never been one for small talk. "Pizza time," he finally said. "Want me to order?"

"No, I'll do it." Josie went through the various coupons, and they settled on toppings and a nearby restaurant that delivered. "One large pepperoni and sausage and one medium veggie," she told the restaurant clerk.

After she'd given the address and placed her phone down, she turned to Maisy. "I have water and milk to drink."

"Milk," Maisy said, shy now.

"Do you have homework?" Dalton asked Maisy.

She bobbed her head. "Reading. Miss Josie helped me with the math."

"But you might want to let your dad go over that with you since I'm a bit rusty," Josie suggested. "She's very smart in math," she said to Dalton. "She even explained a few things to me."

Proud to hear that, Dalton smiled at Maisy. "Okay, after we eat you can read for a while, and I'll check the math when we get home." But he doubted that would be necessary. Josie seemed like a capable woman. Pretty and smart. But what else was going on there?

Satisfied with his suggestion, Maisy became curious. "I like your house, Miss Josie. Our house is boring."

Dalton gave her a mock-affronted frown. "Did you say boring? I beg your pardon. Our house is warm and safe and…boring."

Maisy giggled and got up to walk around. "We don't have all the pretty decorations." She pointed to a picture of a grinning snowman. "Does it ever snow here?"

"Yes," Josie said, smiling at Maisy. "It gets really cold here at times, too, like Flagstaff where you usually live. Do you like snow?"

Maisy glanced at Dalton. "Yes, sometimes. The day my mom died, it was snowing. But…we didn't get to go out and play in it."

Josie gave Dalton a sympathetic look, her green eyes

full of understanding. "Maybe we'll get snow for Christmas," she said. "I'll take you outside, and we'll make snowballs."

"And a snowman," Maisy replied, content once more.

Dalton's heart shattered all over again at the pain he heard in his daughter's words. Would Maisy ever be able to forget that day over a year ago when her mom had been taken from them? He didn't want to remember that day, and he only wished Maisy could wipe it out of her mind, too.

"I'm going to take Luna for a walk," he said. Anything to get away from the pity in Josie's eyes and the hurt in his little girl's heart. Then he shot Josie a signal and mouthed, "We'll check things outside."

She nodded and got Maisy involved in helping her find plates and napkins. Their chatter echoed after him when Dalton shut the front door, Luna by his side.

Taking in the cold night air, he breathed deeply and closed his eyes. The dark memories threatened to overtake him, but Dalton had learned through counseling to work through the memories and to focus on seeing his daughter whole and happy again. Being with Josie did make Maisy laugh, at least.

And Lord, make me whole and happy again, too, he prayed.

Maybe the one prayer he asked for Maisy's sake every day had led him to come to Josie's home tonight. Truth be told, he had a slight crush on the pretty brunette with the shimmering green eyes. She had a knockout smile and a warm heart. She was a good person and, well, she was easy on the eye. He hadn't noticed another woman since Eileen had died, but lately he'd noticed little things about Josie. Those little things added up to a whole package that he couldn't ignore.

Was he ready for that kind of thing? Probably not. Besides, he'd be heading back to Flagstaff after Christmas. He and Maisy could start fresh in a new house, and he'd have a new position as an official K-9 officer.

Dalton cleared his head. He had work to do and a little girl to take care of. No time for such nonsense.

But he couldn't get Josie's sweet smile and the kind way she handled his daughter out of his mind. Someone had sent her what could be perceived as a threatening note. So he told Luna to search, and the slender dog took off like a rocket.

Doing her job without hesitation.

He needed to do the same.

They cleared the front and back yards and were headed back inside when Luna's head went up and a soft growl emitted from her throat. She sniffed the air, and her body turned toward the left. Dalton listened and glanced to the far end of the street, but a shrub blocked his view. Urging Luna forward, he saw a car he didn't remember from before. Too dark to see the make and model.

Dalton heard footsteps pounding, and then someone jumped into the car and took off in the other direction. Had that someone been watching Josie's house?

THREE

Josie glanced up when Dalton and Luna came back inside. "We're all ready. Any sign of the pizza guy?"

"No. Didn't run into anyone," he said, his alert gaze moving over the entire room before settling back on her. He looked distracted. "We'll keep watch," he added, his hand on the blinds covering the front window. "Maybe he'll be here soon, and then we can eat and get out of your hair."

Josie knew something was up, but she didn't say anything. "Okay, well, we can sit and talk or watch television until the pizza gets here."

"Talking is a good idea," Dalton said, turning to face her. "I'd like to get to know you better."

Josie sent him a questioning glance. The man had hardly spoken a complete sentence to her, other than to get Maisy registered and a quick "hello" and "thank you" here and there. "Sure. What would you like to know?"

"Where are you from?"

She didn't want to go down this road, but he was obviously trying to conduct an interrogation. "Texas, but you know that, right?"

"Where in Texas?"

"A town near Waco. Pine Cone."

"You lived in a town called Pine Cone?" Maisy asked with a giggle, her big eyes full of the same inquisitive perusal as her dad's.

Josie swallowed her fears. "Yes. It's so small it only has one traffic light and one main street. Pine Street."

Maisy shook her head and got out her reading book. "Must be a lot of pine trees around there."

"Yes. Tall, giant pines. Not quite as dainty as the ponderosa pines around here."

Josie motioned to Dalton. He ordered Luna to stay, and the big dog curled up next to Maisy. Then he walked over to the counter.

"What's with all the personal questions?" Josie asked.

"I'll need to gather some background information," Dalton said in a low voice.

"Why?"

He put both hands on the counter and stared at her with solemn gray eyes. "Relax. Just as a precaution."

"No," she said, anger and dread clawing at her throat. "You're going to do a background *check*, aren't you? I had to go through that process in order to open the day care and…everything checked out."

He tapped the counter. "If you're being threatened, I need to know who could be after you. Someone from home, maybe."

Josie didn't want to delve into thinking about anyone from home coming after her. She hadn't told anyone where she was going, and the people she'd known had to have forgotten her by now. Even her bitter, heartbroken and widowed mother-in-law Janine Callahan, who was too sick with grief to plot something like this.

"And why do you think it would be someone from Texas?" she countered, hoping he was wrong. She'd tried to keep her past in the past. "It could be an angry parent."

"Yes, that's true. Have you had a disagreement with any of the parents recently?"

Josie shook her head. "No. We've only been open a few months, and usually if a parent has a complaint, we handle it immediately and try to make it right. If we're aware of it."

He processed that for a minute and then said, "Maybe someone is upset with you or someone else at the day care, but they haven't shared that with you."

"Why would they go about things in this way?" she asked. "This seems extreme, considering we've had nothing but good reviews and our clients send people to us. You know that firsthand."

"I agree," he said. "I'm gathering facts, Josie. Not accusing you or anyone on your staff."

"Are you worried about a repeat of what happened with Patrick?" she asked, concerned about the little boy's abduction attempt. Maisy had been upset when Patrick went missing. The girl didn't need to worry about the happenings at the day care, too.

"That incident did come to mind," he replied. "But we know who tried to take Patrick."

"Okay," she said, inhaling to calm her nerves. But her home and business both now held a sinister sheen that reminded her of why she'd left Texas. "What do you think?"

"I don't know. It could be a prank, or it could be that they're after one of your employees. Anyone working with you having relationship problems? Any hint of domestic violence?"

"No," she said, wishing he'd back off. "You know my aunt. She's one of the nicest people in the world. Same with my uncle. We have four other workers who've all had extensive background checks, and they're all trained to work with children. They're good people. We were thorough in making sure they were suitable to work at the day care."

"I can believe that," he said. "Let's table this for now."

Thankfully, the doorbell rang. But Josie's heart sped out of control and she jumped. Then she rushed around Dalton, a wad of cash in her hand.

"No, let me," he said, pulling out his wallet. "I want to check the delivery person, anyway."

"You don't trust my pizza delivery boy, either?"

"Right now, I don't trust anyone, and I'm here to make sure you don't let anyone you don't know into your house."

She'd let *him* in, Josie thought, ragged nerves making her want to scream. But that tension made her appreciate his strong presence. When he opened the door, her regular delivery person looked shocked to see the tall, dark-haired man standing there.

"Oh, hi…uh… Officer," the young man with bright red hair said. "How ya doing?" He glanced around Dalton and smiled at Josie. "Hey, Miss Callahan."

"Hey, Ryan. Good to see you."

Dalton paid the kid and added an extra five. "Thanks, buddy." Then he glanced up and down the street before he shut the door.

After he'd set the two pizza boxes on the counter,

Josie leaned close. "You saw someone out there earlier, didn't you?"

He made sure Maisy wasn't listening and then nodded. "But it could have been a neighbor leaving in a hurry."

"Right," Josie said, wishing she could believe that. "Let's eat before the pizza gets cold," she added to show a sign of bravado.

But she didn't feel brave. And she'd lost her appetite.

"Maybe you should stay next door tonight with your aunt," he suggested.

"I'm a grown woman. I won't let some random letter scare me."

He didn't like that response. "You need to take this seriously."

"Oh, I'm taking it seriously," she replied. "But… there's something you don't know about me, Dalton. I used to cower in fear and try to please everyone. But I've changed. I stand up for myself these days."

He passed out pizza and then stood there staring at her. "I'm glad you're stronger now, but…sometimes it's hard to stand up to someone who's dangerous and deranged. That can get you hurt or worse…killed."

Josie stared down at her pizza, embarrassment heating her skin. She was being insensitive. Dalton's wife had been killed. He was just trying to warn Josie to be careful.

Looking into his stormy eyes, she said, "Thanks for the warning. I'll…call my aunt and tell her what happened and… I'll be careful. I promise."

"Good." He smiled and called Maisy over to the dining table. "Let's eat, honey, and then we have to get home. You've got school tomorrow."

Josie touched his arm. "Thank you, Dalton, for doing this."

"My job," he said. "And… I have to take care of you. You're one of Maisy's favorite people."

Josie felt a new kind of shiver moving down her spine.

The kind a woman got when she realized she might be attracted to a good-looking man.

But she couldn't explore those feelings until she found out who had targeted her at her place of business today. That was urgent. But add to that, Dalton was moving back to Flagstaff in a couple of weeks. Nothing could happen between them.

The next morning, Dalton told Chief Ryder Hayes about what he'd found and showed him the letter, which he'd placed in a letter-sized mailing envelope.

"I dusted it for prints," he said, "but I didn't find anything traceable. So that means whoever left this must have been wearing gloves." He leaned back in his chair. "Josie will alert me if she receives anything else suspicious."

"Best you can do," Chief Hayes replied, his blue eyes pinning Dalton to the spot. "It could be random, but with kids involved, we can't take any chances. I don't want Lily in any danger."

Lily was the chief's little daughter. He'd lost his wife to a murderer a few years ago. They had that in common. But Ryder had found a second chance at love with Sophie, the lead K-9 trainer.

"I'm going to do background checks on everyone who works there," Dalton said. "And I plan to question all of them, too."

"Once a detective…" Chief Hayes smiled and nodded. "I hear Josie's a widow?"

"Yes, sir. She didn't mention that, but I'd heard it also."

Dalton wondered what had happened to her husband. She was awfully young to be a widow. Maybe he'd ask her about that.

Or maybe it was none of his business. He sure didn't like people asking what had happened to his wife.

He was happy for the chief, though. Ryder and Sophie planned to get married in February. Sophie had helped Dalton get acclimated to moving into a new area of law enforcement, and she'd shown him how to bond with Luna. Everyone here worked that way. As a team. He liked that.

Now he sat up and glanced at the chief. "Josie Callahan is a capable, hardworking woman. I can't imagine anyone wanting to come after her."

The chief's gaze hardened. "Part of our job is to be diligent and go with our gut. If you have a hunch that something isn't right, don't hesitant to follow through. Luna will know what to do."

"Yes, sir," Dalton replied.

After grabbing a corner desk, Dalton looked up the Desert Valley Day care website and jotted down the names of the entire staff.

An hour later, he'd cleared several of the employees. Josie had been right. They were all highly qualified to work with children. No arrest reports or criminal activity. Most of them were female, ranging in age from twenty-five to fifty and educated in everything from child development to how to run a mother's-day-out program. One of them had even worked at the church in that capacity.

He'd saved Josie for last, maybe because he felt guilty about checking up on her. But…everyone had a past, and, while he'd been thorough, he knew people from the past could come looking. That's how his wife had died. A drug dealer had come looking for Dalton and had taken Eileen instead. But someone had called 911 and the police had immediately spotted the car. Then a high-speed chase had ensued and…the doped-up driver had lost control of the vehicle. The car had crashed into a stand of ponderosa pines and exploded. The driver and Eileen had been killed.

Maisy had been left alone in the house after Eileen had urged her to run next door. Instead of leaving her mother, his brave daughter had hidden and called for help.

He'd heard the alert on the radio, but Dalton had arrived at the scene too late to save Eileen.

Dalton couldn't let that happen again. He might have missed something that hadn't shown up on the internet search.

He was about to run the check on Josie when fellow rookie Zoe Trent walked in with her partner, Freya, a beautiful brown Belgian Tervuren with some black tips covering her fur. Zoe's long, shiny brown hair matched her partner's. It was a joke around here, but Zoe took it in stride.

"Hey," he said, smiling. "How's it going?"

"Good," she said. "How about you?"

"I can't complain. How's Sean liking his new job?" Sean Murphy was little Patrick's dad. The two had been through a lot.

Dalton's father ran West Construction out of Flagstaff, and Dalton had suggested Zoe's new fiancé, Sean Murphy, get in touch with him to find work. West Construction had offices all over Arizona. Sean was now a regular on the construction crew that worked all over Canyon County. New construction was booming right now, so Sean stayed busy. Since Zoe had been assigned to go back to Mesa once the holidays were over, Sean could easily find work there, too.

Zoe sank down on a chair, Freya at her feet. Luna gave her K-9 friend a lift of the head and a little woof. Freya stared at the other dog and gave a doggie smile in acknowledgment.

"He loves building houses," Zoe said. "Thank you so much for recommending him to your dad. This job is good therapy for his PTSD since your dad doesn't mind his service dog, Angel, being on-site."

"I'm glad it worked out," Dalton replied. Sean Murphy had been injured by an IED while serving in Afghanistan.

Proud of how his family supported returning veterans, he said, "I haven't talked to my folks in a couple of weeks. I'll see them after the holidays since I'm pinch-hitting for some of the other officers."

It didn't feel like Christmas, but he had to keep his spirits up for Maisy's sake. "Sounds like you and Sean are happy."

Zoe's smile said it all. "Great. Better than great. And Patrick is amazing."

Dalton missed that kind of contentment in his own life. When he thought of Josie Callahan, his mind went back to work mode. Changing the subject, he said, "What's up today?"

"We've been going through our paces out on the practice yard at the training center," Zoe said, motioning to Freya. "What're you working on?"

Dalton gave her the specifics. "Strange and certainly a matter of concern."

"Sean won't like hearing this about the day care after what we went through with Patrick, but it might turn out to be nothing much."

"I hope so," Dalton replied. "I'm keeping close to this one, though. Maisy was there alone with Josie Callahan last night."

"I understand," Zoe said. "Let me know if you need me to pick up Maisy or do any groundwork on the case."

After he and Zoe caught up a little more, his cell rang.

"Dalton, it's Josie Callahan."

She sounded out of breath and upset.

"Are you okay?"

"No," she said. "We found another note."

"I'm on my way," Dalton replied, his gut burning.

Luna sensed his agitation and fell in right beside him. Together they hurried out to his patrol car.

FOUR

Josie held the manila envelope away, staring at it as if it might be a bomb. Her fingerprints were all over it. But she'd found some gloves in the nursery and now she could feel her palms sweating against the sticky latex.

But the words made her go cold.

And my wrath shall wax hot, and I will kill you with my sword. Exodus 22:24

The verse had been taken out of context, but Josie got the meaning loud and clear. One note was questionable. Two made it real.

"Miss Josie, are you okay?" her assistant, Heather, asked from the office door, her hazel eyes bright with questions.

Josie dropped the envelope and the offending note made with cutout letters. "I'm going through the mail. Did you happen to notice when the mailman came?"

Heather shook her head, her brown ponytail bouncing. "No, ma'am. We've had people in and out all day. Did you find the envelope with your name on it?"

"Yes," Josie said, trying to stay calm. "I saw it with the mail. Did someone drop it off?"

"I found it wedged inside the door when I opened

this morning," Heather replied. "I thought one of the parents left it."

Josie took a breath. "Thank you. Did you need something?"

Heather stood inside the doorway. "I wanted to check on you. You look tired."

Josie forced a smile. "I am tired. I didn't sleep very much last night but…it's nothing."

"Well, I'm about to take my lunch break, unless you need to go first."

"No, you go ahead," Josie said. She saw the police cruiser pulling up. "There's one of our parents now. I have a conference with Dalton West."

Heather grinned and glanced out the window. "He's a tall drink of water, as my mama likes to say."

Josie managed a tight smile. "Yes, he sure is. You go on and enjoy your lunch. I'll take the late shift."

Heather nodded and greeted Dalton as he appeared in the doorway to Josie's office, then glanced down at Luna. "Hey, there, Luna. Are you fighting crime today?"

Luna glanced at Dalton and then back at Heather, her nose in the air.

"We're on the job," Dalton said, his cheerful tone belying the panic Josie couldn't stop.

Dalton hurried into the office and shut the door. "Show me the note."

She handed him the manila envelope with her name scrolled on it in scraggly bold black. Then she pointed to the folded piece of paper lying beside it.

Dalton pulled a pair of gloves from his equipment belt and opened the envelope. After reading the words pasted there, he looked at her with a stoic stare. "This is serious."

"I'm not sure how to handle it."

"You have to be careful," Dalton replied, his gaze on the note. "Was this sealed?"

"No. Pressed together with the metal fastener. I opened it without gloves. It was with the mail, and I didn't even bother looking at the front."

"The mailman wouldn't have let this get through without a complete address," Dalton said.

"Heather found it by the front door early this morning and put it with the mail. What should I do? I can't allow the children to be in danger, and if I tell the parents, they'll take their children out of my care."

"We'll take it a step at a time. Right now, you're the target, but if it escalates we'll have to warn everyone. How did your aunt take it?"

"She had a doctor's appointment today, so I haven't told her." She sank back in her chair and rubbed her forehead. "I'm concerned about the children."

Dalton placed the note back into the envelope. "Stay calm for now. I'll check the yard again, and I'll dust this the same as I did the last one. But I'm pretty sure we won't find anything. Do you have surveillance cameras?"

"We can't afford those. We have locks on the windows and doors and the playground gates. But they got inside the playground." She glanced out the window, thoughts of someone creeping around causing her to shiver. "My maintenance man is trying to remove that rock embedded by the fence."

"Well, there's no sign of break-ins. We can put a cruiser on the street to watch for anyone suspicious.

Have them circle the block every few minutes after hours."

Josie had the certain sinking sensation that this person would find a way around a patrol car. "Okay. Then what?"

"I think we might want to go ahead and talk to the staff, Josie," he finally said. "I'd planned on questioning them about the first note, but I didn't want to alarm them. If we get them all together, maybe I can scope the room, get a feel for things. Luna can help there, too."

"You think someone on my staff could be doing this?"

"Can't rule anyone out," he replied. "Can you get them all together for a few minutes after closing?"

"I'll try," she said. "Besides my aunt, one other person has the day off."

That got his attention. "Who?"

"Tricia Munson. She works with the babies."

"Why did she take the day off?"

"To attend a funeral," Josie said, ruling out Tricia immediately. But Dalton didn't look so sure. The man must have been a great detective because he had a bulldog's tenacity.

"Who died?"

"Her uncle."

"Did he live here?"

"Yes," Josie said. "His obituary was in the paper this morning. Jeffery Munson. He's a highly respected local businessman."

Dalton must have sensed her disbelief. "I don't mean to sound insensitive," he said. "We have to start somewhere, and any employee acting out of the ordinary is fair game."

"I understand."

"Okay." He stood and held Luna's leash. "Get that meeting together for tonight."

"I'll tell Aunt Marilyn as soon as she gets back from her appointment."

"And I'll get that cruiser over here," Dalton said, his eyes a stormy gray. "Whoever this is, he's a coward. He comes after hours and in the dark of early morning. If I have to, I'll spend the night here. Luna will be glad to do that job."

The sleek dog glanced up at the sound of her name. She did look ready and willing. They both made Josie feel safe.

"Thank you," she said after she'd walked Dalton around the building. Luna didn't alert, so that was a relief. But she could tell the staff was beginning to wonder what was going on.

When they stopped in the front parking lot, Dalton did a scan of the entire yard. "You have a good open area, so nowhere for someone to hide. I'll be here on time to pick up Maisy this afternoon, and I'll do another sweep then."

"Okay," she said. She didn't want to depend on Dalton, but the man made her feel protected.

"I enjoyed last night," he said. "In spite of what brought us together."

"Pizza brought us together," she retorted, not wanting him to read anything into their dinner. "And your daughter's demands," she added with a smile.

He looked sheepish. "Yeah, sorry about that." Then he turned serious. "You spend a lot of time with Maisy. How is she doing, really?"

Josie chose her words carefully. "She misses her mom. Do you two ever talk about what happened?"

His expression hardened. "No. It's too hard to explain. We both went to counseling…after her mother died. I thought Maisy was doing better, but I know she has nightmares. So do I, for that matter."

Josie's heart went out to him. "It's tough. I still have nightmares about my husband's death."

Dalton latched on to that. "How did he die?"

She hadn't meant to say anything, but she trusted Dalton. "He worked at an oil refinery back in Texas. An accident that caused a chemical spill."

An accident that his family blamed on Josie because they considered her a bad wife. But they didn't know where she was now. She almost said something to Dalton, but the possibility of Douglas's mother or brother finding her was slim. His mother was sickly, and his brother had married and moved to Louisiana.

"That's tough," Dalton said. "Any coworkers who might have a grudge against him or you?"

She thought about that. "I didn't know the people he worked with, but…he'd come home with stories. Mostly gossip or news about their wives and children."

"Could you remember any of them?"

"We didn't socialize with them a lot." She grabbed a notepad from her purse. "Douglas mentioned George— George Cleveland—a lot. And Perry Wilcox. Perry was always mad about something and hated his job. Douglas used to go fishing with Rafael Gonzalez. He was a good man from what I remember." She handed him the list. "Douglas got into heated arguments with Perry. He told me Perry Wilcox was a hothead."

"We have to consider anyone who might have a grudge."

She'd blocked out that part of her life, and she didn't want to delve into it again. But she was willing to co-operate. "I hope it's not one of them."

He took another look around. "I have to go. But I'll be back for Maisy, and I'll send that patrol. Meantime, we have an incident file going, so document everything. The letters or anything else you might receive, the time of day, how and where. Keep your phone with you and... Josie, don't go anywhere alone. Call me if you need anything."

"Thanks again," Josie said, trying to absorb his instructions. She watched as he got in the squad car and sped away. Before, she'd always loved the front drive to the day care where she and her aunt had planted shrubs and palm trees and made pretty rock gardens filled with succulents. They'd worked hard to make the arched entryway to the heavy wooden front door welcoming and like a fun castle.

Now, she shivered in the cool breeze and searched the nearby businesses. The rambling day care building looked ominous and dark in spite of the wreath on the door.

When she came back inside, Heather was standing in the hallway. "What was that all about, Miss Josie?"

"We're going to have a meeting tonight after work, and I'll explain," Josie said, paranoia new to her. "Meantime, it's work as usual."

"I don't mind a meeting," Heather retorted. "I was asking what's going on with you and that handsome lawman. He sure likes to look at you."

Josie scoffed at the notion, and then she shook her

head. But she couldn't deny she'd been very much aware of Dalton taking up space in her office. "He was giving me some security tips."

"Right," Heather said with a grin. "We'll go with that."

Josie didn't want to have this conversation. "Back to work," she said on a gentle note. "I'll tell the others about our meeting."

She dreaded telling them anything, but she couldn't keep this from her employees. She only prayed she didn't have to shut this place down because of some lunatic.

Dalton drove around the neighborhood and searched for any signs that might give him a hint of what was going on. These older homes along the main thorough-fare aptly called Desert Valley Road had mostly all been turned into commercial businesses, such as the Desert Valley Medical Clinic where Officer Whitney Godwin Evans's husband, David, used to work.

Dalton was only in Desert Valley because of the K-9 training program he'd completed and his offer to work for the DVPD until after the holidays. But Desert Valley wasn't such a bad place to be. There were good people here.

He thought of Josie Callahan and stifled the surge that shot through his heart. Again, he had that feeling of awareness that he'd gotten the first time he'd met her. She'd been holding a tiny infant while she reassured the baby's frantic mother that she'd take good care of her baby boy.

He'd been smitten with her from the beginning, but he'd tried to squelch those erratic feelings. Maisy needed him, and he wasn't always home to help her.

That's why he'd been so glad to find a day care that allowed older children to attend the after-school and late-shift programs. He didn't want anything to jeopardize that arrangement.

And he sure didn't want any harm to come to the children or Josie and her staff. So he cruised the neighborhood around the day care, located near the town center. The streets were quiet, the modest homes clean and settled.

Then he glanced at a rutted dirt lane that led to a run-down house sitting like a squatter in a rocky, isolated corner lot.

A dark, older-model car was parked at an angle by the house.

It looked like the car he'd noticed driving away from Josie's house last night.

"Let's go investigate," Dalton said to Luna. She woofed her agreement from the backseat.

Dalton wondered if Josie's tormentor could be hiding in plain sight.

FIVE

"This isn't easy," Josie said a few hours later.

She had the whole staff gathered in the break room. Her aunt, whom she'd already told everything, was sitting in the front lobby with the last of the children. Maisy was there with Aunt Marilyn, helping out as usual.

Glancing at the clock, she said, "I hoped Officer West would be able to help me explain this but…you know how it goes with police officers."

Heather's grin brightened, but she wiped her face clean when Josie didn't grin back. Josie had to tell them what was going on to keep them safe and to show them that she wasn't hanging out with Dalton West because she suddenly had a hankering to date a K-9 cop. Not that the notion hadn't entered her mind.

"What is it?" Tricia Munson asked, her brown eyes full of anxiety. "Are you laying some of us off already? Is that why you called me in for this meeting?"

"It's not that," Josie said, sinking down on a chair. "I've received some threatening notes."

"What?" Heather's blankness vanished. "Is that why you've been so preoccupied?"

"Yes," Josie said. "Officer West found one of the notes on the playground yesterday after someone tried to open the back door."

They all started mumbling among themselves.

"Listen, let me finish," Josie said. "I've talked to Aunt Marilyn about this already, but I need you to understand—this might be nothing. I received another note today." She glanced at Heather. "The package you found at the door."

Heather gasped. "I'm so sorry. I had no idea."

"It's not your fault," Josie replied. "We don't know if it's a joke or if it's an upset parent trying to scare me. Or maybe someone else."

"That granny woman sure wasn't happy with anybody in Desert Valley," Floyd, the maintenance man, said. "Could it be her pulling some strings from jail?"

"You mean Patrick Murphy's grandmother, Alice Shepherd?" Tricia asked. "They arrested her after she tried to take Patrick. Surely she isn't starting all over again? She'd be crazy to do that."

Floyd let out a grunt. "I rest my case."

Thinking she needed to school her staff on being sensitive to others' suffering, Josie hadn't even considered Floyd's suggestion. "Mrs. Shepherd is being treated for her mental problems, so I don't think this is coming from her. But I'll mention it to Officer West."

She took a sip of water. "We don't want to scare our parents, but they'll need to know if it keeps happening. Before we alert them, however, you need to keep this among the staff. Officer West wants to check on every parent who has a child here to rule out that possibility. So he might have to interview all of us."

"Does he think it's one of them? Or one of us?" Tricia asked.

"No. He's not accusing anyone. We're being diligent in making sure we've covered every possibility. It could be kids playing pranks."

"Are the notes threatening?" Floyd asked.

"Not in an obvious way," Josie said.

"Can we see them?" another worker asked.

"No. Officer West filed them as evidence, and he's filled out an incident report." Josie stood, ready to end this. "Remember, they've only come to me. No one else is being threatened in a direct way. I've alerted the police, and Officer West is on the case since his daughter attends the after-school program here. Several officers place their children in our care, so the whole department will be aware. He's putting a patrol on the street during the workday and after hours. And if I can find some money in the budget, I might put in a security system."

"I know a guy," Floyd said, coming over to pat her on the arm. "We're all behind you, Josie."

"Thank you, Floyd," she told the older man who seemed like everyone's grandfather. He'd retired from coaching soccer at the high school, and she was blessed to have him. "We're going to be okay, I promise."

But even as she said it, Josie didn't know how she could make such a promise. She'd pray her way through this situation. And hope that Dalton found something soon.

Nothing. He'd found nothing.

The old house was vacant and falling down, and the car looked like it'd been stripped for parts. But Luna had displayed a keen interest in the car. Since they hadn't found any items near the automobile or in the trunk, he couldn't be sure if she'd sniffed something she recognized or if she'd had a false alert from too many squirrels hanging around.

The house was locked, so he didn't search inside. But the place gave him a feeling he didn't like. He'd have to keep an eye on it.

With nothing concrete to connect this place or the abandoned car to the case, he had to move on. But he would alert the chief.

After taking care of that, he headed back to the day care and saw Josie's aunt Marilyn with a cluster of children.

"Daddy," Maisy said, waving. "We're reading. Miss Josie is having a meeting. Can I finish this story?"

He nodded. "Good idea, honey. I need to see Miss Josie, anyway."

Marilyn Carter nodded at him. "They're in the break room."

Dalton hurried back, Luna by his side.

When he walked into the room, several workers were gathered around Josie. "Did I miss the meeting?" he asked.

Josie looked relieved. "We just finished. I waited but…they were anxious to hear what was going on."

Dalton nodded to the half-dozen workers. "I'm sorry I'm late. I'm sure Josie has explained, but if you have any questions—"

Everyone starting talking at once, so Dalton tried to calm all of them, one question at a time. And then he asked them some questions of his own.

* * *

An hour later, Josie locked up and turned to Dalton. "You can't keep escorting me home."

"I don't mind," he said, his gaze moving over her in that way that left her both warm and chilled. "Part of the job."

And he was all about doing his job, she reminded herself. She shouldn't read anything else into this. He needed the extra training with his partner, Luna, and what better way than to find out who was harassing her?

But her need to remain independent kicked in. "I can make it home. It's not that far."

"It's getting dark," he said. "Don't waste time arguing."

"Right." He wanted to get on with his day, too. *Stubborn, meet stubborn.* "Let's go."

"Are you eating with us again, Miss Josie?" Maisy asked from the patrol car, hope in her question.

"No, honey. Your daddy's being a gentleman and making sure I get home okay."

Maisy shrugged and gave her father a disappointed glare. "Why can't she have dinner with us?"

Dalton looked heavenward and then tried to explain. "Because we have our house chores and homework, and Miss Josie is tired and she wants to go home to her house, alone."

"Alone isn't fun," Maisy said with a pout.

"She has a point," Dalton said to Josie.

"But we can't do this," Josie whispered to him. "She might get the wrong idea."

"I know." He did the visual thing, his sharp gaze roaming the street. "It's kind of out of the blue, but I wouldn't mind taking you out to dinner sometime."

Josie blinked. "Did you just ask me on a date?"

He looked sheepish. "Maybe when…things settle down. You know, as friends."

"You'll be gone after Christmas, Dalton. It can't happen. Even as friends."

Giving her a resigned stare, he said, "Right. Forget I asked." Whirling, he added in a gruff command, "Let's get you home safely."

Josie wished things could be different, but she hardly knew the man. Besides, she wanted to stay in Desert Valley, and Dalton planned to move back to Flagstaff.

But…he *had* asked. Probably felt bad that she was alone and being harassed. A shiver moved like a caught spiderweb against her skin. What did this person want from her?

She got in her car, her mind still on Dalton. But when she looked up and saw a red rose lying tucked into one of the windshield wipers, Josie jumped back out.

Parked across the lot, Dalton got out and hurried over. "What is it?"

She pointed to the rose.

His expression grim, Dalton took a pen out of his pocket and lifted the wilted flower from the wiper. It stood out in stark contrast against her white car.

"A card," he said, motioning to the cream-colored square attached to the flower. He flipped the card over.

'Tis the season. Soon, I'll be sending you something special.

"That's definitely a threat," Dalton said. "Josie, I think it's time we question everyone you know here."

Before she could answer, a shot rang out and Dalton tugged her down against the truck and shielded her as glass from her car's windshield exploded all around them.

* * *

Josie shook all the way home.

She kept glancing at Dalton. When they got to her place, he got out with Luna and Maisy at his side. He'd called for backup after someone had shot at her, but the police hadn't found anyone. The shooter had gotten away, and even though they'd scoured the parking lot, they hadn't found any bullets. Josie's car couldn't be driven until she had a new windshield.

"Do you think your aunt would mind if Maisy stays with her while I check your house?"

The girl stared her down. "Daddy told me you're getting an alarm system. I don't mind staying with Miss Marilyn. You need to be safe."

Amazed at Maisy's calm acceptance, Josie said, "You're so patient. A real trooper." The girl had barely flinched when Dalton had hurried to check on her after Josie's windshield had been shot out. But Luna barked incessantly, anxious to do her job.

"Comes with the territory," Maisy said in a mature tone. "Can Luna go with me?"

"I need Luna to work," Dalton said. "She's good at sniffing out trouble spots."

Josie tried to sound animated. "Did my aunt tell you about her dog? He's a tiny Chihuahua named Boo. You'll love him."

Maisy grinned. "I can hold him?"

"Sure." Josie's chuckle was ringed with a frazzled edge. "Let's walk over there."

"She has boys," Maisy pointed out, her nose in the air.

"True, they're not girls for you to play with, but they're fun kids," Josie replied, her gaze hitting on Dalton while she tried to keep things light for Maisy's sake. She noticed Dalton checking the immediate area to make sure no one was lying in wait.

Soon, she had Maisy settled with her aunt, the sound of boys boasting and little Boo barking giving her hope that her world wasn't about to cave in.

"Thank you," she mouthed to Marilyn. Her aunt nodded and held her hands together, prayer style. Her aunt was a good prayer warrior. "We'll talk later."

"Come over for dinner," Aunt Marilyn said. "And bring Dalton with you. We've got a big pot of stew going."

"Thanks," Josie said, thinking it wasn't such a good idea to invite Dalton and Maisy for another meal.

Hurrying back to Dalton, she said, "Aunt Marilyn said we need to come and have dinner with them. No arguments, unless we find something we need to deal with."

His eyes centered on her. "We'll go over every inch of your house and yard. But before dinner, I need you to level with me about your past."

"The yard is clear," he told her a few minutes later.

Josie nodded. In her mind, she'd gone over all the details of her marriage, Douglas's death and the days following. Could that have something to do with this?

"I'll check the bedrooms," he said as they headed inside her house.

Full official mode. He wouldn't take no for an answer, but she wasn't sure what he expected her to say. That her past had finally caught up with her? That her life in Texas had not been a pleasant one?

"All clear," he said when he came back.

She turned on the Christmas-tree lights. "It doesn't feel like a holiday around here."

"Someone threatening you can certainly ruin the joy."

"I won't let them do that," she replied on a determined note. "I've worked too hard for this."

He crowded the small space with a comforting presence that made her feel safe. "Then you'd better tell me why you had to start over here in the first place."

He ordered Luna to heel, and then he walked into the kitchen. And immediately filled it with enough man power to make her want to shrink back.

But she held her ground. "I won't let you steal my joy, either."

"I have to know everything about you so I can figure this out," he said, his eyes moving over her face like a laser. "It's standard procedure. And it could save your life."

He was right. Instead of being aggravated, she should be thankful. She handed him a cup of coffee and then said, "My husband's family resented me even before he died. I was never good enough for them, and I didn't produce grandchildren right away, so they pretty much treated me like the enemy. And after his death, they blamed me for him being distracted the day of the accident. Somehow, they knew we'd had a bad fight that morning before he left for work. After he died, I received a large amount of life insurance money, which my mother-in-law seemed to think I should share with her."

Dalton's eyes held hers in a way that stripped her soul. "Enough money for one of them to come after you?"

"More than enough," she said in a low whisper. "But

I didn't tell them I was coming here. I sold most of my belongings and I left. No one back there could possibly know where I am now."

He gave her a sympathetic stare. "Josie, finding a person is easy with the available technology these days. They might have put a GPS on your car or phone. Or someone could have seen you leaving and tipped them off. If they know you have a relative here, it'd be the first place they'd look."

"I tried to be careful," she said. "I never dreamed someone might come after me. But...no matter who's doing this, we have to stop them."

"We'll keep working on it," Dalton replied. "Sooner or later, they'll either slip up or we'll get a solid lead."

Placing her coffee cup on the counter, she asked, "Dalton, what if it is one of my in-laws? What if they've found me?"

SIX

Dalton tried to be honest. "I can't say for sure until I do some investigating, but they're on the list. Why would they come after you in such a strange way? Cryptic notes, and now shooting at you? Why wouldn't they show up at your door and tell you what they want?"

She finished her coffee and put her cup in the sink. "After we got married, Douglas changed. He became moody and mean, and nothing I did pleased him. I soon figured out he'd married me so he'd have someone to wait on him and pamper him the way his mother did. They blamed me for his bad moods and spread it around that they didn't like that their son married a girl from the trailer park."

Casting her gaze downward, she said, "My mother worked as a maid at the local hotel. She wasn't the best mother ever, and she died not long after I got married. My father left when I was a baby. So I was pretty much a pushover. I wanted to please everyone, but I always failed."

Dalton's heart burned with anger. This kind, gentle woman had been through a lot more than he'd imagined.

"So do you blame yourself for your marriage going bad?"

"I did at first. But I grew stronger as I matured. Going to church helped with that. Aunt Marilyn helped me, too. She'd come and visit and bring me things. I owe her a lot."

She lifted her head up as if to shake away the bad memories. "Anyway, that's my past and so here we are."

"Tell me a little more about your in-laws," he said, wishing he could wipe away the sadness in her eyes.

"While they weren't rich, my in-laws were straitlaced pillars of the community. My father-in-law worked in upper management at the refinery, and he got Douglas a job there after Douglas quit college. Douglas Senior passed away a few months after Douglas died. Janine, my mother-in-law, kept saying Douglas's death had killed her husband, too. My father-in-law was never the same after Douglas died. They quit speaking to me."

"You mentioned more than one in-law. Any other children?"

"Yes. My brother-in-law, Randall, is estranged from his mother now, but he and Douglas stayed close. He was pretty upset when Douglas was killed in that accident. He hated the refinery and refused to work there. He studied to become an electrician, but I don't know if he ever finished school. He worked for a cable company last I heard."

She shook her head. "He pretty much kept to himself, and he had a girlfriend who kept him busy, but right before I left they got married and moved to Louisiana." She wiped at a speck on the counter. "Janine was all alone and she didn't have a lot of money, and she suddenly decided I should share the money I'd received with her."

"Did you?"

"I gave Janine some money, but I explained to her I wanted to use the rest to start my own day care. I'd worked in child care since high school, so I could pay for college, course by course, through the years until I finally got my degree. She laughed at me and told me I'd never succeed."

He watched her face, wondering if one of her in-laws might have come looking for her. But money could bring out the worst in people. "Did *they* ever threaten you before?"

"No." Then she paused. "But...after Douglas's death, she turned on me. They didn't like me, anyway. After he died, his parents seemed to shift into true hatred for me. They implied if I'd been a better wife, Douglas might still be alive. Then when Douglas Senior had a heart attack, Janine poured out her angst on me. She believed the stress of her son's death contributed to my father-in-law's death. And I think she was right."

She inhaled a shaky breath. "She started spreading rumors about me. I quit my job, since my boss kept hearing the rumors and questioned me daily. I knew what would happen next. I'd be fired for not being a fit child care provider. So I took the easy way out. I left." She looked into Dalton's eyes. "I came here with a clean record, and I'd like to keep it that way."

"But you mentioned the insurance money."

"His father never knew about it," she said. "I was so shocked that Douglas had taken out a policy and left it to me that I didn't tell anyone for weeks. But after his dad died, I went to Janine and blurted it out. That's when things got ugly. Janine demanded that I turn over the money to her. Told me she was broke, and that Douglas Senior hadn't left her much of anything."

Dalton saw the apprehension in her eyes.

"I've never seen anyone so angry," she said. "I know she was hurting. She'd lost her son and her husband in a matter of months."

"So you gave her money to appease her?"

She looked surprised and then resolved. "I gave her part of the money, but I'd had enough of Texas and the family, so after I talked to Aunt Marilyn she suggested I should come here for a while. When she told me she'd help me start a day care, I jumped at the chance." She wiped at her eyes. "And here I am. I've been here getting the day care up and running. Why would they wait so long to confront me?"

"They found a way to track you," Dalton said. "But the notes and even being shot at could be coming from a man or a woman. The brother maybe, if she put him up to it."

She started around him, her frown full of doubt. "I don't think it's either of them. My mother-in-law is frail and sickly, so I can't see her doing it," she said. "Randall's trying to improve his life, so why would he try something like this?"

Dalton touched a hand to her arm. "Josie, people who are desperate will do anything, especially when it involves money. Your mother-in-law might be frail and unable to travel, but she could have sent someone to find you."

"And what will they do? Kill me and try to get what's left in my bank account? They can't do that."

"No, but they could take you and force you to get the

money out of the bank and then kill you. Is there any of the money left?"

Ignoring the crouching fear his words provoked, she said, "I have a small savings account and a modest checking account. My aunt and uncle cosigned on the loan and put up a share of the front money. They did that to protect me and because they own some other real estate, including this house."

Dalton could see how much she had riding on this venture. "Maybe they're threatening you, thinking you'll leave and go back to Texas. Then they could work on getting their hands on what they consider to be a fortune."

"Or maybe they want to torment me." She stopped and gasped, her fingers digging into his shirtsleeve. "Dalton, that has to be it. If they keep at this, the parents will remove their children from the day care. I could lose everything. What if this *isn't* about getting to the money? What if they want to ruin me?"

An hour later, Josie sat with her aunt and uncle in their den. The boys and Maisy were in another part of the house, watching a movie. They'd had a quiet dinner, but Josie could barely eat.

"I'm sorry," she said now. "I can't believe this is happening."

"Now don't go jumping ahead," her uncle Jack said. "Let Dalton do his job."

"He's right, honey," Marilyn said. "This doesn't mean someone is out to do you in. I know your life with Douglas was hard, but he's gone now. He can't hurt you anymore. Nor can his mama or his brother. We're not gonna let that happen."

Josie whirled from her aunt to Dalton. "Douglas was cruel and irrational, and he didn't trust me at all. Our marriage was over long before he died. I just didn't have the courage to leave him."

"Did he abuse you?" Dalton asked, an edge in his voice that made her uncle sit up and take notice.

"No," she said. "He didn't love me. He drank too much and flirted with other women and complained about his job. He was careless and cynical and...he didn't trust anyone. And because of that, I cowered and became some kind of passive person that I didn't even recognize."

"But you're okay," he reminded her, the admiration in his eyes warming her. "You're doing great. Use your strength to keep your head clear. We've had three messages and now a near-shooting, so this is serious. And it'll probably get worse. You told me you'd changed, and I believe you."

"She sure has changed," Marilyn said with a chuckle, her dark curls bobbing around her face. "She stared down contractors and inspectors and town council members to get our business up and running, and she worked hard on finding a good team to take care of our children. I'm very proud of her and I know if my sister was alive, she'd be proud of her, too."

"Thank you, Aunt Marilyn," Josie said, touched. "But don't sing my praises too much. I'm so worried right now I don't think I'll be worth much come morning. My focus is on the day care and the children."

"Why don't you stay with us tonight?" her aunt asked. "We have plenty of room."

Josie shook her head. "No. I'll be okay. My house isn't that big, and I've got locks on all the windows and doors, thanks to my wonderful landlord." She smiled at her uncle. "Now, I need to get home and I'm sure Dalton feels the same way."

"I don't mind," he said, standing. "But Maisy does have school tomorrow, and it's party day. She'll be wired when she gets home."

"Oh, that's right," Marilyn said. "School's out for the Christmas break. We'll be busy with extra kids all next week."

"I'll go get Maisy for you," Jack said. Then he turned and gave Dalton a serious appraisal. "If you ever need to bring Maisy to us, she's welcome here. We have a room that's all girl—Marilyn's getaway room. It's like a spa and a boutique all rolled up in one—as my wife likes to say. Maisy viewed it earlier tonight, so I know she'd be comfortable there."

"Thank you," Dalton said, appreciation in his eyes. "It's good to know she's got people like you to look after her." Then he looked at Josie. "And I'm glad you have these two next door."

"All the more reason to be extra-careful," Josie replied after her uncle went down the long hallway to the other wing of the house. "We have to take care of Maisy and the other children, first and foremost. I was looking forward to our party for the kids next week and then the couple of days we'll have off during Christmas."

"You can still look forward to this special time of year," Marilyn said as they walked to the door. "We're gonna have faith and get through this. God led you here so He's not gonna abandon you now."

Josie wanted to believe that with all her heart. But after Dalton and Maisy escorted her home, she couldn't shake the sense of dread.

Dalton checked the house again, Luna already learning the routine. "I'll do a sweep of the yard, front and back, before I leave," he told her. "Make sure you're locked in tight." Then he handed her a card. "Call me if you see or hear anything that scares you."

He scared her. The way he cared about her safety was a whole new experience for Josie. No man had ever tried so hard to show her that he wanted to protect her, and this man barely knew her. His kindness was so overwhelming that she wanted to push him away and tell him that she didn't deserve his protection.

But her aunt would shun that notion. She'd always been Josie's champion, even when her own mother hadn't encouraged her. No wonder Josie had married a bully of a man who treated her like a doormat. She'd cowered from her bitter mother for years. But after counseling at church and being with people who encouraged her, she wasn't a doormat anymore. She'd learned that she could fight for herself and still come out on the other side. Unlike her mother, who'd never found the strength to get on with her life after Josie's father had left.

She'd fight now. But she'd fight smart. "I promise I'll keep my phone on my pillow," she told Dalton. "I'll leave lights on and I won't go outside. If I do, I'll call my uncle. And… I did take some self-defense crash courses after Douglas died."

"All of that is good," Dalton said. "Still, be careful."

"I will," she said.

He checked the yard and came back for Maisy. "Let's get you home, Ladybug."

Josie smiled at the endearment. But Maisy looked

up at her with big, solemn eyes. "You could come and stay with us, Miss Josie."

Josie heard the catch in the girl's suggestion. Maisy was putting on that brave front. Even though they'd tried so hard to shield her from what was really going on, the kid had a keen intuition.

But Maisy also had enough sense to know this was about more than beefing up security.

She hated putting this child through any more trauma. Her eyes met Dalton's, sympathy piercing her heart. "That's so sweet of you, Maisy. But I have everything I need right here. You don't have to worry. Your dad has coached me on what I need to do. He's being very smart, practicing on me and letting Luna get in some practice, too."

Maisy glanced at her daddy. "Sometimes, even things we've practiced can still get messed up."

Dalton's frown ripped at Josie's consciousness. "Maisy, what do you mean by that, honey?"

Maisy's stoic expression turned to cautious. "Nothing. But…people get hurt all the time. Sometimes, you can't protect them."

Dalton's tanned skin turned pale. "You're right. But we can't stop trying. And I'm going to do my best to protect you and Miss Josie and everyone else around here."

"I don't want to leave here," Maisy said. "I like living here. I don't like Flagstaff."

Realization clutched at Josie and she saw the resolve in Dalton's eyes, too. "But we talked about this," he said, his tone soft. "We'll find a nice new neighborhood and start fresh with Luna. She'll watch out for us."

Luna's ears pricked up, and she gave Maisy a loving stare, as if she knew exactly what the little girl was feeling. Which she probably did.

"I don't like it there," Maisy said. Then she rushed to Josie and hugged her close. "I like it here better."

Dalton's jaw clenched. Josie could see the pain in his stormy gray eyes. "We'll talk about this later, okay? We have to get home right now."

Josie hugged Maisy close and told her she'd see her tomorrow. "Remember, I need you to help me pass out cookies and Christmas ornaments."

Maisy smiled at that. "Okay."

But Dalton wasn't smiling. He nodded and turned with a stiff back and hurried his daughter to the car.

Josie had never felt so alone.

And she'd never seen such hurt in a man's eyes. Maisy's heartfelt pleas had broken him in two.

Dalton West carried a lot of burdens on his broad shoulders. And now, he'd added her to that load.

She hoped this would end soon. They could all use a break. But her instincts told her this was just the beginning.

SEVEN

Dalton checked in with Josie the next afternoon when he picked up Maisy. He hoped she'd had a safe, restful night. He'd wanted to call her and offer to give her a ride to work, but he'd decided that could come across as unprofessional. Besides, she had already planned to ride to work with her aunt. So he waited all day and hoped he'd see her.

He found Josie in the nursery, holding a toddler against her shoulder while she rocked in a big comfortable chair. The sight of her sitting there with a child in her arms caused him to imagine things he had no business thinking about. Sure, he'd known her for months now, but he hadn't really *known* her until this week when they'd been forced together by some kind of sick person's handiwork.

He'd been smitten with her from the start, but Dalton had ignored those little tremors of attraction. Now, he couldn't deny that he liked Josie Callahan a lot. But... where could that admission take him? She was building a life here, and he wanted to go back to Flagstaff where Maisy could be surrounded by family. His mother kept calling and asking if they were coming home for Christmas.

Watching Josie right now, he didn't want to go anywhere. When she glanced up and saw him leaning against the doorjamb, her smile went wide and his heart went flip-flop.

"Hi," he said, crossing his arms against his chest. "He's a cutie."

She nodded and carefully stood, her hands holding the chunky little boy across his back. "He played himself out. His mom's on her way."

After putting the sleeping toddler in one of the cribs lined up along the room, she turned to Dalton and motioned to the wide hallway.

"How are you?" he asked, not knowing what else to say.

"Okay. Nothing happened last night. I didn't sleep very well, and I kept getting up to check the windows. I haven't seen any notes today, either. Do you think they could have given up?"

Dalton doubted that. "No, I think they're retreating because they've seen us together."

Her crestfallen face said it all. "I'd hoped…"

"I know," he said quietly, since her staff seemed intent on listening. "But you still need to be careful and stay aware. For now, you made it through today."

"We did," she said, her smile unsure. "We had a great day with all the kids, and tonight we're all meeting at my aunt's house for a staff party. You're welcome to stop by."

Surprised and tempted, he said, "But I'm not on staff."

"You almost are," she said. "You seem to have assigned yourself as my personal bodyguard."

"Tired of me already?"

She blushed a becoming pink. "I didn't say that. But you do have a life, and I'm sure you don't need me in it."

"You might be wrong about that," he said, surprising both of them.

She stood there, her green eyes shimmering while she stared at him. Dalton felt a sizzle that reminded him of heat lightning moving over the desert. His mind filled with something sweet and right and welcome.

And then a preschooler running down the hallway screamed, and the moment was gone. Josie looked away and grabbed the escaping, giggling bundle of energy and lifted him up with a smile and a "Whoa!"

Whoa was right. Dalton had to gather his thoughts, so he turned to go find Maisy. Best if he got out of here right now. As long as Josie was safe, he could relax.

But…he'd never forget that moment that had just happened.

Lightning had hit him, and now a monsoon of emotion was pouring through what had been the dry gully of his soul. And he had to wonder—*Is this what it feels like when God touches your heart with hope?*

Josie headed to her aunt's car. Her uncle had picked up Marilyn earlier, since they had some shopping to do. A lot of parents would need to work right up to Christmas, so they'd have a big group of children early next week, and then she'd have four days to celebrate with her family.

Thankful that her aunt and uncle had taken her in and helped her so much, she looked forward to a big Christmas dinner. Praying that she'd have that without any threatening letters or any more gunshots, she let out a breath. When her cell rang, she absently picked it up.

"Hello?"

Nothing.

"Hello?" Josie said again, her eyes on the traffic light, which glowed red.

Nothing. But she heard breathing.

"Who is this?" she asked, her heart rate speeding up. When the light turned green, she eased through the intersection.

The caller ended the call and her phone beeped.

By the time she pulled into her driveway, Josie had talked herself into believing the call had been a wrong number. Calming her jitters, she got ready for the party next door, and then she gathered the casserole she'd made and hurried to greet her coworkers.

But an hour later, after two more voiceless calls, she knew her tormentor had moved one step closer to her. Somehow, this person had found her cell number.

Dalton checked in with the patrol officer the chief had authorized to cruise the block surrounding Josie's house. So far, nothing was out of the ordinary. He believed the patrolman, but Dalton couldn't help but worry about Josie.

She should be at her aunt's staff party right now. The party she'd invited him to attend. He wasn't going, of course.

Dalton sat in the tiny apartment he'd rented three months ago, wondering if he'd made the right decision switching from detective to the K-9 unit. His chief back in Flagstaff had encouraged him to try something new after his wife had been killed.

Might help you to heal, Dalton. K-9s are not only good partners and officers, but they provide companionship. Both you and Maisy could benefit from that."

The chief had been right. Maisy had taken to Luna the first time he'd been allowed to bring the dog home. Now he couldn't imagine not having Luna around. She was smart, quick and she protected Maisy without question. He trusted the pound puppy that had been trained from a young age with his life.

But had he done the right thing, bringing Maisy here?

He watched his daughter now. They'd had a quick supper of soup and sandwiches, and now she sat staring up at the meager Christmas tree.

His heart hurting for her, he looked up from the paper he'd been trying to read and asked, "Hey, Ladybug, what do you think? Did we do okay on the tree?"

"It's really pretty, Daddy," she replied, Luna by her side. "But it's sure tiny." Then she glanced back. "Remember that big one you brought home, and we had to cut it over and over so it would fit by the fireplace. Mom and I laughed at you about that."

Dalton swallowed the emotions welling up inside him. "I do remember. What? About three years ago? But we got that tree down to size, didn't we?"

She nodded, her hand touching Luna's sleek fur. "That was the best time."

Dalton got up and went to sit on the floor beside her, his gaze on the few presents he'd managed to get wrapped. "Honey, I wish I could give you a big tree this year. But once we're back home, I'll buy you the prettiest tree we can find."

Maisy turned to stare up at him. "It's okay. I don't mind a little tree if we can stay here."

Dalton had been afraid that topic would resurface. "Honey, we've talked about this. I need to get back to Flagstaff so Luna and I can do our jobs."

"But why can't you do that here?"

Dalton tugged at one of her trailing curls. "Well, the Desert Valley Police Department isn't as big as the one in Flagstaff. We train here, and then we're sent out all over the state."

"Could you work close to here?" she asked. "That way we could stay?"

Dalton hadn't considered that. "I don't know. That depends on a lot of things. Why do you want to stay here so much?"

He thought he knew the answer, but he prayed she'd open up to him, anyway.

She pushed at her hair and swiped a hand across her nose. "I like it here. I like going to the day care 'cause Miss Josie and Miss Marilyn let me help out."

"And you're good at helping," Dalton replied, watching her for any changes in her expression or mood. "But you don't have to take care of everyone."

Bobbing her head, she said, "I don't mind. I need to make sure they're all safe."

"Is this about Patrick?" Dalton asked. "Because he's safe now and he's improving every day."

"But...we almost lost him."

Dalton motioned to her, and she scooted into his arms. "I know it's scary sometimes, what I do. And... I can't promise I'll be able to save everyone who needs my help. But you know I'll give it my best shot, right?"

She nodded again. Then she looked up at him with big, misty eyes. "We couldn't save Mommy."

Dalton took in a breath, his lungs burning with a

scorching heat. "I know," he said, kissing the top of her head. "I'm so sorry."

Maisy stared up at him, and then she pulled away. "No, you don't understand. I didn't save her, either." Then she got up and ran to her bedroom and slammed the door.

Dalton was headed after her when his cell buzzed.

Josie.

He stared at his daughter's shut door.

Then he answered the call.

"Dalton West."

"I hope I'm not calling at a bad time," Josie said, her tone hesitant.

"Uh… I do need to check on Maisy, but I can talk for a minute."

"Someone is calling my cell and then dropping the calls."

"You mean, hanging up?"

"Yes. They don't speak. They just…breathe."

He kept an eye on Maisy's bedroom door. "Do you want me to come over?"

"No. But you can add that to the police report. It has to be the same person who left me those notes and the rose."

"And shot out your windshield." He walked toward Maisy's door. "Where are you now?"

"I'm at my aunt's house. The party is winding down, and I'm about to go home."

"Ask your uncle to go with you."

"I will. Just wanted to let you know." Then she said, "Dalton, are you okay?"

Could she read him that well already?

"Not really," he said. "I need to go check on Maisy. She's having a bad night."

"Go," Josie said. "I'm fine. We'll talk later."

"Can I call you once I get Maisy settled?"

"Yes," she said. "I'd appreciate that." Then she added, "I'm sending a little prayer for both of you."

"Thanks," he said. "I think we'll need that now more than ever."

An hour later, Josie's cell buzzed again.

She let out a held breath when she saw it was Dalton. "Hello," she said, sinking onto the couch. She had every light in the house on and all the outside lights shining into the front and back yards.

"Hi," he said, his voice sounding weary. "Any more calls?"

"No." She shivered in spite of the heater blasting through the overhead vents. "I hope they're done for the night. Or maybe forever."

"They have your private number now, so no, they're not done."

She detected irritation in his voice. "I realize that, Dalton. That's why I called you in the first place. Look, it's late and you sound tired—"

"No," he interrupted. "I'm sorry. It's Maisy. She's begging to stay in Desert Valley and I think… I think she's becoming too attached to the day care and…to you."

Surprised that he'd told her anything regarding his daughter, Josie shifted on the couch. "It's understandable after what you've both been through. She feels safe here, and she knows I will do my best to keep her safe when she's in my care."

"But what if you can't?" he blurted out.

So that was it? Josie's eyes burned with unshed tears for Maisy. "Are you saying you don't think the day care is safe now?"

She heard a rush of breath. "No, I'm not saying that. I'm not making any sense. She seems so overprotective of the younger children and I think—"

"She is overprotective," Josie replied before she could take it back. "She's afraid, Dalton. Because no one could save her mother."

"You mean, *I* couldn't save my wife," he said, his words gruff. "Is that what you're saying? Does Maisy talk to you about that?"

"She's made a few comments."

"You should have told me this sooner."

"I probably should have, but… I didn't want to upset you."

"She's my daughter. You can't keep things like that from me."

"No, that's not it," she replied, getting up to pace around the den. "Dalton, it's none of my business. I'm sorry. Look, you're obviously concerned about Maisy—"

A noise outside stopped her cold.

"But?" he said, as if he needed to hear her reasoning. "Josie?"

Another bump and then footsteps. "I think someone's in my yard."

"Listen, hang up and call 911. I can't leave Maisy, so I'm calling Whitney. She lives right around the corner. Okay?"

"Okay." She did as he said and listened to the silence of the house. A crash sounded somewhere outside, causing dogs to bark all along the street. A light went out in the backyard. Then she heard more footsteps, fast now. Hurrying. Another crash and the fence gate slamming shut. Were they coming around to the front of the house?

She stayed on the line with 911 and prayed her stalker wouldn't come inside her home.

EIGHT

Officer Whitney Godwin Evans circled back to the front of Josie's house, her K-9 partner, Hunter, moving ahead of her with a sure stride as the pointer did his job.

"They're gone," Whitney said, her gaze scanning the street.

"But someone was here?" Josie asked, wishing she hadn't scared the whole neighborhood.

Her uncle stood beside her while her aunt Marilyn stood on the porch of their house to make sure none of her rambunctious boys escaped to investigate on their own.

"Someone was definitely here," Whitney said, her blue eyes bright underneath the porch light. "Hunter sniffed all around the back fence and followed the trail to the front. They must have gotten in a car down the street."

"Did they do any damage?" Jack asked, his hand on Josie's shoulder.

Whitney pushed up her K-9 cap and lifted her blond hair off her neck. "Broke out a security light and…left you a message."

Josie searched but didn't see anything in Whitney's hand. "Where it is? What did it say?"

Whitney gave her an apologetic stare. "They scrawled it on the back fence."

"What?" Jack moved closer to Josie.

"Can you show me?" she asked Whitney, dreading what she would see.

"Sure, but don't touch anything. We might find some trace evidence if we dust the fence for fingerprints. Or we could stumble on something in the grass and dirt back there."

She guided Josie and her uncle around to the back-yard. "I'm having flashbacks of when this kind of thing happened to me here," Whitney said. "I thought I'd se-cured my yard but…people who want in can always find a way."

Jack grunted. "I think I'll sell the place. Too danger-ous."

"I'm sorry," Josie said, wishing she hadn't brought this on her aunt and uncle.

"Do not apologize," Jack said, his tone soft. "You re-member how you told us you were stronger now? Well, you have to stay that way, okay?"

She nodded, unable to speak. Whitney held up her flashlight so Josie could see the fence.

Scrawled in red, the message said, *You shouldn't be watching over anyone's children.*

Josie put a hand to her mouth. "They didn't come to steal from me. They came to shut me down."

"Who do you think it is?" Whitney asked, her solemn gaze moving over the bold letters and then back to Josie.

"I can't prove it," Josie replied, "but I'm beginning to suspect my in-laws. My father-in-law died right after my husband was killed. But my mother-in-law blamed both their deaths on me because my marriage was in trouble. My husband had one brother. Randall."

"Does he have a beef with you?" Whitney asked, in full interrogation mode now.

Josie cleared her throat. "I didn't think so, but now I'm wondering how far they'll go to ruin me. I left Texas to get away from my mother-in-law and her lies. But Randall and I always got along. He didn't like how I was being treated, but maybe she's convinced him otherwise. I can't see Janine physically capable of doing all this on her own."

"We've got help on the way," Whitney replied. "We'll do our best to figure it out."

Josie remembered Dalton's sharp words to her. He thought she was putting his daughter in danger. "Well, until we do figure it out, I think I should close down the day care."

"Honey, do you think that's wise?" Jack asked.

"I don't see what else I can do," she replied. "I don't want to scare the children or put them in danger."

Whitney touched a hand to her arm. "You've only got a couple of days next week, and a lot of parents are depending on you to be open—including me. If you stick to your routine, we might be able to nab this person."

"Or someone might get hurt. Or worse."

Whitney nodded. "Let me see if I can arrange things where one of us can be there for the two days you're open before the holidays. How's that?"

"That's not routine," Josie pointed out.

"No, but it might make them slip up," Whitney said. "Especially if they don't know we're there."

Josie could almost see the wheels turning inside

Whitney's brain. "Well, several of you do have children in my care."

"That's right. They've probably been well aware of that, so they only strike when they think we're not around dropping off or picking up kids. We can change that up a bit."

"Be careful," Jack said.

"Always," Whitney replied. "Okay, we'll go over things here but…honestly, I doubt we'll get anything solid. From what Dalton's told us, they're covering their tracks. I'll call Dalton and give him a report. He'll be concerned."

Josie thanked Whitney and went next door with her uncle.

"You're staying with us until this is over," Marilyn insisted. "No arguments."

Josie didn't have the energy to argue. "Thank you," she said.

She wondered if Dalton would go along with Whitney's idea or if he'd pull Maisy out of the day care for good.

Dalton paced the floor, his phone in his hand. When it rang, he immediately answered Whitney's call. "Tell me."

"She's fine."

He listened while Whitney went over the details. Rubbing his forehead in an absentminded massage that wasn't really helping his developing headache, he said, "Thanks. I'll read over your incident report in the morning and file it with what I have so far. Still nothing on fingerprints or any other evidence from the day care, and I agree with you. Probably won't find anything since this person seems so thorough on covering his tracks."

"Hey, you might want to call Josie. She's thinking about shutting down the day care early for the holidays. She's worried about the kids."

Then she told him her idea.

"I did suggest that to her if things got worse," he replied, referring to putting an undercover officer inside the day care. "I can't be the one. I'm pretty sure whoever's behind all this has been watching and knows I've been on the case."

"They've seen all of us there," Whitney replied. "Sophie and Ryder, David and me. You. And Zoe and Sean. Actually, it's probably the best guarded day care in the state."

Dalton smiled at that. "You could be right. But one of us needs to be there 24/7 for the few days before Christmas. Or maybe all of us. Even if they see us. That kind of presence should scare them off or make them mess up."

Deciding they'd talk to Chief Hayes in the morning to get the go-ahead, Dalton ended the call.

Should he call Josie? He'd been harsh with her before because he was so upset about Maisy. He thought back to his big talk with Maisy. He'd knocked on his daughter's door and…she'd run straight into his arms.

"I'm sorry, Daddy."

"I'm sorry, too, honey. I know this is hard for you, but we have to stick together. You know I'd be lost without you, right?"

"And Luna," she added on a sniff. "She's my best friend."

Luna nudged at Maisy's hand, waiting for a response.

Maisy let go of Dalton and held tight to Luna.

Dalton agreed with her there. "Luna is the best. She watches over us and protects us and…she's why we came here."

"She's why I don't want to leave. If you take her to a big city, she might get injured." Maisy had looked up at him. "Sometimes police dogs get shot."

"Sometimes they do," Dalton replied. His job was easy compared to being a father. "Maisy, I can't promise you much in this life, but God watches over all of us."

"Was He watching over Mommy?"

Dalton gulped in a breath that bordered on a sob. A sob he'd long held tightly inside his heart. "I think He was. He watched and He cried because God hates evil. And the people who did this to your mother, to our family, they were the worst kind of evil. But God knew that no matter what those people did to your beautiful mother, He'd take care of her. And us. Honey, He took her home because someone evil took her life. And now your mommy is safe in His arms. He's watching over us and…we have to keep living. We have to hold out hope."

Maisy's face crumpled and her eyes filled with tears. "I did the right thing, Daddy. I called 911, but then they chased the car. And Mommy died in that wreck. If I hadn't called—"

Dalton's eyes filled with tears. "Oh, baby, is that what you think? That this is your fault?"

She bobbed her head, her sobs tearing at Dalton with an agony he didn't think possible. "I'm sorry. I'm trying to do better now. I help Miss Josie take care of the other children."

Dalton could see it all now, and his heart tore into pieces for his sweet, smart daughter. "No, baby, I'm the one who's sorry. I should have realized this. You did the right thing, Maisy. You tried to help your mom. That dangerous man is the one who caused her death. Don't ever forget that."

He held her there and explained to her that she did nothing wrong. They'd both done their best. And then he tried to assure her that she didn't have to be a protector for everyone around her.

"But you are," Maisy pointed out.

"I guess I am," he replied, thinking the apple didn't fall far from the tree.

Finally Maisy lifted her head up to stare at him. "Miss Josie says God loves all of us. I hope He still loves me."

Dalton swallowed back the raw-edged emotion clogging his throat. "He does. He loves you and me and Luna, too. He even loved the people who hurt Mommy. But it's important that you and I always talk and work things out between us. God gives us that grace. He wants to help us, but He expects us to work hard on our own."

"He wants us to pray?"

"Yes," Dalton said, giving her a weak smile. "Prayer is how we talk to God."

"I talk to Mommy that way, too."

"That's good. So do I."

Then his amazing daughter said something he'd never expected. "I think Mommy would like Miss Josie."

Was that her way of asking for approval? Did his daughter want him to get involved with Josie Callahan? Maybe Maisy felt the same kind of guilt he did whenever he thought of having a woman like Josie in his life.

Or was she searching for someone to fill that deep void inside her heart, same as him?

After settling Maisy into bed with Luna in her own bed in the corner of Maisy's room, Dalton waited to hear from Josie.

He stopped pacing now. He and Maisy had crossed a threshold tonight, talking about her mother and God. He understood what his little girl was going through.

Thanking the Lord for that precious conversation, he found Josie's number on his phone. Time for another important conversation.

Josie hit at the pillow and turned over again. It was still early, but she'd told her aunt and uncle she was tired. Now she was in the attic room they'd converted into a nice guest bedroom complete with a small bath. Cozy and comfortable. She'd stayed in this room when she'd first arrived here. Aunt Marilyn kept it off-limits. This was the room she'd shown Maisy last night.

But in spite of the romantic, Victorian-inspired surroundings, Josie couldn't get comfortable.

Would she have to run again? Go somewhere else, far away. Why would Douglas's mother or brother come after her? Had she really been wrong not to hand over the insurance money her husband had left her?

Am I greedy, Lord? Josie prayed for clarity and guidance. She'd used the money to make a new start, and she'd given some to her church back home and the church here in Desert Valley. Other than the little bit she'd given to Janine, the rest was tucked away for a rainy day.

But someone wanted her destroyed.

Who could be that vindictive?

Her phone buzzed against the nightstand wood.

Dalton's number came up.

"Hello," she said. "How are you?"

"I'm okay. I just wanted to check on you and tell you I'm sorry about earlier."

Letting that go, she said, "I can't sleep. Everything is such a mess, Dalton."

"I can't sleep, either," he said. And then he told her about his conversation with Maisy. After that, they talked for well over an hour about a lot of things, but Josie still wasn't sure if Dalton wanted Maisy around her right now. Or ever.

Dalton had just said good-night to Josie when a message from Chief Hayes flashed across his phone screen.

Possible lead on the day care case. Call me first thing tomorrow morning.

NINE

Bright and early the next morning, Dalton sat at his kitchen table reading the report about the car he'd discovered at the old run-down house not far from the day care. He'd asked the chief if one of the crime scene techs could check it out.

The chief had sent him the results after they'd talked on the phone this morning.

"So, I was right about that abandoned car?" he said after the chief told him what they'd found.

"Looks that way," Chief Hayes replied. "We didn't find any insurance or registration information on it. But one of the techs did find an old bill of sale underneath the seat. It was definitely purchased a month or so ago from a used-car lot off I-20 W near Lubbock, Texas. Cash."

"Texas." Dalton's gut burned. "Josie's from a small town near Waco. Pine Cone."

"Well, I think that's a pretty good lead," the chief replied. "That's about all we have, but if someone bought an old used car in a hurry and drove it from Texas to Arizona and then abandoned it, I'd say that person might be on a mission."

Dalton told the chief about Josie's in-laws. "Sounds like we might be on to something. Luna knew it, too. She alerted near the car, but I didn't find anything that was helpful. I'll do some digging around and maybe call the police in Pine Cone. I have a list of other possible suspects from that area, too."

"Careful with that," Chief Hayes warned. "If it's a small town and her in-laws were prominent, the locals won't want to divulge a lot of information."

"I'll keep that in mind," Dalton replied.

"We can't locate the owner of the abandoned house," the chief said. "And you didn't find anything?"

"No," Dalton replied. "Just dust and empty rooms. If anyone has been squatting there, they cleaned up after themselves."

"And left a car behind," Chief Hayes said before ending the call.

Dalton intended to do some work this morning. Being a rookie on short-time until after the holidays, he didn't have a desk to work from. He had to borrow from the department or work from home. Today was Saturday, and after his talk with Maisy last night, he wanted to stick close to her. Maybe do something fun.

But it was early and she was still asleep, so right now he'd see what he could dig up on the Callahan family from Pine Cone, Texas. Including the friends from Douglas Callahan's work place.

And he'd try to call Josie again.

But he wasn't quite sure what he'd say to her.

Josie stumbled downstairs and was greeted by her four wide-awake cousins. The boys ranged in age from five to ten and had more energy than a roadrunner on steroids.

"We want you to live with us forever," the youngest shouted as he launched himself against her. "We love you."

"I love you, too," Josie said, grinning against the headache that threatened to explode. "I need me some of your mama's good strong coffee."

"She's making pancakes and sausages," Ricky said.

Josie wondered if she'd be able to eat a bite. Her whole body ached from tossing and turning, and her eyes burned from lack of sleep.

Two of the boys whizzed by, loaded with electronic devices.

"They are so lame," Bryson, the oldest, said from his perch at the big kitchen island. He looked up at Josie with earnest eyes. "I like Maisy. She's cool."

That got Josie's attention. "Are you two friends?"

"I see her at school and…at the day care."

Josie tried not to show her interest. "She's a sweet little girl."

Bryson shrugged. "Yeah, she's okay."

He got up and headed for the den, nonchalance written all over his face.

"I think he has a crush on Maisy," Marilyn whispered as she handed Josie a cup of coffee. "How'd you sleep, honey?"

"Not so good," Josie replied. "I don't know what I'm going to do."

"If it's too much stress, it might be a good idea to cancel the party."

Josie had thought about this and prayed all night.

"How can we risk the children's safety for a party? It wouldn't be right."

"Maybe the threats will stop," her aunt said. "They shot at you when you were with a police officer."

"But they wrote on the fence. Bold. And Dalton thinks they'll keep at it."

"You and Dalton—"

"Are just friends," Josie said, the coffee warming her insides. "He expects me to take good care of Maisy while she's at the day care, and based on a conversation we had last night, I'm afraid he thinks I can't do that now."

"I'm sure he's worried," Marilyn said. She dished up fluffy pancakes and dashed each with red and green candy sprinkles. "Boys, your breakfast is ready."

"Where's Daddy?" Andy asked as he slammed up onto a barstool.

"Checking on things at the garage before he comes back to take you all Christmas shopping."

Josie enjoyed the extra time with her cousins and nibbled on a pancake and had a bite of sausage. When her cell rang, she got up and gave her aunt an apologetic shrug. Then she hurried to the enclosed porch on the back of the sprawling house.

"Hi."

"Hi," Dalton said. "Listen, can we meet for coffee or something?"

She sighed and stared out at the backyard where her uncle Jack had built an impressive treehouse around a towering pine tree. Maybe if she and Dalton had a conversation away from everything and everyone, they'd be able to communicate regarding Maisy's well-being. She had to be sure. "Where do you want to meet?"

"How about the Cactus Café? They have pretty good coffee."

"Okay, I'll meet you there in about half an hour."

When she turned, her aunt was standing in the doorway. "Dalton?"

"Yes. He wants to meet for coffee. To discuss things."

"Uh-huh. Well, that's good. Do you need a ride?"

"No. I'll take your car if you don't mind."

"Text me when you get there," Marilyn said. Then she heard a crash in the kitchen followed by "Mom's gonna be mad."

Marilyn groaned and hurried to check on her boys.

Josie's nerves tightened when she rode by the day care. Slowing, she checked the front for any signs of an intruder, but was relieved to see a police car sitting in the parking lot.

Then she checked her rearview mirror to make sure no one was following her. It was a cold wintry Saturday with light traffic. Safe so far.

When she pulled up to the Cactus Café, she saw Dalton and Luna waiting patiently by the older-model police car he'd been temporarily issued.

"Where's Maisy?" she asked when she got out of the car.

"A friend invited her to a Christmas party at the church, so she decided to go," he said. "So much for my plans to spend some quality time with her. But at least it gives me some time to talk to you privately right now."

She nodded, wondering what was coming. "I'm sure being with other kids her age at church will do her good," Josie said. Then she stopped short, a hand to her mouth. "And I told myself I wouldn't give unsolicited advice to you anymore."

He shook his head and glanced around the parking lot. "About that, I really am sorry…" Lifting away from his car, he added, "Last night was tough all the way around."

Feeling contrite for doubting him, she said, "Buy me a cup of coffee, Officer, and you can tell me all about it."

Relieved that Josie was willing to listen to his excuses for being so rude, Dalton found them a booth and ordered two coffees and a couple of cinnamon rolls. "You were right. Maisy is holding a lot of anxiety inside that brain of hers."

"I'm sorry," Josie said. "I was trying to help, and I made things worse."

"No, you opened my eyes to what was right in front of me. I know she's still grieving. We both are. But Maisy has it in her head that neither of us did enough to save her mother. Hard to swallow and really hard to explain to a child."

"I can't imagine how tough it must be. It's horrible to lose a loved one, but for a child to lose a parent, it must be a hundred times worse. I didn't want to interfere, and when she'd say something random to me, I thought if I listened to her, it would help."

"What exactly did she say to you?"

Josie took a sip of her coffee, her eyes full of sympathy.

"The other day while you were checking outside she said it was up to *her* to take care of *you*."

"Wow." Dalton's heart cracked a little more. "That's

a big responsibility for such a little girl. But it makes sense now that I know she felt responsible for her mother's death."

"Exactly." She took in a deep breath. "I wanted to talk to you about it, but all of these weird things keep happening and... I couldn't find the right time."

"And I'm too stubborn to listen to someone who's with my daughter practically every day. I'm sorry."

Her forgiving eyes gave him hope. "You have a lot on your mind, so don't apologize."

Dalton pointed to the cinnamon rolls. "Peace offering?" She smiled, and his heart rolled over and started a fast beat.

"I nibbled at a pancake at my aunt's house. I couldn't eat when I first got up, so now I'm hungry."

"Have at it," he said, relief washing over him.

"Now that we've settled that," she said between bites, "I want to hear if the chief's call had anything to do with my stalker. Whitney said she'd fill you in on last night's intruder."

"She did," he said. "I don't like it."

"What are you not telling me, Dalton?"

"Eat up," he said, amazed at her intuitive nature. "Let's enjoy this quiet time together before we step back into the fray."

He didn't want to ruin the moment with the information the chief had given him. He'd tell her about that later.

And he didn't want to tell her that he'd done a thorough search regarding her mother-in-law. A search that had revealed some very surprising news.

TEN

They walked around a trail that wound through a small park near the town center, the sun warm on their skin even with the frosty temperature. Bright lights twinkled on the lamp posts scattered throughout the walkway, and red bows adorned an open-air square pergola near a small man-made brook. A decorated tree sparkling with colorful lights completed the festive atmosphere.

Josie's mood had changed now that she understood what had happened last night. Maybe she'd been right to blurt out her concerns regarding Maisy, since it had forced Dalton to have that talk with his daughter.

But now, she was itching to find out what was going on in his mind. Something had him stewing.

"A storm is coming in the next few days," Dalton said, his hand light on Luna's leash. "We might get snow for Christmas."

Josie grinned and shot him a quick glance. "That would make Maisy happy."

He turned to stare at her. "And what would make you happy?"

Surprised at the intensity of that question, Josie drew back. "Honestly, right now I'd like to feel safe again.

I thought I was building a good life here. I work hard, and I love what I do. I don't want to disappoint anyone, and I don't want to be forced to leave a place I've come to love."

He studied her, his eyes moving over her in a way that left her soul stripped of any facades. "You won't have to leave. I'll make sure of that."

"I hope *I* can make sure of that, too. I hope my reputation will hold through all of this."

He lifted her chin with his thumb. "So if everything were okay? I mean, if none of this was happening and I called you out of the blue to go to dinner, how would that make you feel?"

Josie stared up at him and saw the burning question in his gray eyes. Was he asking her permission to… take things to a new level between them? She wouldn't lie to him, so she took a deep breath and gathered her courage. "That would make me feel very happy, Officer West."

He leaned toward her, his expression full of determination and demand. The pines swayed in a soft wind, causing her blue scarf to lift and flow out around her shoulders. While the air around them was crisp, the warmth in his eyes made her feel safe and comfortable. Too comfortable. But the longing in her soul couldn't be denied.

Josie waited, wondering how his lips would feel on hers.

"And how would you feel if I told you I'd like to kiss you?"

Her whole system buzzed to life. "I… I…uh…think I'd like that, too."

He moved closer and touched his lips to hers in a

sweet, slow exploration that made Josie blush all the way to her toes.

Satisfied, he stepped back and gave her a smile that sizzled her bootstraps. "Okay, then."

Regaining her momentum, she asked, "Are you finished…interrogating me?"

"Not quite, but it's a start."

He guided her, holding a hand on her elbow. "But now we can talk about your situation. I don't know who's sending you the threatening messages, but I can tell you one thing for sure, Josie. It's not your mother-in-law."

Dalton saw the shock registering on her face. Pointing to a bench, he guided her over and waited for her to sit down.

"What did you find out?" she asked, her hands twisting against her knit scarf. "And why didn't you lead with this?"

"First, I did a search and made some calls from home this morning and, second, we needed a break from all that." His gaze moved over her face and settled on her lips. "And I don't regret that decision."

She met his gaze, her expression full of apprehension and caution. "Okay. Go on."

"According to the people I talked to in Pine Cone this morning, your mother-in-law, Janine Callahan, had a stroke and she's been in an assisted living facility for at least six months."

Josie put a hand to her lips. "I had no idea. I didn't keep in touch."

Dalton nodded. "Understandable, but this means we

can rule her out. She can barely speak, according to the woman I talked to in the sheriff's department."

"Did you tell this woman why you were calling?"

"I was discreet," he said. "I know what I'm doing."

Josie sank back on the bench. "Poor Janine."

"That leaves the brother. He moves around a lot. He's not in Louisiana, though."

"I can't see Randall going to all this trouble."

"Well, somebody is. I checked out your husband's coworkers, too. Two of them still work at the refinery and have solid alibis. The third one, Perry Wilcox, is no longer employed there. I'm still trying to locate him."

"Wow, you've sure been busy."

He stood. "Yep. I have to go and pick up Maisy. I'll walk you to your aunt's car." Offering her a hand, he held Luna's leash and waited for Josie to turn back toward the town center. "This was nice."

"Yes. And you were right. I needed some downtime." She gave him a serious look. "What do you recommend I do about the party? The children have been anticipating it for weeks, and the parents need me to be there while they finish up work and shopping before the holidays. But I don't want to endanger anyone."

Dalton thought about his conversation with Whitney.

"I'll clear it with the chief to have myself and some other officer on the premises for the next three days."

"You'd do that?"

He saw the hope in her eyes. "I'll make it happen. And I think I know a way." He reiterated what he and Whitney planned—keep a K-9 officer on the premises at least for the next few days. "I think you need to alert the parents that you've received some concerning mail. Reassure them that you'll have protection for the near future."

She stopped at the end of the path. "Thank you, Dalton. I've relied on your advice throughout this nightmare, and I'll never forget how you've helped me."

"Hey, it's my job," he said, but when he saw the disappointment in her eyes, he tugged her close. "And *you*, Josie. It's you, too." Deciding to lay it all on the line, he added, "I was worried about Maisy, but she loves you, and I think you've been a good influence over her. I was worried about work, but that will take care of itself. I was still grieving but…that won't bring back my wife. I need to move on with my life, and… I'd be crazy if I didn't let you know that… I'd like to have you in my life. We don't have to rush anything but we at least should…try."

He watched as tears misted in her eyes. "Are you sure about that, Dalton? You're not fixating on me, are you? You and Maisy have been through a lot. I need you to be sure. And we haven't even talked about you leaving after Christmas."

"I'm pretty sure," he said, knowing his heart. "I knew it the minute I met you. It's not a fix. It's real. I'd like to see what happens with us. I don't have to take the assignment in Flagstaff."

She looked awestruck. "Really? But how can you be so sure about me?"

"Really. You were holding a little newborn baby. I saw the tenderness in your expression."

"Dalton."

His name on her lips in that sweet way told him she felt the same. But he had to ask. "Are *you* sure?"

"I'm beginning to hope," she said. "But—"

"But we have to get past this thing and decide what happens next, right?"

"Right." She pulled away and glanced toward her car. "I hope we'll figure this out soon and then—"

She stopped and pointed. "Dalton."

The sweetness in her voice had changed to distress. He turned and checked her car.

A flat tire on the front left side and a message scrawled in red on her windshield.

Sacrifices and burnt offerings.

Dalton let out a breath. "How did he manage this in broad daylight?"

Josie stood staring at her car. Then her words sent a chill rushing through Dalton.

"That's taken from Exodus. A sacrifice to the Lord, according to Moses."

The sound of gunshots hit the air. One, two, rapid and sure. Dalton tugged Josie to the ground and held his body over hers. "I think he's trying to make you the sacrifice," he said in Josie's ear, his gun drawn.

"Finally, somebody saw something," Dalton said as he got back inside his patrol car where Josie was waiting.

Thankfully, there *had* been a witness. A woman getting out of her car across from the restaurant had noticed the guy leaving the message, and she'd ducked down when he raised the rifle and started firing. Dalton had seen her watching after the patrol cars had zoomed in, and when he'd questioned her, she'd delivered a good description.

"And she got a good a glimpse of him driving away in a dark-colored sedan," Josie said.

"A man with a beard, skinny and wearing sunshades."

Josie kept staring out into the parking lot. "A man who managed to slash a tire and leave me another cryptic message. A man who obviously carries a big knife or something that can penetrate a tire and a gun that he knows how to use."

That concerned Dalton more than he wanted to let on. This person was getting closer with each act. And carrying yet another weapon that he could use on Josie.

"And he also left a can of spray paint that we're having analyzed. So we have a full report, and an eyewitness who caught him in the act and watched him drive away."

Josie got out of the car and tugged at her scarf. "But she didn't see the license plate number. And I don't know anyone who fits that description. Randall Callahan is hefty and short. It can't be him."

Dalton wanted to make her see how the evidence was stacking up. "She said skinny, not tall. Maybe Randall lost weight."

"But how can we prove it's him?"

"I'm running checks to find his last known location, and we'll go from there," Dalton said. "The rest is paperwork and making sure we have all the accurate information, which we do. I'm still trying to locate Perry Wilcox, too."

"Okay."

Dalton and a bystander had changed the flat tire and put on the spare. They'd searched around the slashed tire but hadn't produced any evidence. A team was searching the parking lot for anything they could send to ballistics. Dalton wasn't holding his breath on finding any DNA or prints. But Luna had alerted and followed the scent two parking spaces over, near a trash bin. She'd emitted the same low growl he'd witnessed when they'd found the old, abandoned car.

The suspect had waited until midmorning when the restaurant wasn't so crowded. But the town center buzzed with Christmas shoppers who were so involved in getting things done they'd probably never even noticed him. A quick spray of paint on the windshield and one quick duck in beside her car to cut into the tire. Then he'd waited for the right time to shoot, but he'd missed, thankfully. When Dalton thought of how close he'd come, he felt sick to his stomach.

"He's been watching you," Dalton told Josie on the way back to her aunt's house. He'd insisted on driving her home. He'd call a friend to give him and Luna a ride back to his car.

Josie stared straight ahead. "He had to have followed me this morning, somehow. And I checked and rechecked."

"It's a small town, Josie. All he had to do was see your car and give you time to make a turn or two."

"Which means I'm not safe anywhere," she said.

Dalton came around the car before she could bolt into the house. "Hey, listen. This is a huge break. He got too close and someone spotted him. We have a description of him and the woman saw him with a rifle. We know it's a male. He's gonna slip up, and then we'll have him."

"And how long do I have to wait for that, Dalton? How long do I put my life on hold or keep putting my kids in danger?"

"I'll be right here with you," Dalton said. "No matter what, Josie. We're in this together."

She stared up at him, defeat in her eyes. "I believe

you, but… I don't know how much more of this I can take."

Dalton wanted to pull her into his arms and hold her tight.

Instead, he took her hand in his and guided her up to the porch. "Don't give up on me, Josie. Remember, no matter what."

ELEVEN

Later that day, Josie's cell buzzed.

Dalton. He'd promised he'd call her and check on her.

She sat on the love seat inside the enclosed sunporch at her aunt's house, trying to read a book. But she'd read the same paragraph about five times. The boys were in bed, and her aunt and uncle were in the den watching television.

After the harrowing morning, Josie helped her aunt wrap some presents and clean the house. But now her mind kept whirling between wanting to kiss Dalton again to wanting to give up and run away from her fears. And him.

"Hi," she said, the memory of their walk through the park helping her keep it together.

"Hi." He sounded breathless. He'd told her he liked to go for long runs sometimes.

"Have you been running?"

"Yeah, but not in the way you'd think. I've been running around all day following leads."

She held her breath, dreading what he might have found. "And?"

"And we've located your former brother-in-law."

Pushing her book out of her lap, Josie stood. "Where?"

"He's living in Utah. Near St. George."

Josie's nerve endings trembled a warning. "That's not that far from us, Dalton. And it can't be a coincidence."

"I know. About two hours at most. I don't have all the details, but I've alerted the authorities there, and they'll question him. Without any solid proof, they can't hold him, so we'll see if he confesses or not."

"What about the spray paint can?"

"It'll take a while to hear back from the state lab on that one. But if it's him, he's probably been coming back and forth, so we can find out what kind of vehicle he drives and put out an alert. If he shows up again, we'll nab him for questioning."

"Could this be over?"

"It could be," he said. "If the authorities there can locate him and question him, then we have something to work with."

"Thank you," she said, caught between relief and despair. "I hope it's not Randall, but if it isn't him, then the nightmare won't be over."

"We'll keep at it," he said. "Meantime, you go on with planning your big party for the kids. You'll have plenty of K-9 officers patrolling next week, and they'll be at the party, too. I told the chief it would be a good PR move to teach the kids all about how we train our partners."

"You're something else, Officer West."

They talked a while longer and then ended on a high note. He told her he'd see her in church tomorrow.

Josie sat there in the dark and accepted what her heart already knew. She was falling for Dalton.

* * *

The next morning, Dalton hurried Maisy out the door to church. Feeling hopeful for the first time in a week or so, he smiled when they got in the car.

"We don't go to church much as my friends do," Maisy said, buckling her seat belt. "Are we going because Christmas is coming?"

"That and because you've been active in some of the church happenings, so I thought it was time I got more involved, too. I know I've missed a lot because of work but I'm going to do better."

Her grin said it all. "I'm glad, Daddy. All the other parents go with their kids."

Dalton silently kicked himself. "I'm sorry I didn't think about that, honey. Daddies get so busy sometimes they don't make the right decisions."

Maisy rolled her eyes. "And…some dads are afraid to go to church."

"You are way too smart for your own good," Dalton replied.

But she was right. He was already sweating just thinking about walking into a crowded sanctuary. He'd gone before only because of Maisy. Now he wanted to go for himself, too.

But after he parked the car and shook a few hands, the friendly atmosphere of the Desert Valley Community Church helped to calm Dalton. When Maisy poked him and pointed to where Josie sat with her relatives, his pulse quickened and he found his strength.

Time to turn back to God. And maybe it was time to forgive himself for not being able to save his wife.

About midway through the service, Dalton's cell

buzzed. Discreetly checking his phone screen, he saw that the chief had called. Then a text.

Urgent. Found Randall Callahan.

Dalton waited until the service was over and then leaned close to Josie. "I have to go. Can you take Maisy with you to your aunt's?"

She nodded, alarm clouding her face.

He'd have to explain later, so he whispered to Maisy that he had to go to work, so she'd be going with Miss Josie. Maisy bobbed her head and smiled up at Josie.

At least he didn't have to worry about her while he headed to the police station.

"Randall Callahan says he only came once to find Josie."

Dalton stared at Chief Hayes, disbelief filtering through shock and hope. "So he admitted that was him I saw running to get into a dark car that first night when all of this started?"

"Yes." The chief got up and stared out the window. "He claims he got transferred to Utah. He's an electrician, and he has to follow the work. A new plant being built."

"And he did admit that he'd tracked Josie down?"

"Yes. Said he wanted to make amends."

"I don't believe him. I'd like to go up to Utah and question him."

"We don't have anything solid, Dalton—especially because you already showed the eyewitness a recent photo of Randall Callahan, and she couldn't be sure he was the man she saw in the parking lot. The Utah authorities have warned him not to set foot in Arizona again. He knows if we see him in Desert Valley, he will be spending time in our jail."

Dalton had to go with that for now. What else could he do?

But it was too close for comfort. And he had to tell Josie that this might finally be over, but that their main suspect wouldn't be held since they couldn't say without a doubt that he was their man. If only the eyewitness they'd interviewed could be sure. Dalton had personally gone to the woman's house and shown her the picture the Utah police had sent to him. But she couldn't verify if Randall Callahan was the man she'd seen shooting at them yesterday.

It was midafternoon by the time Dalton made it to Josie's aunt's house to pick up Maisy. Josie met him at the door, so he pulled her aside. "We need to talk."

"Okay." She took him out to the sunporch. "The kids are upstairs in the playroom. Maisy's teaching the boys how to play Monopoly."

He smiled at that. His daughter sure liked being in charge.

He sat Josie down and told her what he'd learned about Randall Callahan. "It looks like he's our man, but he didn't confess to the harassment, and he claimed he only came here once because he wanted to see you to make amends. Said his mother had gone off the deep end, and she'd blamed it all on you."

"Do you believe him?" she asked, her eyes wide with shock and distrust.

"No." Dalton wouldn't lie to her. "But his wife is vouching for him, too. Said he's been to work and back for the last few weeks, and that he did try to locate you one time but he chickened out when he saw a patrol car in your yard. Either way, the authorities in Utah have warned him to stay away from you."

"Can we be sure he'll do that?"

"According to our contact in Utah, yes. Said he kept repeating that he had a good job and a wife he loves, and he's trying to make a new life. He said he only remembered recently that you'd mentioned relatives in Arizona. He found some old letters after he cleaned out his mother's house."

"So he saw my aunt's address?"

"Yes. We think that's how he found you."

"I forgot about the couple of boxes I'd stored in her attic. It's strange that he wound up so close. Kind of makes me nervous, no matter what."

"He can't hurt you now. He told the interrogators he'd never do something like that to you. He even asked to see you."

"I'm not ready for that yet," she said. "But I do feel a sense of relief that he says it wasn't him. Do I believe him, though?"

"We have to for now. So…we go on as planned. We'll take care of the day care. Then you have the four day holiday weekend. It'll be a test to see if the threats stop. If they do, then we've scared him away."

"For now," she said. "And if it's not him?"

"We'll keep at it."

"But you still might have to leave after Christmas, Dalton."

"About that—"

Maisy burst into the room. "Daddy? When'd you get here?"

Giving Josie an apologetic smile, he said, "A few minutes ago. Ready to go home?"

Maisy nodded. "Yes. The boys won't listen to anything I say."

She hugged Josie and Marilyn, and they said their goodbyes.

"I'll call you tomorrow," Dalton said, wishing he could kiss Josie good-night.

But tomorrow could be a new start for all of them.

Monday and Tuesday morning went by without incident.

On Tuesday afternoon, Josie saw Dalton walk in the door, Luna by his side. He glanced up, searching, and found her. She smiled at him, that now-familiar warmth coursing through her system. The staff had gotten used to having K-9 officers walking around the perimeters of the property. The kids loved it, but after Josie had sent out an email explaining, a few of the parents had refused to bring their kids back. Then the local paper got wind and did an interview with her and the police chief.

Josie didn't blame anyone for their fears, but the chief had assured everyone that they had the situation under control. It was a tough call, since some of their clients didn't have anyone to watch their kids. But the place was like a fortress and the training was good for the rookies, as Dalton kept telling her.

He walked toward her now, his smile soft and sure. "So far, so good," he said. "If we get through tomorrow, I'd say we're clear."

Josie prayed toward that end. "I'm going back to my place tonight," she said. "I'll leave all the security lights on, and I have my aunt and uncle on speed dial."

"I don't like it, but I understand," Dalton said. "However, Luna and I would be willing to sleep on your couch. Or the porch."

"I don't have much of a porch, and my couch is way too small for all six feet of you."

"Too bad." He grinned and let out a sigh. "What are you doing for Christmas?"

"I'll be with my folks next door, of course," she said. Then she looked into his disappointed eyes. "Unless you and Maisy want to spend Christmas Day with me."

"I'd love that," he blurted. Then he looked sheepish. "I wasn't fishing for an invite. But I was hoping."

"Consider it a date," she replied. "Besides, my aunt will have lots of good leftovers."

"The best of both worlds," he replied in a whisper. "I'll have you to myself for a while, and then I'll have leftovers later."

She grinned at that and waved as he and Maisy left. Whitney and Zoe escorted Josie, her aunt and the rest of the staff to their cars.

Josie spent the evening wrapping gifts. She'd managed to pick up a few things when Zoe invited her to go shopping yesterday after work. She'd bought Maisy a scarf, and she'd found a nice pair of gloves for Dalton.

She'd pulled back the covers to go to bed when her cell rang. Her heart filled with dread; Josie didn't recognize the number.

Answering with trepidation, she held her breath.

"The Desert Valley Day care is on fire."

TWELVE

Dalton pulled to the curb, tires screeching as he jumped out of the patrol car. "Maisy, stay with Luna."

His blurry-eyed daughter nodded. "Daddy, don't let it burn down."

"Stay there," he told her. Poor kid was still in her pajamas underneath her puffy coat, but he had to come and he couldn't leave her at home.

When he saw Josie standing with Marilyn and Jack, he hurried over to her. "Josie?"

She turned and fell into his arms, her eyes full of tears. "He tried to burn it down, Dalton."

"I'm so sorry," Dalton said, holding her close. "I thought we had our man but I don't see how Randall would try this knowing we're on to him."

"It had to be Randall," she said, pulling away, her eyes full of anger.

Dalton couldn't comfort her. He'd failed her, and it was evident from the look on her face that she thought that, too.

Zoe hurried up. "I just heard. Do you think it was Callahan?"

"We need to find out," Dalton said. "Call the local police station in Utah." He gave her the number. "Thanks, Zoe."

Zoe hurried off, her phone in her hand.

Chief Hayes rushed toward them from the back of the building. "Started near the fuse box. Electrical."

"Electrical?" Josie tugged at her coat. "Randall's an electrician. What more proof do we need?"

"Unfortunately, a lot more," Chief Hayes said.

Dalton felt as helpless as Josie. "Officer Trent is notifying the authorities in Utah, sir. We should hear soon if Callahan is involved. Meantime, we can put out a BOLO."

Dalton watched as tired firemen walked by and went about cleaning up and putting away their equipment. The fire chief came up to Josie and Marilyn. "We managed to put it out, but the kitchen and back part of the building aren't safe. You'll need to shut it down for repairs."

Josie nodded, her fingers pressed to her lips. When Dalton reached for her, she pushed away and headed to the back of the building. "I want to see how bad it looks."

"I'll go check on her," Marilyn said. "Jack, go see about the boys. They might have driven our SUV away by now."

Her husband hurried to where their big vehicle was parked, but one of the firemen stopped Marilyn to ask her a question. That left Dalton standing alone, the smell of burned wires and scorched wood stifling him. When he heard Luna's agitated bark, he whirled.

And saw the door to the patrol car standing open. Maisy wasn't there.

Josie heard a dog barking in the front parking lot. Wiping at her tears, she turned from the rubble that had once been the storage room and the day care kitchen.

Now she would lose her clients because of fear and not having a place to leave their children. Her life here was over. And for what? Some sort of revenge quest?

When she heard the barking again, she turned and saw a purple backpack lying near the fence. And then she noticed the back gate to the day care property standing open.

With a gasp, she rushed toward the backpack and grabbed it up.

Maisy!

Josie gulped in a breath and turned to find Dalton running toward her, panic on his face. Luna whizzed past him and into the woods, turning to bark before she danced around toward the dark brambles.

Dalton took one look at the backpack and shook his head. "No. No." Then he called out to Luna. "Find. Find Maisy."

Luna barked and lunged forward.

Dalton took off running after her.

Maisy was gone.

Josie held to the backpack and followed him into the woods. She could hear him shouting for help. Luna's barking sounded off in the distance.

Please, Lord, let them find Maisy safe and sound.

But before she could catch up with Dalton, someone grabbed her from behind and clamped a grimy hand over her mouth. Dropping the backpack, Josie struggled, but that only made the man tighten his grip.

"You're coming with me," he said. "We end this tonight."

"Maisy?"

Dalton was hoarse from calling her name. Luna stayed

up ahead, racing through the woods until they came out on the other side of the road.

And into the yard with the abandoned car and old, deserted house.

Dalton swallowed the excruciating pain coursing through him. The pain of failure, the pain of knowing he'd been close to the truth the last time he'd been here and he'd found nothing.

Nothing. But now, his daughter might be in there, hurt. Or worse.

Dear God...

He couldn't finish the words. He hoped God would hear his plea. Luna stopped at the side door of the house. Now she emitted low growls. Her way of warning Dalton while she alerted.

Someone was in there.

Dalton pulled his weapon and prayed Zoe and the chief would follow the trail. His phone buzzed, and he quickly checked the message.

It was Randall Callahan. Josie's brother-in-law remembered someone inquiring about Josie. A coworker of her husband's named Wilson or possibly Wilcox?

Dalton put away his phone, his gut burning. They'd been targeting the wrong man.

Josie. He remembered her holding the backpack, her eyes wide with fear and horror. She'd want to help find Maisy. She loved his daughter, too.

Blinking back his emotions, Dalton slowly made his way to the old, battered door and stared into the window. A flashlight lay on the floor, illuminating enough of the room for him to see Maisy sitting in a chair, her arms tied behind her so she couldn't escape. A slow rage boiled up inside Dalton. He was about to kick down the door when he heard a sound behind him. Dalton turned and found a dirty, scruffy-looking man holding Josie, his arm stretched across her neck.

And a gun jammed against her side.

Josie shouted, "Dalton, get down."

The man shot and missed. She cried out, but he held the gun to her head. "I'll kill her," he shouted to Dalton. "Put down the gun and hold that dog back."

Luna's growls turned to aggressive barks.

Dalton halted her. "Stay." He held his gun out and slowly lowered it to the ground.

When Josie heard cries of "Daddy" from inside the house, she breathed a sigh of relief. Maisy was alive.

"I'm coming," Dalton called. "Maisy, honey, stay right where you are. Don't try to untie your hands. Stay there, baby."

"She can't get away," the man said. "Y'all are gonna have to join her. And then it'll finally be over."

Josie gave Dalton a warning glance. "He's not my brother-in-law. He's—"

"Perry Wilcox," Dalton guessed. "The one missing link that we couldn't find." He nodded toward the man. "You worked with Josie's husband, right?"

The man shoved Josie toward the house. "That's right. I finally found her. This woman ruined my life, so I tried to ruin hers."

"By threatening her with strange notes and letters and shooting at her?" Dalton asked. "And now, kidnapping a child, too?"

"I had to get everyone's attention," the man shouted. "No one ever listens to me."

Dalton kept his eyes on Josie. She stared at him, trying to convey all that she felt at this moment—gratitude, fear for him and Maisy, hope and dread, and love. A love so strong that she knew she had to survive this, somehow.

"He thinks I caused the accident at the refinery," she said, trying to keep her voice steady. "Douglas and I had a horrible fight that day before his shift. Mr. Wilcox cleaned up hazardous spills and…something went wrong."

The man pushed her closer to Dalton. Luna growled low in her throat, her impatience evident in her body language.

"I'll show you what went wrong." Wilcox turned, and Josie felt sick to her stomach. He had a horrid scar on the left side of his face. His skin had been scorched and burned. "This! My marriage ended, and I lost my job." He jerked his arm tighter around Josie. "The accident was Douglas Callahan's fault. In the weeks before it, he always came to work drunk. He told us how horrible Josie was, how she didn't want a family or children. How lazy she was. Not a good wife. He was so mad at her, he couldn't focus and he messed up big-time."

Dalton's eyes held Josie's, an understanding passing between them. "So her actions ruined your life and you had to make her pay, right?"

Wilcox bobbed his head. "Right. I tried to shut down that kiddie corral. And I'm not done."

Dalton inched closer. "You don't have to do this. We can help you. I'll make sure she gets what she deserves." Josie knew Dalton was bargaining, anything, to make the man think he was on his side.

Wilcox shook his head. "I don't care anymore. I can't let her live when my life is over." He pressed the gun into Josie's ribs. "Get inside. I want her to tell me how sorry she is. I want her to beg."

Josie tried to keep breathing. She could get out of this. She had to help Maisy and Dalton. She wouldn't let them die because of this madman and his misguided sense of justice.

"Just take *me*," she said. "Let them go and take me with you. I'll do whatever you want if you let them go."

"Ain't gonna work," he said. "Now let's get inside."

Before the man could force them into the house, they heard a shuffling noise and a door slamming. Startled, Wilcox looked to the left.

It was all the distraction Josie and Dalton needed. Josie elbowed him in the ribs, stomped on his foot and then shoved him back. She dove to the ground a few feet out of his reach. Dalton grabbed his gun and rushed the man. Luna started barking again.

"Attack," Dalton called, rolling away so Luna could do her job.

Maisy came running around the building, holding a large tree branch. When Josie saw the girl, she grabbed her and held her back. "It's okay, Maisy. I'm okay. We're all okay."

Maisy dropped the big limb and turned and fell into Josie's arms, her sobs echoing out over the stark woods. "I kept working at the ropes until I could slip through them."

"You did great, honey."

When they heard more barking, Dalton called off Luna and cuffed Perry Wilcox. "Don't move!"

Then he turned and hurried to his daughter and Josie. "It's over," he said. "It's all over."

Christmas Day

Josie stood in her kitchen and smiled at the man sitting with his daughter on the couch. Dalton and Maisy had opened their presents at home, and now they'd come to spend Christmas with her. Dalton was admiring his gloves, and Maisy was wrapping her scarf in much the same way she'd seen Josie wearing hers.

Josie thanked God for this scene. When Dalton got up to refresh his coffee and grab another cinnamon roll, she couldn't help it. She hugged him close. "Thank you for the hand lotion."

He sniffed her hair. "You always smell so good, it reminded me of you."

"It's so good to be alive," she said. "We're so blessed."

He nuzzled her ear. "Yes."

The horror of her encounter with Perry Wilcox still held her, though. "I'm just glad it's over."

They had Wilcox in custody. The eyewitness had identified him as the man she'd seen in the town center parking lot, and the can of red spray paint left behind was what was used on her fence and her car. The lab had actually found a partial print on the can that was a match.

"We're here, together, and it's cold, but we're warm and safe," Dalton said. "I'm cleared to start my assignment next week in Canyon County instead of Flagstaff. I won't have to leave you."

They glanced at Maisy and Luna, curled up together. Maisy was now reading a book she'd received from Santa, and Luna enjoyed a chew bone from her doggie stocking.

"We have a big day," Josie said. "Zoe, Sean and Patrick are coming over for dinner and bringing Freya, and then we'll go over to my aunt's for even more food."

"I love it," Dalton said. "And I love you."

Josie's heart dipped and lifted. "I thought we were going to take this slow."

"We will," he said. "But I can love you while we do that."

"I love you, too," she admitted. "I love Maisy and I owe Luna my life."

"I'll remind you of that every day for the next fifty years."

She smiled at him, and then he dipped his head to give her a quick but thorough kiss. "Let's hurry up and take this slow."

When the doorbell rang, Maisy jumped up. "May I get it?"

Dalton laughed. "Make sure you know who it is first."

He'd had a talk with his brave daughter. She'd untied her hands in spite of his warnings. Or because of his warnings, since he'd tried to teach her how to survive in any situation. Maisy was bold, but he wanted her to be cautious, too.

Dalton gave Josie another kiss before the house filled with laughter and joy. Freya greeted her friend Luna with a doggie woof and then settled down beside Luna to enjoy the day.

Maisy took Patrick by the hand. "Wanna see what I got for Christmas?"

The little boy grinned and showed her his gift, his speech still slow and stilted but improving. "I got a game."

Zoe hugged Josie and gave her a reassuring smile,

while Dalton offered Sean a drink. "You sure look happy."

"I am," Josie replied. "I can't believe the police department volunteered to throw us a party and help us rebuild the day care."

Sean grinned and held up his drink. "And we're keeping our children with you. We trust you, Josie."

Josie found it hard to speak. "I can't wait to get back to work."

"Well, meantime, your aunt has the situation under control," Zoe said. "She was licensed to care for children in her home for years, and she's still good to go."

After they gathered around the dining table, Josie took Dalton's hand. "Will you say grace?"

Dalton looked sheepish. "Yes, I'll be glad to. I have the best Christmas gift. My family."

When he finished, Maisy screamed and ran to the window. "Daddy, look. It's snowing!"

Josie couldn't believe it. Beautiful, delicate snowflakes fell like lace and covered the ground.

Maisy grabbed Patrick. "This is a perfect Christmas."

Josie looked around the table and then met Dalton's gaze. Maisy was right. After so much pain, they were able to celebrate the gift of Christ together. She was home.

* * * * *

A KILLER CHRISTMAS

Lenora Worth

For He will give His angels charge concerning you
to guard you in all of your ways.
—*Psalms* 91:11

To Terri Reed—you make me proud every day.
I'm so glad to be here with you!

ONE

The full moon grinned down on her with a wintry smile. FBI Tactical K-9 Unit Agent Nina Atkins held on to the leash and kept an eye on the big dog running with her. Sam loved being outside, no matter the weather, no matter the crunch of snow underneath his paws. The three-year-old K-9 rottweiler, a smart but gentle giant that specialized in cadaver detection, had no idea that most humans were terrified of him. Especially the criminal kind.

Tonight, however, they weren't looking for criminals. Nina was just out for a nice run and then home to a long, hot shower. Two weeks before Christmas, and after a harrowing year where one of their own had gone bad and lost his life, thankfully all was quiet around the Billings, Montana, FBI Tactical K-9 Unit headquarters. Special Agent in Charge Max West would be back before Christmas, but right now he was taking some time off with his bride, Katerina. Even tech wiz Dylan O'Leary had taken a few days away to spend some time with the parents of his wife, Zara. So many of her friends and fellow agents had fallen in love lately, Nina's head was spinning. Which was probably why she'd felt the need for a quick run. She lived for her work. No time for romance. Okay, maybe she'd just given up on a love life since her last brief relationship had fizzled out like a mountain stream in a serious drought.

Nina lived about twenty miles from downtown Billings, in the quaint town of Iris Rock. Regardless of her single status, she loved going on these nightly runs through the quiet foothills near the Elk Basin.

"C'mon, Sam," Nina said now, her nose cold. "Just around the bend and then we'll cool down on the way home."

Sam woofed in response, comfortable in his own rich brown fur. But instead of moving on, the big dog came to an abrupt halt that almost threw Nina right over his broad body.

"Sam?"

The rottweiler glanced back at her with his work expression. What kind of scent had he picked up?

Then she heard something.

"I don't know anything. Please, don't do this."

Female. Youngish voice. Scared and shaky.

Giving Sam a hand signal to stay quiet, Nina moved from the narrow gravel jogging path to the snow-covered woods, each footstep slow and calculated. Sam led the way, as quiet as a desert rat.

"I need the key. The senator said you'd give it to me."

Nina and Sam hid behind a copse of trees and dead brambles and watched the two figures a few yards away, standing in an open spot.

A big, tall man was holding a gun on a young woman with long dark hair. The girl was sobbing and wringing her hands out, palms up. Nina recognized that defensive move.

Was he going to shoot her?

Then Nina noticed something else.

A shallow, open pit right behind the girl. Could that be a newly dug grave?

Nina didn't stop to ponder that question, but she knew to be careful, too. Giving Sam another "quiet" signal, she called out, "Hey, everything okay here?"

The girl gasped and stared at her with fear-filled eyes, but stayed frozen to the spot.

The man turned to face her. Nina used a hand signal to allow Sam to bark, hoping to distract the man so the girl could run. The dog did his job, his ferocious bark echoing loudly out over the winter woods. Since she didn't have her weapon, Sam was Nina's only hope right now in stopping the girl from getting shot. That could give her time to call for help.

The man stared at Nina, giving her a good view of his face in the eerie white light from the moon. He shot at her and just missed, and then pivoted back toward the girl, weapon in hand. Sam kept barking. The man looked panicked, so Nina motioned the rottweiler forward, all the while taking in the assailant's appearance.

The big dog growled, but stopped when she signaled him. "My dog is trained to attack," she said. "You should drop that gun now."

The man shook his head and raised the gun, but Nina signaled Sam again. The animal danced and barked, causing a panicked expression on the man's face. He started backing away, but in a lightning-fast move, pivoted and took one quick shot at the girl.

She screamed, grabbed at her shoulder and fell into the open pit behind her as the gunman disappeared into the woods.

Sam kept barking, eager for some action.

Nina pulled out her phone and hurriedly called in the crime, describing the scene and her location. "Suspect somewhere in the Iris Rock woods just off the Eastern trail."

Jumping down into the pit, she breathed a sigh of relief. The girl was still alive, though her pulse was weak. Nina almost sent Sam after the man, but instead ordered him to guard in case the killer came back. Because Nina knew in her gut that he would return. She hoped by then she'd have backup.

She'd need it, and she'd need to pray for protection. He'd left his victim alive, and the girl had seen his face. So had Nina. She and Sam had surprised the man and thrown him off guard long enough to defuse the situation. And because of that, he'd probably come back for all of them.

US Deputy Marshal Thomas Grant brought his big Chevy pickup to a halt just off the edge of the woods. Something was certainly going on. Several police cars and a few big black SUVs sat caddy-cornered off the narrow road ahead, lights flashing to warn any passersby. Official-looking people milled around, some dressed in black and wearing FBI vests. A couple officers had K-9s with them, sniffing here and there.

He decided to investigate, because his gut told him this was more than a traffic stop or an accident. This looked like an all-out manhunt in progress.

Dressed in civilian clothes as he was, he pulled out his ID as soon as he climbed from the truck, and flashed it at the first officer he came into contact with.

"What are you doing here?" the young patrolman asked with a skeptical tone.

"Looking for a wanted man," Thomas replied on a droll note. "He could be in these parts."

The cop nodded and let him through.

Then Thomas spotted her.

A female wearing heavy jogging clothes and a bright purple wool hat hopped up out of a dark, six-foot-long hole in the snow-speckled ground. A big, fierce-looking dog met her and wagged his tail, while she held up her hands to show the crime scene techs what looked like dirt and blood.

Thomas watched as the woman talked to an officer, her hands lifted in the air. Then he glanced to where an ambulance had backed up into the woods. Two EMTs pushed a stretcher carrying a young woman hooked up to an IV toward the waiting bus.

Before he could announce his presence, the jogger glanced over at Thomas and stalked toward him. "May I ask what you're doing here, Deputy Marshal?"

He took in the light blond hair underneath the wool hat and the big brown eyes full of distrust. He had to look down at her, but she stood straight and didn't flinch.

He showed her his credentials even though he'd given the officer his name already. "US Deputy Marshal Thomas Grant. I was passing by and saw the ruckus. I'm looking for a man—."

"Hey, Nina, can you come over here?"

"Hold that thought," she told Thomas with a puzzled glare, before she turned back to a man wearing an official FBI jacket.

"Coming," she said, scooting toward where a group of FBI agents gathered by the open earth. They stood in a cluster and talked among themselves, the woman right in the middle.

Thomas waited and listened, two things he was good at. Soon enough, he'd stitched together the details. The cute blonde had been out jogging and had stumbled across a crime in progress. A man holding a gun on a young girl. The jogger must have called it in.

So the young woman was on the way to the ER and the man was long gone. And from the way the blonde was calling out information and discussing details with the K-9 agents, he'd guess she had to be someone official, too. That and the big dog shadowing her summed it up.

She was an FBI agent. And the dog was obviously her K-9 partner. Off duty and on a run, but now on full speed ahead to find the man who'd tried to kill that girl. A girl she'd obviously tried to save, from what he'd seen.

Before Thomas could corner her, someone shouted out, "Nina, we've found another body. That makes two."

"Coming, Tim." She whirled like a little cyclone and took off.

Thomas's gut burned even hotter. Two bodies and one girl shot?

Could the man who'd done this be the assassin he'd come to Montana to find?

Nina did a final sweep of the scene and then turned to leave for headquarters. She needed to file her report and meet with a sketch artist so they could get an image of the shooter to put out to the local media. The team also now had the gruesome task of helping the medical examiner to identify the two female bodies. They'd already sent out the necessary warnings and alerts to be on the lookout, and she'd talked to SAC Max West a few minutes ago to give him an update. The few agents on holiday duty had come through on doing what needed to be done, and the local sheriff's department was on it, too.

Now if she could factor in why a US Deputy Marshal had suddenly shown up, she might be able to get home and have a good night's sleep. No, that wouldn't happen. She'd seen that gunman's cold black eyes and heard that poor girl screaming. She should probably stay at headquarters and work tonight.

"Okay, Deputy Marshal Grant," she said, marching up to the tall, big-boned man wearing the suede jacket and worn jeans. "I'm Agent Nina Atkins from the FBI Tactical K-9 Unit in Billings. What's your interest in this crime scene? Did you just happen to be in the neighborhood?"

He stared her in the face with a calm scrutiny that made her shiver inside her wicking outerwear. "I happen to be here on a case. Looking for a man who could allegedly be a hired assassin, reported to possibly be last seen in Montana, near Billings. The MO mentioned here tonight sounds like his. I'd hoped you could fill me in so we can compare notes."

Suspicious, Nina gave him a long once-over while she tried to sum him up. "I'm not so sure about that."

"I know your unit," he said. "I was assigned to protecting Esme Dupree earlier this year. She was in the witness protection program, before she bolted on me. I hear she testified against her brother Reginald and that she's married to one of your team members now."

Nina gave him another scrutinizing look, surprise sparking through her system. She did hazily recall his name from that investigation, but then being a new member of the team, she hadn't been front and center on every aspect of the Dupree case, so she'd never met him. Nina felt sure she would have remembered Thomas Grant. "So, Deputy Marshal Grant—"

"Thomas," he said, his stormy gray eyes still and quiet.

"So, Thomas, tell me more about who *you're* looking for and maybe I'll share what I know." She turned to go to her SUV, thinking he'd follow her.

When she looked around to check, she found him right behind her. How did he do that without her hearing him?

"Where're we going?" he asked with a wry smile, and a husky Southern accent that shouted Texas.

"*I'm* going back to headquarters to finish out this night," she retorted. "I've got to get my partner some food and let him rest. But we can talk after I put Sam in his kennel."

She hit the fob button and the rear door to the SUV popped open. After letting Sam inside, Nina made sure he had some water and a treat. Then she turned back to Tall, Blond and Intimidating.

She decided to stake her territory. "I need whatever information you have before I can confirm what happened here tonight."

"Of course. I'll follow you to headquarters," he said, not moving.

He looked so relaxed they could be talking about the weather. He wasn't going to give up.

"Why not tell me here?" she asked.

He glanced around and shrugged. "It's dark and cold, and if my gut is right…there's a storm coming. It's gonna be a long night. I could use some coffee and food. Y'all do have a kitchen there, right?" Then he blocked her in a going-bodyguard way. "Plus, that shooter could be watching."

Nina blinked, taking in that summary and the way his voice got all gravelly and husky again. This man made her nervous, which was silly. She didn't do nervous. But if the marshal had information on the person who'd committed this shooting, she didn't mind spending some time with him. And he had a point.

It wasn't safe in these woods.

"I've got all night," she said. "Follow me."

Thomas did as the lady asked, thinking he'd better not slip up and call her *a lady*. She'd probably deck him. If he wasn't so intent on finding Bernard Russo, he could have enjoyed getting to know Agent Nina Atkins a little better.

But that was probably a bad idea on all accounts. They both had dangerous, stressful jobs. One reason he didn't do long-term dating. That, and him being a nomad of sorts. Women wanted a settle-down kind of guy. He wasn't that.

And he had a feeling this particular woman wasn't a settle-down kind of girl, either.

Better to stick to business and get his man so he could decide where to land for the holidays. Hunting and fishing here in Montana, or maybe surfing and sailing in California? Too many options. Thomas thought about that as they traveled up the interstate to Billings.

A few minutes later, he turned into the drive leading to an impressive building in the center of the city. He'd heard the FBI Tactical K-9 Unit occupied two floors here, one for administration purposes and one for training.

Thomas followed Nina's SUV into a gated garage and found a spot two down from where she parked on the ground-floor level. They walked to the elevator together.

"The few team members we have on holiday duty are in and out," she explained. "We've had some suspicious fires in the downtown area that could be arson, but nothing much else has been going on around here until tonight."

"Well, if we're looking for the same man, your holiday duty might get a little more exciting," he replied, taking in the sight of her in the dull elevator lights.

She was buff and solid muscle, petite but with a stance that didn't mess around. Her hair shone a deep golden blond and went every which way around her face and neck. Her eyes were expressive and sparkling, a muted brown like apple cider and cinnamon.

Boy, did he have it bad. He needed to date more often. He was latching on to this woman like a puppy trying to form a bond.

Nina straightened from leaning on the elevator wall when the door opened. "I think this holiday season has already gotten exciting. We often have a lot of US Marshals coming around, but never one for Christmas. Santa must have decided I've been good this year."

Thomas had to chuckle at that sarcastic remark. Then he turned serious about what they had ahead of them. "Sorry you had to deal with this," he said. "I hope that girl makes it."

The agent gave an appreciative nod. "I'm praying for her to survive. We need to find the man who put a bullet in her shoulder."

If the man who'd shot that girl was indeed Bernard Russo, then they had a deadly killer to track down. A killer who this feisty agent had seen up close.

He could come after her.

And that would not be a good Christmas at all.

TWO

Nina sat down in a small conference room, her laptop on the table. She'd grabbed a quick shower in the locker room and put Sam in the capable hands of one of the trainers for some tender loving care. Now she was ready to get down to business. Thomas handed her a fresh cup of coffee and pulled out an electronic tablet.

"So you go first," she said, still wondering how he'd appeared out of thin air. But when she'd called Max West and given him the lowdown, the SAC had reassured her.

"Thomas Grant is a good man and one of the best in the business. He's been with the US Marshal Office for at least five years, so he's high ranking. You can take his word to the bank and, of course, he has jurisdiction in all fifty states and any US territories. Cooperate with him, but stay focused on your case. He knows to stand back and not overstep. But he is authorized to help out if he needs to. Send me the particulars, too. I can go over the reports at least. And if you need me…"

"Yes, sir. You enjoy your time with Katerina and her dad. I'll keep you posted."

Not that she minded so much that she had a US Marshal to deal with. The man was gorgeous in a way that reminded her of the movie character Thor that she and her friends drooled over. Getting her mind back to business, she let out a sigh and then stifled a yawn. "Sorry, long day. Go ahead."

Thomas opened his tablet. "Is this the man you saw tonight?"

Nina took a good look at the picture and nodded, her heart pumping as she had a flashback. "It sure looks like him. It was dark but the moon was full. He was taller than average. I remember the salt-and-pepper longish hair and the craggy skin." Then she wrapped her arms across her chest and said, "I thought you were going first."

Thomas gave her that wry smile again. "This *is* me going first. I wanted you to identify him. This is Bernard Russo. He's the man I'm looking for. We have reason to believe he's killed several people across the country from Florida to Montana, and who knows where else. He's a hired contractor. An assassin."

"And you're here to find him?"

"Yes. I got a tip that he'd possibly been sighted in Montana. Several assets reported seeing him around the state. He came here either to hide out or to take a job. He killed an informant we'd hidden to testify against a major drug ring in Texas."

"Killed, as in before you could move the informant into the witness protection program?"

"Yes, and we're not proud of it. We were moving him to a new location when someone shot out one of the tires on our transport vehicle and snatched the witness, after shooting two of our officers. They both survived, but didn't see the shooter."

"I took a different jogging path and came up on them tonight," Nina said, a delayed reaction coursing through her body. She set her coffee on the table and held her hands in her lap so he wouldn't see how they were beginning to shake. "I didn't have my weapon. Not even a Taser. I should have at least had that, or pepper spray. I didn't identify myself as FBI, but I did my best to stop him from killing her."

"You had Sam," he replied, his astute eyes watching her.

"Yes, my strongest weapon. That and lots of prayers." Sam was resting in his kennel in the training area while they talked. "I planned to order him to attack, but the man turned and shot at me and then turned the gun on the girl. Then I needed Sam to protect us while I tried to…save her."

She'd taken her shower while Thomas talked to some of the other agents, but she could still see the blood on her clothes and hands, could remember the girl's cold, pale body. A shiver moved down Nina's spine, reminding her how close that poor young woman had come to being murdered.

Help her, Lord. Help this poor girl so we can find out what's going on.

"And you *did* save her," Thomas said, as if he knew exactly what she was thinking. "She's alive because you came along at the right time."

"She's in surgery, so let's hope everything will be okay. He planned to kill her and dump her just like the others."

"So you think the other two females were killed by this same man?"

"I don't know. I'm speculating. But it makes sense

because he purposely brought her to that spot, from what we can tell. I'm waiting to hear from the medical examiner regarding their cause of death and their IDs. We'll have to notify their next of kin, too."

"A grisly undertaking," Thomas replied. "My gut tells me Russo is your man for all three crimes."

"I'll have to wait to concur with you on that, but yes, it's looking like a possibility."

He nodded. "Understood."

She leaned forward. "Sam must have picked up a strong scent, because after the shooter shot the girl and ran away, Sam immediately alerted on the two other graves. Shallow graves, a little over a foot and a half deep. The gunman knew that would keep anyone from detecting the scent of decaying bodies. Until Sam got a whiff anyway. I can't say how long they've been there, but the ME said maybe months."

Putting her head in her hands and raking her wet hair back, she said, "Sam and I have jogged by those woods for months now and…those girls were out there. All alone. Now, I'm questioning if Sam tried to alert me before and I maybe thought he'd seen a squirrel or some other animal. I should have caught this sooner." Lifting her head, she added, "The killer must be using that site as his burial ground since, according to the ME, one body has been there longer than the other one."

"Sam knows his business. He wasn't working when you jogged by before and he could have false alerted, since he was on downtime. But tonight, like you said, he picked up on the dangerous situation. The shooter's scent—maybe a cologne or aftershave, or maybe even from the coat he was wearing—caused Sam to search the area, and then he alerted on the bodies. Which makes it highly likely the same man killed those two."

"Not good news for any family, especially this time of year."

"No," the marshal said, his expression grim. "But it sounds as if you have a strong faith to carry you through. That's a plus."

"I couldn't do this without it," she admitted.

"I hear that," he said, that long Texas drawl moving like gentle fingers across her heart.

Nina didn't talk about her faith much but it was there, instilled in her by a strong, loving family. She was glad to hear Thomas apparently had the same shield.

They continued to talk about the details until she'd given him as much information as she could and he'd done the same for her.

"I think I'm going home," she said, standing to stretch. "I'll pick back up on the details there, since I probably won't get any sleep."

"I've got a room at the Wild Iris Inn," he said. "Sounded like a nice out-of-the-way spot. I didn't want to stay in Billings."

"The inn is the only place available near Iris Rock, and not far from my house," she said with a grin. "But you're in good hands. Miss Claire still works there part-time, but she's turned over management to Penny Potter, soon to be Penny Morrow. Penny plans to marry one of our agents—Zeke Morrow—on Valentine's Day next year."

She went on to tell him how Jake Morrow had been a double agent and how his half brother, Zeke, had come to help track him and had been in on his capture and death. But in spite of the horrible tragedy, several of the team members had somehow found true love. Why Nina had decided to share the joy with the marshal, she didn't know. Except that she wanted to believe in hope and love, even if she didn't have a significant other in her life right now.

And she didn't need anyone. She had enough trouble trying to prove herself as an agent.

"This year was rough for all of you," Thomas said, bringing her back to reality. "I'm glad everyone is safe and sound." They'd reached the doors to the parking garage. "Speaking of that, I'm walking you to your vehicle."

Nina blinked and stared up at him. "I'm parked near you, anyway, and I have Sam."

Thomas shook his head. "Look, let's get this part over with. I know you're strong and capable and tough or you wouldn't be here, but…a killer saw you tonight. You're a witness to an attempted murder by a very dangerous man. You're gonna need someone to watch your back."

She turned when they were almost to her vehicle. "Have you appointed yourself for that job?"

Before he could respond, a shot rang out and the windshield of the car next to them shattered. Thomas threw his body over Nina and pushed her to the ground. Another shot rang out, blasting a nearby wall.

Nina's heart pressed beats against her lungs. She couldn't breathe. And she couldn't get past the sure knowledge that Thomas had probably just saved her life.

An hour later, Nina and Thomas were back inside headquarters filing yet another report, and Thomas was now a partner in this investigation. He didn't mind that, since he needed to be a part of it if Russo was involved.

But that hadn't been established. This pattern didn't match Russo's way of taking care of business.

The shooter was nowhere to be found, and surveillance cameras didn't show anyone sneaking into the garage. So the shooter must have had a good view of where they were parked from an off-site spot. They'd canvassed the whole place and the surrounding buildings, and they'd put out more alerts on Russo. The techs were still trying to establish where he'd been hidden. But the destruction from the shots indicated a shotgun. Which meant he'd been close. Too close.

"He's after you," Thomas said to Nina, when they were alone. "You can't go back to your place tonight."

"I'll bunk here," Nina retorted, obviously not in the mood to be told what to do. "I've done it before. And I intend to keep digging. Dylan O'Leary is our best tech and he'll be back on this tomorrow. He'll do research based on what you've told us. Thanks for your help."

Thomas put his hands on his hips. "Are you dismissing me, Agent Atkins?"

She gave him a tired glare. "It's almost two in the morning. Don't you ever sleep?"

"Do you?"

She stood and paced, her green sweater long and droopy, her jeans old and worn. Locker clothes. But she looked cute in them. "Have you considered that he might have been aiming at you, Thomas?"

He rubbed his jaw. "Always a possibility, and yes, he could have taken both of us out and called it a day. But he missed, which is kind of surprising."

"Do you think he blinked, got the shakes?"

Thomas figured this man knew how to use any kind of weapon. "He could have been interrupted or startled, but why a shotgun? Maybe the darkness and seeing both of us together shook him. He sure wasn't expecting to see me here."

"Now he knows you're in town," she said, her fingers twisting in the cuffs of her sweater. "You might need to bunk here tonight, too."

Thomas hadn't planned on that. "I could hang around."

"That's not what I said."

"And I'm saying I can hang around." Seeing the objection on her heart-shaped face, he held up his hands in defense. "Hey, neither of us is gonna get much sleep. We can get a head start on the facts and get our ducks in a row."

She stared at him, her eyes changing so swiftly he felt as if he was chasing glints of pure copper. "Are you hungry?" she finally asked.

Did this mean she would listen to reason and let him do his job?

"Starving. That snack cake I found in the machine went stale in my stomach a couple hours ago."

"I think we have leftover hamburgers in the fridge. Somebody brought in a whole dozen or so from our favorite downtown eatery."

"Sounds good. Lead me to the kitchen."

Nina shot him another mixed-message glance. "We're in this together now, Deputy Marshal. And I have orders from my SAC to cooperate with you whether I like it or not."

"Won't be the first time a woman has tried to resist my charms," he quipped, hoping to lighten the mood.

"I'm an agent first," she retorted. "And a woman second."

Okey-dokey. "Whatever you say, ma'am."

Thomas followed her through the maze of offices and cubicles, thinking at least he had someone interesting to work with. This one would try her best to keep him on his toes.

And he'd try his best to keep her alive.

THREE

"The girl's awake."

Nina rose from her chair, boots hitting the floor, and followed Dylan O'Leary, the agency's tech expert, down the hallway. "Is she talking?"

Thomas saw them and came out of the chair he'd found in a corner of the big cubicle-filled room. "Identity?"

Dylan kept right on going, his glasses stuck to his nose as always. "Kelly Denton. Twenty-four years old. College student who grew up in Helena and worked for former State Senator Richard Slaton. She'd moved away from Helena this year but went home to visit her parents for Christmas. They've verified that and said she had left a message that she was spending the night with a friend. That was night before last. They're on their way here." Dylan hurried off and then turned back around. "Oh, and don't mention the other girls to her yet. We're still trying to establish if they're connected. She could voluntarily fill in the blanks."

"Got it. We're on our way to investigate." Nina turned to Thomas. "Ready to question our witness?"

"Been ready," he said, grabbing his coat.

Soon, they were in Nina's SUV headed east to the Billings Medical Center.

"How'd you sleep?" Nina asked, recalling how she'd tossed and turned and had nightmares the entire three hours she'd tried to sleep.

"Like a baby," he quipped with a wry smile. "I was exhausted after that long drive from Texas."

"Why'd you drive across the country in the dead of winter?"

"I like long drives. Helps me think. Plus I was trying to track Russo's every step so I could establish that he drove here, too. Found some rental cars he'd used here and there, but nothing concrete. So you didn't see or hear him leaving in a vehicle last night?"

Nina shook her head and merged into traffic. "Nope. He ran away, headed into the woods. I still don't get it. He could have shot me, too."

"Maybe Sam distracted him. Sam would have gone after him, don't you think?"

"Possibly. I'm sure he'd have brought down the man. But I was worried that he'd shoot Sam and return to finish the job. Why do you think he ran like that?"

"He panicked. He wasn't expecting anyone to stumble on the scene."

"Yes. Sam and I did surprise him. I know the woods beyond that spot and across the stream are on private property. Someone owns a hunting lodge up there. He could have hidden in it, possibly, but until we find out who owns that place, we can't get a warrant to look."

"But he shot at you—shot at us—last night," Thomas reminded her. "And missed. Russo's trained never to miss. Something's not right about this whole thing."

"I'm kind of glad he missed," Nina replied, wondering what was bugging Thomas. "So…we both think something's off here, right?"

"He's after Kelly. We'll have to watch the hospital. He might be trying to distract us while he moves in on her."

"We *do* have her surrounded," Nina said. "Agents twenty-four/seven, guarding her room."

"I hope that will keep Russo away."

Thomas didn't sound so confident, but they were dealing with a trained assassin. Nina couldn't blame the marshal for being concerned. "Remember, for all he knows she's dead. We only broadcasted that we were looking for him. Not that he'd tried to kill someone."

"But that kind of news tends to leak," Thomas replied. "We might need to move her, and quickly."

They made it to the hospital without incident and were inside safe and sound in under an hour.

After getting permission from the hospital staff to interrogate Kelly Denton, they went into her room. The guard at the door was a massive sheriff deputy. No one would get past that man.

Nina approached the pale young girl, remembering her there in the moonlight last night. The bullet had just missed her heart and had become lodged in her left shoulder, but the surgery had gone as well as could be expected. Her prognosis was good, barring the killer didn't come back. Now if they could match that bullet the surgeon had dug out to the gun that shot her, they'd have an idea what kind of weapon the killer was carrying. A stretch, but something to hope for.

"Kelly, do you remember me?" Nina asked, hoping the girl would recognize her.

She moved her head and stared with bleary eyes.
"I… I don't know."

"I saw you last night with that man…"

The girl's face turned deadly pale and all the numbers and graphs on the monitor jittered and changed.
"He tried to kill me."

"I know," Nina said, glancing to where Thomas stood by the closed drapery over the window. "I was jogging and I came upon you."

"You saved my life."

"I tried to stop him," Nina said. "But he shot at me and he *did* shoot you." Touching Kelly's hand, she said, "Can you tell us how you wound up with him, so far from Helena?"

"He…he took me when I was walking to my car," the girl said, her whispers full of fear. "I'd just left a restaurant. He was waiting with an open van and he had a gun."

Nina wrote down the name of the place. "And he drove you here to Billings?"

"Yes, he tied me up and put a blindfold on me. I was in the back—a small van."

"Do you know the color or model?"

"No. He shoved me inside and put the blindfold on me and then tied me up. I couldn't get to my purse or phone." She tried to sit up, her eyes wild now. "Where is my phone? I need my phone."

"We didn't find your purse or phone," Nina said, gently lowering her back down. "He probably tossed them."

Thomas shot Nina a knowing glance. "Can you tell us anything else, Kelly?"

The girl lay still, her fingers clutching the light blanket spread over her. Nina glanced at Thomas. She'd worked with enough traumatized women to know when someone was truly terrified.

"He kept asking about a key," Kelly said in a weak voice, her gaze darting down and to the left. "I don't know what he was talking about. I don't know anything. I shouldn't have gone back there."

"Back where?" Thomas asked.

"To Helena. I—I should have stayed away. When can I go home?"

Thomas stepped away from the window. The girl's vitals were going crazy. "Are you sure you don't remember something? A detail we could use?" he asked, keeping his gaze on the beeping machines. "Were you in danger before you left Helena?"

Kelly gripped the blankets, clutching them like a lifeline. "No. I can't talk about this. I just want to go home. When are my parents coming?"

A nurse came in, her expression stern. "Time's up."

"Your parents are on their way," Nina said, wishing she could comfort the girl more and find out what she seemed so afraid of. "You're safe here. We have a guard on your room."

"Is he coming back?" Kelly asked, fear in her eyes. "That man? If he does, he'll kill me! He told me he'd kill me."

"Not if we can help it," Thomas said, honesty in each word. "If you remember anything—or decide to tell us the truth—please tell the deputy and he'll alert us. The more we know, the sooner we can end this and then you'll be safe."

The girl didn't seem so sure. She was frightened, and for good reason. Nina talked to the deputy and felt reassured when he told her one of her team members would be here later with his K-9 partner.

Nina tugged at Thomas's jacket sleeve when they reached the elevator. "Let's stay here a while. We can see her door from the waiting room. And…we can talk to her parents after they arrive and they've seen her. Maybe they can shed some light on whatever she's not telling us."

He nodded. "Okay, but I'm hungry. Let's go down to the cafeteria."

"Didn't you eat one of those pastries from Petrov Bakery? Or maybe even two?"

He gave her a mock frown. "That was breakfast."

"Yes, only two hours ago."

"I have to be fed every two hours."

Nina snorted and shook her head. "Right." Then she said, "Okay, we'll get you fed, but then I'm hanging out here. I'm worried about that girl."

"She's hiding something, no doubt," Thomas said, turning serious in that lightning quick way she'd noticed. "She said she should never have gone back to Helena. She knows about the key and she panicked when she realized she didn't have her phone."

"And you can read minds?" Nina asked in surprise. But she had to agree with him.

"I can read people," Thomas replied. "That girl is scared, of course. But it's more. I think she purposely dropped that bit about the key to give us a hint. She's terrified and that's understandable, but she said she didn't know *anything*. Which to me means she knows a lot."

"You have a point," Nina said, as they hurried through the buffet line. She got a salad and Thomas ordered meat loaf, mashed potatoes with gravy and a giant biscuit. The man knew how to down some serious food. How did he stay in such good shape? "She did seem pretty emphatic about not knowing anything."

"My gut is burning," he retorted.

"Maybe that's just the pastries and the meat loaf," she said with a grin.

"Ha, ha." He chewed on a chunk of meat loaf before he answered. "No, this is my gut telling me I'm right."

"Are you always right?"

"Not always. But about 99 percent of the time."

She had to laugh. He made her do that. "Tell me about you, Deputy Marshal. So I get from the accent and the way you can go all cowboy that you grew up in Texas."

He leaned close, his gray eyes twinkling. "Why, yes ma'am, I sure did. Texas through and through. Went to college in Austin, got my degree in criminal justice, worked in law enforcement in several capacities, applied to become a US Marshal and I've been one for five years now. Based out of Florida for a while, but I had a hankering to come back West."

His smile was pro but his eyes went beyond professional. They turned all smoky and flirtatious in a quicksilver way that made her insides shake like the Jell-O the man at the next table was trying to eat.

"You like your job, don't you?" she asked, to keep the conversation moving. To make his eyes change back to a safe level of gray.

"I do. I mean, chasing bad guys, yeah, what's not to like?"

Nodding, she laughed at that. "Same here. I love being a K-9 officer for the FBI."

"It's dangerous work."

"You mean for a woman."

"I mean for anyone."

Then he did the stern, serious thing again. "What put that chip on your shoulder?"

"Oh, you mean the chip about how hard it is to be a woman in what most consider a man's profession?"

"Yeah, that one."

"I told you I come from a big family, right?"

"Yes."

"Well, I have four brothers. All in law enforcement."

"Ouch. So you joined up because you had to prove yourself to them."

"And to my father, who is a retired sheriff."

"Whoa. Can't they see how good you are at your job?"

"No, what they see is their little sister trying to do a job they think is not suitable for her. And…they're all kind of jealous that I'm in this elite FBI unit when they're locals who work hard."

"They should be proud of you," Thomas said, the passion in his words shaking her. "I never had much of a family. My parents divorced when I was little and I kind of got shoved from my grandparents to my aunts and uncles. My dad worked construction and traveled a little too much, and my mom skipped out on me once they got divorced."

Nina's heart did a little flip. No wonder the man moved around like a nomad. "Do you ever go back to Texas?"

"Yeah. My granddad left me a small ranch there. I head straight to it when I need some downtime. He was a good man, a churchgoer, just not an affectionate man."

Nina wanted to keep talking, but they needed to get back. She stood up and said, "Well, remember, if we get through this, you are definitely coming to my family's house for Christmas."

Then she realized she'd overstepped and wished she could take it back. Maybe they'd be done before Christmas.

He grinned, which only made him even more handsome. "Oh, so you want to make those ornery brothers even more jealous. I mean, who wouldn't be impressed with a US Marshal, right?"

She shook her head at his antics. "Right."

They'd just turned the corner back to the waiting area when a male nurse hurried up to the guard at Kelly Denton's door. When the nurse saw them, he took off running in the other direction.

FOUR

Thomas went into action, tackling the man dressed in hospital scrubs in time to stop him from getting away. Another nurse immediately called security. The hospital would go on lockdown until they cleared this up.

The deputy who'd been guarding Kelly's room didn't miss a beat. He helped Thomas by putting a heavy, booted foot on the man's backbone while Thomas grabbed his hands and cuffed him. Together, they lifted him up and slammed him down in a nearby chair. Thomas searched his scrubs and found a small knife.

Nina held her gun on the man until she knew he was secure. "I'll check on the girl."

By now, nurses and doctors were merging inside the room where Kelly Denton lay sleeping. She woke with a start, her eyes wide. "What's going on?"

"Everything's okay," Nina said, thinking they should have stayed close by. But at least they had a suspect now. Only the man they'd tackled wasn't Russo. "Just a ruckus outside. You're safe." Better not to upset her again so soon.

But she had to wonder if the girl needed to be moved again.

When the medical team had checked and rechecked Kelly, her parents came in. After they'd seen her and were reassured she was on the mend, Nina took them outside and explained what had happened.

"Do you know of any reason someone would want to harm your daughter?" she asked.

"No," they both replied.

"But she's been away for almost a year," her mom added. "Maybe someone followed her to Helena?"

"It's your job to find that out," Mr. Denton said. "I thought she was being protected."

"She is. We've taken the man into custody, but he's not talking. He won't tell us who hired him, but he's not going anywhere, I promise."

"They could send someone else," Kelly's mother whispered, tears in her eyes. "Can't we take her home to Helena?"

Nina glanced at Thomas, who had joined them. He frowned and pondered that. "The doctors aren't ready to release her yet, but when they do, we'll have to send someone with her if the man who shot her is still at large. Do you have any other place you could take her for a few days?"

"My parents live about thirty miles from Helena in a gated community. We could take her there," Mrs. Denton offered.

"I'll call ahead when it's time and if it comes to that," Thomas said. "She could become a possible witness in a federal case. We can help protect her here and… we might have to put her into witness protection if this drags out too long."

The Dentons both seemed confused and frightened

by that. "You don't mean forever, do you?" her mother asked with tears in her eyes.

Nina shot Thomas a thankful glance. "We hope it won't come to that. For now, we'll be in touch to coordinate things as soon as she's clear to leave the hospital. And we'll have someone here to escort all of you to your destination."

"Meantime, we have the deputy and a K-9 team member here, so she'll have two people guarding her door at all times," Thomas added. "And if she tells either of you anything, please let us know. We can't help her if we don't know what we're dealing with."

Kelly's parents nodded, but they looked shell-shocked.

"We can also have her moved to another room," Nina said, promising to talk to the hospital administrators.

She and Thomas went to take care of the details. Soon, everything was in place to move Kelly to a room near the nurses' station, where she could be monitored more closely by both the guards and the staff.

Having assured her parents that Kelly would be safe, and telling them they'd be watched, too, Nina and the marshal went back to headquarters, hoping to question the man they'd taken into custody.

Three hours later, after questioning the noncommunicative suspect and then going over files and trying to establish leads, all they had to go on was the suspect's rap sheet of petty crime, and the fact that he refused to give them any information. Robby Collier was a local who'd been minding his own business in a bar when he'd been offered a job paying a huge amount of money.

He regretted that decision, but said he couldn't tell them anything more. "The man made it pretty clear if I got caught, I was on my own. I don't know nothing except I was supposed to take down the guard at the door."

"I guess you didn't think that part through, either," Nina had noted, before they left him locked up tight.

"He thinks he's safer in lockup than out there," Thomas said now. "This has Russo all over it. He hired someone to bring down the guard, which means he was probably in the hospital, too. I'm surprised he didn't shoot dear Robby on the spot for failing in his mission."

"But they locked the place down," Nina said, regretting that she'd left Sam with the handlers here while they'd gone to the hospital. Sam could have helped chase down the assailant. "He had to get away quick. Why would he send someone so unreliable and, well, green?"

"He messed up and left a witness, something he's never done before. And now, because of one determined K-9 officer, he wants this over and done. He has to know you're FBI by now. You're both still in danger."

"So because the heat's on, he turned to desperate measures and sent that clown to do his dirty work," Nina said.

"Russo knows how to get away in a hurry," Thomas pointed out. "He wouldn't hang around since this mission got botched, too. But…he's not going to give up. Like our Robby, he knows he's in serious danger himself. Whoever hired him has been informed by now that things went bad."

"But how did he know the girl wasn't dead? We haven't released any details to the press."

"The crime scene," Thomas said. "It was active and it got a lot of attention. Anyone could have seen the first responders carting Kelly away. I walked right up. A reporter or newshound could have easily done the same."

"Russo could have still been hanging around, too," she said, glad Sam had picked up his scent. But then, Sam did specialize in cadaver detection and he'd done that job to perfection last night. After that, a lot of people had passed through those woods.

Tired and unable to gather her thoughts, Nina stood up and stretched. "I'm going home tonight. Tim and Zeke checked my place and it's safe. No one's been there that we can tell."

"That you know of," Thomas retorted. "You're safer here."

"I'm safe at my house, too," she replied. "I have security and I have Sam. And I have several weapons."

"A woman after my own heart," he deadpanned. "I'll be two miles down the road, letting Penny Potter and the Wild Iris staff pamper me."

"Good." She kind of wished he'd offered to at least come to her house for coffee. But then, they'd both drunk enough of that dark brew...and she had to resist whatever was brewing between them, too. "I'm going to decorate the tree I brought home the other day before all the needles fall off, and make myself a big cup of hot chocolate. Maybe watch a sappy Christmas movie just for kicks."

In reality she'd grab some popcorn and go back over this bizarre case. But he didn't need to know that.

They walked out together, both searching the area for another sniper, Sam trotting at their feet and two armed guards set up in the parking garage. When they reached their vehicles, Thomas turned to her. "I'm kind of lonely, you know. I haven't had a real Christmas in years. I'd enjoy helping you decorate that dying tree."

Nina's heart betrayed her by bouncing all around her chest. "Are you inviting yourself to dinner, Thomas?"

"Are you asking me to dinner, Nina?"

"No."

He laughed. "Then yes, I'm inviting myself to dinner, but I really only wanted to decorate the tree. But if you insist…"

"I don't recall insisting."

"But you were thinking it, right?"

She wondered how he did that. No wonder bad guys tried to steer clear of him.

"No," she said with a laugh, "I was thinking too bad I don't cook."

He leaned close, his whisper half a step away. "Even better. I do."

She'd never had a man cook for her before. Should she tell him to get lost? Or should she let him follow her home so they could brainstorm this case all over again?

She glanced down at the rottweiler. "What do you think, Sam? Should Thomas cook us dinner, but only because we want to pick his brain later and try to figure out things on this investigation?"

The big dog looked from her to the marshal and let out a woof.

"I think that was a yes," Thomas said, his handsome face full of a triumphant smugness.

"Only because it's Christmas and you're a stranger in a strange land."

"I hear that," he replied. Then he scanned the parking garage. "We sure don't need to be standing here out in the open arguing about it, so let's go."

Nina turned off the security alarm and rushed inside the tiny cottage she'd lived in since she'd arrived in Iris Rock a few months ago. The drive to and from

Billings could be tricky on a night such as this, when a new snowfall seemed imminent. But she'd grown up in the bitter cold of Wyoming and knew how to mount snow tires on her vehicle and how to use her head and her driving skills while braking. She was pretty capable at most things, except when it came to kitchen duty. But she wasn't really serious about letting Thomas cook for her.

"What was I thinking?" she asked Sam. He shadowed her, hoping for his own dinner. "I don't have food and I don't cook. I can't offer him your dinner, right?"

The dog shot her a doleful glance that stated *"Nope."*

Knowing Thomas would be close behind her, she tidied up, clearing away the local paper and some research books and novels off the couch, then hurried to change into jeans and a blue-and-white-striped wool sweater. She was running a comb through her tousled hair and putting on pink lip gloss when the doorbell rang.

She'd never actually invited anyone here before. Especially not a man.

"Mom would be proud," she whispered to Sam.

Sam woofed a positive approval that the person at her door came in peace.

But she checked the peephole, anyway.

Too much tall stood there.

Now she was sweating in her sweater.

"C'mon in," she said, her words deceitfully calm. "I'm going to be honest. I'm not sure I have anything on hand to make an edible meal."

Shrugging out of his heavy coat, Thomas took in the small living room and galley kitchen. Nina watched him for signs of disappointment or regret. But in typical law-

278 A Killer Christmas

man fashion, he seemed to be sizing up security—and taking in information on how she lived.

Heavy beige curtains covered the sliding doors to the tiny backyard that she and Sam loved to play in. The furniture came with the place, and it was mismatched and clunky.

Wishing she'd taken a little time to decorate the rooms with her own sense of style, Nina crossed her arms over her midsection and stood her ground. She worked too much to worry about making it into *Architectural Digest*.

"It ain't much, but it's home," she chirped, motioning to the big doors and several windows. "On good days, I can see the Pryor Mountains, which is kind of cool since I could also see them from my bedroom in Wyoming, growing up."

His stormy eyes widened. "What, you circled the mountain and settled on the other side?"

"Something like that." Looking at her sad little home through the eyes of someone else made Nina self-conscious and almost embarrassed. But she shook that off the way she shook off everything she couldn't deal with. "Let's see what we can round up."

She headed to the refrigerator and stared at the barren shelves. "I see a few carrots and two potatoes." Then she checked the freezer. "And a bag of chicken breasts that might have come with the house."

Thomas snorted and gently moved her aside. "The date on the chicken is still within the safe zone. We'll hope the same with the potatoes and carrots. Do you stock any canned goods?"

She nodded and opened an overhead cabinet by the

refrigerator. "Oh, look, chicken noodle soup and tomato soup. If only we had some crackers."

"We don't need crackers," he stated, already rolling up his sleeves. "You get the decorations ready and I'll get dinner going."

"What exactly do you plan to cook?" she asked, wondering how she'd managed to get in this predicament in the first place.

"The Thomas Grant special, ma'am," he said in his best Texas drawl. "You're gonna love it."

She doubted that, but she'd give it a shot since she couldn't kick him out now. Sam's head moved in ping-pong style back and forth between them. Obviously, he smelled something in the air. Something distinctive and different.

Another human in the kitchen. Or a tad too much of some new and exciting undercurrent.

Soon, Thomas had the chicken and potatoes browning in a big pot, along with some onions and peppers he'd discovered in a crisper drawer with all the joy of a kid opening a present. He hummed while he cooked.

Nina pretended to be unraveling Christmas lights, but she couldn't help glancing over at him. A giant wearing boots had taken over her home. And it was beginning to smell good, which caused her stomach to make strange noises and her heart to do funny jumps and bumps.

Finally, after he'd dismantled cans and rummaged for spices and splashed this and that into the pot, he turned it to simmer and came to sit beside her on the now-too-small floral love seat in front of the tiny electric fireplace. "Chicken noodle soup and biscuits coming up in about a half hour."

"Really?" she asked, surprised. "We could have just opened a can for the soup. And I'm not sure how you managed biscuits."

"Really, I opened two cans for my special soup. And added a few special ingredients."

"I'm almost afraid to ask."

"Then don't."

"And the biscuits?"

"You had flour, milk, eggs and baking powder."

"My mom restocks every time she comes to visit."

"Well, that turned out to be a good thing."

His eyes were so amazing. They'd turned as blue-gray as the storm she'd seen over the big sky at dusk and just as mysterious.

Nina laughed and inhaled. "Well, I have to admit that smells better than the soggy pizza I usually bring home."

"You're almost out of protein bars," he replied. "I didn't throw your last two into the pot."

"I'm so glad you didn't."

They bantered back and forth while they got the lights straightened out and wrapped around the sad little evergreen.

"I think this tree is going to be lost in a burst of color," Thomas stated. "Where did you buy it? 'Cause I think you need a refund."

"Ha, funny." She shrugged. "A kid was selling them to make money to buy a bicycle. I felt sorry for him. He'd obviously scoured the back forty and…found the best of the lot."

"We could find you a prettier tree," Thomas pointed out. "But this one is kind of tugging at my heartstrings in that Charlie Brown kind of way."

"I wish you could see the tree my mom and dad put up each year," she replied, not even thinking about her words. "It's fresh and has to be at least nine feet tall and covers one corner of the den in our log house. Dad fusses every year, but he loves hanging the lights on the tree and along the staircase. We all gather on Christmas Eve and sing carols and hymns, and then we eat a big meal of barbecue and all the trimmings. My brothers and their families all live nearby and I usually show up at the last minute and then...it's Christmas."

"That *is* Christmas," Thomas said, his eyes dark with a longing that tore at Nina's heart. "Sounds wonderful."

"You'll see, Thomas," she said. "My family has a steadfast rule that we can bring anyone we want home for Christmas."

He nodded, but he didn't look so sure about that invitation.

Did he think she was pushing him in the wrong way? Nina wondered. Because she'd done it again. Invited him to go home with her for Christmas. She wouldn't ask anymore.

Or was he too afraid to stop being alone to enjoy being with someone during the holidays?

She was about to ask him that when the buzzer on the stove dinged and caused her to step back.

"Dinner is ready," he said, that distant longing still in his eyes, his smile beautiful but full of resolve and regret. "We'd better eat so we can finish making this tree as special as the one you just described."

FIVE

"I have to admit, that was some pretty good soup. Noodles and potatoes and carrots and…what kind of spices did you put in there?"

Thomas grinned and winked. "You had some ginger and rosemary stashed away in the spice drawer."

Nina hit a hand against her head. "Oh, my mom gave me a whole spice rack last time I was home. I think she was trying to give me a hint. You know, get some spice in your life and find someone and get married and make babies."

"All that from a couple of shakes into the pot?"

"All that and more," she replied, before taking a sip of her hot chocolate. "She also gave me this cocoa mix."

He toasted her with his own. "I think mixing up the recipe in a Mason jar is sweet. It's a mama thing."

Remembering he'd never had that, she nodded. "I have a good family so I shouldn't complain."

Misreading her statement for pity, he put down the mug with a motif of a laughing reindeer centered on it. "Hey, don't apologize or downplay that on my account. I'm okay. I have a good job and I get to travel the whole country having fun."

"Fun? You call some of the things we deal with fun?"

"No. I said I was having fun, not that it is fun."

"Oh, so that makes a big difference."

"I love my job," he admitted with a sheepish shrug. "If I can't have a big family, I can help someone else get home to theirs."

"I guess that's a good way to look at it," she replied, turning serious while her heart did that strange little beat again. "Except those two dead girls never had that chance."

"We'll find him," Thomas said. "I have a steadfast rule. I always get the bad guy."

"I try to enforce that same rule," she said. "But I'm still new to the team. I've been here almost a year now and things are getting better, but I never wanted to up my status by stumbling into something this twisted and strange."

"You were the first officer on the scene. Your SAC is wise to stand back and let you do your job."

"Maybe," she said. And then she asked Thomas something she'd been wondering. "But is he doing that because of my abilities or because *you* just happened along to help out?"

Surprise filled Thomas's eyes. "Does it matter? We're in it together now."

She stood and took their empty mugs to the sink. "But would I be carrying the same clout if you weren't here?"

Irritation shadowed his expression. "Are we seriously having this conversation? Am I a threat to you, Nina?"

"No. But am I an equal to you?"

"You're way above my pay scale, even if you earn less than me," he said, gathering his coat. "I came here for one reason—to bring a killer back to Texas. I can't change the circumstances that brought us together, but I intend to do my job. But you seem to have a one track mind on getting bad guys, so that makes you more valuable than me right now."

In spite of you, she figured he wanted to say. He intended to do his job in spite of her.

Wishing she'd kept her mouth shut, Nina pushed at her hair and then tugged at her sweater. "I'm sorry. I want to do my job, too."

"Then cut that kind of talk," he said, jamming his meaty arms into his coat. "It's been a long day. I think I'll head back to the inn. I would offer to check the place, but I don't want to offend your stubborn need to measure up."

She deserved that, Nina decided. Why had she even let him see her insecurities? That only made her look weak and helpless.

"Thanks, Thomas," she said in a low voice. "For helping with the tree and…for cooking."

"You can enjoy the leftovers tomorrow night," he retorted.

Alone.

The silence shouted that one word between them.

He turned for the door, Nina close behind.

And then the whole house went black.

Sam growled quietly. Nina didn't move, but she crouched low next to her partner. Listening, she heard a noise out in the carport attached to the house. It sounded as if someone had stumbled into the empty trash can. Then she heard the groan of something heavy being shoved aside.

The rottweiler woofed. "Sam, quiet," she ordered. "Stay."

She could hear Thomas by the door. "Nina, stay down."

"I am down," she whispered. "But I don't have my weapon and I never reset the alarm after we came in tonight."

"I've got my weapon," he said. "And he'd have probably disengaged the alarm, anyway."

He came near and grasped her by the arm. "It could be the storm. Where's your circuit breaker?"

"The kitchen, by the door to the carport. But I heard something—"

"I did, too."

"Let's check."

He didn't argue. Together, they stayed down and worked their way to the kitchen. Nina sat and scooted toward the corner where the circuit box was located. "I'll need some light," she whispered.

Thomas followed her and pulled out his phone and handed it to her. Using the faint moonlight creeping through the shuttered blinds, she found the flashlight app and slowly worked her way up the wall.

But before she could check the circuit breaker, the door right beside her jiggled and a shot rang out, splintering the wood and sending fragments flying as Thomas threw her to the floor.

"He's bold," the marshal said, sitting up with his weapon drawn.

"Shoot," she suggested, wishing she had her own gun.

Thomas got in front of Nina on one knee and shot back, adding more bullet holes to the shattered wood.

"I guess if he's dead, we'll have to explain," she whispered. "But I would technically be protecting my castle."

"I'll go and find him," Thomas suggested instead. "If I didn't get him already."

Nina thought about what she'd have done if Thomas hadn't been here. She would have grabbed her weapon and taken control. "Or I could open the door and let Sam do his job."

"Good idea. But both those strategies are risky."

"We need to call for backup."

"The best plan. And if they don't make it in time, I'm shooting to kill."

That's what she would have done. Weapon, backup, shoot to defend and protect.

She made the call with his phone, giving her name, rank and location.

When they heard a bang against the glass sliding doors, Nina ordered Sam to bark and guard. The dog headed in that direction, sounding every bit as fierce as he looked.

"Guess I missed," Thomas said.

"He won't give up," Nina replied.

"What is he doing here?" the marshal retorted. "He has to know we're both in here and armed."

"And that I have security. Not that it matters now."

"He's prowling, for some reason. He didn't get to Kelly, so now he's after us."

Another shot streaked through the air, this time shattering a window just above their heads.

Nina jumped up and looked through the slats of the blinds. "If I can see him, I might be able to ID him as the man in the woods."

"He's toying with us," Thomas answered. "To flush us out."

"He'll shoot us both if we try to get out. And if we don't, he'll keep shooting until he hits one of us."

"Agreed…" The big man shifted and eyed the side door that held a scatter-shot scar. "I'm not sure what his plan is, but he's angry, so he's enjoying this."

Nina moved around the small area where they were crouched. She stood, but Thomas pulled her back down. "Don't try to locate him. He'll be expecting that."

"I wasn't," she said in a weak whisper. "I wanted to grab the hot chocolate my mom made. I don't want it to get shot."

Thomas fell for her just a little bit more after that soft-spoken confession. But he had to protect the stubborn woman so they could share that hot chocolate.

"We'll worry about that later," he said, holding her down. "We'll have to sit right here until help comes."

"I don't want to sit," she replied. "Let me go around the house and at least try to find him. Sam will show me the trail." Sam stood guarding the sliding glass doors.

"We wait until we can't take it anymore," he replied. "It's too risky."

"But I need my weapon. It's what I'd do if I were here alone. I'd get to my weapon and go after him."

"But you're not alone, and right now, I don't want to argue about it."

Nina squirmed and held on to the jar of hot chocolate. "I don't like your being here, but I'm glad you are."

"You are a paradox," he retorted.

Sam's woofs sounded like questions. *"What's the plan?"*

"I vote we make a run for it now," Nina said, her tone decisive. "I won't sit here and wait to die."

"Okay." Thomas helped her up and gave her his coat. "Put this on. We'll go out the kitchen door and use our vehicles as a shield if he starts shooting."

"That'll work," she said, already preparing. She summoned Sam and ordered him to guard. "For now," she told Thomas.

The marshal went ahead and slowly cracked open the side door. The burst of cold air nearly took his breath away, but the blast of the next shot caused him to duck down and slam the door again.

"Are you sure you want to go out there?" he asked Nina.

"What choice do we have?"

"Once we get out, I can circle back and take him," Thomas replied. "If he's still here."

Nina nodded, concern in her eyes. At least she hadn't argued with him.

While Nina hadn't parked her vehicle under the carport, she had pulled it up alongside the open garage. But when Thomas tried to open the door again, and wider this time, it moved only a couple inches.

"He's blocked us in. What do you have in that trash can?"

"I just emptied it," she said. Then she let out a breath. "I have a potting bench right next to it. He must have wedged it against the can."

"Nina?"

She eyed the situation from behind him and then carefully placed her hot chocolate mix in a nearby cabinet. "We're trapped," she said, her tone calm, all things considered. "He's trapping us until he can find a way in."

"But *we'll* find a way *out*," Thomas said. "If I can shove the table away a few more inches and we run fast, we might be able to get out before he returns to the garage. He must be making his way around the house and back."

"It's that or die trying," Nina said. "I need my weapon. I think I can get to it in the linen closet."

"No. No time."

He could tell she wanted to argue, but she clamped her mouth shut and silently glared at him in the muted moonlight. Then she called "Come" to Sam.

"Okay then," Thomas said, glad for another small victory. "On three, we crouch and run toward my truck." He turned and pulled his coat over her head. "Keep that on, okay?" The coat's suede skin and shearling lining might shield her from the shooter's aim if she kept running.

"Okay," she said in a reluctant whisper, followed by, "Thomas, thank you."

"Don't thank me yet," he said. Then he shoved against the door and heard the potting table groaning. Thomas grunted and pushed his way through, ignoring the spattering of shots all around them. Both the trash can and the heavy potting table actually served as deflectors.

Nina hurried along behind him, Sam bringing up the rear in silence. The next shot tore a hole in the tin carport roof. Thomas shoved her ahead of him, behind his truck. "Get underneath," he said, urging her to crawl between the big tires.

"Sam, come," she called again. The K-9 got on his belly and did as he'd been trained to do.

Soon, they were safe under the truck's heavy armor.

Thomas lay on his belly, his chest and head lifted, and listened for the footsteps he knew would be coming. It didn't take long.

"I'll try to sneak around," he whispered against Nina's sweet-smelling hair.

The crunch and cracking of boots hitting snow and dirt stopped him. Too late.

Nina pointed to the left.

Thomas nodded. If he could take aim, he could at least maim the intruder.

The man inched within a few feet from them in a matter of seconds. Nina pointed to Sam. Thomas nodded. What better way to take the man down and keep him alive to talk?

Nina raised herself up, about to sound the attack command, when they heard sirens on the road.

The man turned and took off running. Nina shouted, "Attack!"

Sam bolted from under the truck and went into the woods, following the scent of the stranger. Nina pushed away Thomas's coat and started to follow, but he pulled her back. "Wait for backup."

"Give me your weapon," she shouted. Snow was falling all around them now, and her house was full of bullet holes and scattershot.

Thomas shook his head, glad when Max West stalked toward them and asked, "Agent Atkins, are you all right?"

"Yes, sir," Nina answered. Then she launched into a full report, Sam's fierce barking making her fidget. "I need to pursue the suspect, sir."

Max put his hand on her arm. "We've got it covered. Why don't you let the EMTs check out your injuries?"

"I don't have any injuries," she retorted, anger marking each word.

"Yes, you do," Thomas said, taking her by the arm. She was bleeding from her left shoulder.

SIX

"I'm fine," Nina kept telling everyone. "It's a flesh wound." Sam now stood at attention near where she sat in the back of the open ambulance, with a heavy blanket around her and a big bandage wrapped around her upper left arm. "I'll be okay. I just want to go to bed and sleep for twelve hours."

"Not in this house," Thomas told her. "You're coming to the inn with me."

Nina shook her head. "I want to stay here."

"No," Max said from behind Thomas. "It's either the inn or the bunk room at headquarters. Or I'll take you out to the ranch."

Nina let out a groan of frustration. Three windows shot into rubble and gunshot holes in the side and front doors. The landlord would not be happy, but at least she had renter's insurance. Filing that report would be such fun.

"I'll probably have to move, anyway," she said, with another huff of frustration.

Agent Zeke Morrow strolled up with his Australian shepherd, Cheetah. "Penny has your room ready. We have plenty of dog food and whatever else you might need."

"Isn't that inn getting kind of crowded?" Nina retorted, glaring at Thomas.

"Always room for one more," Zeke replied, his dark eyes solemn and sure. "And I have a temporary apartment not far from there while the house we bought is being renovated, so you're covered if anyone tries to mess with you again."

"I can take care of myself," she said with a weak whine.

"We know," all three men said in weary unison.

Then the SAC leaned over her. "Look, Nina. You're a good agent, but you have a target on your back. Do you really want to sleep here tonight?"

Nina glanced from her shattered little cottage to the man who'd been by her side the whole time. Thomas gave her an understanding glance and waited for her response.

"No," she said, tossing off the blanket. "What I want is to find whoever is behind this. He got away again."

"He had a car right around the corner near the stream that runs along this property. The land on the other side of the stream is fenced and private, but we're working on locating the owner. Sam tracked the shooter to the water and took a bite out of the long trench coat he left behind."

"A DNA petri dish, I hope," Nina said, gaining hope.

"Already on its way to the lab," Thomas replied. "Now, let's go find you some clothes so you can get that sleep you need."

He reached out to help her out of the ambulance. Nina winced when she tried to move her left arm. She'd have a nice bruise just below her shoulder. The bullet had hit her in a bony area, leaving a deep gash that would hold a permanent scar.

"Are you sure you don't need to go to the ER?" Thomas asked, his voice low.

"No. Just a little sore, is all."

"Do you have the pain pills the EMT gave you?"

"Yes," she said. But she didn't intend to take them.

"Okay, I'll drive you to the inn."

"I can take my vehicle."

"You can get your SUV tomorrow once the crime scene techs are done here. Tonight, I'm driving you."

Too tired to argue, she followed him into the shot-up house, past the little tree, which was now toppled over on the floor, its lights and ornaments shattered and crushed. Nina bit her lip, then grabbed her go-bag and her weapon, and allowed him to guide her to his big truck. When he opened the passenger side door, there was a moment when she thought the man was actually going to pick her up and put her inside. But he only stared into her eyes, the storm clouds in his gaze telling her that he was loaded for bear on finding Russo.

Nina tried to hop up onto the seat, but winced in pain.

"I got you," Thomas said, not lifting her, but assisting her with a strong hand that held her with such a sweet strength, Nina's composure almost melted. She got settled and then stared out the window at the yellow crime scene tape now holding her house together.

Thomas got in the truck and put on a cowboy hat. Just like some western hero.

When she looked at the road, news crews were

swarming all around, but the FBI team and the local police held them back from her house and yard.

"They'll keep digging," she said. "They might scare Russo away. I hope the reporters don't find Kelly and lead him right to her."

"Kelly is fine. We checked on her at the hospital. They've moved her to a more secure area and Tim Ramsey and his K-9 partner, Frodo, are guarding her, along with the sheriff's deputy."

Breathing a little sigh of relief, since Tim was good at his job and very capable, she kept staring ahead. "Thomas, Russo's getting sloppy. He wants both of us dead, but…this doesn't seem like a hired killer's MO."

"Agreed," Thomas replied, as he pulled the big truck up close to the inn's carriage drive. "While you rest here, we're going to do more digging. Hopefully, we can figure out who the other two victims were. Someone knows something. I might have to make a trip to Helena and ask around about Kelly's life there."

"I'm going with you if you do," she said, determination adding punch to the words.

"No."

"Yes, Thomas. Yes. You said this is my investigation, that I can do the job. So let me. Either help me or get out of my way."

"Nina," he said, turning toward her in the seat. "This man is dangerous."

"I think I've figured that out, since I witnessed him trying to kill a young girl, and especially when I found the bodies he possibly left nearby. He's tried to kill me twice now, so I get it, Thomas. My job is to get to him before he can kill one of us or Kelly Denton. So if you go to Helena to investigate, I'm going with you. And there will be no discussion on that matter."

Thomas didn't argue with her, but Nina had a feeling there would be more discussions between them.

The next morning, Nina woke up and realized where she was and why she'd spent the night in this beautiful room at the Wild Iris Inn. Sam woofed a greeting and stared at his food bowl with doleful eyes.

Her partner never complained. He'd hold off on eating and relieving himself in order to protect her or anyone else. Glancing at the clock, she noted it was six in the morning. She was usually up and ready to go by this time. When she lifted her arm, her wound reminded her that she'd had a close call the night before.

A knock on the door caused her to bolt straight up, sending pain shooting through her body. Sam stood at attention, but didn't seem too worried. A friendly.

"Just a minute," she said, grabbing a robe she'd tossed into her bag last night to put over her T-shirt and plaid pajama bottoms.

Nina opened the door, expecting Thomas to be standing there. But Penny Potter greeted her with a smile, her dark eyes full of concern. "I have strict orders to keep you out of trouble."

Nina laughed but shook her head. "Let me guess. Thomas Grant?"

"Him, and Max West, too. Both very formidable when they need to be."

"They wouldn't treat a man that way."

Penny put down the tray she carried and stared over at Nina. "You're wrong there. When Zeke lost his brother, it was rough for all of us. You've no doubt heard that Jake was the father of my son, Kevin. I fell in love with his half brother, Zeke. We both had a lot of guilt to deal with." She poured coffee and motioned for Nina to sit at the little wooden bistro-style table by the big bay window. "Max told Zeke to take some time off. Ordered it, actually. And he told both of us to talk to counselors and to make sure Kevin got help, too."

Feeling contrite, Nina nodded. "I'm aware of some of that, yes. Zeke was in a lot of pain."

"Yes, but Max went with us to bury Jake in Utah. He didn't have to do that, but he did. He's a good man who guards his team members like he'd guard anyone else, except with his team he not only guards them, he makes sure they are safe and healthy so they can be the best at the dangerous jobs they do."

Nina took a sip of coffee and stared at the blueberry bagel covered with cream cheese on the pretty floral china. "I'm sorry. I just fought against so many condescending colleagues early in my career that I have to remind myself Max is not that way. He expects the best of us, and I've tried to give that, but right now I'm under pressure. If I fail at this case, I fail all of us."

Penny tossed back her long golden-brown hair and smiled. "You won't fail, but you do need to rest. Zeke told me you've been at this for days now."

"Yes," she admitted. "It did feel good to actually sleep last night." Tearing off some of the bagel, she asked, "So where is the notorious Thomas Grant this morning?"

Probably out getting the jump on her.

"He's at headquarters. Said he had to clear something with Max."

"Really?" Nina wished she knew what that something was. He wouldn't demand they remove her from this investigation, would he? Last night, they'd agreed they were in this together.

Penny leaned close, her smile full of understanding. "I'm talking out of school here, but I don't think you have anything to worry about. The man likes you, a lot. Why else would he have guarded your door all night?"

Thomas parked in the covered garage at the back of the inn's property. Dog-tired and needing a shower, he strolled up to the sunporch that covered the entire back of the big, Victorian-style house.

"Well, you've been a very busy man."

Nina sat there, dressed in jeans and a long cardigan sweater over a white blouse, her hair falling in spiky strands around her chin and neck. Sam lay at her feet, doing his job even if he looked deceptively docile.

"I have at that," Thomas admitted. Sinking down in a cushioned wicker rocking chair, he crossed his ankles and took a long breath. "And I'm exhausted."

"Maybe you should stop sleeping in a chair in front of the door to my room."

"I like sleeping in chairs. Builds character." Then he made a face. "But my back is not happy."

"I'm refreshed and anxious to get back to work," she retorted, a bad attitude all over each syllable. "My arm is sore, but workable."

"That's good," he replied, taking his time because she was so amazing when she was in a snit. Her eyes flashed a dark gold, her foot tapping against the porch floor.

"So, how was your day?" she said with a fake smile. "Mine was really boring."

"My day was productive," he said, wishing he could just catch his man and get away from these strange feelings clawing at his heart. "Are you going to let me explain or would you rather have a hissy fit and get it over with first?"

She got up and crossed her arms over her chest, her eyes shooting sparks. "Explain, Thomas. Now."

"I spent most of today clearing things for *us* to go to Helena together."

Her eyes went wide. "Us? I figured you'd take off without me."

"I did consider that…but I'm not completely stupid. *I* figured you'd hightail it after me."

"You'd be right on that."

He nodded. "I promised Max West I would protect you with my life, then I talked to Dylan O'Leary and some of the other techs and found out that the other two girls have been ID'd and they were both also from Helena."

She forgot to be mad and sank like a rock on the chair next to his. "Wow."

"Yeah, but the *wow* gets even more wowee. They all worked at the state capitol in Helena as interns while they attended school nearby."

Another *wow* and he had her listening.

"One girl disappeared earlier this year and the other one about three months ago. The bodies we found have definitely been identified as these two. No doubt there. I have pictures of all three of them now."

"And…can we prove Russo killed them?"

"Based on particles and hair follicles found on the trench coat, and some fibers and epidermis particles we found on Kelly's coat and underneath her nails, we can

prove Russo was with her that night. The lab is compar-
ing fibers they discovered on the remains of the girls,
too, but they haven't come up with a match yet."

"Russo," she said, standing up again. "So he's not as
meticulous as we thought, and we have him for shooting Kelly Denton. When do we leave?"

"First thing tomorrow," Thomas replied. Then he
pulled something out of his coat pocket and handed
it to her.

"The hot chocolate mix?" she said, her eyes widen-
ing, both hands holding tight to the glass jar.

"For tonight." He gave her a Thomas Special grin
and winked. "I'm going to take a shower. I hope Penny
planned something good for dinner. I'm starving."

Nina watched as he walked inside. Then she stared
at the mixture of sugar, cinnamon, powdered chocolate and powdered milk in her hand. He'd found it and
saved it for her. Which meant he'd been back to her
house today.

A wonderful gesture that touched her heart. But she
had to wonder if he'd found something else there that
had him ready to do battle on her behalf.

Nina intended to find out if Thomas knew more than
he was telling her. And if she had to do it over hot chocolate, she would.

SEVEN

"How did you find this place?" Nina asked the next day, after they'd driven the close to four hours to Helena.

Helena was a bustling city that moved on in spite of snow on the ground and Christmas shoppers hurrying here and there. But Thomas had driven straight through without so much as a grunt of impatience.

The tiny condo building held maybe twelve units and was centrally located, near the state capitol. Clean and cozy, their unit consisted of an open den and kitchen with a stunning fireplace and a short hall to two bedrooms, each with its own bath and a slight view of the capitol building.

"We use it…sometimes."

Sam, always curious, sniffed and stared, checking the place out. The big dog gave Nina a questioning glance. Always ready to roll.

But for the moment, Nina was focusing on the man standing across from her.

"Oh, I see." How could she forget one of the main aspects of his job—moving witnesses here and there to keep them safe until they could either obtain a new identity and location, or at least testify and put someone evil away? "So you're been here before?"

"Once or twice."

And he couldn't tell her anything more. Nina wondered what kind of burdens this man carried inside that big heart.

"It's nice."

"And secure," he added. "The entry gate is state-of-the-art and the security system is high tech, too. Plus a lot of the people who live here are either law enforcement or work at the capitol."

Nina dropped her gear and put her hands on her hips, her left arm still smarting from the gunshot wound. "So we start with the capitol?"

"Yes," he said, his expression stern while he lifted curtains and tugged on windows. He was checking the place for vulnerability. The man was a stickler for protocol, but then she was, too. "We'll have to be cautious. Can't go about accusing our state leaders without a good reason."

"No, not after what you told me last night and on the ride here."

They *had* shared cups of hot chocolate last night, after a hearty dinner of baked chicken with wild rice. Penny was a much more discreet innkeeper than her boss, Claire, had ever been. She'd left them to eat and then sent them out on the sunporch, where a woodstove kept things toasty.

Nina had immediately questioned Thomas last night about why he'd gone back to her house. He'd admitted he wanted to see it in the light of day and possibly find something they could use as evidence. The crime scene techs had already compared the shell casings they'd found there to the ones they'd retrieved in the parking garage the night Nina and Thomas had been shot at.

A match that indicated the same shotgun could have been used in both.

"So...that's it. The one thing you were holding back on," she said.

"Not holding back. Just trying to figure some things out."

"Because it doesn't add up, right?"

It was much harder to get in a good shot with a shotgun unless the gunman was at close range, like last night. But at close range, a shotgun could do a lot more damage to either an object or a human. Russo would be the type to take pleasure in blowing someone to pieces. But Russo wouldn't be messing around like this. He'd wait and find the perfect cover and then he'd target his prey and end things, quickly and thoroughly, probably with a high-powered rifle or a silencer gun like the one Nina had seen the other night.

None of this made any sense.

"That means the shooter was close to us the other night in the garage," Nina said to Thomas. "But a pro would have used a rifle with a scope."

"From a safe distance away," Thomas replied, showing her they'd come to the same conclusion. "It would have been quick and clean."

Now she had to wonder if he knew something about the weapon or the shooter that she'd missed. But they both agreed that something was off, at least.

"He probably didn't use a shotgun on the girls," she said now. "He used a silencer when he targeted Kelly Denton, but he was running away and didn't get in a good shot."

Thomas rubbed the back of his neck. "The shotgun is sending a message. I don't know what that means yet, but I hope we'll find out something here."

"Maybe he was just shooting that night to scare us."

"Or maim one of us for life, if not worse."

Nina went still. "Or…there's someone else involved. Someone who's not a professional assassin."

"Bingo."

Thomas opened the refrigerator and then turned to stare at her across the white marble countertop. "I made some calls to the Helena police before we left this morning. They are, of course, aware of the missing girls."

"What else did you find out?" Nina asked, thinking she'd reprimand him later for not telling her until now. "Don't try to protect me, Thomas. I need to know.'

He finally looked her square in the eyes. "They all worked at one time for Senator Slaton."

Nina took in a breath. "What are you saying?"

"I don't know," he replied, doubt in his solemn gaze. "I don't want to speculate."

"So you didn't think to run this by me immediately?"

"Nina, Russo is after you, too, and you've got a wound to prove it. I didn't want to…"

"Scare me? Not telling me scares me even more. The girls are connected and…we might have more than one suspect."

"I didn't want to worry you," he said, the statement full of stubbornness. Then he held up his hand to ward off her glare of aggravation. "If a state senator is involved, you know what that could mean."

"Yes," she retorted, not sure whether to appreciate him or shout at him. "It could mean someone's targeting his staff. Or it could mean something entirely different. If he is involved, it means I'm going to take down a state senator."

"That's it right there," he replied, his eyes going so serious he did begin to scare her. "You're so good at your job you're forgetting to be cautious."

"How can I *not* be cautious when a killer is on my trail, Thomas? I've been as cautious as possible, considering I have a giant Texas shadow hanging over my head. And now we think this goes even deeper. We don't know how the senator could be involved. Maybe he's a victim or he could be a criminal. This isn't about being cautious. This is about doing the jobs we're both trained to do. Together, whether we like it or not."

"I like it," he said in a quick clipped tone. "The together part, I mean."

Nina's breath left her body, but her heart chased after it, needing to get away from that stormy-eyed stare.

"I like *you*," he continued. "I'm going to protect *you*. We need to be clear on that."

Sam shot her a hard, stoic glance. As if the dog was agreeing with the deputy marshal. Great, they were ganging up on her.

She'd almost left Sam behind, because they planned to stay under the radar and a K-9 dog would bring attention to them immediately. But now she was glad she had her faithful partner here to shield her from Thomas Grant. Not in a hostile, take-down way, but in a protect-my-heart-please way.

Swallowing her pride and that burst of warmth and security his nearness gave her, she pushed at her hair and said, "Tell me what the locals gave you so we can get to work and get this over with."

* * *

So she obviously didn't like working with *him*.

And she sure didn't like his trying to protect her.

She wanted this done and over so she could be rid of him.

Fair enough then.

Thomas sat down and stared up at her. "Why don't I take you to lunch and we'll talk?"

"We'll talk here," she said, digging in her heels. Sam sank down at her feet.

Thomas motioned to the chair across from him. After she sat, he said, "The locals did all they could to search for each girl. The cases remain active and they're now aware that we've identified the bodies. They want to know everything we know and they're willing to let us go over their files and compare notes."

"Let's get busy," she said, standing to straighten her clothes. "And we need to talk to Senator Slaton."

Today, she wore a black suit and sensible heels so she'd blend in with government workers. Since he'd rarely seen her dressed up, Thomas acknowledged to himself how pretty she looked, no matter what she wore. But he also reminded himself that her job came first. He'd always felt the same, until now.

Nina didn't have a clue what he was thinking. She was too busy calling the state senator's office.

"He's away on a hunting vacation," she said, turning back to Thomas. "How convenient."

"I wonder what he's hunting?" Thomas replied.

"Yeah, me, too," Nina said, prancing toward the door. "But while the senator's away, we can see what other people have to say."

"And she's a poet."

So they headed to police headquarters, careful to make sure they weren't being followed or watched, and entered the back way. Over the next few hours, they scrolled through reports and files and studied what little evidence had been stored.

"We found one cell phone," a detective told them. "Had the lab analyze it and talked to most of her contacts, but based on some text messages from last December, all we found significant was regarding a party. A very private party."

About three weeks later, the girl went missing.

And they'd never found out where the party took place, since at the time, her friends had claimed they didn't know. A wall of silence, according to one detective. They hadn't realized the two missing girls were connected until now, so of course they needed updates.

"Who did she meet at that party?" Nina asked Thomas now, her eyes scanning the file she'd just opened. "Here's a list of her phone contacts, but there's no information to go on with the names. Maybe we should dig deeper into her phone records or interview some of these contacts."

"I'm sure the locals did that already," Thomas replied, "but it never hurts to go back over things, especially now that we know who we could be dealing with. As for the party, maybe it being so secretive had something to do with her disappearance."

"You mean, like maybe someone on the senator's staff made her disappear?"

"Yeah, like that," Thomas replied with a deadpan look. "Let's keep to the plan and start there first."

"Good idea." Nina called out to where Sam had been

waiting patiently while they studied files. He'd get to visit the Helena K-9 kennels while they did some footwork.

But after an hour or so of getting the runaround at the senator's office and being passed from a secretary to an aide and then hitting brick walls, they left without any relevant information.

"On to the friends list," Nina said.

They started with Mya Gregory, since she'd disappeared first.

Her mother greeted them with red-rimmed eyes and a frail stare. Thomas noticed she looked physically ill.

"We're so sorry for your loss," he said, after Nina had explained why they were there. Mrs. Gregory showed them into a modestly decorated den.

"Thank you," she said, taking her time as she sank down in a chair near a table laden with medical bottles and supplies. Noticing their expressions, she said, "I'm dying of cancer. I'm only talking to you today because… I hope they find out who did this before I die. I'm not afraid to go. I'm ready to see Mya again. But I want justice for my sweet girl, especially now that I know she's never coming back."

Nina leaned forward. "Can you tell us what happened and if you have any information that can help us?"

Mrs. Gregory launched into a detailed timeline. Her husband and she had divorced years ago, but she'd had a steady job and Mya had scholarships and student loans to pay off. "When she got the news about interning at the capitol, she was so happy. She studied political science and took all kinds of government-related classes. She loved being around our state leaders, but then… something went wrong last December. She attended some fancy Christmas party with her friends, and after that she seemed so sad and worried. She wouldn't talk about it, but her whole demeanor changed. She became anxious and secretive."

"And then she went missing," Nina finished, sympathy in her eyes.

"Yes, in early January, right after the spring semester started back up." Mrs. Gregory coughed and Thomas handed her a glass of water from the table. "I tried everything, you know. Talked to the police, gave them all the information I could think of, but… I was shut down at every angle." She sipped the water. "At least now I can bury my baby."

Then she said something that brought Thomas and Nina to full attention. "And maybe now, the threats will stop."

"Threats!"

Nina and Thomas had found a quiet corner café near the condo to have an early dinner. He looked over at her now, taking in the irate expression that only made her more beautiful. "Yeah, imagine that. But in spite of the threats, Mya's mother was smart. She did a pretty good job of digging around in a high-powered world."

Mrs. Gregory had found several of Mya's friends and asked them about the party and why her daughter had seemed so unhappy and distraught after she'd gone to it. None of them could tell her much.

"But someone came to her house and told her to stop digging," Nina replied, checking out the window to where they'd left Sam in the unmarked SUV they'd rented, in sight and with a window cracked open to the chilly night.

"And left threatening messages on her phone."

"The woman is so scared she won't even tell us who it was."

"That's because she wants to live long enough to bury Mya," Thomas reminded her, wishing he could do more for that poor woman and for the upset one sitting across from him.

Nina sank back in the cushioned booth where big clear windows on both sides gave them a view outside and where they could see the whole narrow restaurant and each entryway. "At least she gave us some names. If we find one person who's willing to talk, maybe we'll get to the bottom of this." She took a drink of her sparkling water. "But Thomas, we both know the signs. Someone must have been threatening Mya, too. That means she and the other girl saw something at that party that really shook them up. Kelly Denton has to know what that was, but she's too scared to tell us. Or maybe she's scared because she's the victim."

"Something happened that they couldn't forget," Thomas added. "Something that was so bad, two of them died because of it. And the one left isn't talking."

Nina's head came up. "Thomas, don't you think it strange that Mya's contact list didn't include Kelly and the other girl?"

"They don't necessarily have to know each other," he said, his gut suddenly tightening. "It could be that they purposely avoided each other—a protective kind of thing." Checking out the window he added, "But if they were all interns at the same time and were all at that party together, they could have formed a pact or something. Or they could have a piece of incriminating evidence."

"I don't know if I can eat," Nina said, staring down

at her baked chicken and vegetables. "This smacks of some sort of high-level cover-up."

"You didn't have lunch," Thomas pointed out, unable to stop the feelings of concern. "How's your wound?"

"It's burning like a brand, but I'm okay."

"Try your veggies," he coaxed. "I need you strong and sharp." When that didn't work, he took her hand. "Remember, you saved Kelly's life. I'm going to keep you safe."

She glared at him for a few tense seconds. "I'm not worried about being safe right now, but thanks. I guess I'm just going to have to go with the cowboy-to-the-rescue thing, right?"

"Might be best," he said, wishing she'd see that he wanted to keep her away from this evil. Not just because she was a good officer and needed in Billings, not only because she was a witness to a crime and needed his protection, but also because he really liked being around her and…hoped that maybe one day they could have a quiet meal together with no mayhem involved. "I'm not going to change," he added. "My mama raised me right."

Nina laughed at that. "Yes, she sure did."

Then he put down his water glass and said, "Actually, that's not true. Like I told you, she left me behind after my parents divorced. And my dad didn't know how to deal with me, so I had a lot of mamas, but none of them were really mine to claim."

Nina's expression softened. "Like I said the other night, if we survive this, I'm taking you to my parents' house for Christmas."

"I can't argue with that, since I aim to survive and keep you alive, too."

"As long as we keep doing this together and you understand I don't need a babysitter, we'll be fine."

"I don't want to be your babysitter," he replied, shaking his head. "I need your expertise and I want us to be equal partners. But I'm going to watch after you, Nina."

She opened her mouth to deliver what surely would be a protest and then changed her frown into a little smile. "Okay, Thomas. We'll go with that for now."

"Eat your veggies," he said again, laughing at her in spite of the many questions he had about those three girls.

EIGHT

Nina couldn't believe how Thomas had helped her relax. He'd told her stories of past cases, leaving out names and the bad parts. Told her about his childhood of moving around and never having a real home. Then he got her talking about her brothers and how they'd picked on her without mercy and taught her to be tough.

"I can see that," he said, his gaze washing over her face in a not-so-businesslike way.

His gentle eyes held something that made her blush and wonder what was happening between them.

When they settled on her lips, Nina took a deep breath and pushed her plate away. "It's getting late."

"Yeah, I guess it is."

His statement held so much more than just weary agreement.

He shot her one last glance that held longing and regret, and then his phone buzzed, causing them to part like two guilty teens.

"Thomas Grant," he said into his cell, his gaze still on Nina. But the tender expression on his face changed. "I see. Can we meet and talk about this?"

Nina listened intently and saw a flare of awareness in his eyes. "Well, thank you for the information."

He ended the call and let out a long sigh. "That was one of the friends we tried to contact. Remember Jack Creighton? We talked to him on the phone and he agreed to speak to us in person?"

"Yes," she said. "The last one on our list, out from the city. He knew Mya, right? But he didn't open the door when we got to his house."

"He obviously found the card I stuck in the mailbox," Thomas stated. "And had a change of heart."

"Does he want to see us now?"

"No. He quickly gave me a rundown and then hung up."

"And?"

"He said we needed to find Slaton's son Allen. He implied the senator has kept his misdeeds under wraps for too long."

Nina put her hands on the table and pushed herself up. "Three scared girls and one senator's son. What happened at that party, Thomas?"

"Probably something we don't want to hear about," he replied. Throwing enough money on the table to cover the meal and tip, he took her by the hand and they hurried out of the restaurant.

"I'll report to Dylan," she said, pulling out her phone. "He can do some more research."

Thomas hit the key fob and the SUV's locks clicked open. He was right behind her as they walked across the street. But she heard a thump and a grunt before they reached the vehicle. Whirling, she spotted Thomas hitting the hard pavement. Nina jumped back just as a man charged toward her and knocked her purse to the ground. She went into action and gave the attacker a swift kick in the stomach, and then slugged him with a right hook before she jabbed him with her elbow, screaming at the top of her lungs the whole time.

Inside the SUV, Sam went wild, barking and dancing in the seat. If she could get to the door...

But the man overpowered her and shoved her hard against the big vehicle, his hands reaching for her throat. Nina gasped and prepared to do battle, but before she could trip him up and get to where her weapon remained hidden in her dropped purse, a big swoosh of air hit her and her attacker went down.

Thomas body-slammed the guy, knocking him into the street. Nina breathed deep and rushed to get her gun. The man fell a few feet away, but got up and took off running toward a dark alley, Sam's barks echoing after him. Thomas, still weak, started to follow, but when people came charging out of the restaurant, he turned and yelled to them to get back inside.

Then he passed out and fell to the ground again.

Thomas woke up with a jolt and blinked. When he saw Nina hovering over him, he grabbed her hand. "Are you all right?"

Nina gently pulled his hands away. "I'm fine. Lie back. We're almost to the hospital."

Straining to see, Thomas realized they were in an ambulance. "No, I'm fine. I'm supposed to take care of you."

And he'd failed.

"Thomas, listen to me," she said, using an authoritative voice. "You got hit over the head with a baseball bat. You probably have a concussion."

"I said I'm fine," he lied. In fact, his skull was hammering like a construction crew way behind on the job. "Turn this bus around."

"No. It's my turn to watch over you, you big oaf."

Squinting at her to make sure she was in one piece, he glanced at her hand on his arm. There was a lot of strength in that firm grip. "Did you just call me an oaf?"

"Yes, and I'll call you worse if you move again. The locals are searching for our assailant and Sam is safe with one of their handlers. The man left the bat, but he was wearing gloves, so no good prints to speak of. Witnesses only saw an average-size man wearing a heavy black dress coat and a dark hat pulled low. I saw his face, but he had on dark glasses. I don't think I could identify him."

Thomas blinked again, trying to keep up. Her chatter was nervous and nerve-racking. "If you'll be quiet, I'll lie still," he finally said. "Since you have everything under control."

"Good idea," she replied. "We're at the ER, so hang on."

Thomas fell back and closed his eyes, the image of the attacker going for Nina's throat making a loop inside his head that angered him to no end.

He'd humor her for now…but he wasn't going to spend the night in the hospital.

Thankfully, he convinced the ER doctor of that, too. Soon, they were in a patrol car, being taken back to their vehicle, where they were reunited with Sam. Nina got the rottweiler settled in the back and put Thomas in the passenger seat and hopped up to drive, adjusting the seat from tall to short to accommodate.

"Am I safe with you?" he asked, trying to relieve some of the tension.

"Always," she said. Then she turned to him. "Are you sure you're okay to go back to the condo?"

"Yes. You can keep me awake with your annoying, bossy chatter."

"I'll be glad to, since you looked after me when I got grazed with that bullet."

He'd seen her arm earlier. In her efforts to take down the attacker, she'd caused her wound to start bleeding again. She now wore a fresh bandage under the red stains on her white blouse.

Gritting his teeth, Thomas squelched the frustration of not being able to help her when she'd needed him, and promised himself that wouldn't happen again.

After scanning the area where they parked close to the front door, she had him inside and pointed him toward the couch. Then she checked the backside and small patio, too. "Nothing out of the ordinary, but why do I feel as if we're being watched?"

"Shut the door and bolt it, Nina."

She did that and then set the alarm. Sam cleared the rooms while Thomas fell into a pile on the couch.

She scooted around in the tiny kitchen and came to sit down beside him. "Hot tea," she said, shoving a mug at him. "Drink it."

"I don't like hot tea."

"It's herbal, so it won't mess with your head. Drink it."

"*You're* messing with my head," he retorted. "Nina,

maybe it's the knocking I took, but you look so beautiful."

"You definitely have a concussion." She put the tea down and stared at him. "Thomas, you scared me."

"I was trying to save you, but you saved yourself and me."

"Are you going to pout about that? You've saved me a couple of times already, so you're still ahead."

He took her hand, thinking because he was weak and woozy he'd milk this for all it was worth. "I'm not pouting. In fact, while we're sitting here doing nothing, you can do that research on what Jack Creighton told us with such cryptic details. That is, when you're not waiting on me hand and foot."

Even if he couldn't see straight right now, he could at least enjoy watching her.

"I can do that," she said, staring down at his hand over hers. "Right after you take two pain pills. You can rest, but I'm supposed to wake you every few hours."

He liked that idea. But not the medicine. "I don't need pain pills."

"Yes, you do. You know how it works with a slight concussion, I'm sure."

"I do and that's why I don't need pain pills. I have a hard head." Then he motioned toward her arm. "Same way you have tough skin."

"Take your medicine and I'll share what I find out on Jack Creighton."

"You don't play fair."

"All's fair in love and crime."

She called Dylan, knowing he wouldn't mind the late hour. While she waited to see what he could find, she searched for information on Jack Creighton and found a wealth of photos on his social media profile going back well over a year or so.

She checked on Thomas. He was dozing. She'd wake him in a few minutes. Something on her laptop screen caught her attention.

Jack Creighton in a picture with Allen Slaton. A school photo with their names listed. They'd played soccer and football together, the usual prep school activities.

But these photos showed they were friends. Were they still friends? Had Jack called to help them or get them off the trail?

After scrolling through a few more posts and discovering information that would help their case she turned to wake up Thomas.

The man lay there watching her, his eyes open and lucid. Too lucid.

"I like the way you bite your lower lip when you're researching," he said, his voice gravelly with sleep.

"I can see you're going to live," she retorted with a drip of sarcasm to hide the treacherous tremor of her pulse. "Do you want to keep lying there with that flirty look on your face, or do you want to know what Dylan and I have found?"

"I don't know," he said, slowly raising himself with a grimace. "I sure enjoy flirting with you even though it's not very professional." Then he chuckled. "You know, if you closed that laptop, you'd be off duty. Then we wouldn't have to follow the rules."

She stood and leaned over him, thinking she might actually flirt back, then shook her head and sat down on the couch. "Easy, cowboy. When you hear what I found, you'll forget all about me."

"No, I won't," he said, rubbing a hand over his beautifully tousled hair. "Work first. Then we can get back to the good stuff."

For the first time in her career, Nina wished work didn't have to come first. Which only proved it should, in spite of the Texas-bred distraction sitting next to her.

"I found out about the party," she said, figuring that would get his mind back on the job.

It did. He frowned at her, obviously going on full alert. "Tell me everything." Then he glanced toward the kitchen. "I'm kind of hungry, so I'll eat while you report."

"I'll make you a sandwich while I talk," she replied, thinking this domestication stuff sure was cozy. And deciding his grocery bill must be huge.

But she went on with her report. While she found the ham and cheese and pickles and bread they'd bought earlier, she said, "The party was held last year, a week before Christmas, at a private club on the other side of town. A chateau owned by a corporation. A fraternity and a sorority put it together. And guess who attended?"

Thomas took the sandwich she'd slapped together and cut in half. "Let me see—our three girls and this Jack dude and… Allen Slaton?"

"Yes, all of the above, along with about thirty others," she said with a solemn stare. "Dylan located the other girl's father. Her mother passed away a few years ago, but Kristen Banks's dad is still here in Helena. We can try to contact him first thing tomorrow."

"Sounds like a plan," Thomas said, admiration in his eyes. "This sandwich is great."

"It's just bread and ham, cheese and mustard, Thomas."

"But you cooked for me. And added pickles."

"Don't get used to that."

He finished his sandwich, then went to the bathroom to freshen up. She pulled out a bag of cookies he'd nabbed at the nearby grocery store, thinking she needed something to nibble on instead of his enticing lips. When he came back they ate cookies, drank coffee and talked about the investigation for a few minutes, developing a solid plan for the next day. Then he tugged her down onto the couch.

"I'm ready to do some serious flirting," he announced.

Nina's heart did a somersault. "I haven't flirted in so long I'm not sure how to respond."

Sam yawned from his spot on the rug by the window.

"Just be you," Thomas said, and then he laughed and pulled her close. "We're a good team, Nina. Thank you for saving yourself tonight and for taking care of me."

"My job," she said, her voice turning mushy. "But this... Thomas... I'm not so good at this."

He leaned close, his incredible eyes holding her gaze. "We'll learn together, and once this is all over...we'll be pros in the relationship department, too."

Then he kissed her, a soft warm whisper on her lips that shot a sizzle all the way to her heart. Pulling back just a breath, he said, "Meantime, you know what they say. Practice makes perfect."

Nina kissed him again for good measure.

NINE

Jeffrey Banks looked as haggard and tired as Mya Gregory's mother, but he wasn't sick, physically. The man was suffering from grief. At first he was wary, but after they showed him their badges and explained why they needed to talk to him, he told them about how he'd raised Kristen alone after his wife died.

"She wanted to be a nurse like her mom but she also liked politics so she wound up working for Senator Slaton—just a temporary part-time thing. She had one more year of college when she...just disappeared."

"I'm so sorry," Nina said. "We want to find justice for these girls."

"So now that she's dead, everyone comes running," he said on a grim note while they stood in the hallway of his modest, two-story home. "Nobody seemed to care before."

"We care," Nina said, wishing she could ease his pain. "That's why we're here. We want to find the people who did this."

"I already talked to that other detective about a week ago," Mr. Banks said, rubbing his salt-and-pepper beard. "He wanted to go through her things, but I told him not without a search warrant. And I had my shotgun in his face to prove it."

Nina glanced at Thomas, both of them taking note of the shotgun comment. "Who was this detective? Did he give you a name?"

"No. He looked mighty young. Clean-cut. I don't believe he was any kind of law officer. You know how you get a bad vibe with people? I never saw a badge and he never actually told me his name, so we didn't get very far into the conversation. He left when my 12-gauge and I refused to let him in my house."

"Have you traveled anywhere recently?" Thomas asked. "Been on any hunting trips?"

The man looked at him as if he'd gone mad. "No, sir. I rarely get out Helena. I'm a maintenance worker with the highway department. Do you have a warrant to search my house?"

"No." Thomas showed him a picture of Russo. "Is this the man who questioned you?"

"Nawh. Too old and too tall."

"How about this one?" she asked, showing him a picture of Allen Slaton.

"That might be him, yes."

Nina jotted notes. Mya's mother had said someone threatened her over the phone. Could that be the same person who'd tried to get past Mr. Banks? Someone else who was looking for clues? Slaton? Russo would have shot Mr. Banks and searched the house, making it look like a robbery. Not his style to back down. Mr. Banks owned a shotgun, but a lot of people did and Thomas hadn't pushed him on that issue. She ruled out the possibility of his lying. What purpose would the man have to go to Billings and shoot at them?

No, this was looking more and more like the senator or his son. Or maybe both.

Nina took a chance and went down another path. "Did Kristen ever mention anything about a key?"

Mr. Banks looked surprised, his eyebrows rising. "She had lots of keys—to her car, her gym locker, her apartment."

"Did she confide in you?" Thomas asked. "About her life? Did she seem distant, or worried about anything?"

Mr. Banks stood up straight. "My daughter was a good girl. Loved the outdoors. Never met a stranger." Then he looked down at the floor. "But yes, something was eating at her when she came by at Christmas last year. I figured she had boyfriend problems. She quit jogging or taking long walks, and joined a gym, which wasn't like her. She hated gyms."

He shook his head, his eyes watering. "The gym called me about two weeks ago and said she had a locker and that her membership needed to be renewed in a month." He blinked back tears. "I didn't tell them my little girl had been missing for almost a year." Giving in to the tears, he gulped, "Now I have to tell them she won't be coming back at all."

"So she joined this gym after Christmas?" Thomas asked, his tone gentle.

"Yeah. Now that I think about it, I might have that locker key. She left it here last time I saw her. She must have forgotten it."

A buzz moved through Nina's system as she glanced over at Thomas. "Can you find the key?"

"I'll be right back." Mr. Banks pivoted and shuffled to the rear of the house.

"I think we're getting somewhere," Thomas said in a

whisper. "If Allen Slaton came here, he must have had a very good reason."

Mr. Banks returned with the key, and instead of handing it over, he told them to follow him to the gym, just down the road. So they did, and Sam went inside with them.

And came up empty.

"Nothing in there," Kristen's father said. "I guess I'll never know why someone had to murder my baby."

He left, not bothering to shut the locker or tell the gym employees that his daughter was deceased.

Sam sniffed, but didn't alert. The locker didn't give them any answers. Had someone beat them here with another key?

"If Kristen was hiding something here, it's gone now," Nina said. "Let's ask around."

No one at the gym could remember Kristen or what might have been in her locker, so no help there. Nina and Thomas left, defeated but still determined.

"We've asked around at the capitol and we've talked to as many contacts as we could," Thomas said, once they were back in the vehicle. Nina was still driving, since his headaches seemed to come and go. "I think we need to get back to Billings."

Nina didn't want to give up, but they couldn't stay here indefinitely, and the locals hadn't found the man who'd attacked them last night. Not yet, anyway.

"I hate to admit defeat but…we keep running into roadblocks, and Senator Slaton is obviously making himself unavailable. Plus we can't seem to locate his son. But Mr. Banks might be able to ID him, so that's good."

"Which means this trip wasn't wasted," Thomas replied, while she headed out into midday traffic. "The senator and his son are now on our suspect list and we know the girls were at that party, along with Allen Slaton and the Creighton boy. We also have reason to believe Kristen Banks might have hidden something in her gym locker, but I don't think she ever worked out in that gym. Maybe we should go back and talk to Jack Creighton again, shake him up enough that he'll tell us everything."

"Someone came after us last night, so that means someone knows we're here and why," Nina reminded him. "I just feel like we're so close."

They made it back to the condo without incident and Thomas turned to stare at her. "I discovered one more important thing on this trip," he said, leaning close, his sleepy eyes moving over her face. "I really like flirting with you and kissing you."

Nina's blush warmed the truck. "Yeah, there is that."

He moved closer, but her phone buzzed. "Hold that kiss," she said with a smile, her heart going weak. "Atkins," she said into the phone, her eyes still on Thomas.

"Nina, it's Dylan."

"Hey," she said. "I'm putting you on speaker."

"Good, 'cause you'll both want to hear this," he replied. "We just found some information that's kind of significant. The land where you came across Russo and Kelly Denton and found those dead girls, well, it's part of an estate that's owned by Senator Richard Slaton. And we have reason to believe he's at his hunting lodge across the stream from the crime scene and that he's been there for days."

Nina's gaze slammed into Thomas's. "We're getting ready to return there now." Then she added, "And

Dylan, make sure security is beefed up at the hospital. He could be coming for Kelly Denton."

She ended the call and they hurried to get their belongings so they could head back to Billings. Thomas's phone rang when they were about to close down the condo.

"What now?" he said, before taking the call. Putting it on speaker as Nina had done, he said, "Thomas Grant."

"Marshal, I remembered something."

Mya's mother.

"What's that, Mrs. Gregory?"

"I found a key and I think it belongs to a safety deposit box or something. I have a rental receipt. Mya must have rented the box for some reason."

Nina's heart hammered with so many mixed emotions she couldn't catch up with herself. The direction this investigation seemed to be headed made her ill with grief for those poor girls, but the relationship between Thomas and her had her on edge in a different way. Now she was worried about something happening to him. Silly, since the man could certainly take care of himself.

Is this how it begins? she wondered as they sped across town to Mrs. Gregory's house. *This burning in the heart, this wanting to do everything within your power to save another person's pain?*

Is this what falling in love feels like?

Pushing at her hair, she glanced over at Thomas. She had met him only days ago and yet she felt such a connection with him, such a sweet security and the confidence that she could trust him with her life. And with her heart.

Oh, no. This couldn't be happening. She couldn't fall for the Texan. He understood her job, but he did the same kind of work. They'd always be in some sort of competition. He could turn out like her brothers and father, always teasing her and making her feel as if she didn't measure up.

But he hasn't done that, she thought. And she knew he wouldn't. Thomas respected her even when he was trying to protect her.

They reached Mrs. Gregory's short driveway, and Nina had to put this new realization on the rear burner while she backed the SUV in for security measures. This could be over soon and Thomas would go back to his world.

And leave her to take care of herself.

They got out, Sam with them, and Nina ordered the dog to guard the front porch. Sam would bark at anyone who approached.

They knocked and Mrs. Gregory opened the door, her eyes wide and red-rimmed. "Thank you for coming," she said, glancing back. "I...hated to bother you, but I had to—to let you know."

Nina glanced at Thomas. Something was off. Sam's ears were lifted and he seemed to be alerting, his gaze on the frail woman.

Nina decided they needed to get inside, fast. Sam must be picking up on the woman's fear.

"What do you have for us?" she asked, once they'd stepped inside. Thomas scanned the tiny living and dining area and sent Nina a subtle nod.

"I went through some of Mya's things. It was hard

but… I thought maybe I'd find something important. I found a receipt for what looks like a bank box."

Nina took a pair of tweezers from her coat pocket and held up the receipt Mrs. Gregory had handed her. "Looks like she rented a safety deposit box."

Thomas kept a visual on the rooms, but Nina could tell he was getting antsy. Sam stood just outside the open door and emitted a low growl. Now they were both on edge.

"You mentioned a key," he said to the woman, his gaze moving over the house.

She nodded, tears forming in her eyes, her hands trembling. "Yes, here it is." Taking the key from her pocket, she handed it to Thomas. "I'm sorry."

Nina quickly put it and the receipt in two clear evidence bags she'd had tucked into her pocket. "You have nothing to be sorry about. You're doing the right thing. This might help us figure out what Mya was hiding. What she was so depressed and upset about."

Sam growled low.

Mrs. Gregory shook her head, but before she could speak, a man wearing a dark coat stepped out of the tiny hall bathroom.

"I'd like to know the answer to that myself," he said, his gun trained on all of them. "Mrs. Gregory and I have had such a good visit today. But… I really wanted to see both of you, too, so I *convinced* her to call you. And I especially wanted to take that key…right out of your hands. Before I kill you both."

"Russo," Thomas said, disgust in his voice.

Nina recognized him immediately and went for her weapon, but the gunman pressed his weapon against Mrs. Gregory's skinny back. "We've been waiting for you. I really needed all three of you here. Makes things so much easier."

Behind them, Nina heard another low growl. Sam knew this man, too. "So you'll make it look like we were involved, or that we came here to confront Mrs. Gregory and this frail little woman took both of us down?"

"Something like that," Russo said, his voice polite and quiet. "I'll figure out the details later."

He shoved Mrs. Gregory toward them. "Shut the door so that feral animal doesn't take a bite out of me."

Nina turned toward the doorway, hoping she could sic Sam on the man before he took this any further. Then she heard harsh, ragged laughter, and glanced back to see Mrs. Gregory's somewhat hysterical expression.

The woman whirled toward Russo, her skinny finger jabbing into his chest. "Shoot me first, please," she said with a wave of her other hand. "You can do whatever you want with those two nosy know-it-alls. Just put me out of my misery so I can see my daughter again."

She advanced on Russo, surprising all of them enough to distract the man. Thomas didn't waste any time. He plunged forward and Mrs. Gregory, suddenly spry, hopped out of the way and watched with a gleeful satisfaction as Thomas knocked Russo back, both men wrestling with the gun Russo still held. Nina got out her weapon and opened the door wide.

"Sam. Attack!"

Sam took a giant leap and nabbed Russo just as Thomas twisted the other man around. Thomas let go and got out of the way, watching with heaving breath as Sam put a bite hold on Russo's left calf. The man screamed and dropped his gun, fighting and tugging, which only made Sam hold on with all his strength.

Thomas kicked Russo's weapon away and then, his own gun trained on the screaming criminal, glanced to where Mrs. Gregory leaned against a table, all her energy spent.

Nina went to the woman and helped her to the couch. "Are you all right?"

"I'm fine now, honey," she said. "We got him, didn't we? We got the man who killed my Mya."

"I think so," Nina replied. "Thank you for what you did."

Mrs. Gregory sank against the sofa, her voice low, her eyes watery. "I had to do what he asked, but wasn't about to let him hurt either of you. I figured if I got you here, together we'd take care of the rest."

TEN

Three hours later, Nina and Thomas were on their way to the bank to open the safety deposit box, a warrant in hand and an urgency in their actions. They now knew the safety deposit box had been rented by Mya Gregory.

"At least Russo is off the streets," Thomas said, his heart still jumpy from finding Russo standing there behind Mrs. Gregory.

The man had worked his way into her house and made her search her daughter's things. Then he'd forced her to call Thomas and Nina, so he could end it all, leaving with what he needed and no witnesses left. But that had backfired on him.

"Yes," Nina replied with a long sigh. "And we have one feisty woman to thank for that."

"A brave woman," Thomas said. "She risked her life to help us and to save us."

"But…she won't make it much longer, Thomas. Once Mya's remains are released for burial, her mother won't be far behind her."

"We'll check on her," he said, meaning it. "She doesn't have anyone, but I'll make sure and check on her often."

"Me, too," Nina said, thankful that she'd partnered up with a good man. A man who was back in the driver's seat, while she sat here wondering how her heart would ever recover after he left.

Shoving that from her mind, Nina got out of the vehicle, and together they went into the bank. One of the officers took them to the vault where the safety deposit boxes were stored.

The key worked right away and soon they had the box open.

"An envelope," Nina said, picking up the package with gloved hands. "Something's in here."

She opened the taped seal that held the padded yellow envelope together, while Thomas took pictures to verify. Then she pulled out a burner phone and another envelope. This one was white and sealed with heavy tape.

And it had a name written across it.

Kelly Denton. The girl who'd been shot. Nina managed to peel away the tape so they could quickly scan the letter. It told the whole tale. The senator's son had assaulted Kelly, and the two other girls had heard him bragging about it. That had started a chain of events that resulted in a cover-up and now, murder.

"We'd better take this to the police station," Thomas said. "Russo isn't going to talk, because he doesn't know what we know yet. This will hopefully give us enough information to make him tell the truth."

"I hope so. That man is creepy," Nina replied, remembering his craggy face and almost suave demeanor. "I hope he tells us who hired him, although I'm pretty sure I know who that was."

She put the phone and small envelope back into the

bigger one and pressed the seal together, the bank officer her witness.

Thomas followed her out of the room and then the bank officer who'd been standing nearby guided them out the door, probably relieved that they'd been discreet, since they were investigating a possible crime.

Once they were back in the SUV, Thomas turned to her. "So you've got people watching the senator's hunting lodge."

"Yes. If he makes a move, we'll find a way to detain him. And...we're still looking for his missing son. He's probably holed up with his father." She shrugged and tugged at her seat belt. "I'm thinking one or both of them must own a shotgun. Because the shotgun attacks were far from professional grade."

"Agreed. It's all beginning to add up," Thomas said. "Let's get this evidence entered and filed, and then we'll head back to Billings. Maybe there, we can finally pin down the senator and his elusive son."

Late that night, they rolled into the Wild Iris Inn's parking lot. Surprised to find Penny and Zeke still up and sitting in the cozy parlor, Nina sent them a weary smile.

"We thought you might need a snack," Penny said, glancing over at Zeke.

"And an update," he added. "Max gave us the lowdown. Sad situation, but hopefully it'll be over soon."

After taking care of Sam, Nina returned to the dining room, where Penny had set out cheese and crackers, along with brownies and coffee.

"You'll have to teach me to cook," Nina said, fatigue tugging at her.

"I'm still learning myself," Penny admitted. "We have a very good cook who leaves things for me to present to our guests."

As they ate, Nina turned to Zeke. "Russo is willing to take a plea bargain. In fact, he's begging for one."

"I would imagine so," Zeke replied. "No movement from the lodge. It's well hidden, so that explains why not many people even knew it was there."

"But you believe the senator is hiding out there?" Thomas asked, his hand tight on his coffee cup.

"And maybe the son, too."

Nina nibbled on an oatmeal cookie. "No one connected with the Senator would tell us where the senator was, but we got the impression they knew."

"They either have no idea or they know to keep quiet," Thomas said.

"And Kelly Denton?" Nina asked, worried for the girl's safety even though Russo was out of the picture.

"Safe," Zeke said. "We moved her to another location, just in case. If the son's around, he'll come after her. Probably with a shotgun."

"Why did they send Russo after us if they know Kelly's here?" Nina asked, shaking her head.

"You saw him up close," Thomas replied, his eyes going soft as he looked at her. "And me, well, he knows I'm here to take him, one way or another. I'm thinking Senator Slaton has been trying to cover for his son's misdeeds, and he got angry when Russo botched killing Kelly Denton and put us on his trail. He's obviously been protecting Allen all this time. Killing off the girls was an attempt to end it for good."

"So the senator and his son decided to take matters into their own hands by trying to scare us off the trail.

Tried to get to Kelly Denton and then sent Russo to take care of us."

"Yeah, something like that," Thomas replied. "They sent an amateur to the hospital and then sent Russo to take care of us when the attempts to scare us didn't work."

Nina shook her head. "Kelly was so scared she wouldn't tell us anything. She's been traumatized into silence. This happens to young girls a lot. Some never tell anyone at all. When she and the other girls started receiving threats, I think she just shut down."

Zeke nodded. "We kept so much protection on that girl, they didn't stand a chance. I'm glad for that."

Nina nodded, careful to keep her voice low. But Penny, used to the secrecy of their work, had gone upstairs to check on her two-year-old son, Kevin. "So did Max brief the team on the contents of the box—the letter that Mya had hidden, along with the phone?"

Zeke gave her a grim glance. "Yes. But give me the details again."

Thomas sat down, a brownie in his hand. "In a nutshell, Allen Slaton drugged a girl, attacked her and then bragged about it to his friends."

"Allen Slaton assaulted Kelly Denton at the Christmas party."

"And the victim was so afraid, she held the truth inside." Nina's stomach recoiled again. "He bragged to his buddies, but he didn't realize Mya Gregory had her phone set on Record, to capture something else going on at the party. When she and her friend Kristen Banks checked their video to post it, they heard Allen Slaton's voice in the background and realized what he'd done.

They found Kelly later and helped her get back to her apartment. Then they told her they knew the truth."

Zeke's frown said it all. "I guess that bond helped Kelly to cope even if she was afraid to come forward."

Nina nodded. "One of the boys saw them leaving together and got concerned. Allen Slaton asked him to watch them and track their moves. That's when he realized they probably knew."

Nina took a sip of water. "The girls came up with a plan to move the phone around, hiding it here and there. After they received some cryptic threats, Kelly Denton wrote a letter but kept it hidden, explaining what had happened to her at the party. Allen Slaton had put drugs in her drink and taken advantage of her. But she thought she'd never be able to prove it, and she was terrified, so she tried to let it go. Once the boys who were with Slaton heard there was a recording of him describing the whole thing, the three girls started receiving threats, and feared for their lives. So they did what they could to put the truth together with the evidence, only they kept it hidden, thinking they'd use it when the time was right. But one of the girls got tired of the threats and took it to another level. She started blackmailing Allen Slaton."

"The Gregory girl," Zeke said, his tone grim. "She made it worse."

"Her mom was dying of cancer. They needed the money," Nina replied. "Mrs. Gregory obviously doesn't know the truth. She thought Mya worked extra jobs to help her. We aren't going to tell her unless we have to. Knowing her daughter did this to try and save her will only make it worse for her. She'll blame herself."

"It's all there in Kelly's letter," Thomas said. "She

refused to tell us the truth, because she was so scared. They threatened to kill her parents. Now she's agreed to testify. But only when she knows the senator and his son are in custody and no threat to her and her family."

"Which we hope will be soon," Zeke said, getting up. "We've got people ready to go. But you two need to rest."

Nina and Thomas both stood.

"We're rested," she said. "And now we're ready."

Thomas gave Zeke an unapologetic grin. "You heard the agent."

Nina's emotions took a tumble deep inside her heart. He'd backed her up. Thomas knew she wanted in on this and he hadn't tried to stop her. She loved him—for that and oh, so many more reasons.

When she looked up and met his gaze, she saw so much in his golden-brown eyes. Would he leave after this? Would she ever see him again? Thomas gave her that slight grin and a quick wink.

Zeke's astute gaze moved from her to Thomas and back, but he didn't seem surprised. "Okay, then. Get into your gear and load up. It's gonna be a long night."

Thomas's gut burned with a new sensation. Something had passed between Nina and him back there. Something important.

He loved her.

Crazy, since they'd met under the worst of circumstances and had been thrown together to find the truth about a grim, tragic investigation. But no wonder he loved the woman. She was stubborn and spunky and…a really good FBI agent.

As they traipsed through the woods now, feet falling

on soft snow with a hardly a sound, he wanted to protect her even more. But Thomas had to let Nina do her
job. He'd have her back and she'd do the same for him.

That was the thing that had connected them.

Could they make this work after the fallout from this
strange case had settled down?

He sure prayed so. He prayed for a lot of things as
the FBI K-9 agents spread out around the perimeter of
the Slaton lodge, careful to stay in the shadows. Those
girls didn't deserve this and their parents had suffered
in the worst kind of way. Thomas prayed for the peace
beyond understanding for Mya's dying mother and Kristen's bitter, grieving father. Kelly had a second chance
and he prayed for her to get past this, too. Fear and
grief had held her captive, but now she could seek the
help she needed.

Glancing over at Nina, Thomas took in her tactical
gear and the way her shoulders rose in a rigid, down-
to-business mode.

And he prayed they could work on their kisses a little
bit more after this was all over.

He saw Nina check Sam. The big dog stood at the
ready, wearing protective gear, too. Then his earbud
crackled to life and he stood at attention, suited in his
bulletproof vest and carrying a high-powered rifle.

"Let's get on with this," she said through her mic,
giving him one last glance. "I'm ready for something
good to happen."

"I hear that," Thomas said, and they moved in on
the lodge.

Tim Ramsey and his German shepherd partner,
Frodo, approached on the right. "We have movement

in the front of the structure. Looks like a big den or great room."

"Have we identified the subjects?" Thomas asked through the radio.

Max spoke up from his command post a few yards into the woods. "Positive on both senator and son. We're moving in."

They spread out, two by two. Nina and Thomas took the front door. Two locals used a battering ram to get them in.

After that, everything became a blur of voices shouting, dogs barking and the whole house lighting up inside and out as they did a sweep of both levels.

Nina rushed ahead of Thomas, her gun drawn and Sam moving up front. They could hear an agent coming from another part of the house, telling the senator to get down on the floor.

Nina made it through the front door, just before someone rushed at her from a hallway and knocked her off her feet. Allen Slaton.

Sam started barking. Nina shouted, "Hands up. Down on the floor."

The younger Slaton did as she ordered, defiance mixed with fright in his pretty-boy features.

Nina called to Sam, "Guard!"

Sam stood between the boy and the door, the rottweiler growling. The kid looked terrified, his eyes wide, his hair on end. "Dad?" he called. "Dad? I can't get away."

He tried to stand.

Thomas stood behind Nina, his boots hitting on the wooden entryway, his weapon raised. "Stop right there, son. Hands up. Don't do anything stupid."

Allen Slaton started to cry, and sank to his knees. "Dad?"

Sam growled again and held his position, his snout aimed at the boy, who was now kneeling with his hands in the air.

Nina stepped between the dog and the young man. "It's over." Then she shot a relieved glance at Thomas and read the boy his rights, while the other agents brought the senator into the den just off the front hallway and sat him on a chair.

Nina commanded Sam to stay and then turned to Allen Slaton. Thomas watched as she went to pat him down.

The boy raised his arms, but quickly went for something in his back pocket, his expression full of rage and fear, his eyes on Nina. Thomas saw the weapon and didn't think twice.

"Nina, look out," he shouted. And then, after making sure she was safe, he shot Allen Slaton.

ELEVEN

"You did it again." Ignoring all the action around them, Nina stared up at Thomas, her heart beginning to slow down, her pulse less jumpy now.

"Yep. Just can't seem to stop myself from protecting you." He grinned, but she saw the darkness in his eyes, along with something else that made her want to hold him tight. "I'm sorry the boy is dead, but I had no choice. He could have killed you."

"But he didn't. I had my weapon and I had Sam." Instead of fussing at Thomas, she leaned up and gave him a quick peck on the jaw. "And now I have you."

She turned to get back into the fray, but his hand on her arm stopped her. "Are you sure about that? I mean, I don't back down."

"Neither do I, cowboy. As soon as we tie up these loose ends, we're going home for Christmas."

Thomas watched her walk away, that tough-girl stride colliding with the softness of her gentle kiss.

"We're gonna need your statement and…well, you know the drill," Max West said without preamble from behind Thomas.

"Understood," he answered, turning to find the man's eyes wide with realization. Thomas wondered if Max had witnessed that quick breach of protocol. "I'll call my people and explain. I know the routine. I hate this part of the job, though. I killed that young man."

"Yes, because he had a weapon and he pulled it out after both Nina and you warned him." Max looked to the patrol car where a shocked and dazed Senator Richard Slaton sat with handcuffs on his wrists. "The irony is that they hired a known assassin to kill three innocent girls—all to protect their good name and the status quo. In his desire to shield his son, the senator broke the law and tried to cover it all up. Now his only son is dead, and the senator will probably be in prison for a long, long time.

"Russo's talking now and Slaton is beyond caring about his precious image anymore," Max finished. "We've got reports to file and then we can close this one out." Rubbing the back of his neck, he added, "I've got to move on to these possible-arson fires. Tim's taking the lead on that one, thankfully. His K-9 partner's expertise is in sniffing out accelerants."

"Tim's a good agent. But then, your whole team seems solid." Thomas hesitated and then said, "If you're done with us, Nina and I want to go talk to Kelly Denton and let her know she's safe."

"Okay," Max said, turning to get back to work. Then he pivoted and gave Thomas a hard stare. "Don't take her away from us, Deputy Marshal."

Thomas pondered that for a moment. "You mean Agent Atkins? Hadn't planned on it. I've always had a hankering to live in Montana. Now seems like a good time to act on that notion."

Max cracked a quick, fleeting grin. "Does Agent Atkins know that yet?"

"No, not yet, but I aim to fill her in real soon."

A couple hours later, dawn started a gentle approach over the mountains, coloring the snow-tipped peaks in a shimmering pink-gold light.

Thomas stood with Nina at the door of her room at the inn. He wanted to hold her and kiss her and tell her he'd never leave her. But that would scare her away...

They'd gone to tell Kelly Denton and her parents that Allen Slaton was dead and that both Russo and the senator were in jail. Even if the senator got out on bail, Kelly would be safe. The FBI and US Marshal Department would make sure of that.

Right now, he was concerned about Nina. She took helping people to heart.

"If you ask me again if I'm okay, I might deck you," she said, reading his mind with all the precision of a high-powered flashlight.

"*Are* you okay?" he asked anyway.

She fisted her hand and knocked on his biceps twice. "I guess that didn't really hurt you at all, did it?"

"Told you I'm tough," he said, gathering her into his arms. "I've died a thousand deaths since I met you, but I sure like being around you."

Nina knew that feeling. Wanting to protect him and take care of him and never let him go out there again. But then, he was big and brawny and...beautiful. Why did love hurt and heal all at the same time?

"Think you can handle me, cowboy?"

He tugged her close and grinned down at her. "Yes, ma'am. I'll give it my best shot."

"Then kiss me like you mean it," she quipped.

He did, and then he followed her inside and held her close on the love seat by the fire. "Let's watch the sunrise coming over the mountaintop," he said. "Then I'll let you get some sleep."

Nina stirred and sat straight up, remembering where she was and why she wasn't at her little house anymore. She'd have to get that fixed soon. Then she smelled fresh coffee and bacon. A knock at her door made her hurry and freshen up while Sam's ears perked up.

"Come in," she called, stepping out of the tiny bathroom, her warm robe cocooning her.

She was having a good dream.

And in it, a tall Texan was standing at the door with breakfast and a red rose on a tray.

"Can I keep you?" she asked in a husky squeak of delight.

Thomas smiled at her. "I don't come cheap. I like a lot of groceries. Even Penny's complaining about that."

"I think I can manage buying more food," Nina said, getting up and wishing she'd brought pretty clothes to the inn with her.

Then she glanced around. Sam sat watching them probably amazed at the sizzle of something more than bacon moving through the small space. "Ah, Thomas, where did you sleep? Not out in front of my door, I hope."

"I went to my room and was out like a light," he said, while he arranged the tray on the bistro table by the bay window. Then he petted the rottweiler on the head.

"But Sam told me I really missed out on a lot. Said you snore. Told me it's the cutest thing, so delicate and—"

A throw pillow hit him upside his head. Dodging it, he said, "Hey, don't mess up this wonderful breakfast Penny and I prepared for you."

"I don't snore." Nina marched toward him and glanced at the clock. "It's late. I should get to work."

"Max said your vacation officially starts today, remember?"

She let out a little breath. "I'd forgotten I have five days off. And it's two days until Christmas. No wonder my mom's been calling."

"You might want to let her know you're safe and sound and you'll be home for Christmas," Thomas said as he set out plates full of eggs, bacon and toast. With some fruit on the side. Then he held out the rose with a flourish.

The man was full of surprises.

Nina took a sniff and let the sweet scent surround her, then sank into a chair and tried to drain her coffee. Putting down the dainty Christmas cup, she said, "Uh, Thomas…"

He stood across from her and stared down at her. "Yes, I'd love to go home with you for Christmas and meet your family. And no, you can't back out of it now because I'm pretty sure one day in the future, they will become my family, too."

Was he proposing to her?

Did she want him to propose to her?

"You're kind of confident," she said, hoping she didn't look as confused as she felt, and wishing she could be as confident as him. She'd never been impulsive, but now she wanted to dive right into breakfast and into being with Thomas.

He sat down and grabbed a piece of toast. He looked fresh and alive, and he smelled like the pines in high country. He wore a button-up shirt and jeans.

Off duty but on the prowl.

She liked him. Loved him. "Are you sure about all of this?"

How was she going to survive having him around her judgmental, outspoken family?

He leaned back and chewed on his toast, his eyes moving over her in a catlike fashion. "I'm pretty sure that I want to spend some time with you, no guns and no regrets."

"I have to figure out things, Thomas."

"About me? About us?"

"Yes, and about my house. It's a mess. I need to go by there and probably meet with the landlord and the insurance people." She stared at her bacon. "This is happening so fast."

"Eat your breakfast," he said, as calm as a sleeping lion. "Call your mom. Your landlord is aware of what happened to your house. He promises to have someone out to look at it today. You can figure out the insurance stuff and get with your landlord and then grab what you need to go home for Christmas."

"You talked to my landlord?"

"Max had Dylan talk to him, since you were kind of busy."

"Five or six days busy," she said. "We've only known each other a week. Isn't that kind of strange?"

Thomas stopped eating and stood up. "Okay, if you're not comfortable with me going with you, I'll understand. It won't be the first time I've spent Christmas alone."

Nina's stomach roiled. She'd invited him. She didn't want him to be alone during the holidays. Was he walking out on her? Well, she had told him she wasn't sure.

Feeling like the worst kind of tease, she said, "Thomas?"

"Nina, if you're not ready for this, we can try again once things settle down. I get it. We've been through a lot this past week and you need some time to debrief. Then, of course, I'm a lot to deal with. I have a dangerous job and I travel at the drop of hat. It works for me, but it's never worked in a relationship." Putting a hand on the doorjamb, he added, "Or at least, it hasn't before."

Then he was gone, moving fast for such a big man.

She waited a beat or two and then glanced over at Sam.

The dog looked at the door, woofed, and then set his doleful eyes on her. *"Go after him."*

Nina's heart took over her common sense. Grabbing suede booties to protect her bare feet from the snow, she stumbled down the stairs, still tugging one on.

Thomas was headed for the front door.

She rushed toward it and slammed it shut, then turned to see his surprised expression. "You big oaf, I want you to...be my date for Christmas. I'm scared and stupid, and I thought you'd be like my brothers and dad, but you're not. You accept me, Thomas. You get me. We both have the kind of careers that scare normal people, so I'm okay with you having to leave." Grabbing him by the collar, she added, "But don't you ever walk away from me again."

He let out a breath, his gaze softening with relief. "I had to be sure."

She yanked him into her arms and kissed him.

"Did that make you sure?"

"I don't know. Maybe a few more times."

Kissing him again, she breathed a thankful prayer.

"Will it always be like this?" she asked.

"Probably worse." He kissed her back. "And better."

"Okay, I can live with that," she said. "Let me get changed and we'll get going. We've got lots to do today."

Christmas Day

Nina showed Thomas the turn to the winding road up the mountain. Her entire family was waiting for them.

"They'll try to pick you apart," she warned, her tone shaky. "We could go somewhere else for Christmas."

"You're not getting cold feet, are you?" he asked, still amazed that she'd taken a leap of faith. "I mean, we brought gifts and I've got on my game face."

"No, I want you to be here. I want to be here with you. But you've heard how my brothers are. They'll test you to the limit."

"Bring it."

"My dad will do a background check on you."

"I don't mind that a bit."

"My mom will ask you fifty questions."

"I'll give her fifty answers."

The big cabin was a solid, rambling, worn, towering structure that looked as if it had been carved into the mountainside. Snow-covered and decorated with pine wreaths draped in bright red bows, it looked like the perfect Christmas card.

"They'll all be staring out the window," she said as the two of them got out of the truck.

Thomas met her by her door and whispered, "Then let's give them something to talk about."

He kissed her and then turned to face the house. "Nina, in spite of the horror that brought us together, I'm thanking God right now. This is the best Christmas I've ever had."

Sam danced around while they kissed again. Then the big dog woofed and stared up at them. *It's about time.*

Before they could part, the front door opened and one tiny woman and five domineering men rushed out to greet them.

Thomas grinned and shook hands and felt as if his heart had been rearranged and tied up with one of those bright red bows.

"Welcome home," Nina's mom said, hugging her daughter tight. But she was looking at Thomas.

* * * * *

Terri Reed's romance and romantic suspense novels have appeared on the *Publishers Weekly* top twenty-five and Nielsen BookScan's top one hundred lists, and have been featured in *USA TODAY*, *Christian Fiction Magazine* and *RT Book Reviews*. Her books have been finalists for the Romance Writers of America RITA® Award and the National Readers' Choice Award, and finalists three times for the American Christian Fiction Writers Carol Award. Contact Terri at terrireed.com or PO Box 19555, Portland, OR 97224.

Visit the Author Profile page
at Harlequin.com for more titles.

YULETIDE STALKING

Terri Reed

Have I not commanded you?
Be strong and courageous. Do not be afraid;
do not be discouraged, for the Lord your God
will be with you wherever you go.
—*Joshua* 1:9

Thank you to my family
for all the love and support you show me every day.

ONE

The cold December night air smelled of burned rubber and the lingering acrid odor of consuming flames. If not for the quick response of the Billings, Montana, fire department, the downtown tire store would have been a total loss.

Agent Tim Ramsey, a junior member of the FBI Tactical K-9 Unit headquartered in Billings, sat back on his haunches next to his canine partner. The three-year-old German shepherd, named Frodo, specialized in accelerant detection. They both had on booties to protect the scene and themselves.

This was the third fire in as many weeks. The first two were residential properties on the outskirts of town. A knot of frustration formed in Tim's chest. With Christmas just a few days away, the last thing anyone needed was a firebug on the loose.

Frodo kept his intense gaze on the floor, using his primary alert of sitting at attention. This was the dog's way of letting Tim know he smelled something of interest in the ash-covered area at the back corner of the store. It was the same area the firefighters suspected was the point of origin. Frodo and Tim's job was to root out the cause.

Tim trusted Frodo's keen sense of smell with his life. The dog's ability to detect odors and differentiate them with accuracy was what made Frodo and other canines so valuable in law enforcement.

With gloved hands, Tim gently sifted through the rubble, looking for clues. He lifted a piece of burned rubber. His stomach sank. Beneath lay the remnants of what he suspected was the cause of the fire. He knew what the forensic team would find upon analysis of the debris: cigarette ash, fibers from pillow stuffing and fragments of a generic matchbook. And trace elements of gasoline, just like in the other two fires. All indicators of arson.

Tim tagged the evidence with yellow markers, rose and addressed the Billings fire chief. "Sir, I believe our serial arsonist has struck again."

He could only hope and pray they caught the fiend before more fires were set, or the holiday season would go up in smoke and lives could be in jeopardy.

Christmas music drifted into the kitchen of the Billings Homeless Shelter. Trying to relax and enjoy this special time of year, Vickie Petrov hummed along to the upbeat tune as she rolled out more dough for her family's famous biscuits.

As was their tradition, she and her parents were serving the homeless on Christmas Eve. Because they owned a bakery, they made biscuits and pies, while other eateries in town provided turkeys and all the side dishes for the meal.

Vickie preferred to stay behind the scenes, where no

one paid any attention to her. Wiping her brow with the
sleeve of her thermal shirt, she glanced out the small
window above the sink. Fat snowflakes fell from the
sky. An involuntary tremor of dread worked over her
limbs. Another white Christmas.

Having grown up in Billings, she was accustomed to
the cold winters. Though she enjoyed bundling up, hiding beneath layers of sweaters, scarves and big jackets
that kept her warm and safe, she preferred the bluebell
sky of summer, where there were no nightmares lurk-
ing in the shadows.

Winter always brought back memories of…things
she'd rather forget.

Another shiver chased over her skin. She shoved
it away. She was safe here. No need to let the past in-
trude on such a festive night. Still, she couldn't shake
the strange sense of dread that had camped out in her
chest for months now. There was no reason to believe
she was being watched or followed, yet everywhere
she went, the small hairs at the base of her neck would
quiver with fear.

More than once, she thought she'd glimpsed Ken's
face in the crowd. But then she'd look again and he
wouldn't be there. It was just her imagination run amok.
Ken was most likely in California, living the dream he
professed to deserve.

Forcing him and the simmering anger clogged with
fear from her mind, she used the round cutter mold and
cut out two dozen biscuits, then set them on a baking
sheet and popped them in the oven.

The double doors of the kitchen swung open and
her mother strode through, with two plastic bags of
garbage in tow.

Affection filled Vickie. "Here, Mom, let me take care of that."

Irena Petrov relinquished her hold on the bags. Beneath her white baker's apron, she wore a sweater with a Christmas motif of reindeer romping in a meadow, strands of colored lights adorning their antlers. Her silver hair was twisted into a fancy bun at the nape of her neck.

Her clear blue-gray eyes danced with joy. "I wish you'd come out and join the festivities. Your father and Pastor John are setting up a karaoke machine so they can sing Christmas carols."

Vickie laughed. "I'll come watch when the singing starts."

"Okay, then." Irena checked on the pies. "These look wonderful, Vic. You do us proud with your baking." A shadow crossed her mother's face. "I wish you'd reconsider going back to college to get your business degree. I want you to be fully ready to take over the bakery one day."

Vickie forced herself not to flinch at the reminder of her broken dreams of graduating from the prestigious college that had granted her a scholarship. "I will be ready, Mom. The online courses I'm taking will prepare me just fine."

"You're alone too much," Irena chided gently. "It's been three years since you came home. Don't you think it's time to try again? You'll never find a nice young man to marry working behind the counter at the bakery."

"You never know, Mom," Vickie teased. "Daddy was behind the counter in his family's bakery when you met him."

Irena's face softened with love. "True. But that was in the old country." Her parents had immigrated to America from the Ukraine shortly after they married. "The world has changed so much since then. Why don't you try one of those online dating sites?"

Vickie sighed. "Mom, I'm not ready to date."

She feared she'd never be. Of course, her mom and dad didn't know the whole truth. She'd wanted to protect them from the depth of her pain. After the assault by her date, Ken, during her third year at the prestigious college in Boston, she doubted she'd ever be ready to let a man close again.

Yanking open the back door, she stepped outside with the two bags of garbage. Caution whispered across her flesh, raising goose bumps everywhere. She glanced around. She was alone. Safe.

Refusing to give in to the old fear, she set the bags on the ground so she could use both hands to lift the heavy lid of the Dumpster. Her skin prickled from the frigid temperature. The cold metal against her palms nearly made her lose her grip.

The smell of burning cigarettes close by mingled with the stench of trash. Vickie wrinkled her nose, feeling the hairs at the back of her neck rising in alarm. Unease twisted in her stomach. Anxious to get back inside, she quickly hefted the two bags into the container and then let the lid fall back in place with a noisy clank.

Before she could return to the safety of the kitchen, two strong bands of steel wrapped around her middle, trapping her forearms at her sides. Terror jolted through her brain like electricity. Her heart slammed into her ribs.

A scream built in her chest.

Her brain fought through the stunned panic. She'd taken self-defense classes at the local community center, determined to never again let anyone hurt her.

She bent her elbows, cupped her left hand over her right fist and used her right elbow as a battering ram into her attacker's rib cage as she twisted to face him where she'd be able to use her knees, feet and hands to strike out, to disable him.

Her assailant grunted, released her and bolted, running away into the dark.

Thrown off balance, Vickie stumbled, catching herself so she didn't take a header into the snow. She covered her heart with a hand and sent up a prayer of gratitude for her safety even as her mind grappled with what had just happened. Who was the man? Why had he grabbed her?

For a fleeting moment, an image of Ken's face reared up in her mind. That wasn't possible. She was mixing up the past with the present.

Trembling, she hurried toward the shelter's back door. She had to call the police. They had to catch the guy so he didn't attack someone else. She prayed the cops would believe her. The last time she'd dealt with law enforcement hadn't gone well.

A soft popping sound froze her in place with her hand on the doorknob. Fire ignited in the debris near the Dumpster. Flames shot up the side of the building, consuming the shelter's back wall in seconds.

Adrenaline spiking, she yanked open the back door and ran inside, screaming, *"Fire!"*

Tim secured a weather and bulletproof vest around Frodo's torso and attached the lead to the loop on his collar before releasing the dog from his special compartment in the black FBI-issued SUV. Keeping the dog at his side, he headed to the latest fire scene.

Cold air seeped beneath the collar of his thick black jacket emblazoned with the FBI Tactical K-9 Unit on the breast pocket. He was thankful he'd pulled on a black knit beanie to protect his head and ears from the icy temperature.

With a nod at the police officers stationed around the perimeter, he and Frodo walked past the barriers keeping the horde of people congregating on the sidewalk out of the firefighters' way and headed into the action. Heat emanated from the homeless shelter as the firefighters worked to put out the inferno.

Assessing the situation, he noted the amount of damage to the back side of the building. The flames had traveled up to the second floor. Black smoked curled into the night sky.

Fire Chief Ed Clark waved Tim over to where he stood. "I'm glad you're here. The fire burned hot and fast. We got to the blaze quickly. It seems our arsonist has struck again. We have a witness," Chief Clark stated and walked toward a group of civilians huddled together apart from the rest of the crowd.

Tim and Frodo followed the chief. If the witness could identify the firebug, that would be an appreciated Christmas gift, indeed.

"Miss Petrov," Chief Clark said. "This is Agent Ramsey from the FBI. He and his partner help with our fire investigations. Can you please tell him what you told me?"

Tim halted beside the chief, and Frodo sat at his side. Surprise washed over Tim. He recognized Irena and

Sasha Petrov. The Petrov Bakery was a favorite with the FBI Tactical K-9 Unit.

Then his gaze landed on the pretty ash-blond woman sandwiched between her parents. Tim had tried on several occasions to engage in conversation with her, but she hadn't reciprocated the effort.

Not that he was interested in pursuing anything. He was a confirmed bachelor. He'd learned the painful lesson of what happened when he let his heart get attached. Giving away a part of himself only to have it flung back in his face wasn't something he ever intended to repeat.

"Mr. and Mrs. Petrov." He smiled encouragingly at Vickie, hoping to assuage her usual skittishness. She stared at him with big blue eyes from beneath the brim of her snow parka's hood. "Miss Petrov. You all were here at the shelter tonight?"

"Yes, we help feed the homeless on Christmas," Sasha explained. He was a tall, slender man with a graying goatee and silver hair slicked back from his high forehead. "It's tradition."

"A nice one." The church Tim went to collected coats for the homeless. He'd donated several new ones. Every act of kindness helped those in need.

"Go on, Vic," Irena urged. She was several inches shorter than her husband and her daughter. She wore a red wool coat with a matching felt hat covering her head. "Tell the agent what happened."

Vickie lifted her chin as if steeling herself to talk to him. There was apprehension in her gaze. "I was taking out the garbage when I smelled cigarette smoke."

"Did you smell gasoline, too?" Anticipation revved in Tim's veins. "So you saw the person?"

She frowned. "No gasoline. It all happened so fast. I only caught a glimpse of his face in the shadows."

"Maybe with the help of a forensic artist, you'd be able to describe him enough for us to get an ID." This could be the break in the case they needed.

"I could try." Her tone suggested she doubted her success.

Tim had seen the FBI forensic artist work wonders with witnesses who were convinced they had nothing to offer. "You saw the guy start the fire?"

He glanced at the shelter. The flames had rapidly crawled up the building. Not the same modus operandi as the previous fires. But he wouldn't know for sure until the fire chief gave him the all clear to work the scene, which might not be until tomorrow.

"No. I only heard it after…"

Tim focused back on her. "After?"

"Maybe he dropped the cigarette when he grabbed me."

Her softly spoken words clanged through Tim's brain like a fire alarm. "He grabbed you? Why didn't you lead with that?" This took things to a whole new level.

Irena gasped. "You didn't tell us. Are you okay?"

Sasha put a protective arm around his daughter. "Did he hurt you?"

"I'm fine." Vickie leaned into her father. "I jabbed him with my elbow and he ran off."

"Impressive." Tim was relieved she was unharmed. "Good for you. Not many people would keep their head enough to react appropriately. Did the man say anything?"

"No, nothing. Like I said, he ran off. The fire started seconds later."

"She came inside yelling there was a fire, and got everyone out safely," Irena said, pride lacing her words.

Tim met Vickie's gaze. Respect for her grew tenfold. "You're a hero."

Her chin dipped in a shy way that Tim found endearing. "No. I did what anyone would have done."

"All the same, you saved lives tonight," Tim said. He admired how genuinely self-effacing she was, not at all trying to gain the limelight for acting quickly.

She gave him a soft smile. He could tell she was pleased by his words and for some odd reason that made him happy.

"Sir! You must stay back," A patrol officer restrained a tall man with a bald head who was trying to push his way past the barrier.

Vickie sucked in a breath and shrank back, practically hiding behind her parents.

Tim's heart rate picked up. "Is that the man who attacked you?"

Could this be the firebug?

TWO

"No." Vickie slipped out from behind her parents, embarrassed by her reflex to hide from the man pointing toward her. "That's Greg Sherman, the neighborhood day security guard." She couldn't let Tim think Greg was the man who'd attacked her. She paused.

A chill chased down her spine.

He wasn't, was he?

She'd have recognized him, right?

She had to admit Greg and her assailant were both tall and bulky. But that could describe so many men. Besides, Greg wouldn't hurt her.

But she'd thought the same of Ken once upon a time. She'd been wrong. Was she wrong now?

Fear tightened a noose around her throat.

She glanced at Greg. He waved. She automatically raised her hand in response before she thought better of encouraging him. Her fingers curled into a fist.

Tim leveled a pointed look at her. "He's a friend of yours?"

More like an irritant. A harmless one, or so she'd thought until now. Her shoulder muscles tightened. "Our relationship is complicated. I've known him forever."

"If Greg works days, what's he doing here tonight?" Tim asked. Without waiting for an answer, he turned and, with his dog at his side, strode toward the barricade line.

From over her mother's head, Vickie watched Tim stop to address Greg and keep him from forcing his way past the cordoned-off zone. She should have guessed he would show up. He always appeared out of the blue when she least expected him. Most likely he was the cause of the unsettled feeling she'd had lately.

She really wished he'd take the hint and go away. She'd turned down every one of his many invitations to dinner, the movies and other outings since she returned from college three years ago. Had he finally realized she wasn't interested and attacked her for it? Her pulse sped up.

But why now? And why would he want to hurt the shelter?

After a few moments of intense conversation, Tim and his partner walked away, leaving Greg behind the barricade. What had they talked about?

Her?

She blew out a breath of frustration and watched Tim talk to the Billings police chief, no doubt telling him about the attack. Would Chief Fielding take her seriously? She pressed her lips together.

Jamming her hands into her pockets to keep from fidgeting, she struggled to calm herself. Her nerves were strung out from all the attention focused on her. It had taken every ounce of self-possession not to squirm under Tim's regard while he'd questioned her. And his words of praise had made her heart bump against her breastbone in a funny way.

Just as it did every time he came into the bakery. He always started up a conversation, usually about the weather or about the different pastries. She knew he liked his coffee with almond milk creamer and had a preference for apricot filling. He seemed like a nice guy. Kind and considerate. But then again, what did she know?

She'd thought the same thing of Ken. He'd been an intern with one of the college's leading researchers, on track to graduate magna cum laude when they'd met in the library. He'd been charming and attentive and she'd been so flattered when he asked her out.

Three dates later, he tried to force himself on her. If not for the grace of God and her roommate's timely arrival, he'd have finished what he'd started.

Afterward, he'd taunted her, calling her a tease for not giving him what he wanted. What he deserved. He'd turned into someone else and made her question herself. How had she not seen him for who he really was? Had she been blinded by his suave demeanor and gentlemanly ways?

When she'd reported him to campus police, they blew her off, believing his lies that she was trying to ruin his reputation because he'd refused her advances. As if she were the one in the wrong. She'd even shown the dean and the officer the bruises left by Ken's hands, but the marks hadn't swayed either man whom she'd thought were there to protect her. Instead, they'd dismissed the bruises, saying the dark spots could have been from anything and didn't prove Ken had assaulted her. She wasn't sure what pull Ken had with the school, but whatever it was, it was enough to keep him from trouble.

She'd found out the hard way that she'd made a mistake in trusting those in authority. A mistake she wouldn't make again.

Even with a handsome FBI agent.

Tim and the police chief were now talking with Lacey Klems, who ran the shelter, and Pastor John, both of whom were clearly upset. Vickie's heart went out to the dozens of people who had nowhere else to stay on this frosty Christmas Eve.

There had to be a way to find the displaced individuals warm accommodations for the foreseeable future, until the shelter could be repaired.

Another commotion from the opposite direction drew her attention.

"I demand to be let through. Who's in charge here?" A short, rotund man in a trench coat that touched the toes of his black wing tipped shoes, and a fur hat, gestured widely toward the building. His voice carried as he shouted at the police officer keeping him out of the cordoned-off area.

Vickie pulled a face. "What is Mr. Johnson doing here?"

"I believe he owns this building," her dad replied.

As well as the one they rented for the bakery. Vickie wasn't a fan of their landlord.

Pastor John and Lacey Klems hurried to the blockade.

Vickie's father sighed. "I should go help Pastor and Ms. Klems. Mr. Johnson can be a bear to deal with. He's been unreasonable since summer. I'm not sure what has him so prickly."

"We'll both go." Vickie's mom tucked her arm

around her husband's. The two marched over to show support to their pastor and friend.

Feeling vulnerable and conspicuous standing by herself, Vickie hurried to catch up. Pride for her parents filled her chest. They were good, steady people with hearts of gold. And they were still very much in love even after thirty-plus years of marriage. She wanted a relationship such as theirs, but doubted she'd ever find someone to whom she could risk giving her heart.

As she stepped next to her parents, she heard Mr. Johnson say, "I knew this wasn't a good idea."

Lacey fiddled with the wool scarf around her neck. "Barry, please, you know as well as I do how much the city needs the shelter."

"So you keep telling me," Mr. Johnson huffed. "Serving so many meals in one night. Did the oven explode? Did someone leave the gas stove on?"

"No, sir." Vickie's dad stepped up. "We don't know what exactly happened."

Mr. Johnson narrowed his gaze on him. "What are you doing here?"

"We provided the biscuits and dessert for the Christmas meal." Though her father kept his voice polite, she knew that tone. It was the one he used when their supplier tried to short them on the good chocolate.

Mr. Johnson turned to address the Billings patrol officer standing nearby. "Did they cause this?"

Vickie gasped. Anger spread through her chest, overheating her beneath her parka. How dare their landlord accuse them of starting the fire! The man was a miser and a bully. She always dreaded the days he came to the bakery to collect his rent. He'd help himself to a pastry or two, uninvited, as if getting free food was his due.

The patrolman raised his eyebrows. "The fire investigation hasn't been done yet, sir."

"Barry, the fire didn't start in the kitchen," Pastor John told him. "Please, don't jump to conclusions. We—"

"You told me you could handle this," Mr. Johnson said, before he could finish speaking. "We'll have to seriously reconsider the future of the shelter once the building is repaired."

"Now, Barr—" The clergyman stopped speaking as Mr. Johnson raised a hand.

"Don't *now Barry* me," Mr. Johnson said. "I was reluctant to allow the shelter into the building to begin with and apparently I was right to be concerned." He gestured to the smoldering structure.

Knowing the loss of the shelter would be a terrible blow to the pastor, Vickie tapped into the adrenaline coursing through her veins and stepped beyond her fear of drawing attention to herself to say, "There's no way anyone could have predicted a fire."

He stared down his wide nose. "Except one happened, now, didn't it?"

"Barry, there's no need to snap at Vickie," Pastor John said.

Tim and Frodo came over. For some reason their presence gave her a measure of comfort as she scooted to the side to make room for them.

"What's the problem here?" Tim asked.

"Who are you?" Mr. Johnson countered. "Are you in charge?"

"FBI agent Tim Ramsey." He showed the man his badge. "We're investigating the fire. What is your purpose here?"

"That's my building," Mr. Johnson said. "This is going to raise my insurance rates and has ruined my Christmas celebration with my family."

Vickie couldn't believe the landlord's level of insensitivity. Surely he realized the inconvenience to his evening was not nearly as devastating as it was to those who called the shelter home for the night.

"This fire has ruined everyone's Christmas," Tim stated in a firm tone. "Without the shelter, most of these people will be struggling to find somewhere safe to get out of the cold."

Vickie wanted to applaud Tim for putting Mr. Johnson in his place and validating her thoughts. Admiration for the agent spread through her chest like frosting on cookies. She met his gaze and offered him a smile of appreciation. Something flared in his eyes, sending ribbons of warmth winding through her. The unsettling sensation knocked her back a step.

"I want to know who started this fire," Mr. Johnson demanded. "I'll have to file a claim."

Tim turned his attention back to the landlord. "Sir, you'll receive a copy of the report once it is finished."

Mr. Johnson harrumphed. "My nephew, Joseph, is a firefighter. I'm sure he'll fill me in on what I need to know."

For a moment Tim's eyes narrowed. "Until we release the scene, you will stand back behind the barricade and let us do our jobs."

Vickie fought to hide a smile. She shouldn't gloat over Tim's dressing down the arrogant Mr. Johnson, but she was relieved someone had no qualms about standing up to the bully.

Turning away from the man in dismissal, Tim addressed Vickie and her parents. "You're free to go."

"Thank you, Agent Ramsey," her dad said, and shook his hand. "We won't be leaving quite yet." He turned to Pastor John. "We can open the bakery and provide sandwiches for everyone."

Pastor John clapped her dad on the back. "You are a good man, Sasha. Let's round everyone up and head over there."

"Vickie," Tim said, stopping her from following her parents, Pastor John and Lacey Klems. "I'll come by the bakery tomorrow to arrange for you to sit with a forensic artist."

"But tomorrow is Christmas Day," she said. "Surely it can wait until the twenty-sixth."

"Crime doesn't observe the holidays," Tim said softly.

Her stomach churned. "What will happen to all the people who were counting on staying at the shelter?"

Tim's lips pressed together in a grim line. "I don't know. Police Chief Fielding will make arrangements. I'm sure he'll contact the Red Cross."

Vickie slid her gaze back to Mr. Johnson, who was now on the phone, no doubt with his insurance company. She wondered how many buildings he owned in Billings. And if there was a space for a makeshift shelter. She bit the inside of her lip. The man's altruism was a shallow well, but she had to try.

"Are you okay?" Tim asked.

She stared into his blue-green eyes. His question sparked a fire of determination in her belly. She needed to be strong, to stand up for those who couldn't. Bravery wasn't her strong suit, but tonight she needed to find her courage. "No, I'm not."

The concern darkening Tim's expression sent her pulse thundering. It was his job to be concerned, she reminded herself, and focused her attention on Mr. Johnson. As soon as he finished his call, Vickie waved to him. "Mr. Johnson, can I speak to you?"

His brow crinkled with apparent irritation. He walked to the barricade separating them. "What now?"

She could feel Tim's curious gaze on her. His presence gave her strength. Gathering her courage, she said, "Would you have a space in one of your other buildings that could be made into a temporary shelter?"

He frowned. "What do I look like? A charity?"

"It's a sound idea," Tim said. "How many buildings do you own? Are they full?"

Mr. Johnson snorted. "I'd have to check with my leasing agent to see what empty space we have and what the rent would be."

"Rent?" Vickie couldn't stomach the man's greediness. "Really? On Christmas Eve?" She turned away from him in disgust. "Maybe the high school gym could accommodate everyone for tonight? I'll go ask Chief Fielding."

Tim put his hand on her arm, keeping her from walking away. "Mr. Johnson, get your leasing agent on the phone now."

"And ruin his Christmas, too?" The older man shook his head. "I can't help you."

Tim stepped closer, towering over the landlord, and lowered his voice. "Sir, the community would appreciate your generosity and goodwill in helping out those less fortunate. I'm sure the media would report such kindness in the face of this tragedy." He shrugged. "Or they might report your refusal to help."

Mr. Johnson's eyes widened. He pushed forward a step. "Are you threatening me?"

Frodo let out a low growl. The man jumped back.

"Not at all," Tim stated. "Just reminding you this incident tonight will make the news. In fact…" He tipped his head toward where the local news crew were filming the shelter fire and interviewing bystanders. "What kind of man do you want to be viewed as?"

Mr. Johnson's lip curled as he yanked his cell phone from his pocket. "I'll see what I can do." He turned away to talk to his leasing agent.

"Wow," Vickie said beneath her breath, so only Tim would hear. "You handled him well."

He cupped her elbow and drew her away from the crowd of people. "Sometimes people need a nudge to do the right thing."

"Sad but true."

"You'll need to prepare yourself as well," Tim told her. "The news people will want to talk to you, too."

Anxiety twisted in her gut. "I don't want to be on camera. What if the man who attacked me decides to come after me again?"

"Don't worry. I won't let anything happen to you," he told her. "I've already spoken to Police Chief Fielding and he will have a patrol officer stationed outside your house."

She'd rather have Tim and his dog for protection. She blinked in surprise at the realization. He was a law officer. The representation of everything she'd come to loathe after the attack at college. She'd turned to the authorities for help but had been brushed off as if she didn't matter.

Did she really want to rely on this man for her safety?

It was better than the alternative.

At least Tim seemed to take her seriously.

"Agent Ramsey," Mr. Johnson called out, drawing their attention.

Tim's warm hand settled on the small of Vickie's back. Surprise washed over her and she nearly lost her footing on the icy sidewalk. He steadied her and guided her toward the barricade. Her mouth went dry and her heart raced. She hadn't let anyone get this physically close in a very long time.

"Yes?" Tim said, as they drew to a halt.

Looking as if he had swallowed a lemon, Mr. Johnson said, "One of my buildings a few blocks from here has space. You can relocate the shelter on a purely temporary basis. The leasing agent will meet you there with the keys."

Delighted by the news, Vickie could have hugged the man, but instead, she smiled. "Thank you, Mr. Johnson."

His gaze flicked to her and away. "A couple of days at most. I'm a businessman, not a philanthropist."

Vickie and Tim shared a glance. *No news flash there.*

"Either way, the gesture is appreciated," she said.

Mr. Johnson made a noise in his throat and left.

"Merry Christmas," she called after him.

"I'll tell Police Chief Fielding and help him organize a crew to transition everyone over," Tim said.

"I'll go tell my parents and Pastor John," Vickie replied.

As she hurried to where they stood talking to the many displaced shelter occupants, the now familiar sensation of being watched shimmied down her spine. She glanced behind her at Tim, but he had his back to her.

Looking around, she met several curious glances from those on the other side of the barricade and from many of the firefighters, who's faces were obscured by their masks, now wrapping up their hoses and putting away their equipment. She searched each face, half afraid to find herself locking eyes with Ken. But he wasn't in the crowd. There was no way he'd be in Billings. She hadn't seen him in three years. It was her imagination. Or her fear that one day she would see him again.

There was nothing concrete to warrant the tingling chill tiptoeing over her flesh.

Yet she couldn't stop the questions bouncing around her head. Was her attacker among the gawkers? Watching her, waiting for another moment to grab her? Would she ever feel safe again?

THREE

"Make way!" Two volunteers squeezed through the front doors of the new, temporary homeless shelter carrying a leather couch, the last of the salvageable furniture from the old shelter.

Standing in the narrow entryway, Tim hooked an arm around Vickie's waist and drew her up against his chest while he tucked Frodo next to his leg.

She stiffened and glanced at him before quickly looking away. He kept his hold loose so as not to crush her, but had a hard time ignoring the awareness zinging through him from the close contact. She'd shed her jacket an hour ago as they'd worked to make the donated space habitable.

She barely reached his chin. Her blond hair hung loose about her shoulders, and though the lingering odor of the fire clung to her, there was a hint of sugar and apples in the silky strands teasing his senses.

He noticed one of the firefighters giving her the once-over and wanted to growl at him like a possessive dog with a bone. So not the way he should be feeling. But given someone had attacked her tonight, he decided he could be a bit territorial.

In a protective way, of course. Nothing personal. He wasn't looking for anything personal. He was content with his life. Adding in any kind of relationship would only complicate things. He didn't like complications.

Once the path was clear, he released his hold on her. She stepped away with a shy smile that packed a powerful punch. "Thanks."

"Anytime." He tugged on the collar of his uniform. "At least the heat is working in here."

She dropped her gaze to Frodo. "He's a handsome dog. May I pet him?"

"Of course."

She hesitated with her hand poised in the air. "He won't bite?"

"Not unless I command him to," Tim replied with a smile. "His specialty is arson investigations. He alerts on accelerants."

Tentatively, Vickie held her hand out for the German shepherd to sniff. Then crouching slightly to reach him, she ran her palm over his sleek head and rubbed him behind the ears. "You're a good boy." She looked at Tim. "How old is he?"

"He'll be three on New Year's Eve."

"How long have you had him?"

"The FBI purchased him when he was ten months old. We've been together for the past two years."

She straightened. "I'm thankful you and Frodo are here." She blinked as if surprised by the admission.

He struggled to suppress a chuckle. It wasn't every day a pretty woman told him she was glad he was around and it wasn't contrived.

She leveled her shoulders and met his gaze. "It was

amazing you were able to convince Mr. Johnson to open up the building for the shelter."

"Considering he'd latched on to the idea of letting the media know of his generosity, I think it's safe to say he realized the benefits of charity," Tim replied.

She laughed, the sound soft and pleasing. He liked it.

"I don't think it was a coincidence the building was empty," she said. "God arranged this. He knew we'd need it tonight."

Puzzled by her logic, he said, "But if God knew we'd need a new shelter, then why did He let the old one burn?"

"I wish I knew. God's ways are a mystery. But I have to believe everything happens for a reason even if we don't understand."

He mulled over her words. He believed in God and His son. Yet he'd seen so much evil and heartache through the years, he couldn't comprehend the point of it all. "I'm not sure I have that same level of faith."

"A little faith can grow."

He grinned. "Like a mustard seed."

She grinned back. "Exactly. Sunday school?"

"Vacation Bible school, actually."

"Me, too. Every summer. My favorite was the summer I was ten. The theme was pirates. I still have my pirate hat. I was quite the scallywag." In the dim glow of the overhead lights Tim could see her cheeks turning pink.

He pictured her as a young girl sporting a tricorn hat with a feather plume and brandishing a rubber sword. Did she still have a playful side? So far he'd witnessed her stellar work ethic and her compassion and kindness toward others. She'd handled herself like a pro tonight with the media. He'd sensed her nervousness, but it hadn't shown as she'd recounted witnessing the blaze igniting.

"Here you are." Sasha Petrov emerged from the atrium. "Come inside. Pastor John wants to say a few words before we disperse."

They followed her father into the large open space in the center of the building where rows of cots dominated one side of the area, while tables and benches were in the center, and a few couches had been arranged in front of a television off to the other side of the room. Tim and Frodo stayed close to Vickie as they squeezed into the crowd.

"Thank you, everyone, for your help." Pastor John stood on a chair and addressed the many people who had come forward to help relocate the residents of the Billings Homeless Shelter.

The show of support from the community impressed Tim, especially those from Pastor John's congregation. As many as fifty families had arrived within a half hour of when the call for help had gone out.

"The Petrovs have offered to bring over Christmas sandwiches tomorrow. Let's give them a round of applause," Pastor John said.

Tim clapped and leaned close to Vickie to say, "Your family is very generous."

Her eyes glowed with delight. "My parents bake and cook. And feeding others is a joy to them. I think it's a perfect way to show God's love on Christmas Day."

He couldn't agree more. Too bad he'd be on duty tomorrow. But at least Vickie would be safe with her family. He'd make sure there was a police presence both at the bakery and at the shelter.

"Please go home and enjoy your families for Christmas," Pastor John said. "God bless you all and Merry Christmas."

Amid a chorus of Merry Christmases and chatter, the crowd dispersed. Tim placed his hand to the small of Vickie's back again and guided her and Frodo across the atrium to where her parents were gathered with Pastor John and Lacey Klems.

"Agent Ramsey, you're still here?" Irena said.

"Yes, ma'am," Tim replied. "I won't be allowed to inspect the fire scene until it's safe for us." Once the embers had cooled and there was no chance of a secondary flare-up, he and Frodo would search for the point of origin and the cause of the fire.

"We appreciate your work, Agent Ramsey," Sasha said, and held out his hand.

Clasping it firmly, Tim said, "Thank you, sir."

"Yes, we are grateful for your help tonight." Pastor John held out his hand in turn and Tim shook it.

"Please keep us informed on the progress you make in the investigation," Lacey said.

"I will, ma'am," Tim assured the shelter director. With a nod, she moved away with the pastor to say goodnight to more people.

Sasha put his arm around Irena. "Time to head home, my love. Morning will come faster than we'd like."

Irena addressed her daughter. "Coming, Vickie?"

"Yes. But I need to find my coat," she said. "I don't remember where I set it when we came in."

"You laid it on a chair in the entryway," Tim reminded her. Reluctance twisted in his stomach. He wasn't ready to see her walk out the door just yet. To her parents, he said, "I'll drive her home."

He told himself he was just doing his job. Protect and serve. Keeping a witness safe. All part of his duties as an officer of the law.

"Not necessary," Vickie said.

"Maybe not, but I'd like to make sure you arrive safely," he improvised. "And I can confirm that a Billings patrol officer is on guard."

"Thank you, Agent Ramsey," Irena said. "I trust you'll take good care of our daughter." She patted Vickie's arm with a gleam in her eyes. "We'll see you at home."

Vickie watched her parents leave before turning back to him. She tilted her head to the side. There was wariness in her eyes. "Are you always so attentive to victims of crimes?"

"When a witness is in danger," he told her. Though in truth, he rarely saw the people involved. He dealt with the evidence. The charred remains. "Until we catch the arsonist, you won't be safe."

Her face paled at the reminder. "Right. Because he doesn't know if I can identify him or not." They walked toward the entryway. "Maybe I should talk to the news people again and let them know for certain I didn't get a clear look at the man's face."

"We could do that," Tim told her. "But you may still be able to help us find him. We won't know for sure until you meet with Brian, the forensic artist."

Vickie stopped. The row of chairs lined against the wall were empty. They searched the building for it but to no avail. She sighed. "My coat's gone. Bummer. Maybe it will turn up later. Someone probably grabbed it by mistake."

Though Tim wasn't surprised someone had taken off

with her coat with so many people coming and going from the place, he felt bad just the same. "Was there anything of value in the pockets?"

"No, thankfully. I left my purse and wallet with all my credit cards at home."

He took off his outer jacket. "You can wear mine."

"But you'll be cold," she protested.

"I'll be fine," he assured her. "Let's get you home."

He helped her into his jacket. She had to push the sleeves up at the elbows in order for her hands to come out of the sleeves. She pulled the collar up close and seemed to burrow into it with a sigh that sounded suspiciously like contentment, and it stirred a yearning inside him he didn't want to examine. Best to ignore any soft emotions right now.

They left the building and stepped into the quiet night. Snow blanketed the world in white but the sky was clear at the moment. There was no one around, only a few cars parked along the curb. He'd left his SUV in the lot of the building across the road.

The unmistakable sound of an engine turning over down the block echoed in the stillness, but no headlights came on.

Uneasiness slinked up his spine and settled in the muscles of his neck. He urged Vickie and Frodo across the street at a quick pace.

The squeal of tires on the slick pavement rent the air.

Frodo barked a warning.

A dark sedan pulled away from the curb and barreled toward them, a hulking, inky shadow racing to take them down.

Releasing Frodo's lead, Tim shouted the command, "Sidewalk!"

Frodo immediately darted out of the road, freeing Tim to grab Vickie. He lifted her off her feet and tucked her into his chest as he dived out of the way, taking them both to the ground. He gritted his teeth as the sedan zoomed past them, barely missing their legs. Frodo's angry barks bounced off the icy pavement.

Sitting up quickly, Tim stared after the vehicle, straining to make out the license number in the glow of the taillights. The plate had been removed. Frustration churned in his gut.

Vickie righted herself but remained within the circle of his arms. "What just happened?"

His gut clenched with dread and anger. "Somebody tried to kill us."

"How can you be sure?" Her voice trembled and her body shook within his embrace. "Maybe the driver didn't see us."

"Maybe." Though he doubted that was the case. He shifted and winced.

"You're hurt!" She quickly disengaged herself from his arms. "We need to get you to the hospital."

Though he appreciated her concern, the only place they were going was to her home. He slowly rose, testing the various places that ached. "I'm just banged up. Nothing broken." He helped her to her feet. "Come on, we need to get off the street before that maniac decides to return."

"You can't know for sure he was trying to hurt us," she said.

She really didn't want to believe her life was in danger. Tim understood. He didn't have to be a mind reader to know she was a woman who saw the good in others. She had a sweet and gentle nature. He wished he could protect her from the reality of the situation but he couldn't. He was sure that car had intentionally tried to hit them. Though he could have been the target, he'd made enough enemies over the years, he was convinced the arsonist Vickie had seen had been behind the wheel.

"Either way, we're reporting the car," he said.

After helping her into his SUV and securing Frodo in his compartment, Tim called 911, identified himself and explained the situation to the dispatcher. They waited for the Billings Police Department to arrive and take their statements about the incident.

Then he drove Vickie to the Petrovs' home, keeping an alert eye out for the sedan. After circling the block to make sure they hadn't been followed, he pulled into the driveway of the two-story house on a tree-lined street. Colored Christmas lights hung from the eaves. A large decorative Christmas tree was showcased in the front window.

Tim was gratified to see a marked patrol car parked across the street. He walked Vickie to the porch. "You'll be safe tonight. If the officer sees anything suspicious, he'll call for backup."

"Thank you for all you've done for me," she said. The warm glow of the porch light shone on her hair, highlighting the blond strands.

"Just doing my job." He stared into her blue-gray eyes and realized he could easily lose himself in the stormy depths. So pretty and sweet.

She hesitated. "You probably have a family waiting for you at home, right?"

"No. No one." Was she fishing?

"No girlfriend expecting you to come by?" she pressed.

She *was* fishing. His ego puffed up a bit and lifted one corner of his mouth. "Not in a very long time."

As one of the only single agents left on the team, he'd opted to be on call tonight and on duty tomorrow, allowing all his teammates to enjoy the holiday with their loved ones. Seemed the least he could do, since he had no family to speak of. Only Frodo.

Standing here with Vickie, his body still humming with residual adrenaline, he couldn't say he regretted being on duty tonight.

Vickie tilted her head again. "What happened to her? Your girlfriend from a long time ago?"

"She moved on without me." He expected to feel the old anger stir, but it didn't. Odd. And yet, looking at Vickie, it was hard for him to think of any other woman.

Vickie cleared her throat. "What about your parents?"

"My folks divorced when I was a kid." There'd been a time when the subject of his parents made bitterness well up. Now he felt only a sad resignation. He'd never have a close, loving relationship with his parents.

"I'm sorry," she said. "That must have been hard."

"It was. They each remarried and started new families. I bounced back and forth between them until I went away to college."

"That's rough," she murmured.

He shrugged. "It was a long time ago. Now my family is the team and Frodo."

"You could stay here with us." Her cheeks turned bright red beneath the porch light. "I mean, to have a late Christmas Eve dinner. You have to eat, right?" she added quickly.

He studied her. "What is up with you and Greg Sherman? He acted like you and he were involved."

She tucked in her chin. "We're not... Our relationship isn't like that. We're acquaintances at most. We went to grade school and high school together. I hadn't seen him in years until he took the job as security guard."

Tim couldn't believe how strangely relieved he was to hear her say that. It made no sense why he should care one way or the other. "He made it sound like there was more between you."

She huffed out an irritated sigh. "He'd like more. He keeps asking me out and I keep turning him down."

Motive to hurt her? Tim's heart rate ticked up. But why set the fire? "Do you think he could be the one who attacked you?"

She bit at her lip. "I considered it, but..."

"But?"

She hesitated, as if debating with herself, then she gave her head a sharp shake. "The man's face was in shadows. It happened so fast."

Acid burned in Tim's gut. Had he let the arsonist walk away? "Do you know what kind of car Greg drives?"

"No, I don't. He's always walking when he comes into the bakery."

"I'll look into Greg. See if he has an alibi." Not just for tonight, but for each fire. "When you work with the forensic artist we'll have a better idea of whether you saw the man's face or not. The subconscious can reveal a lot even when we don't think we've seen anything."

"I hope that's true," she said with a tremble in her voice. "I really want this creep caught."

"Me, too. We'll get him." Tim wouldn't rest until the

man responsible for trying to hurt Vickie and burning up much of the city was brought to justice.

"You didn't answer my question. Will you stay?"

The desire to say yes welled up, making his chest tight. As much as he'd like to spend time with Vickie and her parents, he had a job to do.

The eager expectancy in her face undid him. What was it about this woman that made him want to please her?

He glanced up, seeking help from above, and discovered a sprig of mistletoe hanging over the porch. Uh-oh.

Time to retreat before he did something he'd regret, like kiss her.

FOUR

A simple yes or no would suffice. Vickie didn't understand why Tim wasn't responding to her invitation to come inside for a late dinner.

He stared at the porch ceiling, his face losing its color. She glanced up to see what had affected him so adversely.

A mistletoe ball entwined with red and silver ribbons hung over their heads.

Her stomach clenched with a burst of alarm. She reared back, stumbling against the closed front door. Clearly, she wasn't as good at containing her reaction to the mistletoe as Tim.

Why, oh why, did her dad insist on putting that thing there every year?

She knew exactly why. So he had an extra excuse to kiss her mother every time they crossed the threshold. After thirty years of marriage, her dad was still a hopeless romantic.

In the chaos of the evening, Vickie had completely forgotten about the offending plant taunting her each time she entered and left the house. No wonder poor Tim blanched and now quickly edged backward toward the steps, hoping to make a speedy exit. She didn't blame him. Being trapped into a silly tradition of kissing beneath the green decoration wasn't her idea of a good time. And apparently not Tim's, either.

"Never mind about dinner," she said, willing to let him off the hook so they could both escape the embarrassment of not wanting to share a kiss, despite the uncomfortable burn of disappointment leaching through her. "You have work to do. You should go. I'm sure your dog needs you."

Now my family is the team and Frodo. The thought of him alone with only his dog as a companion made her want to hug him. A reaction she really shouldn't be having about him.

He smiled slightly. "Yes. I should go. Work. Fire." He stepped down the first stair. "I'll see you tomorrow."

She couldn't help the tiny thrill to know she'd see him the next day. She clamped her mouth shut. Silly. He meant when she worked with the forensic artist. He obviously wasn't interested in her on a personal level.

The thought depressed her, which was totally ridiculous. She wasn't interested in him, either, regardless of how handsome and kind she found him, which could all be an illusion designed to trick her. She wouldn't be taken in again by a chiseled jaw and thoughtfulness.

"Good night." She fled inside and closed the door with a snap, then let out a breath. Her knees felt shaky. It was the residual adrenaline from the day, not because of Tim. *Yeah, sure.*

"Vickie?" her mother called from the kitchen. The delicious aroma of her traditional borscht soup, made from beets, broth and a host of winter vegetables, filled the house.

"Yes, Mom. Coming." She decided she'd not tell her parents about the car incident. No need to worry them unduly.

Besides, she wasn't sure the vehicle had been aiming for them. Maybe the person behind the wheel had been drunk or hadn't seen her and Tim. There had to be another explanation other than someone trying to kill them. Despite her reasoning, a tremor of apprehension skated across her skin.

She could only pray that tomorrow she'd be able to give a detailed enough description of the man who'd attacked her and started the homeless shelter fire.

And tried to run her and Tim down.

She had to trust Tim would succeed in capturing the villain.

Maybe this time justice wouldn't fail her.

Tim and Frodo returned to the remains of the Billings Homeless Shelter fire. The temperature had dropped and more snow fell from the sky, making the scene a soupy mess. Kind of how Tim felt.

When he'd glanced up and spotted the mistletoe hanging from the porch over him and Vickie, the thought of kissing Vickie had taken hold of his imagination and shook it until the yearning to kiss her had been overwhelming.

He'd barely managed to retreat before giving in. And judging from the way Vickie had reacted once she'd realized they were standing beneath the decoration, she wouldn't have been amenable to fulfilling the Christmas tradition.

Which was good. For them both.

With effort, he put Vickie and his scattered feelings

about her aside as he donned gloves and booties for him and Frodo before releasing the dog from the SUV and grabbing his evidence collection kit.

The fire chief and several other firefighters were still on scene, wrapping up their hoses and gathering other equipment.

"Chief," Tim said in greeting.

"Agent Ramsey, good timing," Clark replied. "The fire's cold." He rolled his neck as if to relieve his tension. "It's a wonder the whole building wasn't consumed. But thankfully, the call to dispatch came quickly." The chief gestured to the blackened remains. "You two can do your thing. Let me know what you find."

"Yes, sir." To Frodo, Tim said, "Seek." The cue word was to let the dog know they were going to work now.

Tim and Frodo picked their way through the rubble of ash and debris covered in snow to the back door of the shelter and the Dumpster. Vickie had stated the fire had started in this area. The scorch pattern from the ground behind the Dumpster and up the side of the building was odd.

Not like the three arson cases he'd worked this month. Maybe they were dealing with a different perpetrator.

He poked around the rubble, not finding anything of note. Frodo sniffed the edges of the Dumpster and let out a loud bark, then sat at attention.

Tim squatted down to see what had the dog alerting. Beneath the back edge of the Dumpster were remnants of a matchbook and a tiny portion of a cigarette filter. Okay.

Tim's heart rate kicked up. So the same method of

combustion was used, but why had it burned hotter and faster?

He bagged the evidence, placed a marker in the spot with a number to correspond to the evidence bag, and stood to stare at the structure, taking in the unusual burn pattern. Definitely some sort of accelerant had been used, but not gasoline this time.

"Good job, Frodo."

The dog let out a quick bark in response to the praise. Then he set his nose to the ground and sniffed. Tim let out the German shepherd's lead, letting him explore a wider diameter of the cordoned-off area. Frodo halted a few feet away, then sat, once again alerting to something on the ground. Tim hurried over to inspect his find.

A dark glob on the pavement had drawn Frodo's attention.

Using a small chisel from his tool kit, Tim pried the substance free to allow for examination. Though the crime lab would confirm his analysis, he knew without a doubt that he was looking at a drop of a highly flammable type of petroleum wax. The accelerant used in this fire. He slipped the substance into a pint-size arson evidence solid material collection container and marked the spot on the ground.

His educated guess would be the arsonist had coated the back wall of the shelter with the wax and left a trail to the matchbook, so that when the cigarette burned down and the matches ignited, the wax caught fire. Tim told the chief and his men as much.

"Clever and dangerous," the chief said. "We've got to catch this guy."

A murmur of agreement went through the group.

"Our witness is set to work with a forensic artist,"

Tim told them. "The FBI will be operating closely with the Billings police department."

And if all went well, they'd have their arsonist by the New Year.

Christmas morning dawned with a clear sky and the world carpeted in pristine white snow. Vickie glanced out her bedroom window overlooking the neighborhood, enjoying the peaceful serenity of the quiet street and the festively decorated homes. A few chimneys had plumes of smoke spiraling into the air, signaling that the day had already begun in many households.

The only thing marring the postcard-like scene was the police cruiser sitting across the street from her house.

She expected the sight to make her uneasy, scared, but having the police officer present was a reminder Tim had kept his promise of making sure she and her family were protected. That they were safe.

She turned away from the window. Normally on Christmas morning she'd head downstairs in her pajamas to have breakfast with her parents. But today she dressed with care, because she would be seeing Tim.

And the forensic artist. To catch a criminal.

Seeing Tim wasn't a big deal and not why she'd chosen her new green sweater. As she applied a touch of lipstick, she made a face at herself in the vanity mirror. "Get over yourself."

The sound of the doorbell sent her heart rate skipping.

A few moments later her mother opened the bedroom door to say, "Agent Ramsey and his dog are here. Looking very handsome. The agent, that is." She laughed. "The dog, too, actually. You should invite Agent Ramsey to breakfast."

"I doubt he'll have time for breakfast."

"Are you all right? You look a bit pale."

Vickie waved away her mother's concern. "I'm fine. I just didn't sleep well." Not to mention how nervous she was to recreate a mental image of her attacker. She prayed she could give enough of a description for Tim to arrest him.

Taking her hand, her mom drew her close. "That's understandable. Yesterday was traumatic. But today is Christmas Day. A day of new beginnings."

Vickie wanted to believe she had the chance to begin again; however, she wouldn't feel safe until the police caught the man responsible for the fire. The man who had attacked her and then possibly tried to run her down. Though she wasn't convinced the car incident had been intentional. But Tim was. And she trusted him to know. It was his job, after all. To know things like that.

Not wanting to cause her mother any more worry, Vickie suppressed a shiver and took a calming breath. She'd become stronger over the past few years. She would get through this.

Her mom tugged her hand. "Come along. You don't want to keep your young man waiting."

Vickie groaned. "He's not my young man, Mom. Please don't say things like that in front of Agent Ramsey."

Irena grinned. "Touchy, touchy."

Holding on to her composure, Vickie followed her downstairs. Tim and her father were in the living room, talking. Both men turned as they entered. Vickie's heart gave a little knock against her ribs at the sight of the handsome agent. His brown hair flopped over his forehead in a cute way that made her want to reach out and brush it back. Her fingers curled at her sides.

He wore civilian clothes—dark wash jeans, a button-down plaid shirt beneath a warm, shearling-lined leather jacket. He held a small wrapped box in his hands. For her?

Swallowing back the sudden delight, she dropped her gaze. At Tim's booted feet lay his muscular German shepherd. The dog stared at her with dark, intelligent eyes. The pair made a striking picture.

Tim smiled and his blue eyes glowed with appreciation. "Good morning, Vickie. Merry Christmas."

Heat flushed through her cheeks. "Merry Christmas."

He extended the gift. "This was on your porch. It had your name on it." He frowned. "The patrol officer didn't see anyone drop it off, so it must have been there from before you returned home last night and we hadn't noticed."

Disappointment surged and she fought the emotion back. Of course he wasn't bringing her a present. She stared at the package. Who would leave her a gift? And why?

"Well, open it," her father said. "Maybe there's a card inside."

"Ooh, a mysterious admirer," her mother quipped.

Reluctantly, Vickie took the package and carefully unwrapped the festive paper to reveal a black box. She lifted the lid. A small gold cross on a delicate chain lay nestled in the batting. Her hand trembled. Her mind rebelled. It couldn't be. She forced herself not to flinch.

"That's pretty. You used to have a cross like that when you were in college," her mother said. "Whatever happened to it?"

"I lost it." She'd realized she was missing her cross the day after Ken assaulted her. She'd figured it had come off during the struggle, but she hadn't found it in the apartment. Then she'd packed up and returned home, never thinking about the necklace again.

"Is there a note?" Tim asked.

"No. No note." She slammed the lid shut and met his concerned gaze. Now was not the time or place for her to discuss the past. No matter how distressing she found the gift. "Shouldn't we go?"

His gaze never wavered. "Brian, the forensic artist, won't be available until tomorrow."

The news was both a relief and a disappointment. She wanted to get this part over with, but now, with this box in her hand making her skin crawl with anxiety, she wanted nothing more than to hole up inside her parents' house and forget the past existed. "You could have called to tell me."

Tugging at the collar of his shirt, he said, "I could have. But I thought it would be better for me to tell you in person."

Interesting. And a bit disconcerting. Was he attracted to her, too? The thought left her feeling unbalanced. Or was that caused only by the box in her hand. "Thank you."

Her mom nudged her in the side. *Oh, right. Breakfast.* "Would you like to stay for Christmas breakfast?"

Tim hesitated a fraction of a second before he nodded. "I'd like that very much."

Warmth spread through her chest. She would, too.

"Good." She set the little black box on the mantel, glad to not be touching it. If only she could put it from her mind as easily. "Here, let me take your coat."

He slipped his outerwear from his wide shoulders and handed it to her. The jacket retained his body heat and a faint spicy aroma.

Her father clapped Tim on the back. "We can't thank you enough for your help yesterday."

"All part of the job," Tim replied, his gaze on her.

Feeling as though he could see right through her to the hidden torment bubbling inside, Vickie headed toward the hall closet to hang up his outerwear. She held it to her chest for a moment and again breathed in the lingering scent of Tim's aftershave clinging to the leather collar. The material was so warm and inviting. She had the strongest urge to slip the jacket around her, as if doing so would keep her safe.

The sight of the cross necklace loomed in her mind like a neon sign. Her hands tightened, bunching up Tim's coat. Who sent it? Why? She wanted to believe it was a benevolent gift, but she couldn't shake the alarming feeling the present held more malice than goodwill.

Quickly, she grabbed a hanger and hung up the coat. Security wouldn't be found in a coat or in the arms of an attractive FBI agent.

The scuff of a shoe on the hardwood floor sent Vickie's heart jumping. She spun from the closet door, her fists raised high so that her forearms protected her face.

"Whoa!" Tim said, his hands held up, his palms facing her. "I didn't mean to startle you."

Recapturing the breath that had leaped out of her, Vickie lowered her arms and tried to school her features into a neutral expression. "You didn't."

He cocked an eyebrow. "Right."

Caught. She sighed. "I'm a little jumpy."

"Understandable, given the circumstances of the past twelve hours."

He had no idea. The necklace was a reminder of a time in her life she'd worked so hard to forget. "Thank you for keeping your promise of a police presence last night."

A hard glint entered his blue eyes. "You'll have protection until we catch this guy."

Such a different response than she'd received from the police when she'd reported Ken's assault. "We appreciate your care."

"You'll have a police escort any time you leave the house. I don't want to take any chances the guy in the car makes another attempt to run you down."

Her stomach lurched at the reminder. She glanced toward the kitchen, where her parents were busy putting the last touches on their Christmas breakfast. "Shh. I didn't tell my parents about that."

His eyes widened. "I'm surprised. I thought you and your parents were close."

"We are," she told him in a fierce voice. "I love them beyond measure. Which is why I need to protect them."

"They should know what's happening," he insisted.

"It could have easily been an accident. Or you could have been the intended target." The skepticism and resolved gleam in his eyes told her he wasn't buying her rationale. "But even if that car meant to mow me down, why make my parents worry about something they can't do anything about?" She touched his arm. "Please. I don't want to upset them any more than I have to."

He shook his head in clear disapproval and stared at her for several moments.

She entwined her fingers together, waiting for him to either argue with her or flat out ignore her plea.

Finally, he stilled and narrowed his gaze. "It's your call."

She blinked in surprise. It took her a moment to recover. She hadn't expected him to acquiesce so easily. Men in authority, like him, usually wanted to be in control. Nevertheless, she was grateful he understood. She squeezed his arm. "Thank you."

"For now," he amended. "If anything else happens, you'll need to let them know. They would be devastated if you ended up hurt."

His words rang ominously between them. Anxiety ate at her gut. He was right, of course, which was why she would do everything in her power to keep them all from being hurt.

"Tell me about the necklace," Tim said. "It upset you. Why?"

"It's creepy that someone would leave it on the porch," she stated.

"I agree, but there's something more, because your face lost all of its color the second you opened the box and saw what was inside."

Her uncontrollable response had betrayed her. How could she tell Tim about Ken? Would he dismiss her claim of being attacked, as everyone else had? "I was surprised. Why would someone send me a gift and not leave a note with it?"

"Like your mother said, a secret admirer?" His eyebrows rose. "Or maybe not-so-secret. Greg?"

The thought had merit. She was panicking for nothing. Of course the necklace was from Greg. "But why a cross?"

"Because anyone who knows you knows you are a person of faith," Tim said.

She supposed he was right. There was no reason for her to read more into the gold charm and chain than a nice gesture. "Why would Greg leave it on the porch? He came to the shelter last night."

"Maybe he came by here before going to the shelter," Tim reasoned. "I'll find out. You don't have to worry. I'll take care of it."

His determination and thoughtfulness endeared him to her even more than he already was—which scared her nearly as much as knowing there was a serial arsonist out there who wanted to silence her.

FIVE

Tim sat at the square table in the Petrovs' dining room with Vickie on his right, looking beautiful in green, with her blond hair loose about her shoulders. He couldn't help but notice how she fidgeted in her seat.

He only wished there was some way for him to ease Vickie's worry. Arresting the maniac would make her feel safe. Make them all feel safe.

The unsigned gift was a concern, but Tim was sure Greg was the sender. The man had made it clear he thought he had a claim on Vickie.

Not likely. She was too good for Greg. Too good for Tim, too, for that matter. She deserved someone well-adjusted and willing to give everything to her. That wasn't Tim. He'd tried going all in before with disastrous results. He wasn't willing to try again.

The other seats at the table were taken by Irena and Sasha. Frodo lay near the back door, his head resting on his crossed paws.

The delicious breakfast of sweet rolls with raspberry jam and butter, poached eggs and sausage, along with potato dumplings, would keep Tim going all day and into the next. But it was the lively conversation and the comfortable way the Petrov family welcomed him and Frodo into their home that filled him with yearning.

He couldn't remember the last time he'd had a home-cooked meal that didn't involve one or more of his fellow agents. The Tactical K-9 Unit members were as close as he came to having family, but sitting here with Vickie and her parents stirred a need to belong to something more. To *someone* more.

His chest tightened. He knew from painful experience what happened when he let down his guard and gave in to the need for more. Heartbreak waited at the end that path. A path he wouldn't travel again.

Sasha stretched. "As always, my dear, scrumptious."

Irena touched her husband's arm with a loving smile. "I'm glad you enjoyed your breakfast. Now you may help with the dishes." She rose and gathered the empty plates and took them to the sink in the kitchen.

Sasha pushed back his chair. "Vickie, why don't you and Tim visit in the living room while your mother and I deal with the cleanup?"

Tim stood. "I can help."

Sasha waved him off. "You're our guest. Please. This won't take long. Then we can play a game or two before we head to the bakery. We're going to provide food for the homeless shelter again."

The thought of staying with the Petrovs for merriment and serving the people staying at the shelter appealed to Tim, but he was scheduled to work. "I can't stay. I'm on duty again today. I need to get to headquarters." He'd make sure an officer stayed close to the family all day.

"Isn't today a federal holiday?" Vickie asked.

"It is, but someone needs to be available to take any

calls that come in," Tim told her. "I'm due to relieve the morning shift."

Sasha stuck out his hand. "Ah. Well, I wish you a Merry Christmas then."

Tim shook his hand. He liked the older gentleman. "Thank you, sir. Merry Christmas to you, as well."

Irena returned to the dining table and linked her arm through her husband's. "Thank you for taking time to spend with us this morning."

"My pleasure," Tim replied. "This was the best Christmas breakfast I've ever eaten."

Irena beamed. "That's so sweet of you to say." She turned to Vickie. "Offer our guest some chocolate to take with him."

"Yes, Mom." Vickie rose and gestured for him to follow her to the living room.

He whistled and Frodo jumped to his feet. They followed her.

Tim had noticed the large decorated tree showcased in front of the bay windows, and liked the colorful ornaments. And the three Christmas stockings hanging above the gas fireplace from gold-plated mantel holders that spelled out the word *joy.*

The room was cozy and festive, just as a home should be at Christmas. He liked it. His apartment had no decorations, no tree and certainly no stocking waiting for treats.

"Do you always work the holidays?" Vickie asked. She went to the tree and plucked a small wrapped gift from a branch.

"Usually," he said. "That way the others who have family can spend time with their loved ones."

She stopped in front of him. "It makes me sad to think of you alone at Christmas."

He appreciated her concern. "I'm not alone. I have Frodo."

"That's an interesting name to choose for your partner," she commented. "A fan of Tolkien?"

"Yes. Very much so. Frodo was brave and determined. Qualities I saw in this guy when I met him," Tim said, with a glance at the dog sitting beside him.

Vickie held out the present. "This chocolate comes from the Ukraine. My parents have it shipped over every year, and we give a box to those we care about."

He closed his hand around the gift and her warm, slender fingers. "I'm honored to be included in the category of people you care about."

A blush tinged her cheeks. She slipped her hand away. "After all you did for us and the homeless shelter yesterday, you'll receive chocolate every year."

He held her gaze. "I do love chocolate."

"It's good for the heart."

Though he knew she meant physically healthy, he couldn't help the way her words wound around him, making him want to open his heart to her. A dangerous idea that wouldn't serve him well. He wasn't looking for romance. She was a victim of a crime and it was his job to protect her. Nothing more. He didn't need to be with her to make sure she was protected, no matter how much he enjoyed spending time with her.

Yet he found himself saying, "When you head to the shelter, let me know. I'll come help you."

Her eyes widened. "That would be lovely. Thank you."

She opened the front door.

They both glanced up at the decorative ball of mistletoe hanging from the porch eave, then their gazes met and held for a moment before they both grinned.

"My dad's doing," she said. "He and Mom are hopeless romantics."

A chuckle escaped him. The Petrovs were a charming family. Especially Vickie. "I'll see you later." He ducked out the door, careful to skirt around the mistletoe and moved quickly across the porch. No need to stop and linger even if he'd like to.

Later that afternoon at the bakery, Vickie finished packing the last box of food ready to be taken to the temporary homeless shelter. Slipping into her father's office, she called the number Tim had given her for his cell phone. Her heart beat in her ears as she waited for him to answer, eager to hear his voice.

His voice mail picked up. She kept her disappointment in check as she left a message that she was heading to the shelter.

When she stepped out of the office, her mom was checking on the fruit pies in the oven. "These have another fifteen minutes or so to go."

Vickie glanced at the clock on the wall. Four thirty. "We told Pastor John we'd be there at five. How about I take over the boxes and you and Dad can bring the pies when they're ready to be transported?"

Concern darkened her mother's eyes. "We all came together. How will you get to the shelter?"

"I'll ask Officer Reeves to drive me."

Tim had made good, once again, on his promise of making sure they had a guard to keep them safe. Officer Reeves sat in the dining area enjoying her mom's coffee cake. He was a rookie with the Billings police department and very nice. He readily agreed to accompany Vickie to the shelter.

Bundled for the cold, Vickie and the policeman left the bakery in his patrol car, then had to park on the other side of the snowed-covered grass because the plows had pushed all the snow to the sides of the street, blocking the parking spaces. The crunch of their booted feet on the salt-covered sidewalk masked the sound of the surprising amount of traffic on the roads, considering it was Christmas Day.

"Thank you for helping me with these," Vickie said, nodding toward the box in Officer Reeves's hands, while she adjusted the one she carried.

"No problem," he replied. His held condiments and two containers filled with her mom's potato salad. "The fresh air is good for the soul." He grinned. "At least that is what my grandmother always tells me."

"Wise words." Vickie adjusted her grip on the box filled with sweet rolls, savory rolls, sandwich breads and an array of deli meats and cheeses.

A slither of sensation along her nape raised the fine hairs at the base of her skull. She glanced behind her. No one was there.

Paranoid much? she asked herself. She studied the cars passing by on the street, remembering the squeal of tires when the dark sedan had tried to run her and Tim down.

"It would be shorter cutting across the community park than staying on the sidewalk," Vickie said, as they neared the corner where the street diverged around the tree-filled green space.

The sense of being watched shivered across her flesh, again urging her to move quickly into the park. Officer Reeves marched along a few paces behind her.

An odd sound had her glancing back to ask if he was okay, but the words died on her tongue. The officer was face-first in the snow, the box he'd been carrying beside him. Had he fallen?

She spun awkwardly, intending to rush to his aid, but was stopped by hands clamping down on her shoulders and dragging her backward. She dropped the box in her arms as a wave of fear crashed into her, stealing her breath.

Jerking and twisting in an effort to free herself, she jabbed her elbows backward, but her assailant kept out of reach. An arm wrapped around her neck, pressing painfully against her throat.

A male voice hissed into her ear, "You'll pay for talking to the cops."

Clawing at the arm choking her, she tried to make sense of his words. *Pay?* "Please! Let me go."

Panic fueled by adrenaline infused her. She couldn't be a victim. Not again.

Save me, Lord.

She kicked backward and tore at the arm holding her. Her attacker lifted her off her feet and slammed her to the ground, burying her face into the snow. Icy wetness stung her cheeks and slipped beneath the collar of her coat. She kicked and punched as best she could, but the lack of oxygen caused the world to swim and fade. She was being choked and smothered.

Please, Lord, I don't want to die like this.

From a distance she heard a dog's furious barking.

Spots danced before her eyes. Her lungs ached. Terror ripped at her mind. She despaired of ever seeing Tim or her parents again as the world went dark.

SIX

Horror electrified Tim's blood as he brought his SUV to a screeching halt at the curb beside the community park. A man wearing a black hoodie and ski mask had Vickie on the ground in a chokehold.

Using the fob on his key chain, Tim popped open Frodo's compartment. The dog bolted from the vehicle and sprinted forward in a burst of muscle and ferocious barking.

The assailant shot to his feet and ran in the opposite direction.

Tim jumped from his SUV. Heart hammering in his chest, he raced through the snow. "Halt! FBI!"

Frodo leaped in the air and bit down on the man's arm. The suspect let out a howl of pain, then twisted out of the jacket he wore, leaving Frodo with a mouthful of material. The dog spat it out and resumed his chase, easily gaining on the perpetrator.

When the assailant darted into the street, running directly into the path of the traffic, Tim feared for his partner's safety and gave a sharp whistle. Frodo wheeled around and raced back to his side.

Using his cell phone to call the Billings police department, Tim quickly gave the dispatcher the suspect's description and requested an ambulance.

Tim checked the fallen officer for signs of life and was grateful to feel a pulse. A bloodied gash marred the back of the young man's head. A heavy-duty flashlight with blood on it lay next to him.

Next, Tim hurried to Vickie's side. She stirred as he gathered her in his arms. He brushed back a clump of wet, matted hair from her forehead, where a red knot was forming.

She blinked up at him as if she didn't trust what she was seeing. "You're here."

"I'm so sorry," he said. "I shouldn't have left your side."

"Not your fault." She struggled to stand. He helped her to her feet, tucking her into his side. She rubbed at her throat. "He came out of nowhere." Her eyes widened with alarm. "Officer Reeves?"

"Breathing. He took a nasty conk on the back of the head," Tim told her. "Help is on the way." A siren punctuated his words. "Did the attacker say anything?"

Fear clouded her eyes. "He said, 'You'll pay for talking to the cops.'"

"He *is* afraid you can identify him."

A tremble worked over her body. "I can't believe this is happening to me."

He hugged her closer in reassurance. He couldn't help it. "The arsonist is determined to get away with his crimes. You're the only witness who can put him behind bars."

She bit her lip. "But how can you be certain it was him?"

Tim met her gaze. "Is there a reason to think there is someone else out there who wants to hurt you?"

Distress flickered in her eyes before she looked away. "I don't think so."

She didn't sound convincing. "What aren't you telling me?"

Before she could answer, officers and an ambulance were on scene. He reluctantly released her to the EMTs' care. They sat her on the bumper of the ambulance while they checked her head and neck, determining the damage was superficial. He hovered close, unwilling to let her out of his reach.

What was wrong with him?

He gave himself a mental shake. He needed to snap out of it.

Officer Reeves was placed on a gurney. He'd regained consciousness.

"I'm sorry, Agent Ramsey," he said. "I never saw him coming."

"We'll get him," Tim promised the younger man, as the paramedics wheeled him to the ambulance and took him to the hospital.

Tim turned back to Vickie as Police Chief Fielding approached.

Grasping Vickie's hand as she recounted the harrowing incident to the chief, Tim admired her strength and fortitude in the face of such a horrible experience.

He sent up a prayer of thanksgiving that he and Frodo had arrived in time to stop the assailant from doing permanent damage. The thought of losing Vickie sent Tim's pulse skyrocketing. He chose not to analyze the meaning beyond the knowledge that he'd come to care for her.

When Chief Fielding released them from the scene, telling Vickie investigators might contact her and Tim later with more questions, Tim helped her into his SUV.

He then gathered the spilled contents of the two boxes and arranged for another Billings police officer to deliver the food to the shelter.

After he climbed into the driver's seat, he handed Vickie his phone. "Call your parents. Let them know what happened and that you are all right."

She made a face, but took the phone. "They are going to freak out."

"This is a freaky situation," he reminded her.

"True." She dialed. A few moments later she had them on the phone. As he listened to her calmly explain what had happened, he was struck once again by how very much he respected this sweet woman. She had a core of steel, but was also vulnerable and kind. She tried so hard to keep everyone around her comfortable, often to her own detriment.

When she clicked off and passed back his phone, he impulsively took her hand. "It's okay to be afraid. To ask for help and to let others be strong."

She laced her fingers through his. Surprise jolted Tim. Not only was Vickie accepting his touch after being physically attacked, but she was reciprocating. Her show of apparent trust in him sent warmth flooding through his chest.

"I don't want to be a burden on anyone."

His gaze dropped involuntarily to her lips. "You could never be." Why did his voice sound husky?

"Thank you."

He lifted his gaze to her trusting eyes. He wanted to say it was all part of the job, but somewhere along the way she'd become more than a job. "Let's get you home."

"Sounds good to me," she said.

On the drive to her house, Vickie was silent. Tim could only imagine how hard this was on her. She was being brave and stoic and he wanted to pull her into his arms and kiss away the little worry lines around her mouth and at the corners of her pretty eyes. He was in such deep water.

"If you and Frodo…" She hesitated, then shuddered as he brought the SUV to a halt in the driveway of her family home. "That man tried to kill me."

Battling back his own terror at how close the suspect had come to achieving his goal, Tim turned off the engine and gripped the steering wheel tight. "He didn't succeed. And he won't."

"How can you be so sure?"

"I just am." He had to believe he could stop this criminal before he hurt her or anyone else. He noted the police cruiser parked on the other side of the road with a clear view of the street.

Tim climbed out of the vehicle and came around to her side just as she stepped out. She swayed slightly as if the blood had rushed from her head. He wrapped an arm around her waist and was gratified when she leaned into him. He released Frodo, who did a quick sweep of the yard before joining them on the porch.

As Vickie unlocked the front door, Tim glanced up at the ball of mistletoe.

He couldn't stop himself from impulsively leaning close and placing a gentle kiss on her honey-blond hair.

She stilled and then slowly turned her face toward him. Her eyes were huge with obvious surprise and her lips parted on an inhaled breath.

He smiled and pointed up. "I couldn't resist."

She smiled softly. "Silly tradition."

"But a nice one," he replied, and reached past her to open the door.

A flush of pink heightened the color of her cheeks as she stepped inside the house. He and Frodo followed. Frodo settled himself on the threshold of the living room.

Vickie moved to the gas fireplace and hit the switch, igniting a warming flame. She stood in front of the mantel, hugging her arms around her middle as she stared into the dancing fire with an unfocused gaze.

"Vickie, we'll catch him, I promise you."

She turned to face him. "I want to believe that. It's just..." She tugged on her bottom lip with her teeth.

For a moment he was distracted, wanting to take her in his arms and kiss away whatever was causing her to abuse her lip. "It's just what? You can tell me."

"It was a long time ago," she said, her voice sounding so fragile.

He frowned with unease and moved closer, but kept his hands at his sides, afraid he'd spook her. "Let me help," he coaxed in a gentle tone.

She pulled in a shuddering breath and spoke on her exhalation. "During my third year of college," she said, her voice barely above a whisper, "I was assaulted by the guy I was dating."

Tim's heart clutched. Anger on her behalf exploded within his chest. "Did he—?"

She shook her head. "No. But that was his intent."

His fingers curled at his sides. "Did you report the assault?"

"Yes." A grim light entered her eyes. "But no one

believed me. It was his word against mine. And because
he didn't actually succeed at what he wanted to do, there
was *'no harm done.'*" She made air quotes with her fingers and a scoffing sound. "At least that was what the
campus police and the school dean told me."

Outraged, Tim shook his head. "That shouldn't have
happened."

Her smile broke his heart for its bitterness. "Doesn't
matter now. I left school and never saw him again."

"What was his name?"

"Ken Leland. He was a big man on campus. Set
to graduate with honors." Her shoulders wilted. "I
shouldn't have gone out with him. The local police were
willing to investigate when I went to them. They questioned Ken." She let out a bitter laugh. "But whatever
he'd said to them had the officers insinuating I'd led Ken
on and he'd misunderstood my intentions."

"It sounds like he was good at manipulation. Don't
blame yourself," he said. "Not everyone is who they
seem, but many are. All you can ever do is pray you're
making the best decision you can and then trust God
has your back."

"Do you really believe that?"

He searched his heart before finally answering. "Yes.
There are times when I've had a split second to make a
choice that could end or save a life, usually my own or
Frodo's. I do the best I can and leave the rest to God."

Her gaze turned contemplative. "When I think back
on that night, I can see God did intervene. My roommate came home, which forced Ken to escape out the
back. I just wish I hadn't had to go through the rest."

"God doesn't always keep us from the bad things
in life, but He does promise to be there with us." The

words came out of some long-ago Sunday school lesson. He could apply those words to his own life, he realized with a start. Having his family torn apart and ripped out from under him as a kid had left scars, but God had never abandoned him, even if he felt abandoned.

The soft look of affection on her face made his stomach clench. "Thank you. I needed to hear that."

So had he. He reached for her hand and held her gaze. "Sometimes we need to be reminded of God's love and power."

The front door opened and her parents rushed inside, forcing him to release her and step back.

Her mother hurried to her side and embraced her. "Are you okay? We couldn't believe it when we heard you'd been assaulted on your way to the shelter."

"I'm fine, Mom," she told them. "Some bruises. Thankfully, Tim and Frodo saved me."

Sasha engulfed her in a hug, then turned to Tim. "We owe you another debt of gratitude, Agent Ramsey."

"Not at all, sir." He wouldn't tell the man that protecting Vickie was something he longed to do forever. But acknowledging his budding feelings for her was a mistake he couldn't afford. He didn't need to be tangling up their lives and hearts amid such chaos. The forced proximity and heightened emotions weren't the foundations to build a romance on. Even if he wanted to. Which he didn't. Right?

"Tim, would you please stay for dinner?" Vickie asked, her eyes soft with pleading.

There was no way he could refuse her even if he wanted to. He needed to stay close to her because the arsonist had escalated to an attempted murderer. This was work. Nothing personal about it.

* * *

The next morning, Vickie and her parents opened the bakery as they did every day. Only today, Vickie's nerves were on edge as she readied the front of the store for the day's customers. A new police officer was stationed in the dining area. His presence eased some of her tension, but sleep had been elusive last night. Her mind had wanted to replay the assault every time she closed her eyes. Fatigue and worry were a combustible combination.

To distract herself from the trauma, she concentrated on Tim. On his kindness, his strength and integrity. So much different than she'd expected, considering he was an officer of the law. She realized now how silly she'd been assuming all those in authority were like the school dean and campus officer who'd made her feel small and worthless when she'd reported Ken's assault.

Tim was good and fair and full of honor. He made her feel safe and cared for. Cherished even. But did she dare risk opening her heart to him? The question made a different kind of tension form a knot in her chest.

The bell over the entrance door chimed when Tim stepped into the shop, and her heart leaped with the urge to rush into his arms. He looked handsome in khaki pants and a thick, warm-looking jacket with the FBI logo on the breast pocket. She wanted to believe he could keep her safe, but doubts swirled around her like wisps of smoke.

She wiped her trembling hands on the apron covering her jeans and shirt. "Good morning. Where's Frodo?"

"Good morning to you, too. He's sitting out front." Tim leaned against the counter. "Is this an okay time for you to take a break and come to headquarters with me? Brian's all set up and waiting."

She swallowed hard. Anxiety twisted her insides into knots. "I didn't see the man's face the night of fire. And yesterday, as you saw, he had a mask on. He came at me from behind."

Tim gathered her hands in his larger ones. Warmth spread up her arms, wrapping around her. She wanted to step away, to deny how much she needed his strength, but her feet and her heart wouldn't cooperate. "You said you'd caught a glimpse of him. You might have caught a glimpse of his eyes. The shape of his face. You'd be surprised by how much can be gleaned from that."

"I don't know how much more of this I can take."

He pulled her close. Surprise washed over her as she instinctively stiffened, expecting fear and panic to flood her. Ever since Ken's assault, she didn't like to be touched or hugged by anyone besides her parents. Strangely, within the circle of Tim's embrace, she found solace. With a sigh, she melted against him.

"You're doing great," he said, his voice rumbling in his chest. "I'm not going to let anything happen to you. Or your family."

As much as she appreciated his words, she knew he couldn't make that guarantee.

SEVEN

Tim reluctantly released Vickie. It was time for them to leave, despite how much he would prefer to continue holding her.

Knowing what he did of her traumatic past and the way she'd been let down by the campus security and the college dean, he didn't blame her for being wary of trusting law enforcement. He could only hope she'd come to trust him.

He opened the bakery's front door so Vickie could exit in front of him. The winter sun glinted in her light-colored hair peeking out beneath her hat, and her cheeks grew rosy from the frosty weather. She was so pretty it made his heart ache.

To distract himself from her charms, he bent to untie Frodo's lead from the metal bike rack outside the bake-shop.

Vickie held out her hand for the dog to sniff. Frodo brushed up against her, lapping up the attention. His partner apparently liked her, too. The dog didn't give approval to many people.

They neared the corner as the traffic light turned red, forcing them to halt. A prickling at the base of Tim's neck sent his senses on alert. He had the distinct impression they were being watched. Slipping his arm around Vickie, he drew her closer as he scanned the area.

"What's wrong?" A tremble punctuated her words.

"I don't know. Maybe nothing."

She gestured with her chin. "Is that Greg?"

Caution tightened the muscle of his shoulders. "Where?"

She looked up at him, her blue-gray eyes troubled. "Across the street."

Tim searched the crowded sidewalk opposite. Sure enough, there was Greg Sherman, the neighborhood security guard, staring at them from the other side of the busy street. His bald head was covered by a dark beanie, and his wide shoulders were squeezed into his security guard uniform jacket. Had he been following them? The man had dodged Tim's calls, and now he was here. An unlikely coincidence.

"Let's go have a chat with old Greg," he said, as soon as the light changed and the Walk sign flashed. He steered both Vickie and Frodo onto the crosswalk.

Greg spun on the balls of his booted feet and darted down the nearest side street. Tim wanted to give pursuit, but with Vickie in tow that wasn't a possibility. Why was Greg following them? But more importantly, why had he run away?

Vickie was surprised to realize the six-story brick structure in the heart of downtown looked like any other office building. There were no markings to indicate this was where the FBI Tactical K-9 Unit had its headquarters. She was even more stunned when Tim took her to a large training center taking up the ground floor.

He handed Frodo off to a trainer, who led the German shepherd away.

"How many dogs are used by your unit?" she asked.

"There are eight working dogs and seven puppies of various ages training to become working dogs." An emotion Vickie couldn't quite decipher passed across his face. "Last spring one of our agents went missing. We thought he'd been kidnapped but—" He broke off, his jaw tensing.

Vickie's heart lurched. Something bad had obviously happened to his fellow agent to cause Tim to be so upset. She laid a hand on his arm. "I'm sorry."

His eyes were grim when he met her gaze. "He turned bad. Started working for a crime syndicate. But we didn't know that at first, so in honor of Jake—his name was Jake Morrow—the other agents started collecting puppies to train so we could build up the existing FBI K-9 program."

She swallowed past the lump in her throat. "You used the past tense. Did something happen to Jake?"

He nodded. "Jake was killed. In the end, he did the right thing and protected his own son from being murdered, by sacrificing his own life."

Her stomach dropped. "That's so sad and horrifying. I'm sorry for you and your team's loss."

He covered her hand with his, making her realize she still held on to him. Though she probably should release her grasp, she didn't want to let go. He anchored her, gave her a lifeline in the storm that had overtaken her world.

"Thank you. It hurt. All of us," he said. "But life goes on. And I have to trust that somehow this is all a part of God's plan."

Her heart ached for him and his fellow agents. "I will pray God will heal the wound left by Jake Morrow's choices." Just as she prayed every night that God would heal her own wounds from Ken's assault and the authorities not believing her.

"I'd appreciate that." Tim placed his hand to the small of Vickie's back. "We should get upstairs."

Awareness spread through her and settled in her cheeks. She hoped no one noticed her blush.

Tim led her to the second floor, past cubicles to a conference room that also served as the kitchen area. At the conference table sat a man with salt-and-pepper hair. He wore jeans and a button-down shirt with no tie. He held an electronic tablet, which he set aside with a smile. "Hello." He rose and held out his hand. "I'm Brian Ames."

He had kind eyes, she decided as she shook his hand. "Vickie Petrov."

Brian gestured to the chair beside him. "Have a seat, and we can get started."

Flutters of tensions pranced like little reindeer feet along her nerves as she sat. She linked her fingers together to keep them from shaking. She looked at Tim, desperate to hold on to his promise that he'd protect her and her family.

He put his hand on her shoulder. "It will be all right. I've already given Brian my description of the man who attacked you. He'll combine our details."

She hoped this worked. She stared at her hands and willed her heart to slow down. *Please, Lord, help me to remember.*

"Agent Ramsey, it would be better if you left us," Brian said. "Miss Petrov doesn't need any distractions."

Startled by the man's proclamation, Vickie looked anxiously at Tim.

Tim's eyebrows hitched up. "Right. I'll be back when you're done." He stepped out of the conference room and shut the door behind him.

She gave Brian a weak smile. "I really didn't get more than a fleeting glimpse of the man who attacked me."

"Sometimes that is enough," he assured her, and picked up the stylus for the notebook. "I understand you were attacked twice."

"Yes." She hated the helpless sensation crawling through her.

"Do you think it was the same man both times?"

There was no reason to think it wasn't, was there? "I believe so."

Brian nodded. "What I'm doing is building a composite sketch. At first all I want is for you to tell me your impressions of the attacker. Big boned. Wiry. That sort of thing. Then we'll start working on the face and build on the details Agent Ramsey has already given me."

Her mouth turned to cotton with the weight of responsibility pressing down on her shoulders. It was up to her to help Tim capture the villain. She could only do this with God's help.

"He was big. Bulky. Taller than me." She closed her eyes. "He was just a black blob. He wore a hoodie covering his head and a ski mask." Her eyes flew open. "He had a beard. The night of the fire, I'm sure I saw hair or at least heavy stubble." She shook her head as doubts infiltrated her mind. "I think. Or it could have just been shadows."

"We can start there." Using the stylus, he went to

work on the computer. "Walk me through the night of the fire."

Closing her eyes, she prepared herself to relive the assault. But her mind didn't want to cooperate. Instead of recalling the Christmas Eve attacker, her brain took her back to her dorm room three years ago. Ken slamming her against the wall, his groping hands. His stale breath and wild eyes.

Vickie banished the past and tried to concentrate on the present. With her breath expanding in her lungs, she did as Brian asked, recounting the shelter fire, going through each moment as best she could.

Her brain grew tired as the artist showed her dozens of different facial aspects on the tablet, expecting her to pick the closest match to the man she'd seen. But the more images she looked at, the more muddled her memory became as she saw Ken in each feature.

Forty minutes later, Brian tilted his electronic tablet toward her. "What do you think?"

She blinked at the image. There were no eyes or nose, only full lips surrounded by a shadowed jaw beneath a hoodie.

Her heart sank. How would they find the fiend now?

The vague image the forensic artist held up made Tim's stomach drop with disappointment. Apparently Vickie really hadn't seen her attacker's face clearly enough to give more than the barest details of a round head with smooth cheeks tucked inside a dark hoodie. Even adding in his description of the masked attacker hadn't yielded the desired result.

"I'm sorry." Her voice trembled.

Stuffing his frustration into a dark corner, Tim held

out his hand. "It's okay. You did great. We'll find him anyway."

She hesitated before slipping her hand into his. Her slender fingers wrapped around his and held on tight as they walked down the hall to his boss's office. It shouldn't feel so right to have her so close. It shouldn't feel so gratifying.

Special Agent Max West rose as they entered his office, and came around the desk to greet them. Tall and formidable looking, Max was fair and brave and willing to put his own life on the line for his team. Tim couldn't have asked for a better boss. Max had recently become engaged to a nice woman he'd met while working the case to find Jake Morrow.

Max wasn't the only one who'd survived the ordeal and come through to the other side with love. It seemed the whole team had found someone to give their heart to.

Not Tim. He would be the lone holdout no matter what. But with Vickie's palm pressed against his, he was having trouble remembering why he wanted no part of love.

Whoa! Love?

No.

Affection, yes. He held a good amount of affection for the lovely lady at his side. That was a long way from the *L* word.

Vickie's raised eyebrows brought Tim's head out of the clouds. "Max, this is Vickie Petrov," he stated.

"Miss Petrov, Tim has spoken highly of you." Max hitched a hip on the edge of his desk. "We all appreciate your family's bakery."

A pleased glow lit her eyes. "Thank you, sir. We appreciate your business."

Max shifted his gaze to Tim. "Success?"

"Unfortunately, it was too dark for Vickie to see her attacker's face the night of the shelter fire. He wore a ski mask during yesterday's attack. And we're having trouble tracking down the car that tried to run us over. The plates had been removed," Tim explained.

"I wish I could have been more helpful," Vickie stated with remorse.

Max held up a hand. "Do not feel bad about this. And please, trust that we will do everything in our power to keep you and your family safe."

Vickie glanced at Tim. "I'm learning to."

Tim stood taller and widened his stance. He usually didn't need to have his ego stroked, but hearing her words was satisfying and thrilling.

They said goodbye to Max. On their way out of the building, they ran into fellow agent Nina Atkins. She wore khakis and a dark, long-sleeved T-shirt with the FBI Tactical Team logo on the pocket, and her blond hair peeked out from beneath a knit cap. Beside her stood her partner, a large rottweiler named Sam.

"Nina, this is Vickie Petrov. Vickie, this is Agent Nina Atkins."

"Hi, Nina," Vickie said. "You've been into the bakery."

Nina's brown eyes sparkled. "I thought I recognized you. Is everything okay?"

"Working on it," Tim said.

"Let me know if I can help." Nina waved and took Sam outside.

Tim decided to have Frodo remain in his kennel.

He didn't want to have to leave the dog out in the cold while he and Vickie were inside the bakery. Instead of walking back, they took his SUV.

When they entered the bakery the bell over the door announced their arrival. Warmth wrapped around Tim, along with the scents of fresh baking bread and sweets. His stomach rumbled, reminding him it was lunchtime.

"I'll fix you a sandwich," Vickie murmured as she passed him.

He barked a laugh. This assignment definitely had its perks.

As she passed her mother, who was waiting on a steady stream of noontime customers, Vickie paused long enough to drop a kiss on her cheek. The quick greeting gave him an unexpected bump of his heart. They really were a tight-knit family. He automatically reached down to pet Frodo, belatedly remembering he'd left him at the training center.

He followed Vickie to the back of the bakery, where the real artistry happened. He'd never been on this side of the counter and he took in the racks of baked goods, and long counter spaces where Sasha was rolling out dough. Two college-age young men worked nearby, one manning the large oven and the other washing dishes.

Vickie donned protective gloves and set about making two ham and cheese sandwiches on thick slices of crusty bread.

"Can I help?" he asked.

"No, you may not," she replied. "In fact, you shouldn't be back here. Why don't you grab a table and I'll bring them out?"

Nodding, he made his way to the front part of the eatery. He spied an empty table just as Greg, the security guard, walked through the front door. Their gazes collided. For a second, Tim was sure Greg was going to bolt again, but the man squared his shoulders and lumbered forward as if to get in line to order food.

Tim blocked his path. "Why were you following us this morning?"

Greg narrowed his gaze. "Vickie is a friend. I'm worried about her."

"Then why did you run off when we approached you?" Tim wasn't buying his claim of worry.

"I received a call." The man's voice took on a defensive tone. "I had to go do my job."

"I'll verify that," he warned.

Greg frowned. "Go ahead. I've nothing to hide."

"Good. Then you won't mind going to the police station to answer some formal questions," Tim challenged.

"Why? I haven't done anything wrong," the security guard said. "What kind of questions?"

Before Tim could respond, a shrill alarm sounded, bouncing off the bakery walls. Smoke billowed out of the kitchen area. His heart jackknifed in his chest. He had to save Vickie!

"Everyone out," Tim yelled, as he ran for the kitchen. He paused to grab Irena by the shoulders to prevent her from heading for her husband and daughter. "Out the front."

"But Sasha! Vickie—"

Greg took her hand and helped to usher the crowd out the front door.

Tim grabbed a dish towel from the counter and placed it over his nose and mouth as he ran into the smoke.

EIGHT

Eyes watering from the billowing smoke and flames crawling up the back door of the bakery, Vickie grabbed the fire extinguisher and sprayed white foam at the terrifying wall of fire.

The sharp sound of a fire truck siren penetrated the blaring of the smoke alarm attached to the ceiling. No doubt Tim or her mom had called 911.

Her dad beat at the flames with a wet towel. The two employees had raced toward the front of the store the second they'd realized they were danger to help make sure all the patrons exited safely.

"Dad!" she yelled, unsuccessfully trying to be heard over the cacophony. She wanted to grab him and push him to safety, but the fire extinguisher required both hands. Using her shoulder, she butted him aside. "Go!"

He put his big hands on her shoulders and dragged her with him toward the front of the shop. Then Tim was there with a cloth wrapped around his face so that only his eyes were visible. He took the extinguisher from her and pointed for her and her father to leave.

No way. If it wasn't safe for her, then it wasn't safe for him. Heart pumping with adrenaline, she snagged his elbow and tugged him with her. They made it out to the street as the fire engine rolled past and turned down the alley to the back of the bakery.

Drawing in cleansing breaths of cold air, she searched the crowd for her mom. Vickie sighed with relief to see her parents embracing, safe and unharmed, as were their employees.

"Come on." Tim clasped Vickie's hand. They ran down the alley. The engine roared to a stop as men and women in turnout gear jumped out. Tim drew Vickie to the opposite side of the narrow passage, several feet from the fire.

"Stay here," he instructed, before hustling forward to talk to the fire chief.

This was the arsonist's work. The man had warned her to stop talking to the police. He'd done this as a kind of punishment. Another message. A way of letting her know he could make good on his claim that he could get to her. To the people she loved.

"Vickie!"

She turned to see her parents hurrying toward her. Each had a blanket from the fire department covering their shoulders. When they reached her, her father engulfed her in a hug, while her mother secured a blanket around her.

Irena touched her cheek. "I was so worried."

"I'm fine, Mom." She stepped back to look at them. "Tim got us out safely." He'd risked his own skin for her and her family. She'd be forever grateful. The man was proving she could trust him in ways she'd never thought possible.

"Where *is* Agent Ramsey?" her father asked. "I need to talk to him."

"He's speaking with the fire chief." She gestured to where the two stood near the fire engine. As if he sensed her attention on him, Tim met her gaze. She waved for him to come join her and her parents. He held up one finger, indicating to wait a moment.

A firefighter in turnout gear rounded the back end of the truck and strode over to Vickie and her parents. She couldn't make out his features behind the Plexiglas mask and aspirator covering his face. "It's not safe for you to be here." He pointed toward the opening of the alley, where police were setting up a barricade. "You need to move to the street."

Vickie tucked in her chin. There was something familiar about the firefighter's voice but she couldn't be sure because of the respirator muffling his words. She didn't like the brusque way he delivered the command and the accompanying hand gesture, as if he were shooing them away like pesky insects.

"We will, sir. Thank you," Sasha said, taking Vickie and her mother by the elbow. "We'll wait for Agent Ramsey on the sidewalk."

A few minutes later Tim joined them. "They have the fire under control."

"Agent Ramsey," Sasha said. "You need to speak to Colin. He may have seen something."

At Tim's confused look, Vickie interjected, "He's one of our employees."

"Okay. Right. One of the two young men I saw earlier. Where is he?"

Sasha beckoned to Colin and Ryan, the college freshmen who helped in the back of the shop, and they hustled over.

"Hey, boss," Colin said. "Wow, that was wild."

"This is Agent Ramsey of the FBI. Tell him what you saw this morning," Sasha instructed.

The young man wrinkled his nose. "I don't want to get anyone in trouble."

Tim stepped forward. "If you saw something that might help us, I need to know."

"That security guard who hangs around the bakery a lot was in the alley talking with Mr. Johnson about an hour before the fire broke out," Colin said.

Vickie felt her stomach drop. Not only had Greg shown interest in her and she'd rebuffed him, but Mr. Johnson would profit on an insurance claim if the building were damaged. She shared a glance with Tim. An hour before the fire—that was while she was sitting with the forensic artist at the FBI headquarters. Was Greg really the arsonist? Was he working on behalf of Mr. Johnson?

"Thank you," Tim said. "I'll talk to both men." He looked at them all. "Who called 911?"

Both Colin and Ryan shook their heads. Vickie's parents looked at each other, then back to Tim. "Neither of us."

"We've got class soon," Ryan said. "Can we leave? I want to go home and get cleaned up."

Tim shook his head. "Not yet. I will need my partner to release you. He'll be here any minute."

Vickie assumed the trainer was bringing Frodo over. But surely Tim didn't suspect Colin or Ryan of setting the fire.

"Too bad about the bakery," Ryan said. "I liked working for you."

Sasha ran a hand through his graying hair. "I don't

know when you'll be able to come back to work. I'll give you good recommendations," he assured them both.

"Thank you," Colin said. "We'll wait across the street. The bank lobby is warm."

Once the two young men were out of earshot, Vickie said to Tim, "I can assure you those boys didn't set the fire."

"How? How can *you* be as sure as Frodo's ability to smell traces of accelerant, even after a suspect thinks he or she has washed it off?"

Point taken. "I can't, obviously, but I know those guys have no reason to hurt us, or anyone. They have no malice in their hearts. None whatsoever. They've worked for us part-time through high school. We know their families."

Tim reached out and gently gathered her hands in his, a move so unexpected she didn't have a chance to step back. "Vickie, starting fires isn't always about malice. Sometimes, it's about sickness. Sometimes, good old-fashioned greed. Sometimes, we don't get to know the why, we simply count ourselves lucky to figure out who in a case like this, because that means we can stop it from happening again. I sleep better then."

"Well, I hope you have something to read tonight, Agent, because when Frodo gets here, he's going to clear those boys with two sniffs and a wag." She scanned the crowd. "Greg, on the other hand... I hate to think Greg and Mr. Johnson set fire to the bakery. And the homeless shelter." Had Greg been the one to attack her in the park, too?

"We have no proof it was either of them, but it's worth pursuing," Tim told her.

"But why would Mr. Johnson want to burn down his

own buildings?" Irena asked. "And Greg has been so nice to us. We've known the Shermans since the kids were young."

Tim's expression turned grim. "Only Mr. Johnson can answer for sure, but I intend to find out. As for Greg, his feelings for Vickie may be clouding his judgment."

Irena put her arm around Vickie. "Well, I'll talk to his mama."

"Please don't," Tim said quickly. "I don't want to spook Greg. Nor do I want to accuse him of something without proof."

Irena nodded, though Vickie could tell her mother wasn't happy about the situation.

"Mr. Johnson has been on a rampage," Sasha said. "This past summer, when our lease was up, he didn't want to sign another. Instead, he wanted us to rent the building on a month-to-month basis."

Vickie sucked in a quick breath. "Why would he want that?"

"Did you agree to his terms?" Tim asked at the same time.

Her dad nodded. "We had no choice. I wasn't prepared to move. And as to why, I can only guess going month to month allowed him to raise the rent whenever he pleased. Which he has done twice now."

"How can he get away with such a thing?" Vickie asked.

"On a month to month, the law only requires he give a fifteen-day notice before increasing the rent," her father explained. "We've been looking at other locations, but haven't found the right place yet. Looks like we'll need to increase our effort." He turned a sorrowful gaze on the burned-out bakery and Vickie's heart wept for her father.

"I didn't know you were considering moving the bakery." Distress darkened her tone. She shouldn't be surprised they hadn't confided in her. A small voice in her heart whispered that she had done her fair share of keeping secrets from her parents, too.

Her mother placed a hand on her arm. "We didn't want you to worry."

There was a lot of that sentiment going around. Vicki clasped her mom's hand. "I'll help you search for the right place."

"Thank you, dear," Irena said, and pulled her close for a hug.

When she released her, Tim touched Vickie's elbow. "After Frodo and I investigate the scene and the fire chief gives the all clear, you can go inside and gather as much as you can salvage," he said. He looked toward the street. "Frodo's here."

"Thank you, Tim," Vickie said, before he could walk away. "I don't know what we would have done without you."

He seemed to peer through her. "My job is to keep you and your family safe."

He went to talk to one of the police officers. The cop nodded and headed in their direction as Tim took off for his accelerant-detecting dog.

Tim took Frodo's lead from the unit's trainer. "Thanks for driving him over. I didn't want to leave the scene."

"No problem," Faith Rand said, and hurried back to her vehicle.

Frodo lifted his nose to the air.

"Yep, another fire, buddy," Tim said. He grabbed his crime scene kit from his own vehicle. "Okay, boy, let's go to work. I need you to clear a couple of people." He led the dog to the lobby of the bank across the street from the Petrov Bakery, where Colin and Ryan and several other people watched from behind the windows in the heated building.

Tim had Frodo sniff the young men, and when the dog didn't alert, he told them they could leave the scene. Sasha would have their contact information if Tim needed to talk to them again.

When Tim and Frodo reached the sidewalk where the Petrovs stood, the fire chief was already there talking to the family. He clapped Tim on the back. "The scene is yours. I was just telling the Petrovs they could enter through the front door and collect what they can once you're done with your investigation."

"Perfect." Tim turned to Vickie. "I'll text you as soon as Frodo and I have completed our examination of the area."

She frowned. "But the fire started outside. Why can't we go in now?"

"I don't want to confuse Frodo," Tim told her.

He led the German shepherd down the back alley. "Seek," Tim said. Frodo put his nose to the ground and moved steadily closer to the back door of the bakery.

It didn't take long for the dog to find the point of origin. Or the evidence that linked the fire to the other cases of arson: matches, remnants of cotton fibers and the remains of a cigarette.

Feeding Frodo kibble from the pouch at his waist, Tim said a thankful prayer that the arsonist hadn't used paraffin wax as he had on the shelter fire. This burn was a warning for Vickie, making good on his threat, hoping to silence her about what she had witnessed the night of the homeless shelter fire.

Anger burned in Tim's gut. The maniac responsible for terrorizing Vickie would pay for his crimes.

Tim thought through possible scenarios. Was Johnson paying Greg to set the fires? Did Johnson hope to collect the insurance money? Or was Greg setting the fires for his own purposes?

NINE

After helping the Petrovs pack up what they could carry from the bakery, Tim had two police officers escort them home. He wasn't taking any chances. He and Frodo returned to headquarters and went upstairs to Dylan O'Leary's computer cave. The team's tech expert was at his station when they entered.

"Hey, do you have a moment?" Tim asked.

Dylan lifted his hands from the keyboard and spun in his chair to face him. "Of course, bro. What's up?"

Tim smiled at the moniker. Dylan was the closest Tim had ever come to having a brother. They'd been roommates until Dylan had married this past fall. "I need you to do a deep background check on two people." He gave him Barry Johnson's and Greg Sherman's names.

"I need to know financials, criminal history and anything else you can dig up that might be relevant to my arson cases." He supplied him with the dates and properties.

"Sure thing," Dylan said, already turning to his computer.

"Do you mind if I wait?" Tim asked.

"Not at all." His friend opened a drawer. "There's treats here."

"Thanks." Tim grabbed a handful and for the next few minutes put Frodo through a set of exercises. It was best to have the dog work for his food as often as possible, to keep his mind and body active when not out in the field.

When he'd run out of treats, Tim instructed Frodo to a down position, then waited to see what Dylan dredged up on his suspects.

An hour later, the tech expert said, "Greg Sherman has a criminal history. Petty theft five years ago."

"No arson?"

"Nope. And no big deposits in his bank accounts."

Johnson could be paying Greg in cash. "And Mr. Johnson?"

"Barry Johnson has no criminal history. However, he is financially strapped."

"But he owns several properties downtown."

"He does indeed. And all the burned properties belong to him. He's drowning in expenses."

Tim rubbed his chin. "Reason enough to burn down the buildings and commit insurance fraud."

"Can you prove it?" Dylan asked.

"Not yet," Tim said. "But I will."

"Let me know if there is anything else I can do," his buddy told him.

Tim hesitated as some force within brought to mind the man who'd assaulted Vickie in college. "There is something. I want you to find out all you can on a guy named Ken Leland. I want to know where he is and what he's doing."

"Who's this?"

Wanting to respect her privacy, Tim hedged, "A man from Vickie Petrov's past. They attended college together." He gave Dylan the name of the school.

His colleague tilted his head. "Are we using government resources for a personal matter?"

"No, of course not." Tim didn't miss the amusement in his friend's eyes. "It's not like that."

Dylan grinned. "It sure looks like *that* to me. You've got it bad. Not that I blame you. Vickie Petrov is a pretty lady. And nice."

Tim shook his head. "You don't know what you're talking about. I'm protecting Vickie. Nothing more. There's nothing else going on."

"Bro, you can deny your feelings all you want, but it's written all over your face."

Tim's stomach churned. Was he in denial about his feelings for Vickie? "So I care about her. There's no crime in that."

Dylan grew serious. "No. But don't lead her on. I know you, bro. You're a die-hard bachelor."

"I am," Tim confirmed, only the conviction didn't resonate through him as it normally did.

"Be careful. Don't hurt her."

"That's the last thing I want to do." Tim's mouth went dry as his friend's words ricocheted through his brain. He needed to get his head on straight and remember Vickie was a victim of a crime and it was his job to bring the criminal to justice, not to fall for the woman he was protecting.

With resolve to keep his emotions in check, Tim headed for the door. "Come on, Frodo. Time we have a chat with Mr. Johnson."

* * *

"Have a seat, Mr. Johnson." Tim held on to his patience as he instructed the older man with a gesture toward the metal chair pushed up to a matching table in the center of the Billings Police Department's interrogation room. Police Chief Fielding stepped in behind them and closed the door.

The sheen of sweat on Mr. Johnson's brow glistened in the intense glare of the overhead fluorescent lights. His expensive wing tip shoes scuffed along the linoleum floor as he scooted past Frodo with a look of distaste. The dog sniffed the man's shoes and pant leg and then lifted his nose toward his hands. Johnson recoiled, clearly afraid the dog would bite.

After a moment, the German shepherd lost interest in him and lay down near the door.

"I demand to know why you've brought me here," Mr. Johnson said as he plopped his rotund self on the metal chair.

The chief gave a slight nod, indicating for Tim to take the lead and question the suspect.

Tim laid out four file folders. "I'd like to know why several of your buildings have been targeted by an arsonist. And why you didn't mention your other properties the night of the shelter fire."

Mr. Johnson took a handkerchief from the breast pocket of his wool coat and mopped his forehead. Stressed by guilt? "I didn't realize these incidents were connected."

Tim arched an eyebrow. "Don't play me for dumb. I've already checked with your insurance company and you've filed three claims." He opened the first file, which showed the burned-out shell of a three-bedroom, two-bath house on a residential street. "The house on Lazy Willow Lane." Tim opened another file, revealing the charred remains of the back half of a building. "The tire store downtown." He tapped the third file without opening it. Mr. Johnson couldn't deny having seen the damage to the shelter. "The homeless shelter."

The man made a face and looked away from the files. "Someone is out to get me."

Tim didn't buy the rationalization for a second. The property owner stood to gain from the blazes in insurance payouts. "Now Petrov Bakery."

Tim slammed his palm on the table, eliciting a startled yelp from Johnson. Frodo rose to all fours and growled. Tim gave him the stay command with his other hand. "And I'm sure I'll find a way to connect you to the house on Picador Way."

Visibly gathering his composure, Johnson held up a hand. "Now wait a minute." He patted his chest. "You don't think I'm responsible for these fires, do you?" His gaze darted to the police chief. "Why would I want to burn down my own buildings?"

Tim opened the last file folder and turned it so that Mr. Johnson could view the contents. "Your financials. You're in the red by millions. Setting a fire and claiming the insurance money is one of the oldest and most common money scams out there."

Clearly shaken, Johnson shook his head emphatically. "No. I did not set these fires."

Prepared for the denial, Tim said, "I've also talked to your current tenants in your other holdings. It seems you've been very reluctant to renew leases over the past year, demanding they go month to month. And you've increased the rent on all of your tenants. Some have even suggested you wanted them to vacate. Which begs the question, why?"

"I don't have to explain myself to you," Johnson said. "You can't pin these fires on me. You have no proof that I was involved."

"Why did you try to run Vickie Petrov down?" Tim asked the pointed question, hoping to trip him up.

Johnson reared back. "Excuse me? What are you talking about?"

"What were you doing behind Petrov Bakery this morning prior to the fire?"

"I was checking the electrical meter," Johnson said.

Tim made eye contact with Chief Fielding. Okay, then. They were halfway to a confession. Johnson's admission placed him at the scene of the crime.

"The electric company claims the building is draining too much power and is leveling me with fines," Johnson continued. "I'm sure it's the Petrovs who are causing the problem, though I can't prove it. No one else in the building uses much energy."

"Why not talk directly to Sasha Petrov, rather than skulking around the back of the building?"

"I wasn't skulking. I've been keeping tabs on the usage."

"Why was Greg Sherman with you?"

"He's my employee," Johnson said. "I've tasked him with keeping an eye on the meter. If you don't believe me, ask him. Check with the electric company."

"I will," Tim replied. "How much are you paying Greg to set these fires?"

Johnson sputtered. "I am not paying him to set the fires."

"Why would someone target buildings you own?"

Spreading his hands wide, Johnson said, "I don't know."

Tim hammered at him. "Why are you trying to push your tenants out?"

Johnson frowned, but clamped his lips together, clearly unwilling to divulge his motivations.

"Did you send someone to assault Vickie?"

Johnson's eyes widened with shock. "I would never." His gaze narrowed. "You need to talk to Greg. He's got a thing for the Petrov girl. She's trouble. That whole family is trouble."

Anger ignited within Tim's chest. "Enough trouble for you to want them gone?"

Johnson's expression turned bulldoggish. "If you're going continue questioning me, I want my lawyer present. Otherwise I want to leave. I have rights."

Frustrated by the lack of progress in eliciting a confession from Johnson, Tim met Chief Fielding's gaze. The older man shrugged and gestured toward the door.

Tim gathered the files. "Sit tight," he said to Johnson. With Frodo at his heels, he followed Chief Fielding into the hall.

"We don't have enough to hold him," Fielding said. "The insurance companies will be doing their own investigations, and if the FBI wants to make a case against the man, you're going to need to come up with more than you have."

"I know," Tim muttered. "I'm counting on Greg Sherman to provide some answers. Because right now all I have are more questions."

If Barry Johnson really wasn't involved, who was burning down his properties? And why? Was Greg trying to hurt Vickie?

"I'm releasing Johnson," Chief Fielding said. "But I'll warn him not to leave town."

Tim nodded. He didn't like letting the man off the hook, especially without answers.

His phone dinged just then, indicating a text coming in. It was from Dylan.

Tim read: I have the info you asked for.

"I'm heading back to my office," he said to the chief. "Let me know when your officers bring Greg in."

"Will do." Fielding reentered the interrogation room.

Tim and Frodo left the police station and headed to the FBI building a few blocks away. Tim found Dylan in his office. "You found something on Ken Leland?"

"I did." Dylan took off his black-framed glasses and rubbed the lens with a cloth. "Leland didn't graduate from college. He left in the middle of his last semester under mysterious circumstances."

Interesting. Tim leaned against the desk. "Mysterious how?"

Putting his glasses back on, Dylan made a face. "The school is all hush-hush about it. They won't release his records without a warrant."

Since this inquiry into Ken wasn't part of an official investigation, a warrant wouldn't be easy to obtain. "Where is he now?"

"Here's the thing," Dylan said. "Ken Leland disappeared."

Tim was surprised even as a sense of disquiet sneaked beneath the collar of his shirt and tightened the muscles of his shoulders. Agitation churned in his gut. "What do you mean, disappeared?"

Dylan shrugged. "I couldn't find any record of Ken Leland after he left college."

"How could that happen?"

A smirk settled over Dylan's face. "He changed his name. He was clever about it, but not clever enough." Dylan tapped his keyboard and brought up a photo of a dark-haired man with dark eyes. His unsmiling mouth was a flat slash emphasizing a square jaw. "He's going by his mother's maiden name, Benson. Who just happens to be Barry Johnson's wife's sister."

His mind reeling from the news, Tim said, "Let me get this straight. Ken Leland, aka Ken Benson, is Barry Johnson's nephew." A niggling at the back of his mind clamored for attention.

"Yep. And here's where it gets even more interesting." Dylan zoomed out from the photo of Ken to reveal it to be on a driver's license. "Benson dropped his first name and is using his middle name."

"Joseph," Tim stated, staring at the screen. A memory of Mr. Johnson claiming to have a nephew working as a Billings firefighter surfaced and scorched through his brain like a flash of lightning. "He's with BFD."

"How did you know?" Dylan gave a mock pout. "That was my grand finale statement." He clicked a few more keys and another photo appeared, of a man in turnout gear holding his helmet at his side. There was no mistaking Ken Leland, aka Joseph Benson.

Tim had a bad feeling in the pit of his stomach. He felt like he was staring at a jigsaw puzzle. How did the pieces connect? The man who'd assaulted Vickie in college now resided in Billings. And he was a firefighter and nephew to Barry Johnson, landlord to the Petrovs. Coincidence? Unlikely. But to what end?

How did Greg fit in? Who was the arsonist? Had it been Ken or Greg who attacked Vickie in the park?

"We need to bring this guy in for questioning," Tim said. "I'll start the paperwork for a warrant, as well."

"You think he's involved in your case?"

"I don't know what to think."

Tim's cell phone rang. He answered. The man on the other side said, "Sir, this is Officer Wainwright with Billings PD. Chief Fielding asked me to contact you. We've been unable to locate Greg Sherman. He's not at his place of residence."

Tim's stomach dropped. Had Greg skipped town?

"The chief has put out a BOLO on the man," Wainwright continued. "If he's running, we'll catch him."

"I have another suspect I need brought in." Tim gave the officer Joseph Benson's name and the information that he worked for the fire department.

"I'll tell the chief," the officer said, before hanging up.

Tim hoped the "be on the lookout" would net the security guard and Joseph, aka Ken.

"Greg Sherman is missing," he told Dylan.

Tim wanted, needed, to be with Vickie and her family. It wasn't that he didn't trust the Billings police officers stationed in front of her house to keep her safe. His need came from his heart, he realized in a moment of clarity.

A place he'd never thought he'd open again.

But somehow Vickie had infiltrated his defenses. His feelings for her went beyond caring and affection. Despite his resolve not to let himself fall for her, he had. He loved Vickie.

He wasn't sure what that would mean in the future or even if there was a future for them. For now, he had to see her, be with her. He needed to assure himself she was unharmed.

He called the Petrovs' home. The phone just rang. Fear clutched at him, balling his insides into knots. He dialed Vickie's cell and it went directly to voice mail, as if the device had been turned off. Alarm spiraled through his brain and revved up his blood pressure.

"I'm heading to Vickie Petrov's home," he told Dylan.

"Ah."

There was a world of meaning behind the two-letter word, but Tim chose to ignore it. He didn't have time for another lecture.

Gripping Frodo's lead, Tim raced out of the building. A prayer lifted from his lips. "Please, dear God, don't let anything be wrong. Let me be panicking for nothing."

TEN

Vickie stood in the kitchen with confusion and frustration warring within her. She'd left her cell phone on the counter to charge, as she always did when she was home, and now it was gone. Had her mom or dad used it? Why? They had their own cells and the landline if they needed to make a call.

She stepped into the living room, where her parents sat on the couch watching a movie. "Have either of you seen my cell phone?"

Dad picked up the remote and paused the screen. "Is it charging on the counter?"

"It's not there," she replied.

"Could you have taken it upstairs with you earlier?" her mother asked.

"I didn't." At least she didn't remember doing so, but when she'd returned home from working with the forensic artist, she'd been a bit scattered.

Maybe she'd only thought to set it to charging, but had forgotten on her way to her room for a much needed nap. Not that she'd slept. Her thoughts had been in constant motion. Still were… The past and the present kept jumbling together until she wasn't sure which way was up.

Her feelings for Tim clouded her mind and confused her heart. She could have easily taken her cell phone to her room.

"I'll go check upstairs." She hurried to her bedroom, and sure enough, her phone was in her purse.

The sound of the doorbell chime jolted her pulse. Tim? They weren't expecting him, but a flood of anticipation had her hurrying down the stairs. "I'll get it!"

She yanked open the door and stumbled back a step as her gaze collided with Greg Sherman's.

Vickie's heart slammed against her rib cage. Greg Sherman stood on the porch. He didn't have on his security guard uniform. Instead he wore jeans, work boots and a leather jacket. In his arms he held a large picnic basket and a bouquet of flowers.

She looked over his shoulder toward the police cruiser parked across the street. Why had the officers in the vehicle allowed Greg to knock on her door? Had Tim already questioned Greg and released him?

Her father joined her at the doorway, while her mother hovered behind them. Sasha folded his arms over his chest and stared hard at Greg. "What are you doing here?"

"Hello, Mr. Petrov," he said. "Pastor John asked me to bring this basket over." He adjusted it in his arms. "My mom and some of the church ladies got together and made your family a care package."

Irena squeezed in between Vickie and Sasha. "That's so sweet," she cooed. "Why don't you come in?"

Vickie wasn't sure about allowing Greg inside. "Mom," she warned beneath her breath.

Waving away her worry, her mom reached for the basket. "Here, let me take that."

"I'll get it." Her dad clasped the edges of the basket. Her mother opened the lid, revealing two casserole dishes covered with foil, a tossed green salad and a bottle of her mom's favorite sparkling apple cider. Seemed Greg was telling the truth about the food.

"I know my mom's broccoli and cheddar cheese casserole won't be nearly as good as something you would make at the bakery, but it's my favorite." He stepped inside and held out the bouquet of flowers to Vickie. "These are for you."

Reluctant to accept the offering, she hesitated as she shut the door, but remained in place, ready to yank it open again to call for help. "You didn't have to."

A resigned smile stretched his lips. "I want to apologize for everything you and your family have been through." He lowered his voice. "The cops questioned me about the bakery fire."

Wariness made her tighten her fingers around the door handle. "I knew Agent Ramsey wanted to talk to you."

Greg frowned. "I didn't talk to him. But I told the other cops Mr. Johnson had me meet him behind the bakery." Their visitor made a face. "He wanted me to spy on you. Or rather the building. He says the bakery uses too much energy. But that's not true. I checked all the meters for the whole block and the bakery doesn't take any more power than the other businesses."

"We pay the electric bill," Sasha said. "What does it matter to him how much energy we use?"

Shaking his head, Greg said, "Beats me. He's been acting very strange lately. Which is why I've decided to quit." Greg looked at Vickie. "I'm going to join the military. Find my path in life."

Surprise washed through her. She wondered if Tim knew this. And what he thought of it. "That's a big decision."

Greg nodded. "It is. But I feel good about it. Pastor John has been helping me to see I need to change my environment. He has a friend in the army that he's going to have me talk to about joining. It's time I moved on."

Vickie couldn't say she was saddened by the news. Not having to worry about dodging Greg's attention would be welcome. She had a hard time reconciling this version of him with the thought of him being the arsonist or the man who'd attacked her. Was he a good actor?

"Sasha, take the basket into the kitchen," Irena instructed. To Greg, she said, "Please thank your mother and let her know we appreciate the gesture."

"I will."

An awkward silence descended.

"Let me put these pretty flowers in water." Irena took the bouquet from Vickie with a look that clearly said *be nice.*

Keeping distance between them, Vickie led Greg into the living room, hoping he'd leave.

He moved to look out the front window. "Why are the police outside?"

"After everything that has happened lately, Agent Ramsey thought it would be a good idea to have them watching over us." And she sent up a silent prayer that the officers had already alerted him that Greg was here, and Tim was on his way.

"You like Agent Ramsey," Greg said. "It's pretty obvious."

She blinked back her surprise at his observation. Acceptance seeped into her core. She *did* like Tim, more than liked really, but she certainly wasn't going to discuss her feelings with Greg.

Her gaze fell on the black box still sitting on the mantel. She picked it up and held it out to Greg. "I can't accept this."

He tucked in his chin and made no move to take it. "What is it?"

She frowned and popped open the lid. "The necklace you left on the porch Christmas Eve."

He shook his head. "I didn't leave that. It's pretty, though."

She sucked in a quick breath. Her hand shook as his words reverberated through her skull. "You didn't give this to me?"

"No." Concern darkened his eyes. "Are you okay? You look like you might pass out or something."

If Greg didn't leave the necklace, then who did? Her pulse ticked faster with anxiety. She needed to talk to Tim.

"I need to make a phone call." Because she'd left her cell phone upstairs in her room, she hurried to her father's study to use the house landline. She picked up the extension and pressed it to her ear. There was no dial tone. Unease slithered down her spine.

She rushed to the kitchen, where her mom was dishing out food as her father poured apple cider into glasses. Greg had taken a seat at the table.

"Dad, the landline isn't working. Can I use your cell?"

He set the glass and the bottle down. "What do you mean, not working?"

"There's no dial tone," she said.

"I'll get my cell phone," he stated. "I left it in the car when we came home."

"Mine's in my purse," her mom said. "It's hanging in the hall closet."

Before Vickie and her father could step out of the kitchen a loud explosion from the attached garage rocked the house. A wall of hazy smoke quickly filled the living room and invaded the kitchen. The house was on fire!

Adrenaline spiked through Vickie. Fear clogged her throat. She had to save her family. "The back door…"

"The house is burning!" her mom cried.

Greg jumped up, knocking over the chair. "We have to get out!"

Sasha wrapped his arms around Irena and hustled her to the rear door.

But when he tried to turn the handle, it wouldn't budge. He worked the locks, but the door still wouldn't open. "It's been nailed shut from the outside!"

Vickie's breath stalled in her lungs. Someone had closed off their escape route.

The smoke grew denser. Vickie choked, her eyes watering from the toxic haze.

Her mother coughed.

Greg covered his mouth and nose with the crook of one arm.

A loud banging at the front door startled them.

"Fire department! Call out!" A firefighter rushed inside wearing turnout gear, a mask covering his face and carrying a pickax. Greg darted past him to safety.

"Hurry!" The fireman waved them toward the door.

Vickie followed her parents, making sure they made it to the front porch. But before she could get out herself, the firefighter snagged an arm around her waist and dragged her backward. He slammed the front door and shoved her away from him. He jammed the pickax beneath the door handle, effectively keeping anyone from entering, and trapping the two of them inside.

Taking shallow breaths that stung her lungs, Vickie tried to make sense of what was happening.

The firefighter advanced toward her.

She backed up until she hit the staircase. "Are you insane? What are you doing? Who are you?"

The man stopped and picked up a small canister from the floor near the garage door. She hadn't noticed it in her panic. The cylinder emitted billowing smoke. The explosion hadn't been from a fire, after all. There were no flames. An elaborate ruse to get her alone. But why?

The man yanked open the door to the garage and tossed the canister inside, then shut it again. Slowly, he turned to face her and removed his helmet and face-mask.

Vickie's worst nightmare stared at her.

Ken.

ELEVEN

The world tilted. Vickie hadn't been mixing up the past and the present. He was here, in the flesh. Dressed as a fireman. "I don't understand. How can you be here?"

His gaze narrowed. "Fate."

A chill of terror washed over her. She looked for an escape, but the only place she could go was up the stairs. She took another step back. "Why are you doing this?"

"You ruined my life." The malice in his brown eyes cut through her like a sharp knife. "You have to pay." He lunged at her.

Panic revved her blood. He was going to kill her. Spurred into action by the thought, she fled up the staircase, praying she made it to the safety of the bathroom at the end of the hall, where she could lock him out.

Ken pounded up the steps behind her, his heavy footfalls echoing inside her head like nails being pounded into a coffin.

"Please, Lord, help me!" she cried out.

Her parents would alert the police officers. They would come to her rescue. They would call Tim.

She just had to survive long enough for help to reach

her. She didn't want to die. She wanted to live. She wanted to tell Tim…

She reached the bathroom and grabbed the door, putting her weight into shutting it behind her, but Ken was hot on her heels. He outweighed her by at least a hundred pounds and easily pushed the door inward, sending her stumbling backward. With one giant hand, he shoved her to the floor.

She scrambled away from him, but there was nowhere to go. "Stop! You have to stop."

Looming over her like some monster from a horror movie, he said, "I won't stop until you're dead."

"What did I do to you?" He was the one who had assaulted her. He'd taken so much from her. Her dreams. Her sense of self. Her ability to trust.

"You took everything away from me!" He slammed his fist into the wall, leaving a gaping hole.

His words made no sense. How could she reason with him when he was clearly out of his mind?

But she had to try if she wanted to live. *Keep him talking*, she told herself. Give the authorities time to rescue her. "How did I ruin your life?"

"You were a tease," he growled. "You were just like the others. All teases. Letting a guy think you wanted him, only to refuse."

There were others he'd assaulted? She shuddered with dread and revulsion. "I never led you on."

"Yes, you did," he insisted. "And then you went running to the dean."

"Dean Abernathy didn't believe me. No one believed me."

Ken laughed, a horrible sound that bounced off the pale yellow walls. "Of course they didn't. They believed me. But when the others came forward after they heard about what you'd claimed—" He clenched his fists. "Not even my parents' money could make them accept my version of things. They expelled me. I couldn't graduate or get my degree. If it weren't for my uncle, I'd be jobless and homeless."

"But you have a life now," she pointed out, trying to make sense of what he was telling her. Other women had filed complaints against Ken and the dean had had to expel him. She'd cut off all ties to the school so had not heard about this. "You're helping people as a firefighter."

"That's right," he said. "And I'm good at it. But then I saw you. Of all the places to land in the world… I'd forgotten you were from here." His mouth stretched into a thin line. "It was as if Fate had decided to throw me a bone. A bone I intend to bury. It's time for you to die."

He advanced on her.

Terror flooded her system. The words of her self-defense instructor echoed through her head. *If you can't run away, then don't go down without a fight.*

There was no way she would let Ken win. He'd taken too much from her already. Her gaze snagged on her curling iron at the edge of the counter near her head. She pushed to her feet and grabbed the iron.

"Get out of the way!" Tim shouted to the other cars as he drove through the late afternoon traffic. He had to reach Vickie, to assure himself she and her parents were safe.

With Greg Sherman in the wind and the discovery that Ken Leland was in town, Tim wouldn't take any chances. His heart thumped, urging him to go faster. He hit the switch that turned on the strobe lights attached to the roof of his vehicle.

As Tim brought his SUV to a halt outside the Petrov home, several things hit him at once. Mr. and Mrs. Petrov were running out the front door in a wave of smoke. The door slammed shut behind them. Greg Sherman stood on the lawn, doubled over, gagging and coughing. A police cruiser sat at the curb with two officers sitting inside, not moving.

Alarmed by the scene, Tim jumped from his vehicle, released Frodo from his compartment, then raced to the cruiser. Frodo barked and paced while Tim skidded to a halt, then yanked open the driver's-side door. The officers were unconscious. Or worse, dead.

He reached inside to check the nearest man's neck and found a pulse. Then he checked the other one. Both alive.

"Agent Ramsey!" Sasha Petrov ran toward him. He coughed as he forced out his words. "Vickie's still inside."

With his heart dropping to his toes, Tim grabbed his cell phone and dialed 911. He handed the device to Sasha. "Get help."

Then Tim, with Frodo at his heels, rushed for the front door. It wouldn't budge. He used his shoulder as a battering ram and still the door held.

"Agent Ramsey," Greg yelled. "There's a fireman in there. He and Vickie are trapped inside."

Not trapped. Ken was extracting some sort of revenge on Vickie.

Gripped by the certain knowledge that he had to act fast, Tim spied a garden gnome peeking out of the snow-covered flowerbed. He heaved it at the window, shattering the pane into thousands of pieces that rained down to litter the snow.

Not wanting Frodo to cut his paws on broken glass, Tim gave the command, "Stay."

Then he climbed through the opening, his pants snagging and ripping on shards of glass clinging to the window frame. Inside the house, a layer of smoke hung in the air, but he saw no flames. He released his sidearm from its holster.

A scream came from upstairs. *Vickie!*

Pushing aside his panic, Tim ran for the staircase and noticed the front door. Anger erupted in his chest at the sight of the pickax wedged beneath the handle. He yanked the offending object away, then opened the door and let out a sharp whistle as he turned and sprinted up the stairs. Frodo raced inside and slipped past him.

A cacophony of noise filled the house. Frodo growling. A man cursing.

Tim reached the landing. Vickie stood in the doorway of the bathroom, holding a curling iron like a baseball bat and swinging at the man dressed as a fireman. He held up his hands in defense while shaking his leg in a useless attempt to dislodge Frodo. The dog's teeth were clenched around his ankle in a bite and hold. Frodo dragged the man toward Tim.

From outside the house, the wail of sirens announced backup had arrived.

"Ken!" Tim shouted, drawing his attention.

The man swiveled toward him, his gaze wild. "Call off your dog!"

"Let Vickie go." Tim met her panicked gaze and motioned with his free hand. "Come to me."

She slid along the wall past Ken, who grabbed at her. "No!"

Vickie dodged Ken's reach. Frodo swung his powerful head back and forth. Off balance, Ken fell to the floor.

Tim tucked Vickie behind him, while keeping his gun aimed at Ken's heart. Then he let out a short whistle. Frodo released his captive and backed up, growling and baring his teeth.

"Hands on your head," Tim shouted. "On your knees."

Ken hesitated, his eyes on Frodo.

"Do it!" Tim commanded. "Or I release him."

Slowly, Ken went to his knees and placed his laced fingers on the back of his head. "All right, already. Call off your dog."

"Ramsey!" Chief Fielding's voice carried up the staircase.

"Up here." Tim waited until several officers rushed up the stairs, followed by the chief.

"Come," Tim instructed Frodo. The dog immediately obeyed, allowing the officers to take Ken into custody and lead him away in handcuffs.

Once they were alone, Vickie shook like a leaf in a windstorm. After holstering his weapon, Tim rubbed her arms. She stared up at him with wide, unfocused eyes. Shock. He drew her to his chest and held her. "You're safe now."

She took a shuddering breath. "I was so scared. I thought I was going to die."

"You held him off with a curling iron." He couldn't keep the pride and awe from his voice.

"It was the only thing within reach," she said. "Not

that I could have done much damage against a man in heavy gear. But his head was my target."

"Hey, whatever works. You're alive."

"You saved me." She smiled and looked toward Frodo. "You both did."

"You were doing a great job of fending for yourself." Tim's heart continued to beat at a fast clip. He knew it wasn't just from the adrenaline, but because he still held her in his arms.

"Agent Ramsey, everything okay?" Chief Fielding's voice traveled up the stairs. "We're taking the suspect to the station."

Reluctantly, Tim released his hold on Vickie. "We need to go. You'll have to give a statement. And I want to question Ken Leland."

Keeping a hand to her back, Tim escorted her downstairs and to the porch. Her parents waited by the chief's squad car. Greg Sherman was talking with officers. An ambulance was leaving the scene, most likely taking the two unconscious officers to the hospital. Ken Leland sat in the back of a cruiser as it sped away down the street.

Vickie melted into Tim for a moment. He met her gaze, then glanced up at the ball of mistletoe hanging overhead.

"Tradition." He leaned close, intending to kiss her lips, but at the last second she turned her head. His kiss landed on her soft cheek. Confusion infused him. Why had she turned away?

She stepped out of his reach. "Thank you for everything," she whispered, and then hurried down the stairs to the waiting arms of her family.

As he and Frodo walked to his SUV, Tim wondered when or if he'd see Vickie Petrov again. The thought of not doing so shattered his heart as effectively as the garden gnome had shattered the window.

After leaving the Petrov home, he followed the police cruiser transporting Ken Leland, aka Joseph Benson, to the police station. Vickie would give her statement at the scene. If the investigation required more, she'd go to the station at a later date.

The drive into town gave Tim time to process the kiss. Or rather the nonkiss.

What had he been thinking?

He hadn't been. That was the problem. From the second he'd realized she was in peril, his brain had gone offline and his heart had taken over. The sight of her brandishing that curling iron at Ken was imprinted on Tim's mind. She'd looked achingly beautiful and terrified at the same time.

Pride and admiration filled his chest. She had so much strength and courage. She hadn't wilted beneath the terror of Ken's assault. Tim thanked God he and Frodo had arrived in time, before the situation had turned deadly. The tangible relief continued to pulse through his veins.

And the moment he and Vickie had passed beneath the mistletoe, he'd given in to the overwhelming need to kiss her.

However, she'd made it perfectly clear she wasn't receptive to his attention when she'd turned away from him.

Don't lead her on, bro. You're a confirmed bachelor.

Dylan's words echoed in his head as he waited for Ken to be brought to the interrogation room. For so many years now, Tim had used the phrase "confirmed bachelor" as a shield against getting involved. But now the words rang hollow.

But it didn't matter. Vickie wasn't interested in him. This was a place he'd been before. He'd survived last time he'd fallen in love and that love hadn't been returned. And he would survive now.

Shoring up his defenses might take him a few days, but he would do it. No need to pine for something that had never really started. Once this case was closed, he'd file away all thoughts of Vickie, too.

"Good job, Tim," Special Agent in Charge Max West said as he joined Tim in the hallway. Beside Max, his partner, a regal looking boxer named Opal, came to a halt.

"Thank you, sir." Doing a good job was important. And what Tim needed to focus on. Not the pretty baker who'd stolen his heart.

Max gestured with his chin toward the closed door of another interrogation room. "Chief Fielding had Johnson brought back in. The guy is seated in there with his lawyer. I've already had a chat with him. He's pinning all the arson on his nephew."

"And what about the assaults on Vickie?" Tim asked.

"Johnson claims ignorance," Max said.

Chief Fielding joined them outside the room.

"Any word on your officers?" Max asked him.

Fielding nodded. "Both men will be fine. Their coffee had been drugged with a sedative. They'd stopped at a diner on the way to the house," the chief told them. "The waitress at the diner places Ken there at the same time."

"Here's our suspect now," Max said, as two officers escorted Ken from booking.

Beside Max his partner, Opal, let out a low growl.

The hair on Frodo's back rose as he bared his teeth.

Ken's turnout gear had been removed and he now wore civilian clothes. His brown eyes stared at Tim with unveiled hatred. Tim and Max, along with the dogs, stepped out of the way as the officers led Ken into the room and forced Ken to sit, and linked his cuffed hands to a chain threaded through a ring in the middle of the table.

Tim and Max stepped in to the small space after the two officers left and took seats across from Ken, while Chief Fielding leaned against a wall. Tim would imagine the three of them made an intimidating picture, yet Ken appeared unfazed.

Not even the presence of the two dogs—Frodo sitting at attention next to Tim, with his dark eyes trained on Leland, and Opal, who sat at Max's side staring just as intently—seemed to bother him.

"We have you solid for assault and attempted murder," Tim said, as evenly as he could, but the anger he felt leached through each word. "You're going to prison for a long time."

Ken held his gaze, his lip curling ever so slightly.

Max spoke. "But you could do yourself a favor by cooperating. Maybe make those years a little less torturous. Tell us about the fires."

"I don't know what you're talking about," Ken spat.

Tim laid out the photos of the five fires they suspected he had ignited. "All of these places belong to your uncle, Barry Johnson." They'd finally found the connection on the other residential property. The deed was in Barry Johnson's wife's name.

Ken flicked a glance at the row of images. He shook

his head and leaned back. He moved his arms as if to cross them over his chest, but the chain yanked his arms back to the table.

"Just so you know," Max said. "Your uncle is in another room right now. You think he's going to take the blame for the fires? He's serving you up like fish on a platter."

Tim detected a spark of apprehension in Ken's gaze. "He's going to walk away from this with money in his pockets, while you rot in jail."

Ken's jawed worked.

"We have officers at your apartment tearing the place apart," Max said. "We'll have all the evidence we need to convict you of five counts of arson on top of the charges of assault and attempted murder. You have few precious seconds to come clean. If we leave this room without hearing your story, your uncle walks a free man while you go directly to jail."

Sweat dripped down the side of Ken's face. He seemed to be internally debating with himself. Finally, he said, "It was all Uncle Barry. If you find anything in my apartment, he put it there to set me up."

It seemed the two relatives were willing to sell each other out. "Why would he want to burn down his own properties?"

Ken snorted. "He's got a gambling addiction. He needs the cash."

"So you did the deeds in exchange for what?" Max asked.

"You can't prove I did anything," Ken retorted. "Even if you find something in my apartment, it's only circumstantial."

"When did you decide to go after Vickie?" Tim interjected. "Was it before or after you set the fire at the homeless shelter?"

Nostrils flaring, Ken stayed silent. Rage seethed in his brown eyes.

"Did your uncle tell you she was there?" Max pressed.

"She saw you and you were afraid she'd ID you," Tim continued. "You decided to silence her. It was your opportunity to make her pay for getting you kicked out of college."

Ken lifted his chin. "I want a lawyer."

Tim's fingers curled. Not even a lawyer could get Ken out of this hot water. "We'll get you your lawyer. But with Vickie's testimony and mine, there's only one way this goes."

Chief Fielding pushed away from the wall. "I'll have the prisoner escorted to his cell while he waits for his attorney."

Tim and Max led the dogs out of the police station. Fresh snow fell as they walked to their respective vehicles.

"Take a week off," Max told Tim. "You deserve it."

"Thanks. I will." Though he had no idea what he and Frodo would do. Maybe fly down to Florida to visit his mother and her family. Frodo didn't mind flying and a little sunshine and time away from Montana and a certain pretty baker might be just the remedy Tim needed.

TWELVE

Scrubbing the display case in the bakery's new location, Vickie figured Tim was too busy to check in with her. A week after New Year's and she hadn't heard from him. She'd hoped he'd stop by or at least call to update her on Ken's arrest.

But with Ken safely incarcerated at the county jail, Tim had no reason to come see her. In fact, none of the FBI agents had stopped by. Granted, the bakery was no longer within walking distance of the federal building downtown. It still stung that Tim hadn't come to the grand reopening or made any sort of contact.

Which made her regret for not kissing him much more potent. But in that moment, as she'd realized what he was about to do, a bout of shyness had gripped her. People were watching them, most especially her parents. Not wanting to be a spectacle, she'd shied away from meeting his lips with her own.

Dumb. Why hadn't she just gone with her feelings and not cared what anyone else thought?

Tim must believe she wasn't interested in him.

She couldn't stop thinking about him. She longed to see him. To hear his voice. To spend time with him.

Somewhere along the way she'd fallen for the handsome agent. The knowledge had been drilled home the moment he'd come barreling up the staircase after Frodo to rescue her from Ken. Her heart had wept with joy.

But now she was only sad. Sad that she'd missed an opportunity that might not come again.

The bell over the door of the new shop jingled at the arrival of an early morning customer. Pasting on a smile she didn't feel, she lifted her gaze in greeting.

Agent Nina Atkins and a tall, handsome man walked up to the counter. Vickie was glad to see her and had to hold back from immediately asking about Tim. "Hello, Agent Atkins. Welcome to our new location."

"Hello, Vickie." Nina glanced around with approval. "Nice. Bigger than the last place."

"Yes. We are enjoying the space. How are you?"

Nina beamed. "I'm great." She tucked her arm through the man's. "This is US Deputy Marshal Thomas Grant. He just relocated to Billings. Finally."

The man chuckled. "You make it sound like it took a year instead of a few weeks."

"It was a *long* few weeks." Nina glanced up at him with love shining in her eyes.

A stab of jealousy hit Vickie in the chest. She dropped her gaze and wiped at an imaginary speck on the counter. She wanted what they had. To be that in love and unafraid to let anyone see her feelings. "Can I take your order?"

"I'd like two dozen pastries," Nina said. "For our staff meeting."

Vickie's heart clenched. Tim would be there. As she set about the task of loading a pastry box with a variety of sweet treats, she worked up her courage to ask about Tim. "How's Agent Ramsey?"

"He just returned from a visit to his mom's in Florida," Nina replied.

Vickie nearly dropped an apple fritter. Tim had been out of town. Her pulse sped up. Maybe he'd call her now. She finished packing two pink boxes stamped with Petrov Bakery on the top and handed them to Thomas, then took Nina's credit card.

Vickie processed the transaction and handed the card back. "Tell everyone hello for me."

"Of course." Nina stared at her for a moment. "I'm sure Tim will come to see the new place soon."

Vickie bit her lip and darted a glance at Thomas, wishing she and Nina were alone. "That would be nice."

Nina nodded, but didn't move. Instead, she turned to Thomas. "I'll be right out." She gave him a gentle push.

His gaze bounced between the two women and then a light dawned in his eyes. "Ah. Okay. Yes. I'll wait in the car."

Nina motioned for her to follow her to a quiet corner table. When Vickie started straightening the salt and pepper shakers, the agent reached over and placed her hand on hers. "Are you okay? After all you've been through since Christmas..."

Vickie needed someone to confide in. The blond woman sitting across from her seemed so kind and caring. Safe. "I don't know what to do about Tim. Or rather, my feelings for him."

A slow smile spread over the agent's pretty face. "You've fallen for him."

Vickie nodded. "I have."

"Call him," Nina said. "Or better yet, come see him."

"I don't think I could do that," Vickie confessed, as nerves twisted her insides.

"Of course you can," Nina stated with confidence.

᠂ou're brave and strong and shouldn't let fear win."
She rose. "I better get going."

"Thank you. I'll keep what you've said in mind."

Fear had won too many times throughout Vickie's life.
It was time to be courageous and risk her heart for love.

Tim sat at his desk inside the Tactical K-9 Unit's
headquarters doing paperwork. He grabbed the last of
the apricot scone he'd snagged to save for an afternoon
snack and popped the bite of goodness into his mouth.
The tart flavor of the apricot mixed with sugar burst
on his tongue.

For a moment he allowed his heart to ache with
longing to go to the place where the baked good came
from—Petrov Bakery. To see Vickie.

But he was still trying to put her out of his mind
and his heart.

He'd managed pretty well while he was out of town,
but now that he was back, he kept hoping he'd see her
everywhere he went. He'd driven by the new bakery location several times, but forced himself not to stop. It
would only be awkward and torturous to see her again.

Then this morning Nina had brought in boxes of
treats and told everyone Vickie had said hello. The blanket statement hadn't been directed at him. He'd had to
bite his tongue to keep from asking how she was doing.
It was none of his business now.

His phone rang. When he answered, one of the dog
trainers said, "You're needed in the training center."

Alarm set Tim's heart hammering. Frodo was downstairs in his kennel. Had something happened to him?

He hurried downstairs and skidded to a halt. The

center was empty save for Vickie Petrov sitting in the middle of the training center floor.

She looked lovely in jeans and a bright blue sweater that brought out the blue in her eyes. Her blond hair was tied back in a low ponytail and a pink hue brightened her cheeks. A black-masked ball of fawn-colored fluff tumbled over Vickie's outstretched legs.

Tim sat down next to her and held out his fingers for the puppy to sniff. "What's going on here? Who's this?"

"This is Piper. She's a Belgian Malinois," Vickie said, scooping the pup into her hands and depositing her on his lap. "She's a rescue from the animal shelter."

Surprised, he steadied the puppy, his fingers curling into the soft fur. "I didn't know you wanted a pet."

"She's not for me. Though I would like a lapdog one day."

"If she's not yours then…"

"She's a thank-you. To you and the FBI."

He tucked a strand of her blond hair behind her ear. "A thank-you?"

Her eyes held his captive. "If it weren't for you and Frodo, I wouldn't be alive. Ken would have won."

Unable to stop himself, Tim reached for her hand. "I thank God you're safe."

"Me, too." She squeezed his fingers. "I remembered what you told me about your team members bringing in puppies in honor of Agent Morrow."

Tim's breath hitched. "Yes, many of the others have adopted and donated a puppy or a young dog to the K-9 program."

"I'm going to foster her until she's old enough to be trained as a K-9 officer. The trainers said this breed make great protection dogs." Vickie gave him a shy smile that made his heart thump in his chest. "I'm going to sponsor her in your name."

Stunned by her words, he felt warmth spread through him. "My name?"

She lifted her chin. "You're my hero."

Touched by her words and the gesture, he had to work through the emotions clogging his throat. "That's very generous of you."

The puppy chewed on the zipper of his jacket. He lifted the pup up and stared into her dark eyes. "She's a cutie."

When Vickie didn't respond, he lowered the puppy to the floor between them. "You okay?"

She nodded. "I am. Now." Her mouth kicked up at the corners. "I owe Nina a debt of gratitude."

"How so?"

"When she came by the bakery this morning, she told me I shouldn't let fear win. She's right. I don't want to be afraid anymore. I want to live life to the fullest." Vicki laid a hand on Tim's arm. "You taught me I can be brave even if I don't think I can be."

"You've always been brave, Vickie," he assured her.

A pleased smile touched her lips. "When my parents immigrated from the Ukraine to the United States, they adopted their new Christian church's tradition of Christmas in December. But they didn't want to abandon their family's custom of celebrating the birth of Jesus in January."

"Today?" he guessed.

She nodded. "It's become a holiday for the Ukraine, much like it is here in the US," Vickie explained. "But it has something to do with the difference between the Julian calendar and the Gregorian calendar, both of which date back thousands of years." She shrugged. "Tradition is tradition, as my father would say. Growing up, I loved having two celebrations."

"I would imagine so."

From the front pocket of her jeans, she tugged a sprig of greenery out and held it up for him to see. He sucked in a surprised breath. Mistletoe.

"It's tradition to kiss the one you love beneath the mistletoe."

His pulse leaped. "So I've heard."

She lowered her gaze and fingered the sprig. "I should have let you kiss me."

With the crook of his finger, he lifted her chin. The vulnerability in her eyes made his chest ache. "Are you saying you love me, Vickie?"

"I am."

Elation filled his heart.

"I'd understand if you don't feel the same." Her voice trembled. "We hardly know each other."

He cupped her cheek. "I love you, too."

Her eyes widened. "You do?"

"Yes, I do." His heart swelled with love for this wondrous woman. He traced his thumb over her lower lip. "I didn't think I'd ever wanted to go down this path again, but you've made me realize how much I was holding back from life. I was too afraid to love again and not be loved in return."

"We were both afraid."

"But not anymore." His voice rang with the conviction filling his soul. "Your heart is safe with me, Vickie."

Delight shone bright in her eyes. "As is your heart with me." She held the mistletoe over his head. "Tradition."

"Who are we to buck tradition?" Yet he refrained from moving, letting her take the lead.

Slowly, she leaned close and pressed her lips to his. He couldn't stop the groan of pleasure from escaping as he slid a hand to the back of her head, deepening the kiss until they were both breathless.

The puppy yipped and pawed at Vickie.

They broke apart with a laugh. The puppy settled in Vickie's lap to gnaw at her fingers before dozing off. A sign the dog trusted her, just as Tim trusted her. He wanted to claim Vickie for his own. To have and to hold. He wanted the whole shebang. A little house, a picket fence and kids. "I have a question for you."

She snuggled the little animal. "Yes?"

He wanted to do this right, make their romance special. Not rush her. He wanted them to have the kind of future he'd only ever dreamed about, but never thought would be possible. "Do you have plans for Valentine's Day?"

A demure smile played on her lush mouth. "Are you asking me for a date?"

He took her hand. "Yes. For this Valentine's Day." He kissed one knuckle. "And the next." He kissed another knuckle. "And the next and the next...." He kissed each knuckle and then turned her palm over to place a kiss in the center.

Delight bubbled in her voice. "Yes!"

He hugged her close. "I was hoping you'd say that."

She pulled back to look into his face, her eyes filled with love. "Merry Christmas."

"Merry Christmas." He dipped his head and kissed her again.

* * * * *

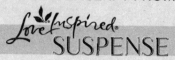
"I have your new identities." US marshal Jonathan Mast
sat across the table from Julia in the hotel where she and
her children had been holed up for the last five days.

The Luchadors wanted to kill William so he wouldn't
testify against their leader. As much as Julia didn't trust
law enforcement, she had to rely on the US Marshals and
their witness protection program to keep her family safe.
No wonder her nerves were stretched thin.

"We're ready to transport you and the children,"
Jonathan Mast continued. "We'll fly into Kansas City
tonight, then drive to Topeka and north to Yoder."

"What's in Kansas?"

Jonathan pulled out his phone and accessed a
photograph. He handed the cell to Julia. "Abraham King
will watch over you in Kansas."

Julia studied the picture. The man looked to be in his midthirties with a square face and deep-set eyes beneath dark brows. His nose appeared a bit off center, as if it had been broken. Lips pulled tight and no hint of a smile on his angular face.

"Mr. King doesn't look happy."

Jonathan shrugged. "Law enforcement photos are never flattering."

Her stomach tightened. "He's a cop?"

"Past tense. He left the force three years ago."

Once a cop, always a cop. Her ex had been a police officer. He'd protected others but failed to show that same sense of concern when it came to his own family. The marshal seemed oblivious to her unease.

"Abe is an old friend," Jonathan continued. "A widower from my police-force days who owns a farm and has a spare house on his property. He lives in a rural Amish community."

"Amish?"

"That's right."

"Bonnets and buggies?" she asked.

He smiled weakly. "You'll be off the grid, Mrs. Bradford. No one will look for you there."

Don't miss
Amish Safe House *by Debby Giusti,*
available February 2019 wherever
Love Inspired® *Suspense books and ebooks are sold.*

LISEXP0119